My BUDDY KiLLER CROC

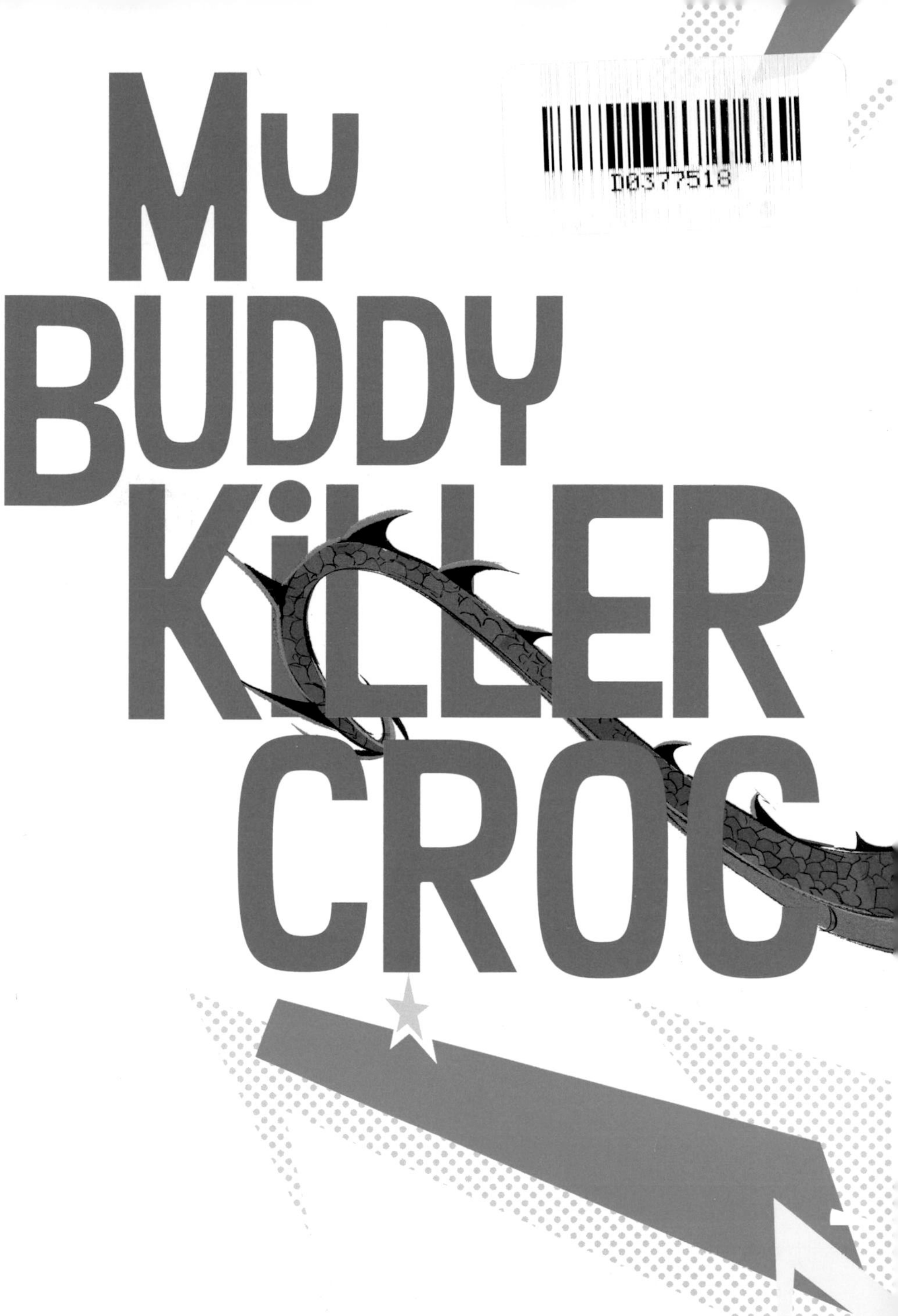

WRITTEN BY **SARA FARIZAN**

DRAWN BY **NICOLETTA BALDARI**

LETTERED BY **BECCA CAREY**

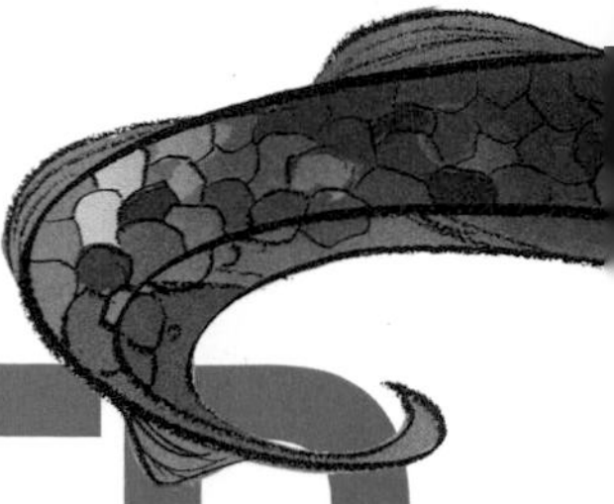

BUDDY KiLLER CROC

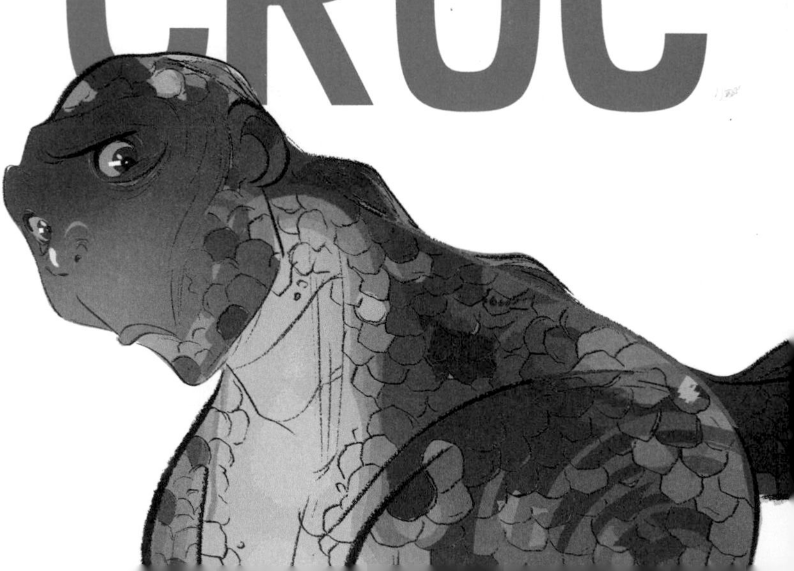

Kristy Quinn Editor
Courtney Jordan Associate Editor
Steve Cook Design Director - Books
Amie Brockway-Metcalf Publication Design
Danielle Ramondelli Publication Production

Marie Javins Editor-in-Chief, DC Comics

Anne DePies Senior VP - General Manager
Jim Lee Publisher & Chief Creative Officer
Don Falletti VP - Manufacturing Operations & Workflow Management
Lawrence Ganem VP - Talent Services
Alison Gill Senior VP - Manufacturing & Operations
Jeffrey Kaufman VP - Editorial Strategy & Programming
Nick J. Napolitano VP - Manufacturing Administration & Design
Nancy Spears VP - Revenue

MY BUDDY, KILLER CROC

DC Comics, 2900 West Alameda Ave., Burbank, CA 91505

Printed by LSC Communications, Crawfordsville, IN, USA. 7/22/22.

First Printing.

ISBN: 978-1-77950-124-0

PEFC Certified

This product is from
sustainably managed
forests and controlled
sources

PEFC/29-31-337   www.pefc.org

Library of Congress Cataloging-in-Publication Data

Names: Farizan, Sara, writer. | Baldari, Nicoletta, illustrator. | Carey,
    Becca, letterer.
Title: My buddy, Killer Croc / written by Sara Farizan ; drawn by Nicoletta
    Baldari ; lettered by Becca Carey.
Description: Burbank, CA : DC Comics, [2022] | Audience: Ages 8-12 |
    Audience: Grades 4-6 | Summary: Andy feels a little out of place when he
    moves to Gotham, feeling less excited about meeting Batman than he is
    about seeing his childhood hero, the wrestler Waylon Jones...a.k.a.
    Killer Croc, the super-villain who teaches him how to put the bullies in
    their place.
Identifiers: LCCN 2022013283 | ISBN 9781779501240 (trade paperback)
Subjects: CYAC: Graphic novels. | Supervillains—Fiction. |
    Friendship—Fiction. | Bullying—Fiction. | LCGFT: Superhero comics. |
    Graphic novels.
Classification: LCC PZ7.7.F365 My 2022 | DDC 741.5/973—dc23/eng/20220331
LC record available at https://lccn.loc.gov/2022013283

DEDiCATiON

To Meredith Goldstein, my Batman
buddy for life.
　　　　　—Sara

　　　To Stefano, for always being close
　　　to me. And to Tommaso, for having
　　　been present during the making of
　　　this book—from my heart, to my
　　　belly, to my arms.
　　　　　　　—Nicoletta

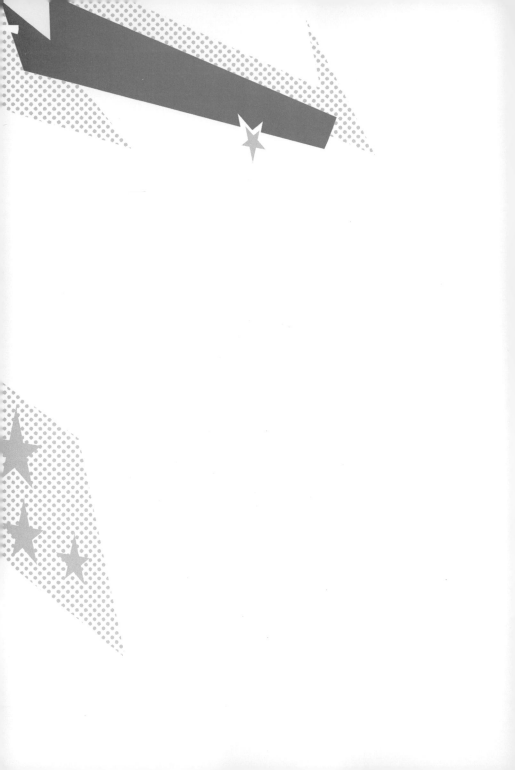

TABLE OF CONTENTS

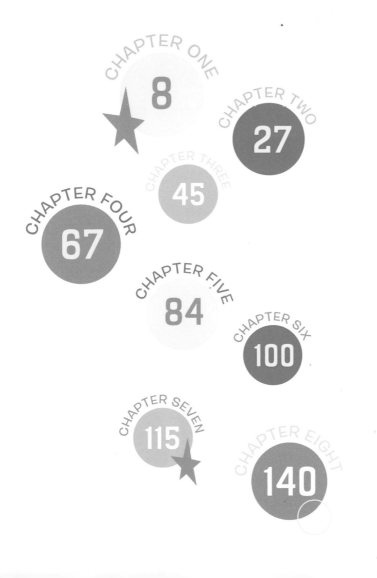

CHAPTER ONE

★ 8

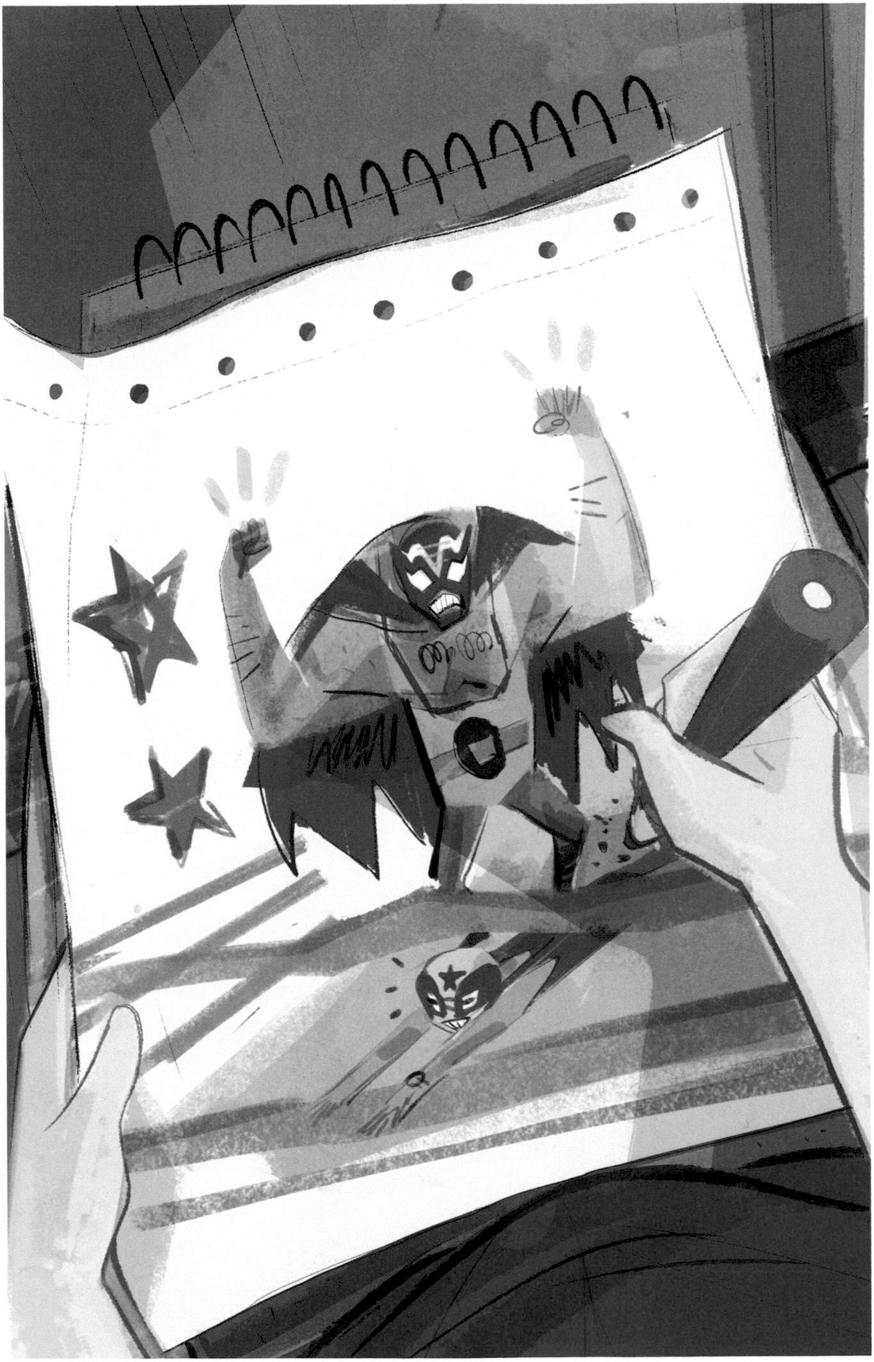

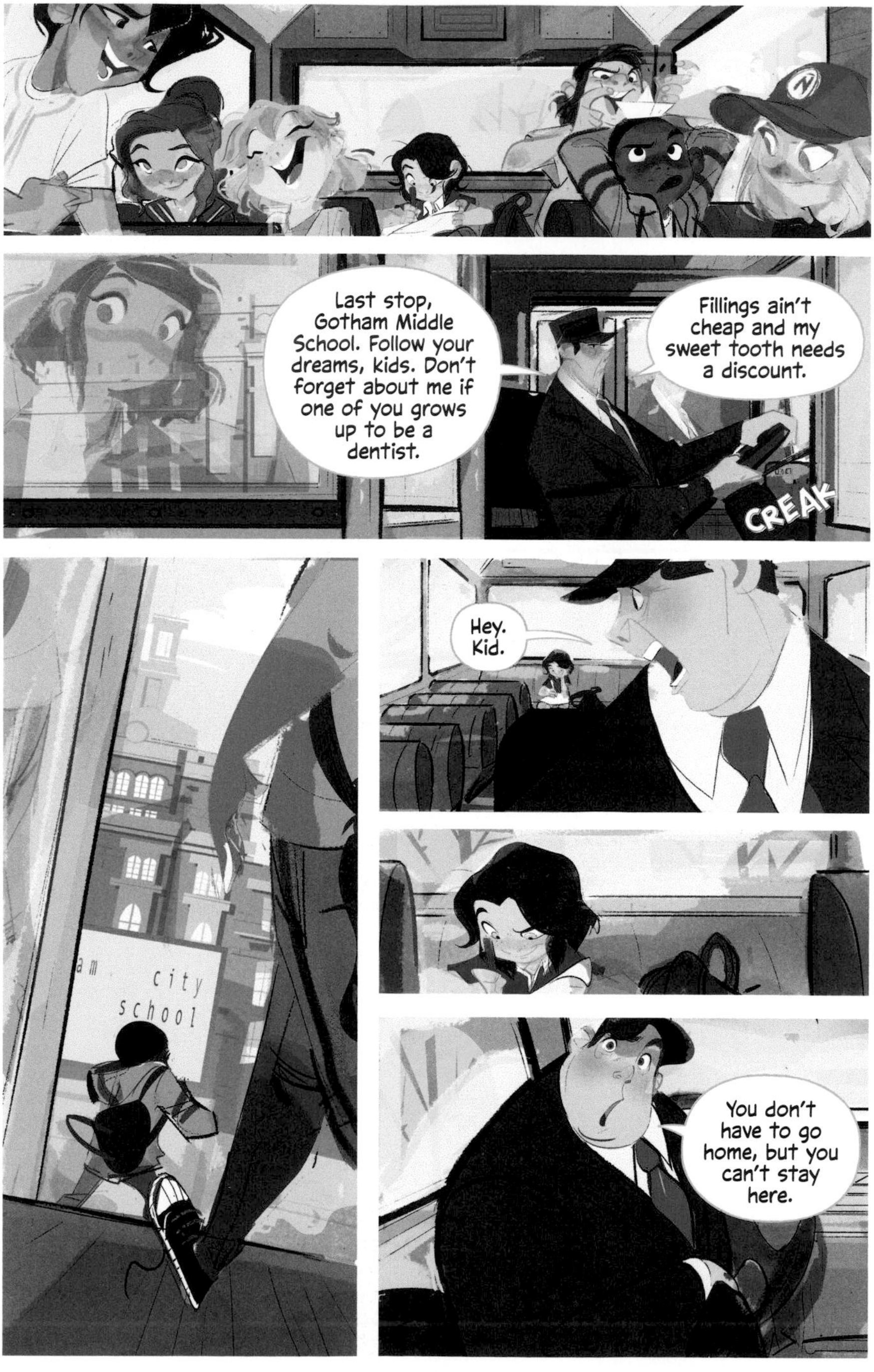
Last stop, Gotham Middle School. Follow your dreams, kids. Don't forget about me if one of you grows up to be a dentist.
Fillings ain't cheap and my sweet tooth needs a discount.
CREAK
am city school
Hey. Kid.
You don't have to go home, but you can't stay here.

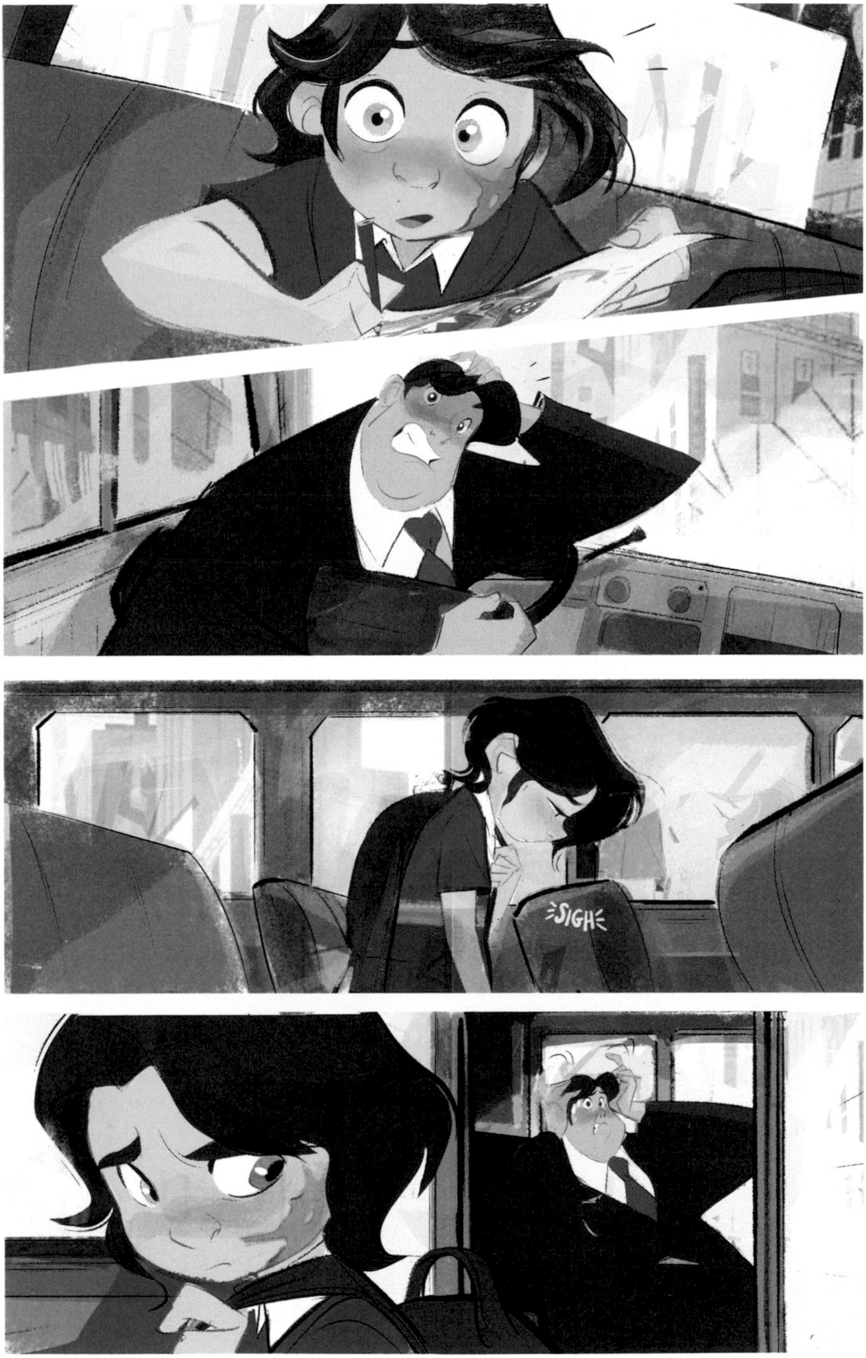
SIGH

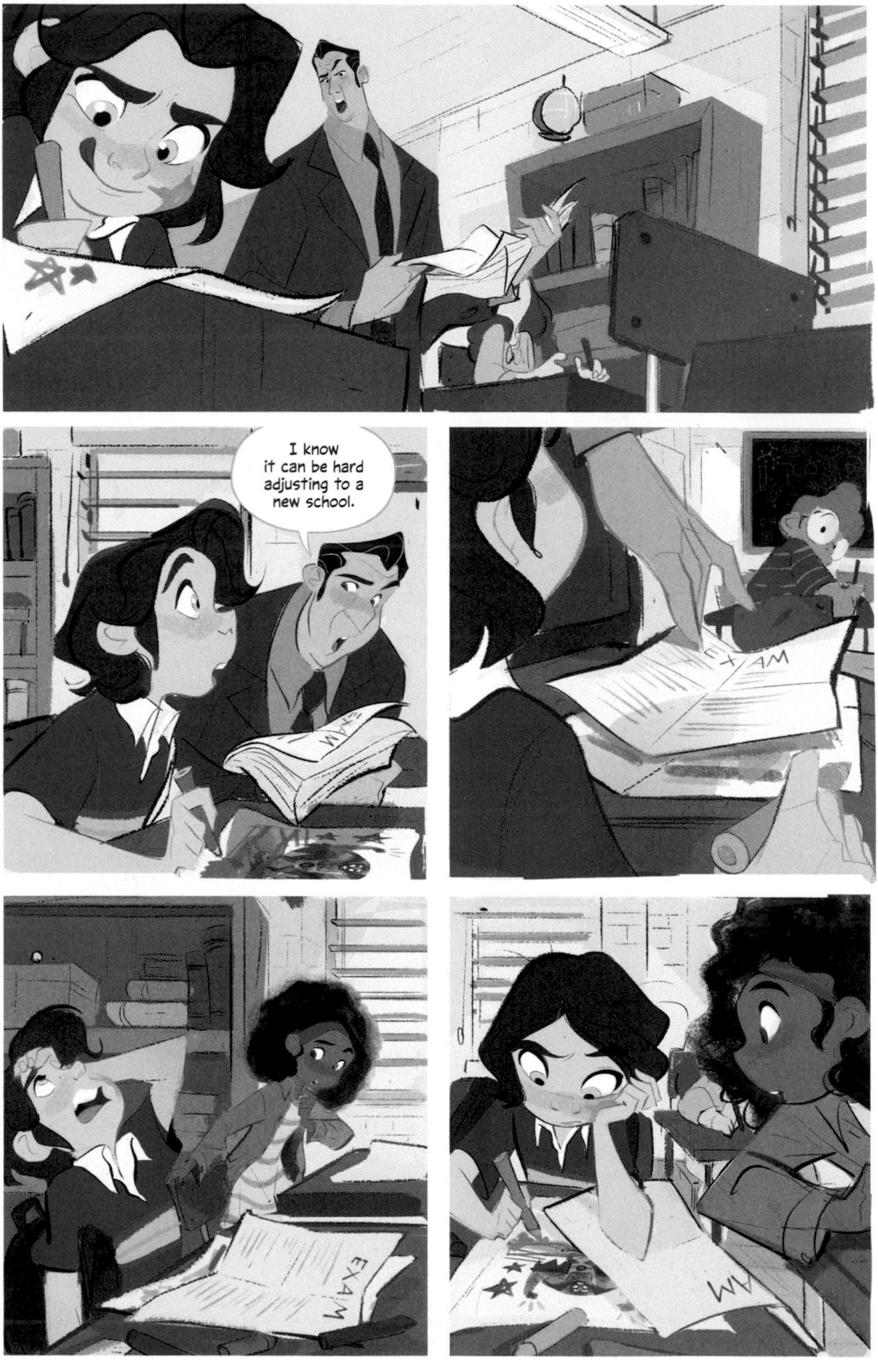
I know it can be hard adjusting to a new school.
EXAM

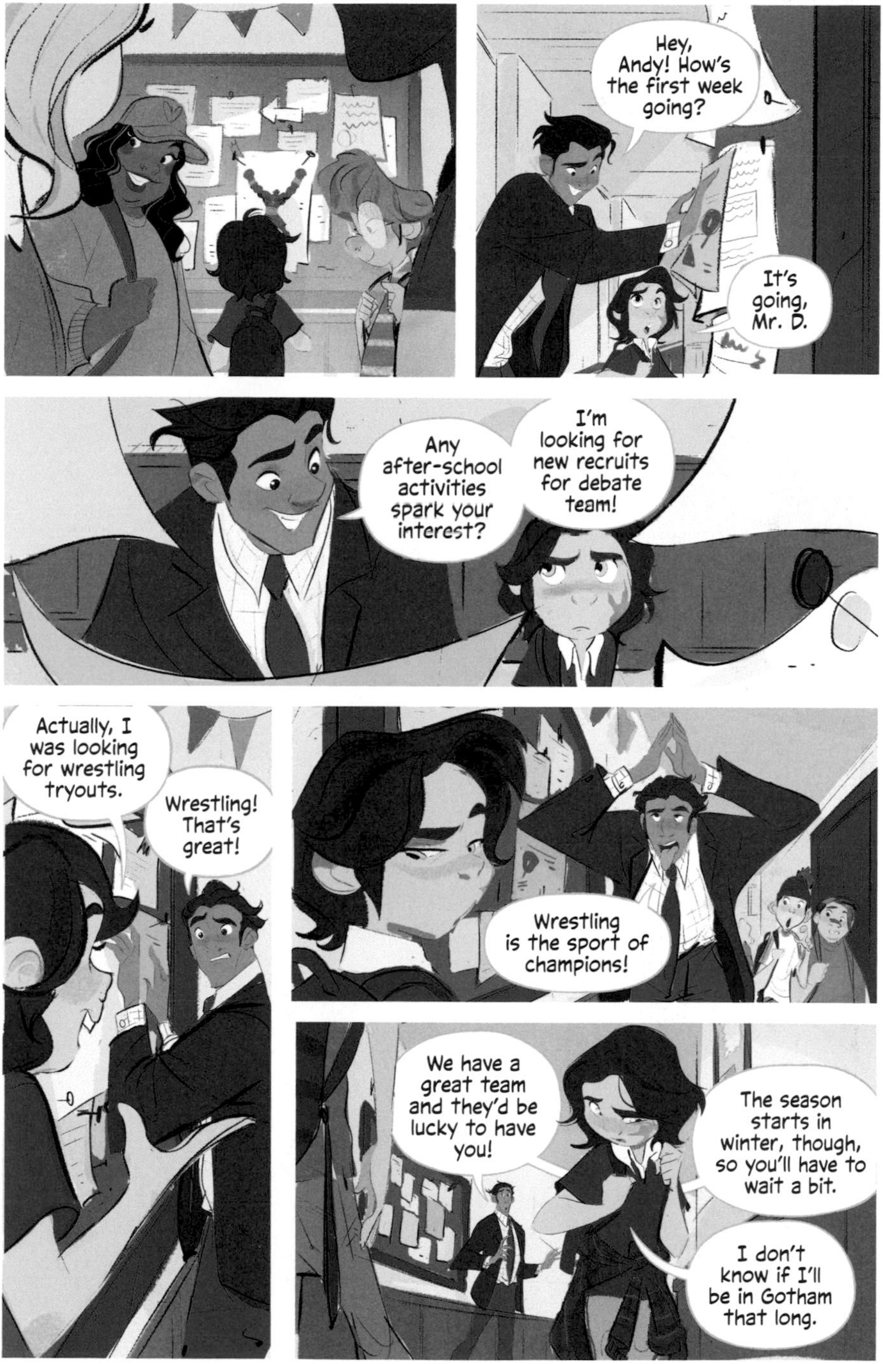
Hey, Andy! How's the first week going?
It's going, Mr. D.
Any after-school activities spark your interest?
I'm looking for new recruits for debate team!
Actually, I was looking for wrestling tryouts.
Wrestling! That's great!
Wrestling is the sport of champions!
We have a great team and they'd be lucky to have you!
The season starts in winter, though, so you'll have to wait a bit.
I don't know if I'll be in Gotham that long.

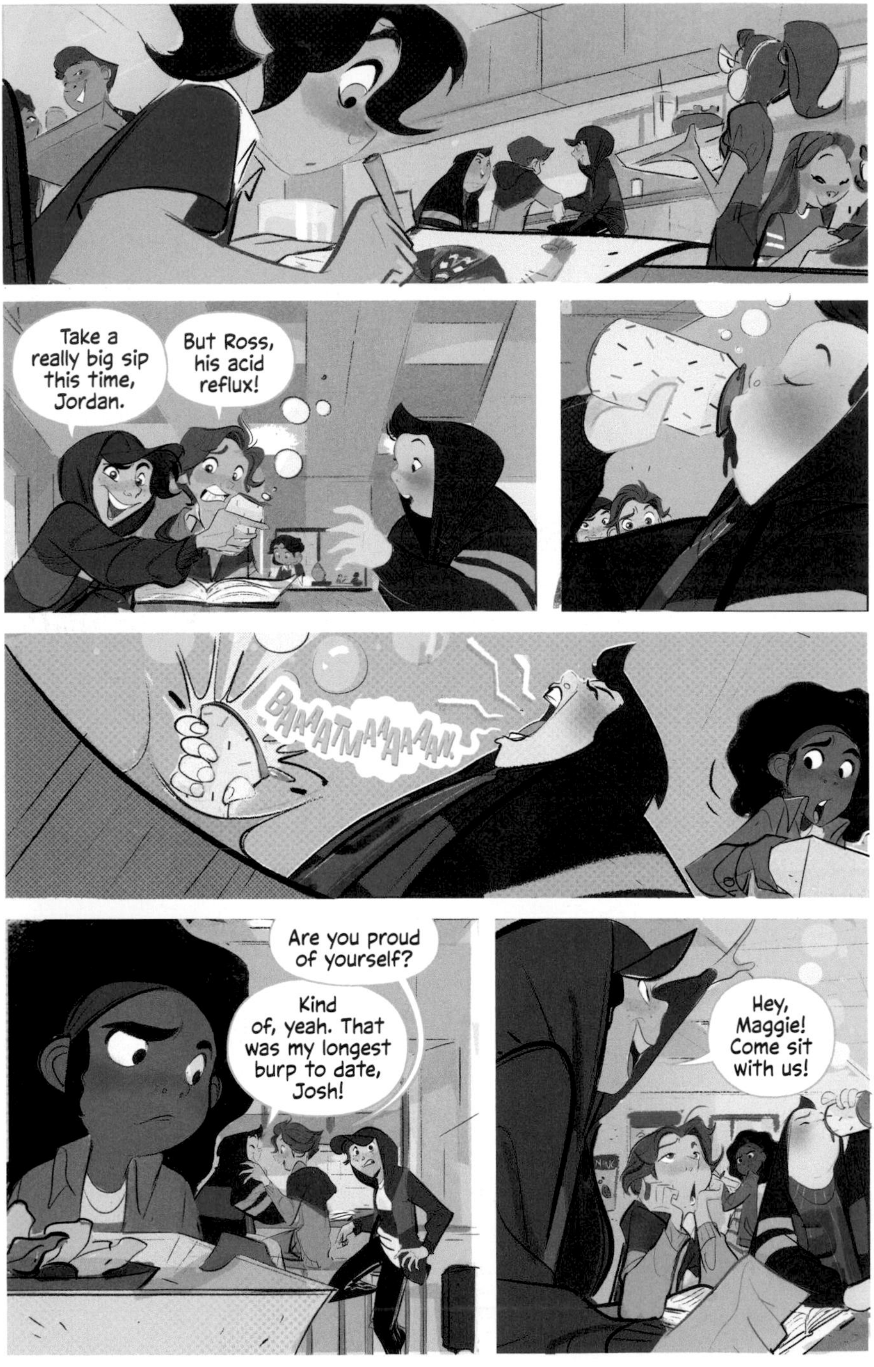
Take a really big sip this time, Jordan.
But Ross, his acid reflux!
BAAAATMAAAAAAN!
Are you proud of yourself?
Kind of, yeah. That was my longest burp to date, Josh!
Hey, Maggie! Come sit with us!

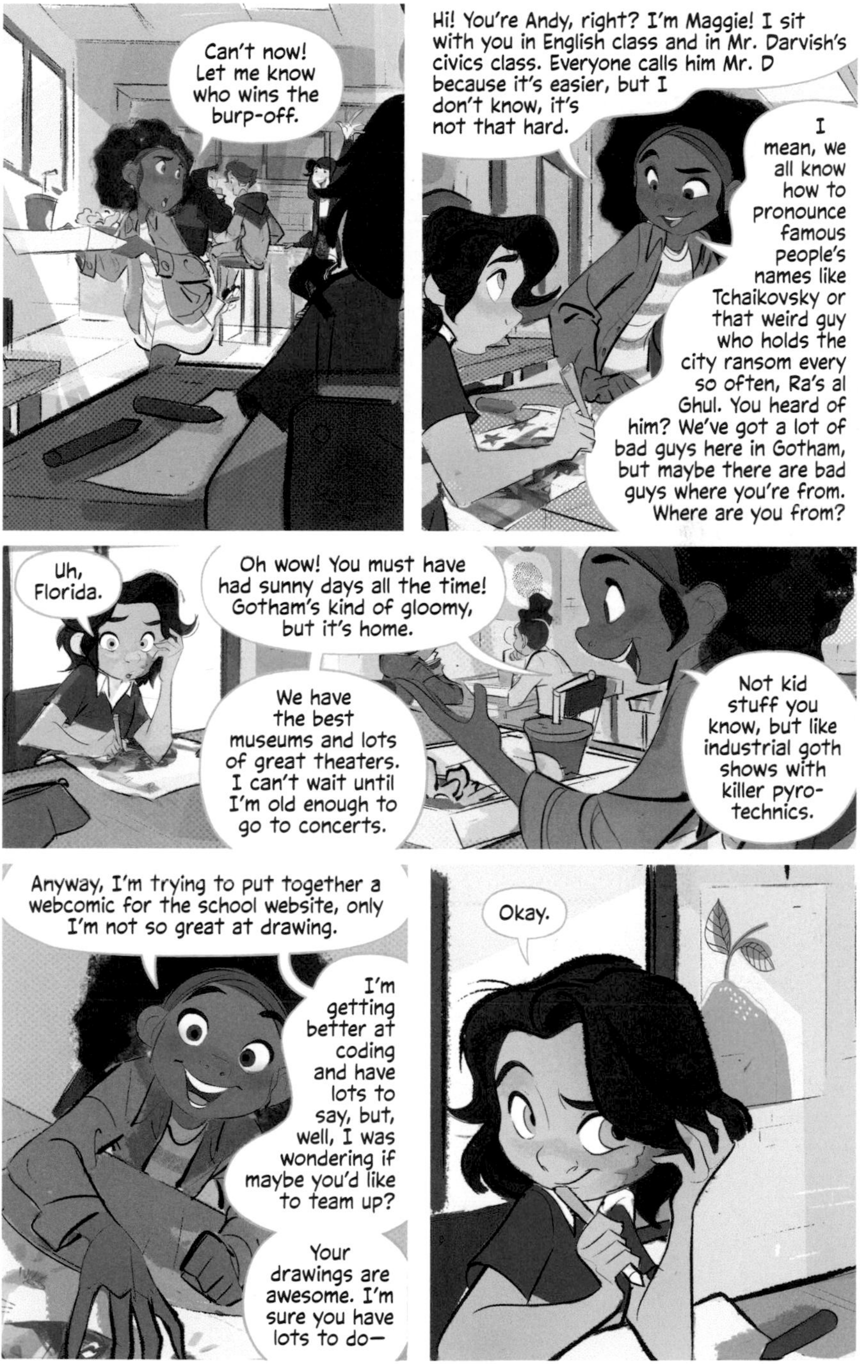
Can't now! Let me know who wins the burp-off.
Hi! You're Andy, right? I'm Maggie! I sit with you in English class and in Mr. Darvish's civics class. Everyone calls him Mr. D because it's easier, but I don't know, it's not that hard.
I mean, we all know how to pronounce famous people's names like Tchaikovsky or that weird guy who holds the city ransom every so often, Ra's al Ghul. You heard of him? We've got a lot of bad guys here in Gotham, but maybe there are bad guys where you're from. Where are you from?
Uh, Florida.
Oh wow! You must have had sunny days all the time! Gotham's kind of gloomy, but it's home.
We have the best museums and lots of great theaters. I can't wait until I'm old enough to go to concerts.
Not kid stuff you know, but like industrial goth shows with killer pyro-technics.
Anyway, I'm trying to put together a webcomic for the school website, only I'm not so great at drawing.
I'm getting better at coding and have lots to say, but, well, I was wondering if maybe you'd like to team up?
Your drawings are awesome. I'm sure you have lots to do—
Okay.

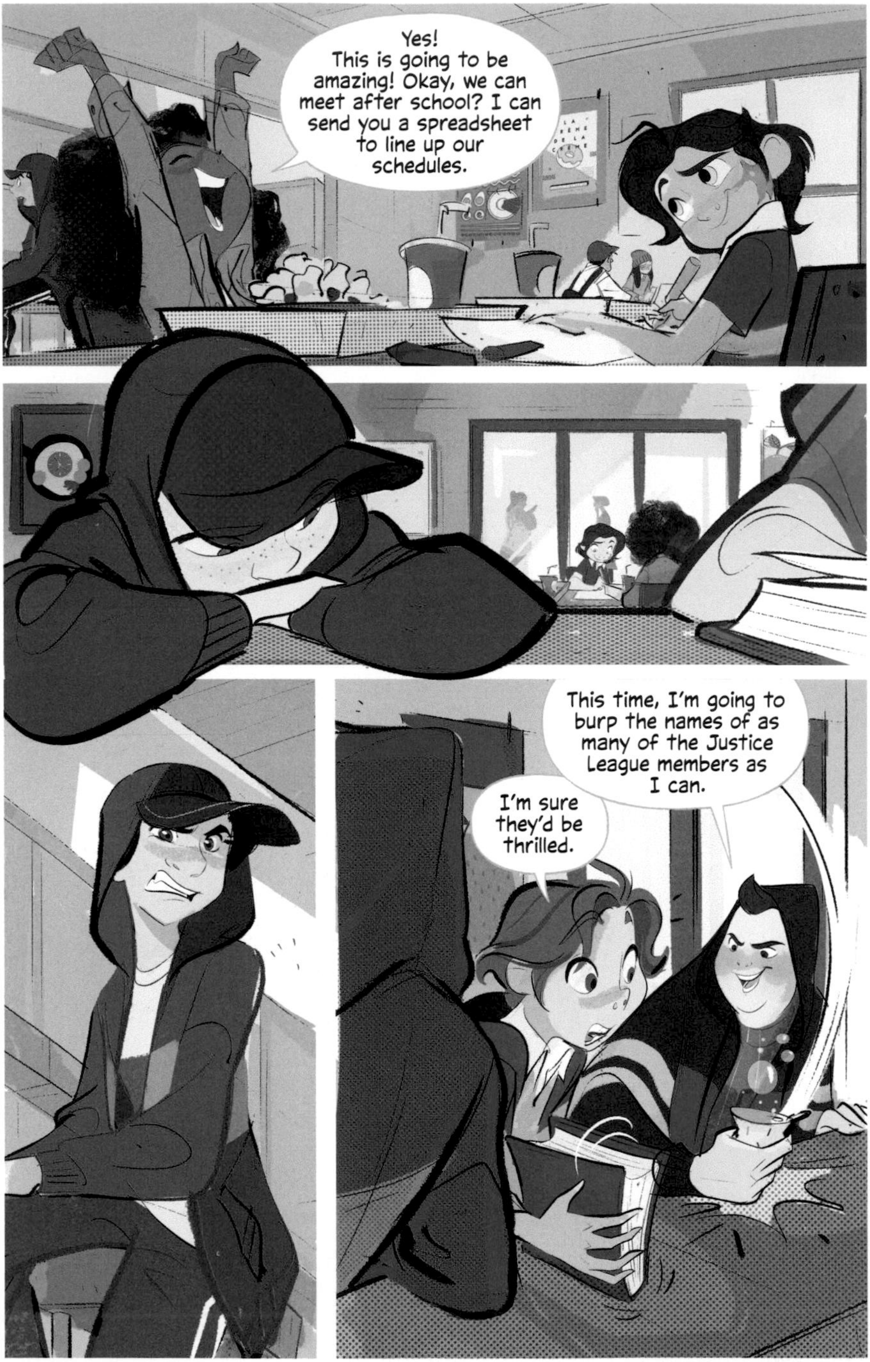
Yes! This is going to be amazing! Okay, we can meet after school? I can send you a spreadsheet to line up our schedules.
This time, I'm going to burp the names of as many of the Justice League members as I can.
I'm sure they'd be thrilled.

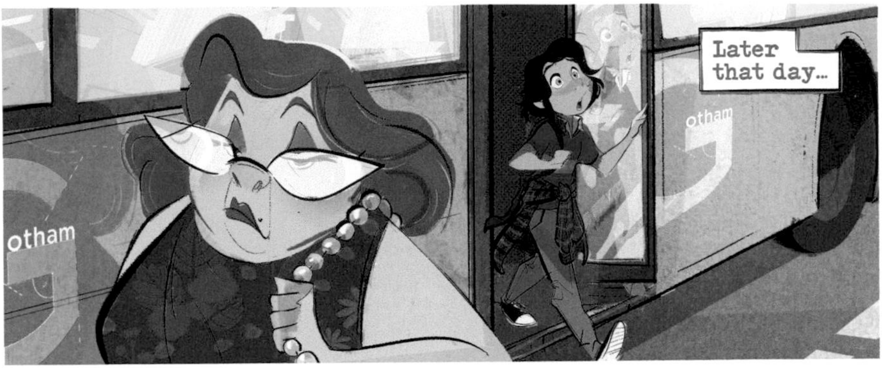
Later that day...
otham
otham

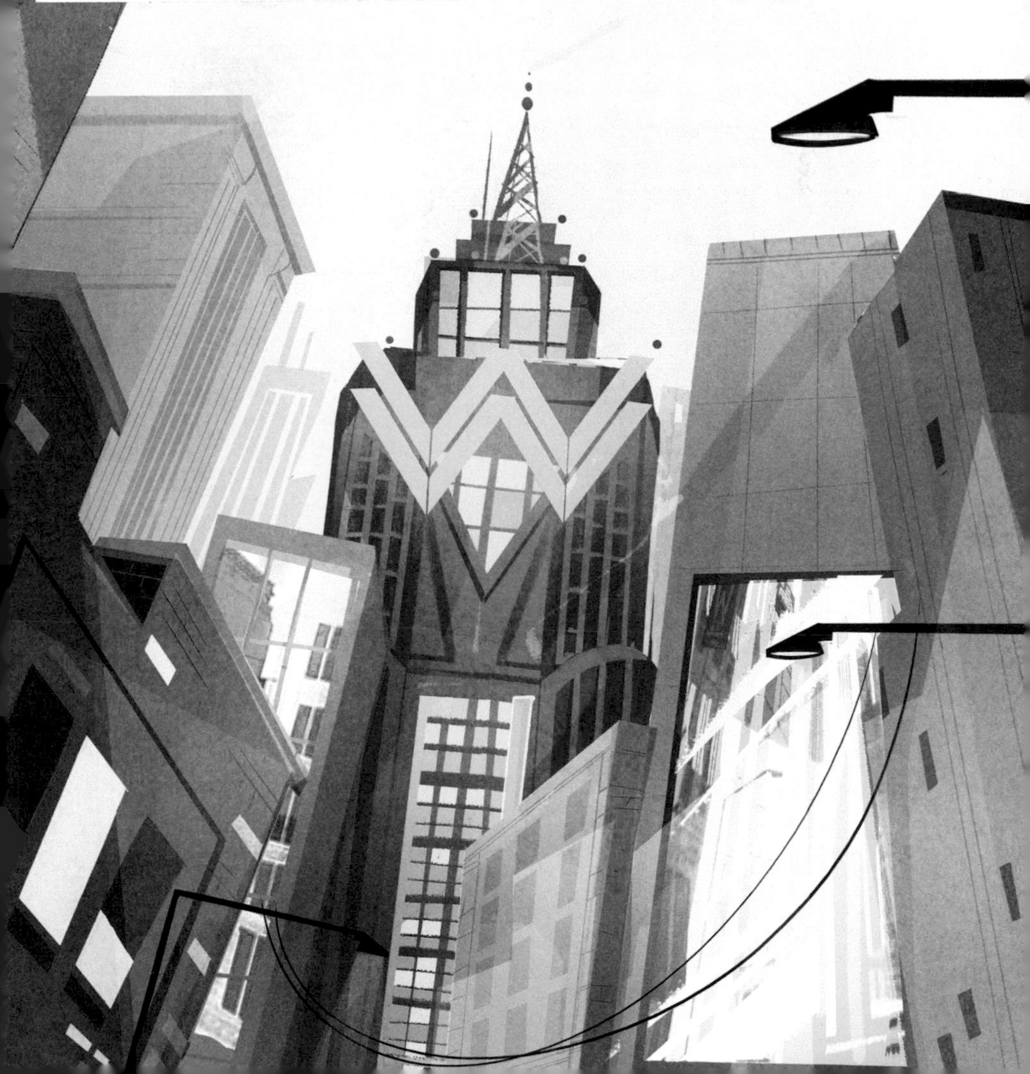

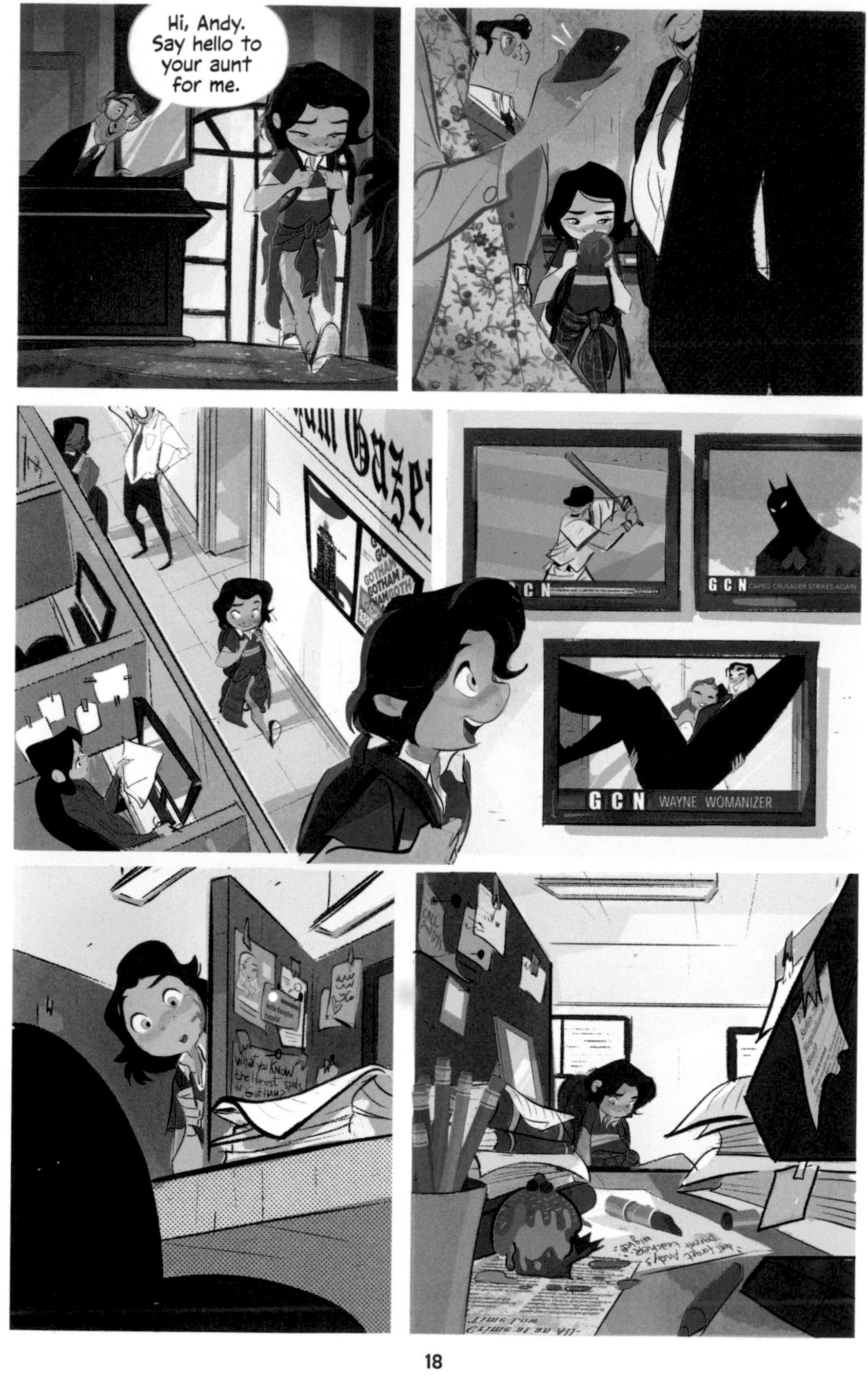
Hi, Andy. Say hello to your aunt for me.
GCN CAPED CRUSADER STRIKES AGAIN
GCN WAYNE WOMANIZER

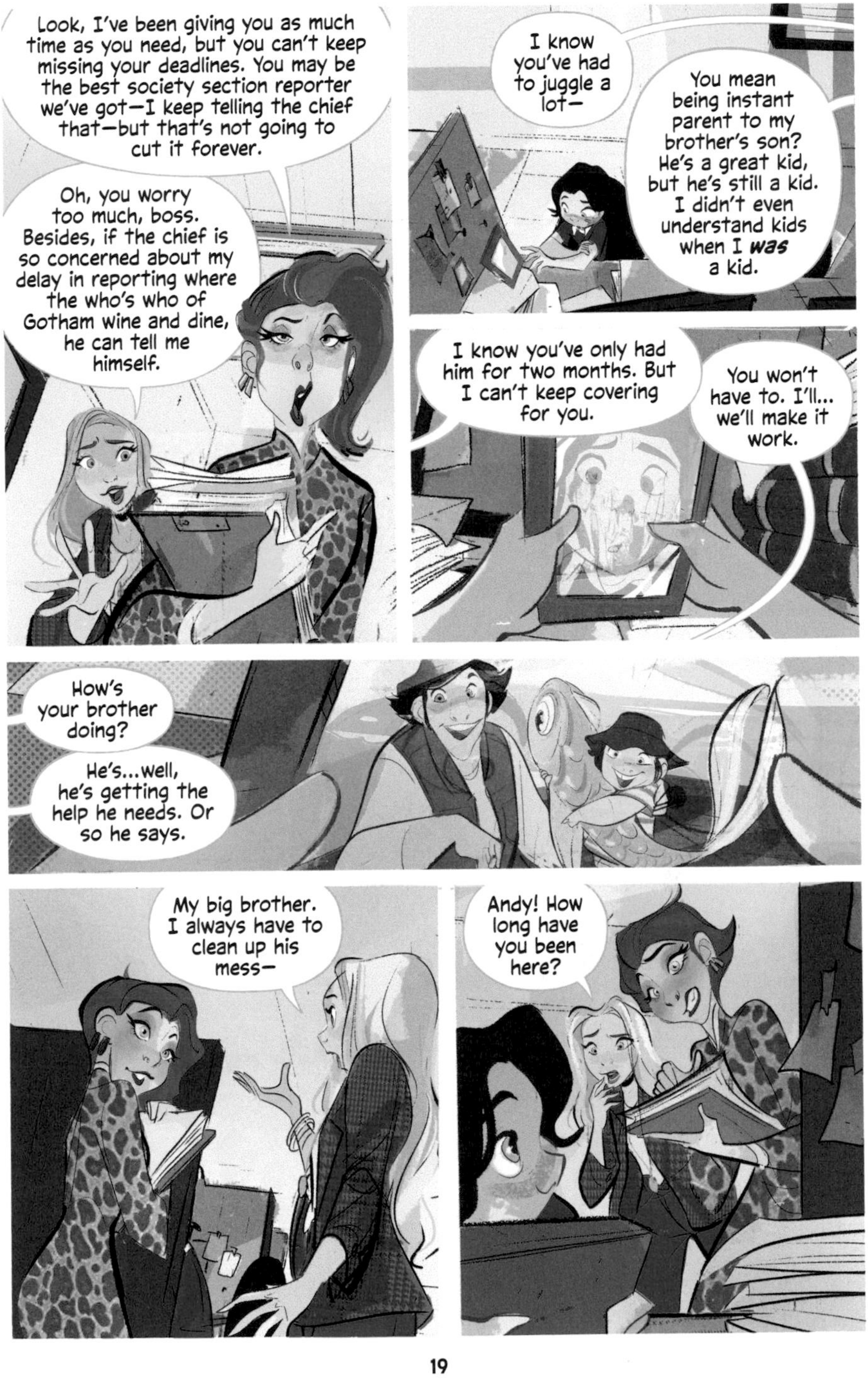

Look, I've been giving you as much time as you need, but you can't keep missing your deadlines. You may be the best society section reporter we've got—I keep telling the chief that—but that's not going to cut it forever.
Oh, you worry too much, boss. Besides, if the chief is so concerned about my delay in reporting where the who's who of Gotham wine and dine, he can tell me himself.
I know you've had to juggle a lot—
You mean being instant parent to my brother's son? He's a great kid, but he's still a kid. I didn't even understand kids when I *was* a kid.
I know you've only had him for two months. But I can't keep covering for you.
You won't have to. I'll... we'll make it work.
How's your brother doing?
He's...well, he's getting the help he needs. Or so he says.
My big brother. I always have to clean up his mess—
Andy! How long have you been here?

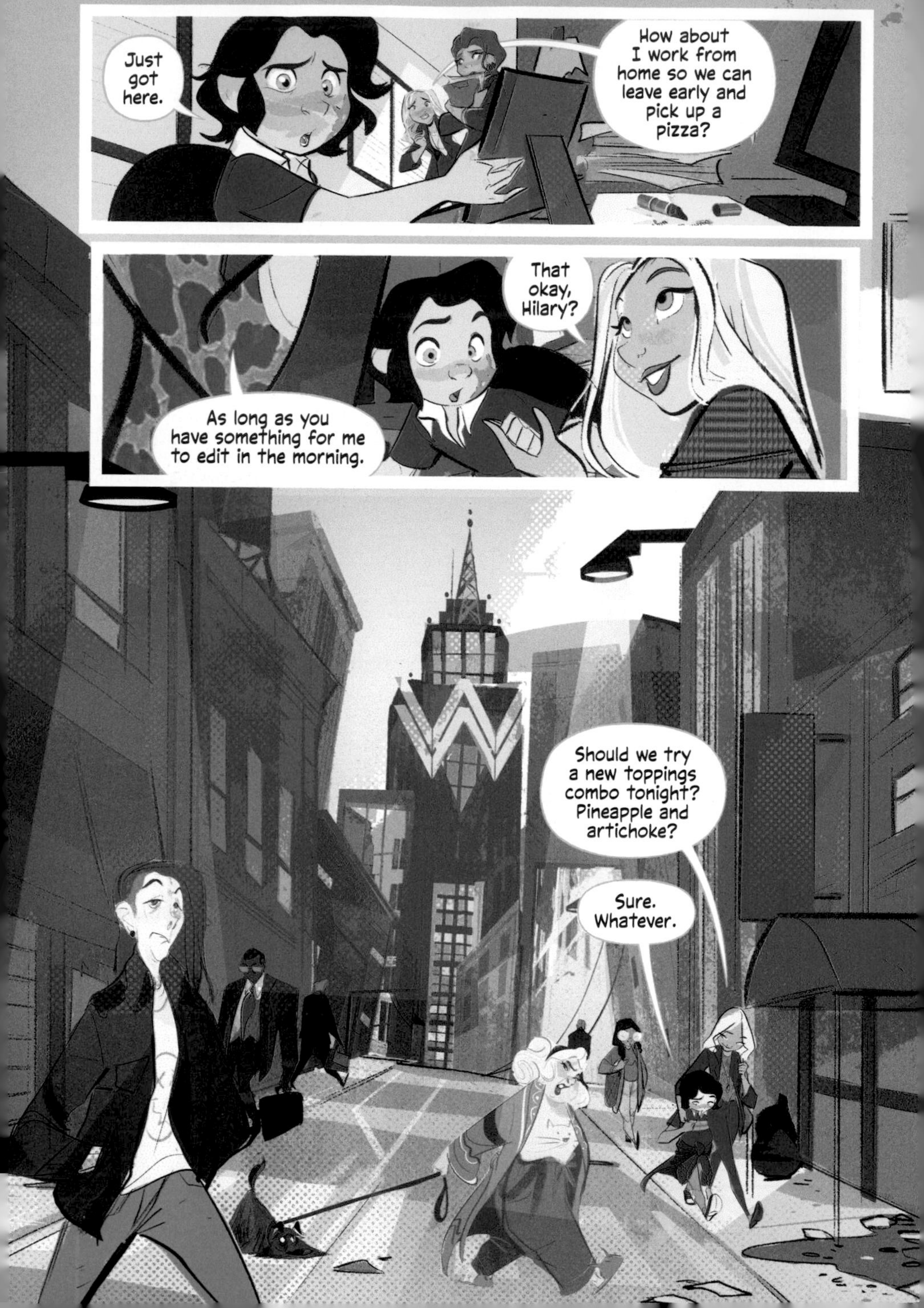
Just got here.
How about I work from home so we can leave early and pick up a pizza?
That okay, Hilary?
As long as you have something for me to edit in the morning.
Should we try a new toppings combo tonight? Pineapple and artichoke?
Sure. Whatever.

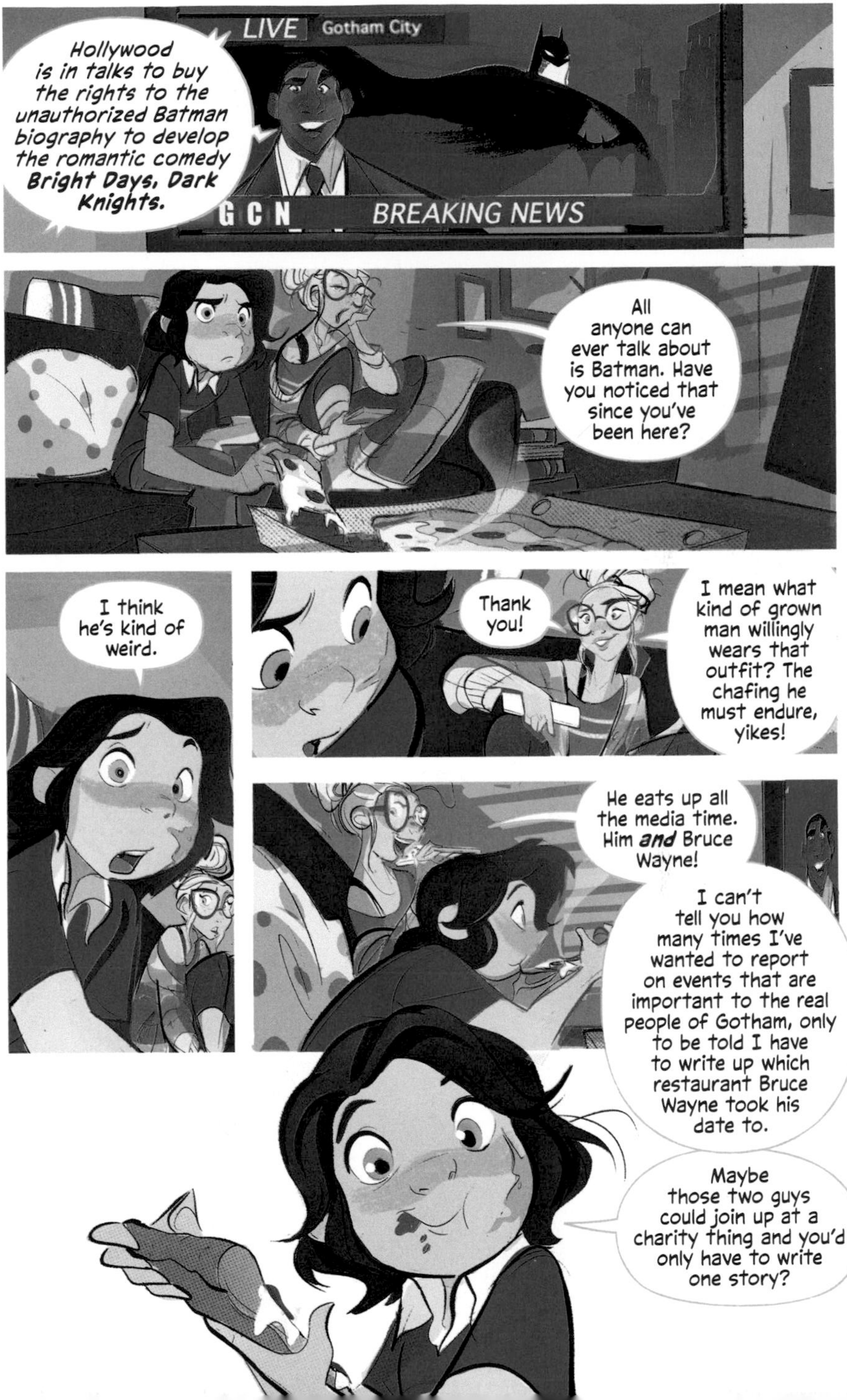
LIVE Gotham City
Hollywood is in talks to buy the rights to the unauthorized Batman biography to develop the romantic comedy Bright Days, Dark Knights.
GCN BREAKING NEWS
All anyone can ever talk about is Batman. Have you noticed that since you've been here?
I think he's kind of weird.
Thank you!
I mean what kind of grown man willingly wears that outfit? The chafing he must endure, yikes!
He eats up all the media time. Him and Bruce Wayne!
I can't tell you how many times I've wanted to report on events that are important to the real people of Gotham, only to be told I have to write up which restaurant Bruce Wayne took his date to.
Maybe those two guys could join up at a charity thing and you'd only have to write one story?

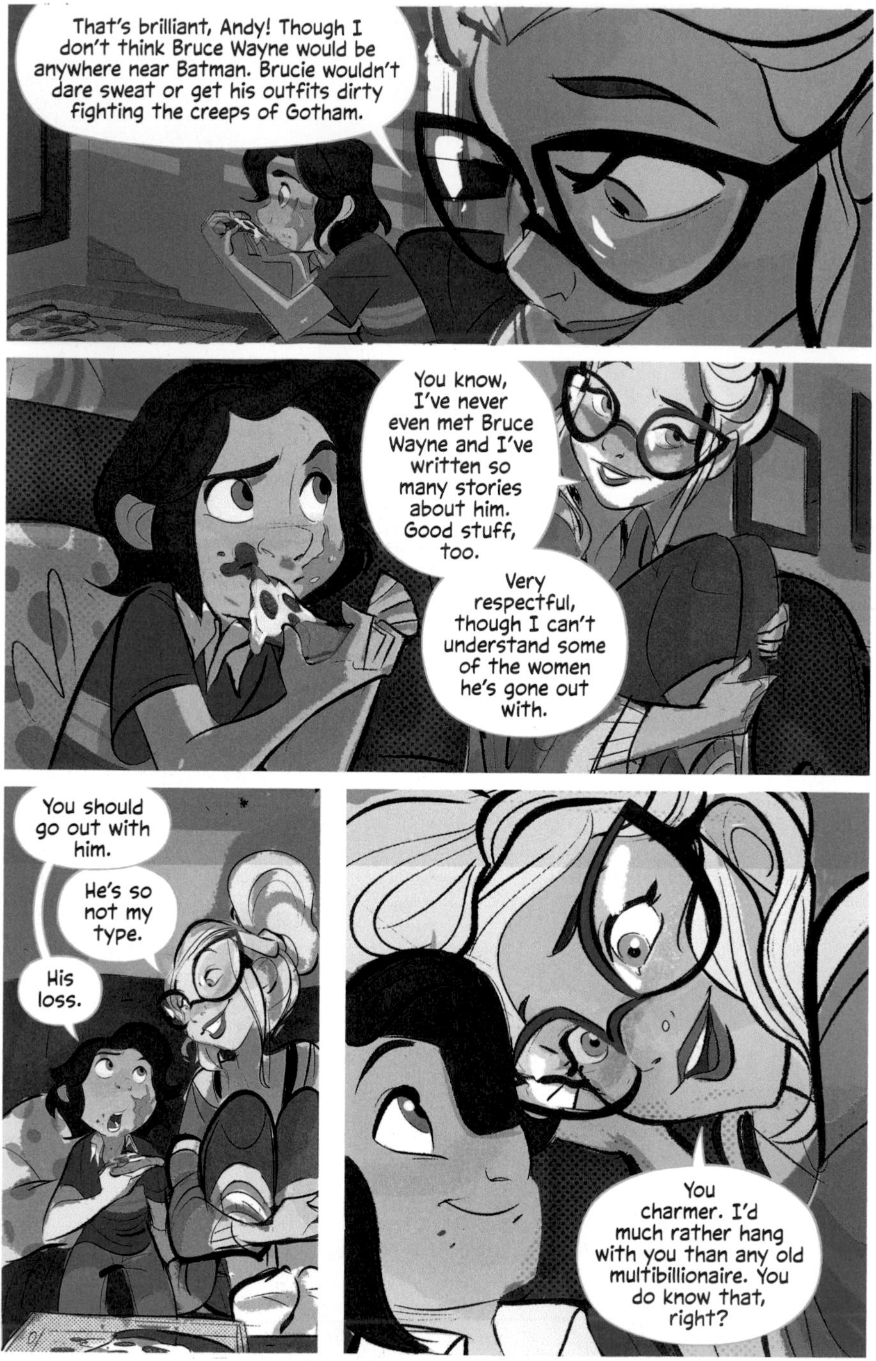
That's brilliant, Andy! Though I don't think Bruce Wayne would be anywhere near Batman. Brucie wouldn't dare sweat or get his outfits dirty fighting the creeps of Gotham.
You know, I've never even met Bruce Wayne and I've written so many stories about him. Good stuff, too.
Very respectful, though I can't understand some of the women he's gone out with.
You should go out with him.
He's so not my type.
His loss.
You charmer. I'd much rather hang with you than any old multibillionaire. You do know that, right?

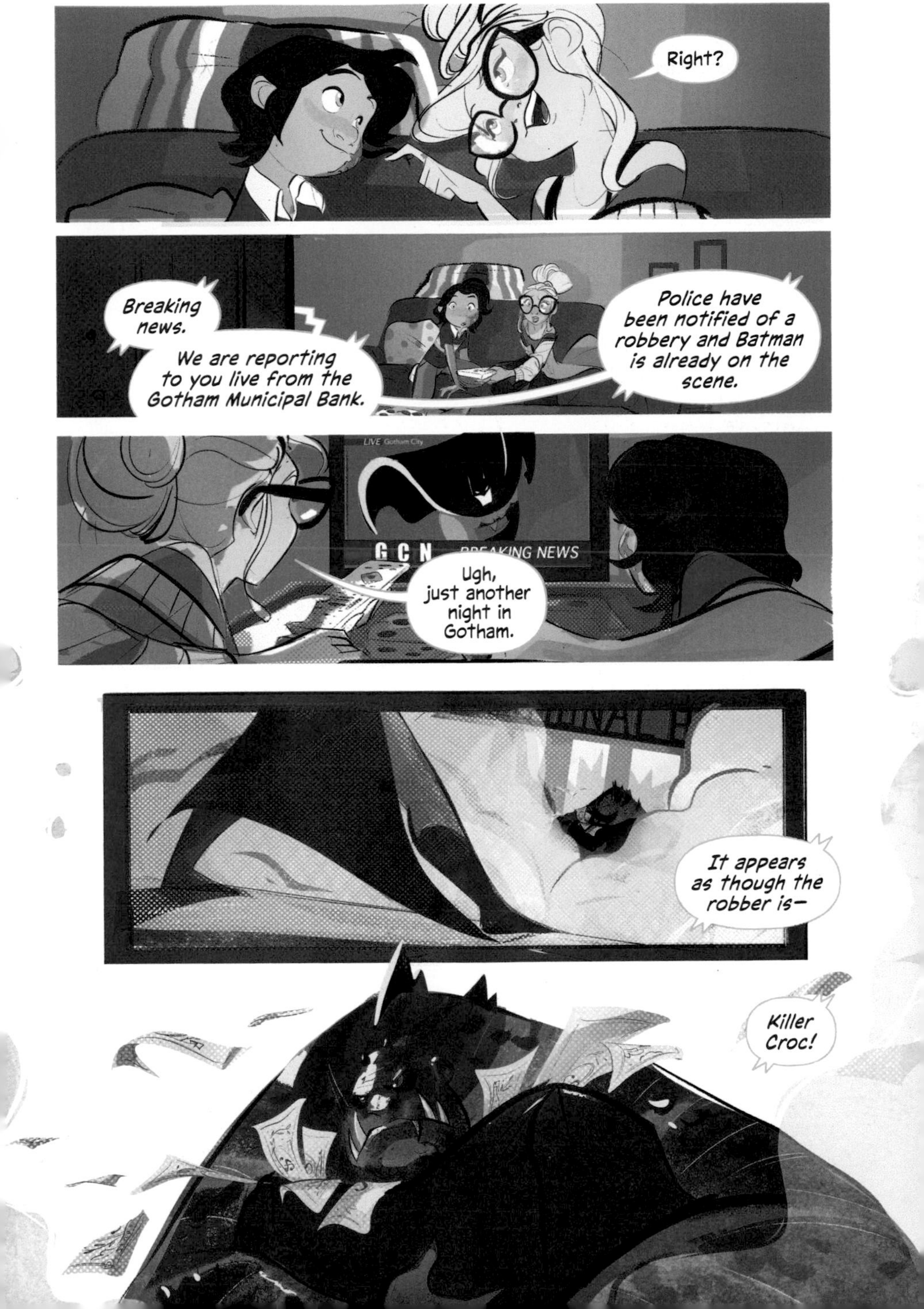

Right?
Breaking news.
We are reporting to you live from the Gotham Municipal Bank.
Police have been notified of a robbery and Batman is already on the scene.
LIVE Gotham City
GCN BREAKING NEWS
Ugh, just another night in Gotham.
It appears as though the robber is—
Killer Croc!

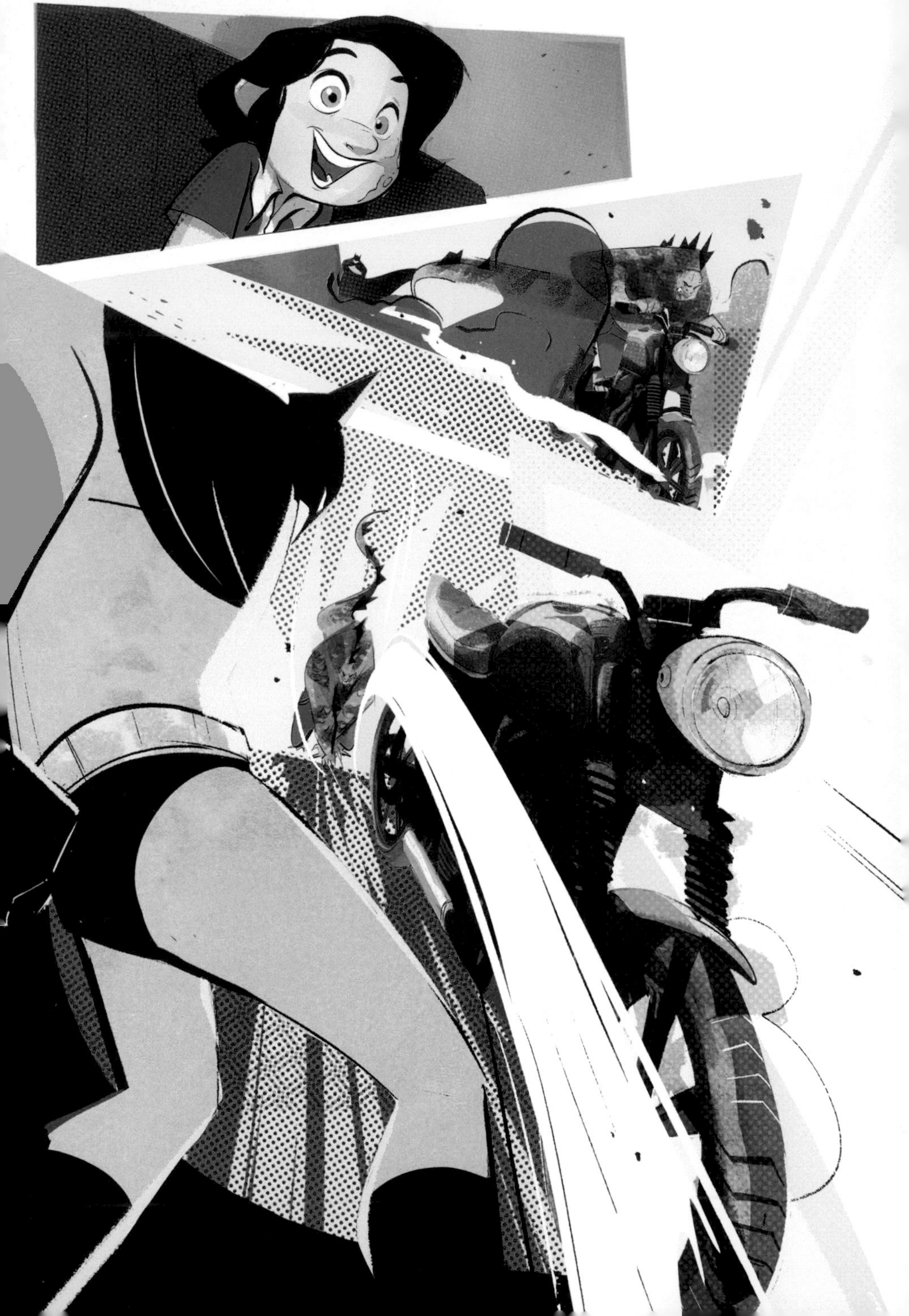

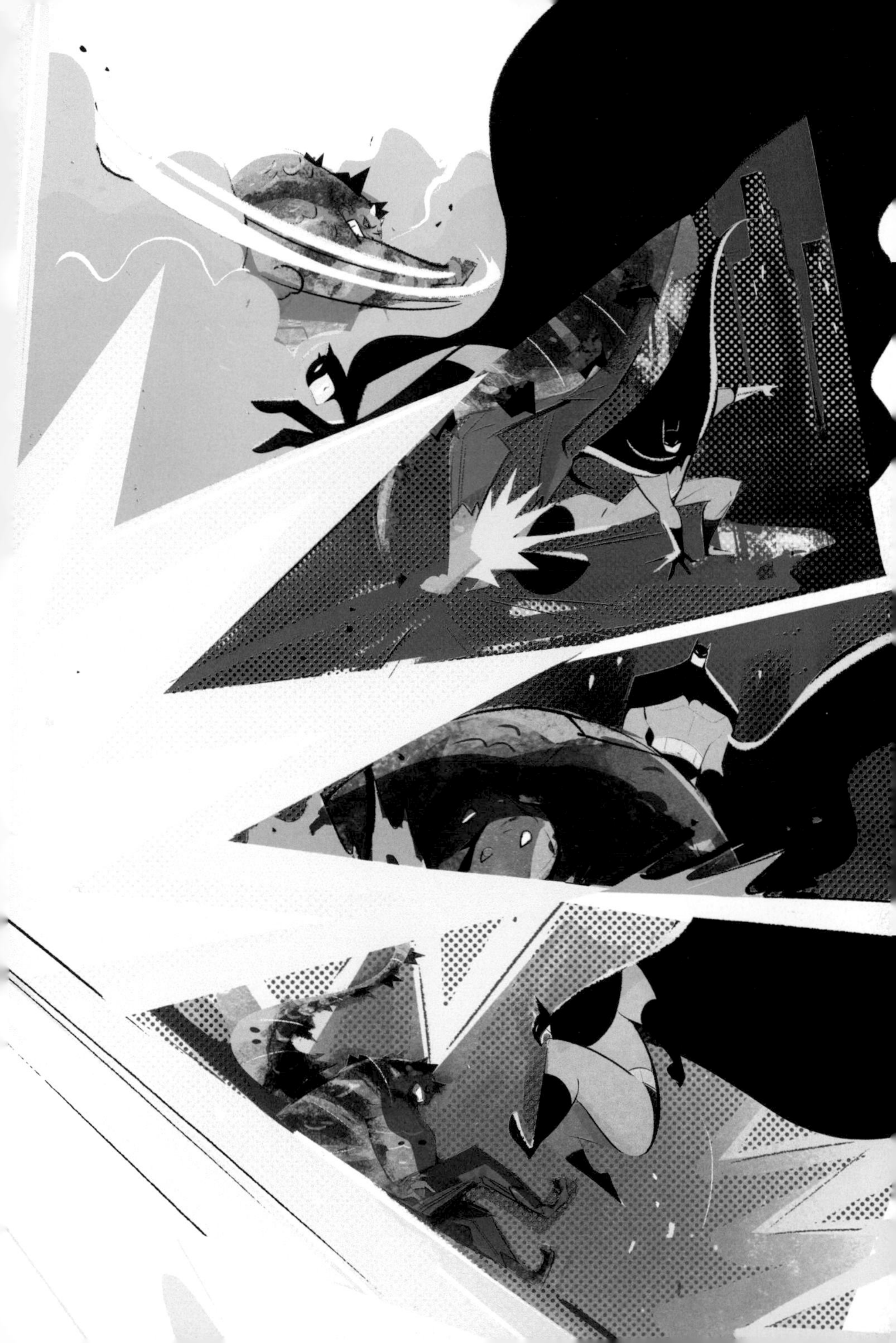

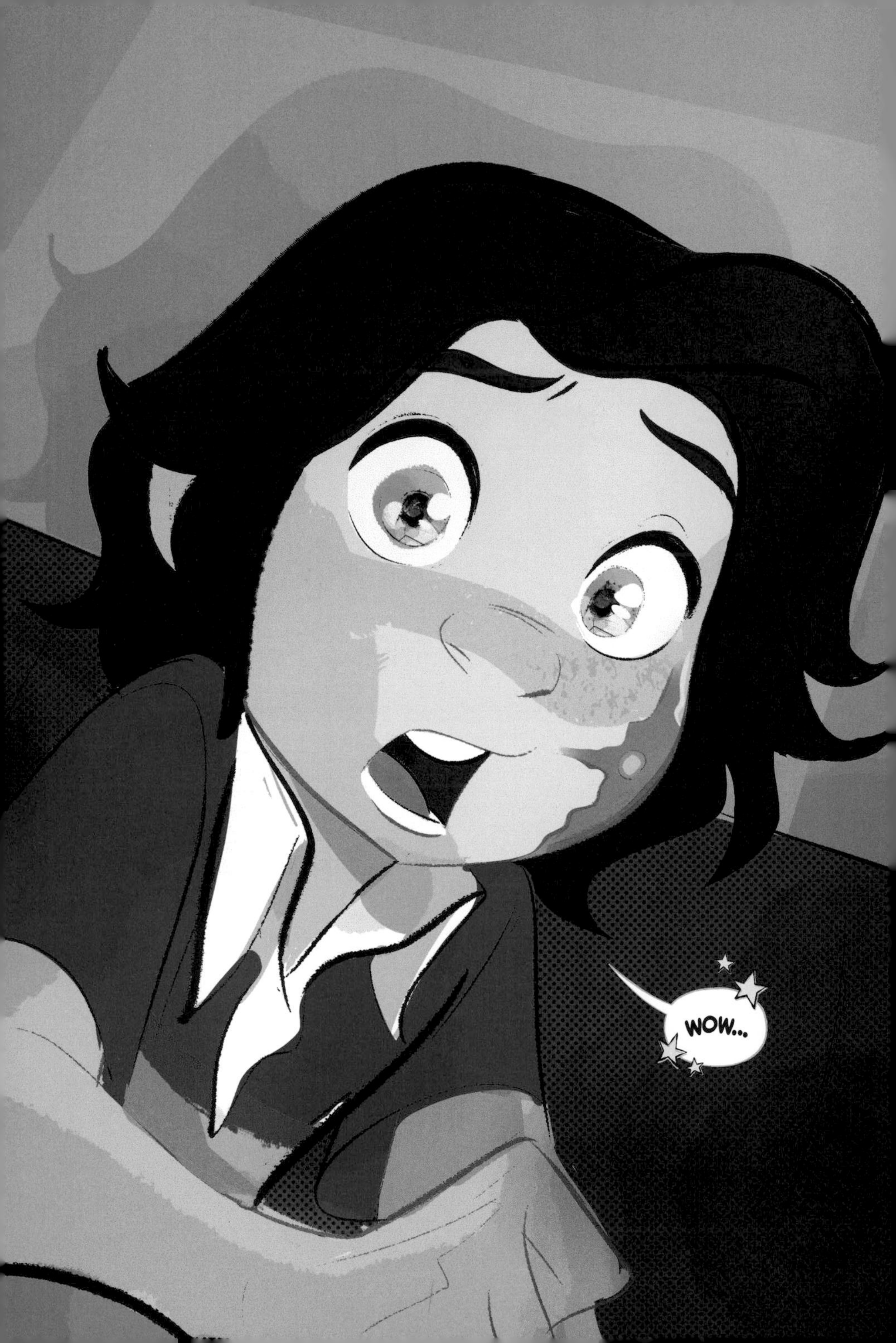
WOW...

CHAPTER TWO
27

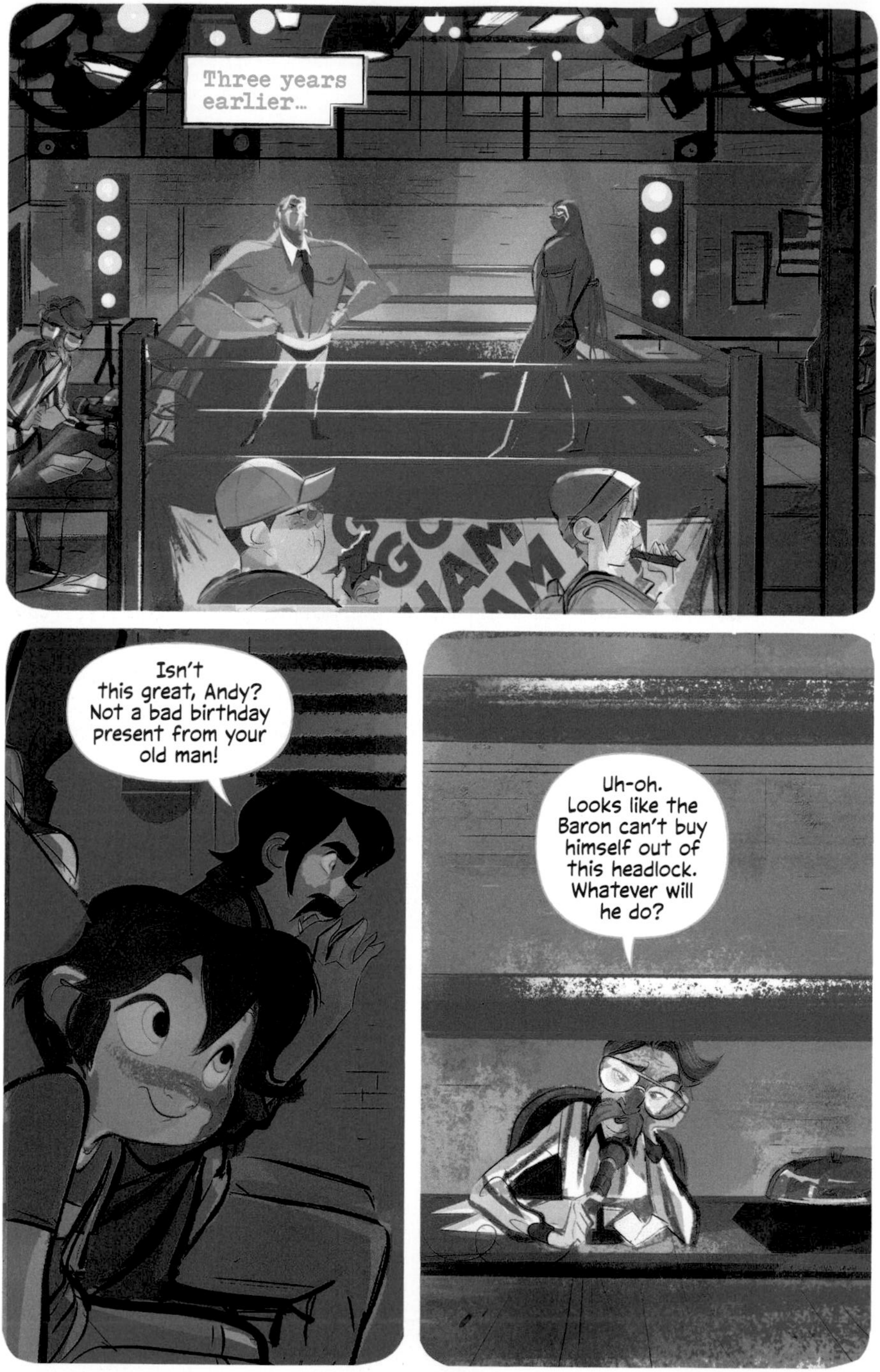
Three years earlier...
Isn't this great, Andy? Not a bad birthday present from your old man!
Uh-oh. Looks like the Baron can't buy himself out of this headlock. Whatever will he do?

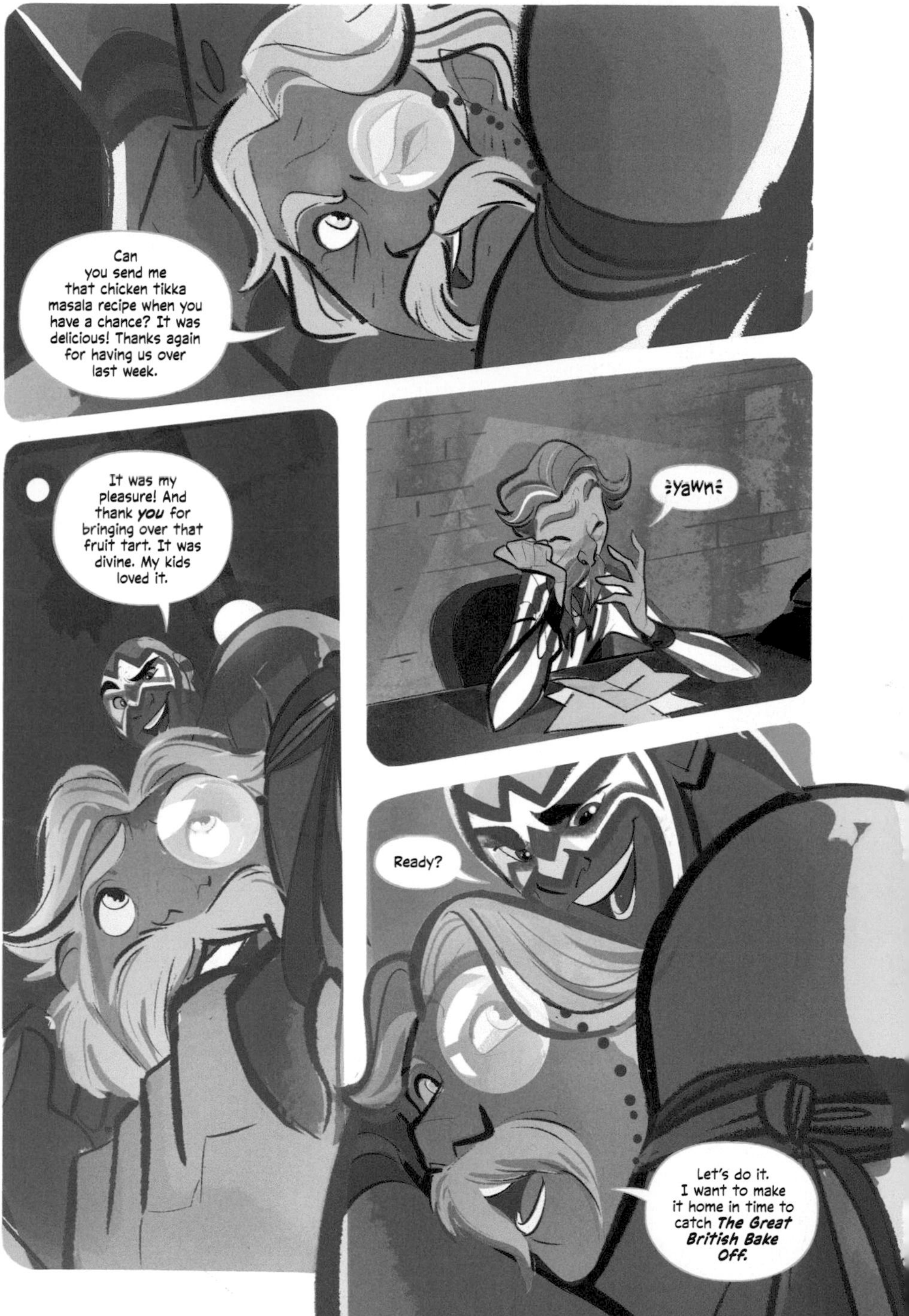
Can you send me that chicken tikka masala recipe when you have a chance? It was delicious! Thanks again for having us over last week.
It was my pleasure! And thank *you* for bringing over that fruit tart. It was divine. My kids loved it.
yawn
Ready?
Let's do it. I want to make it home in time to catch ***The Great British Bake Off.***

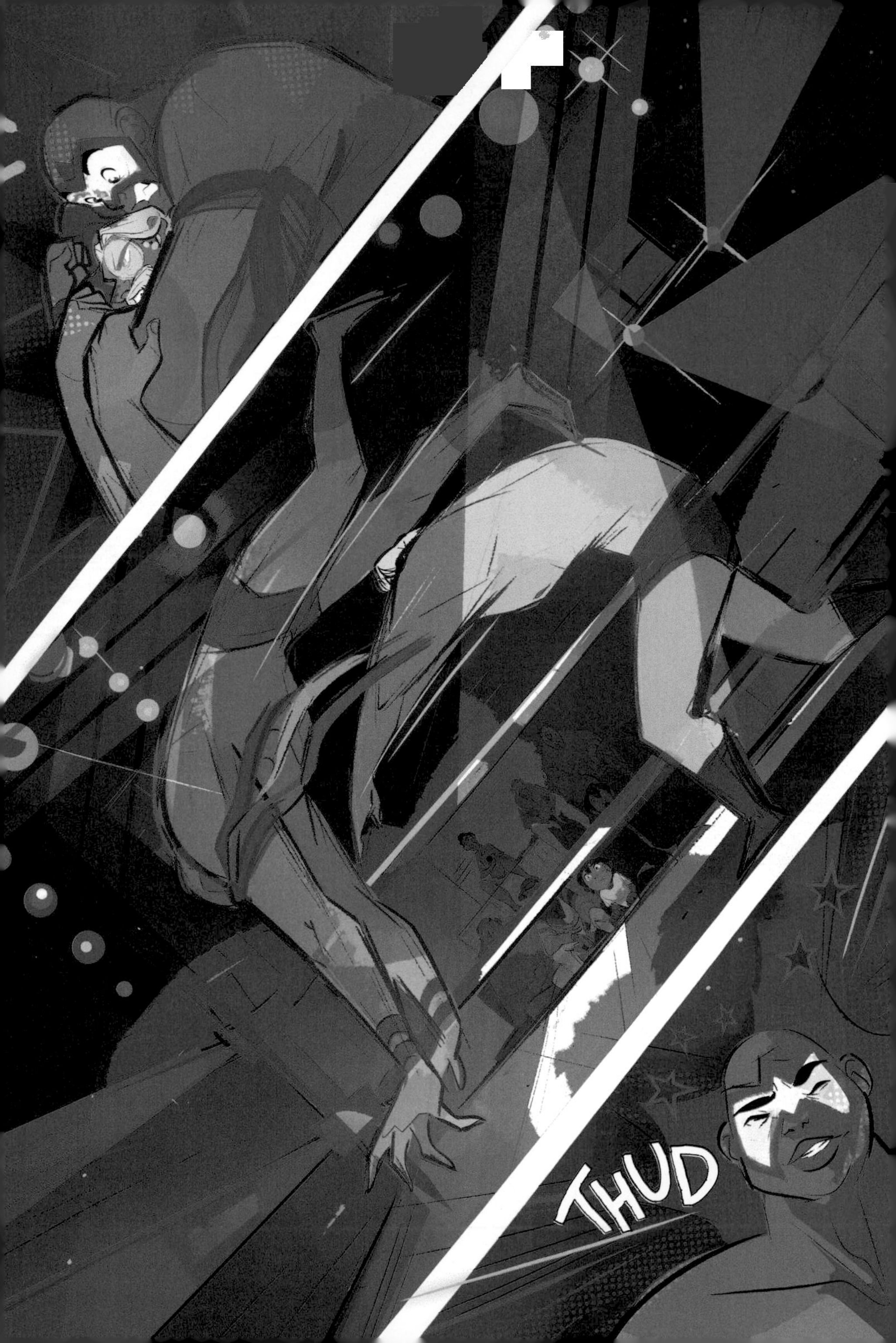
THUD

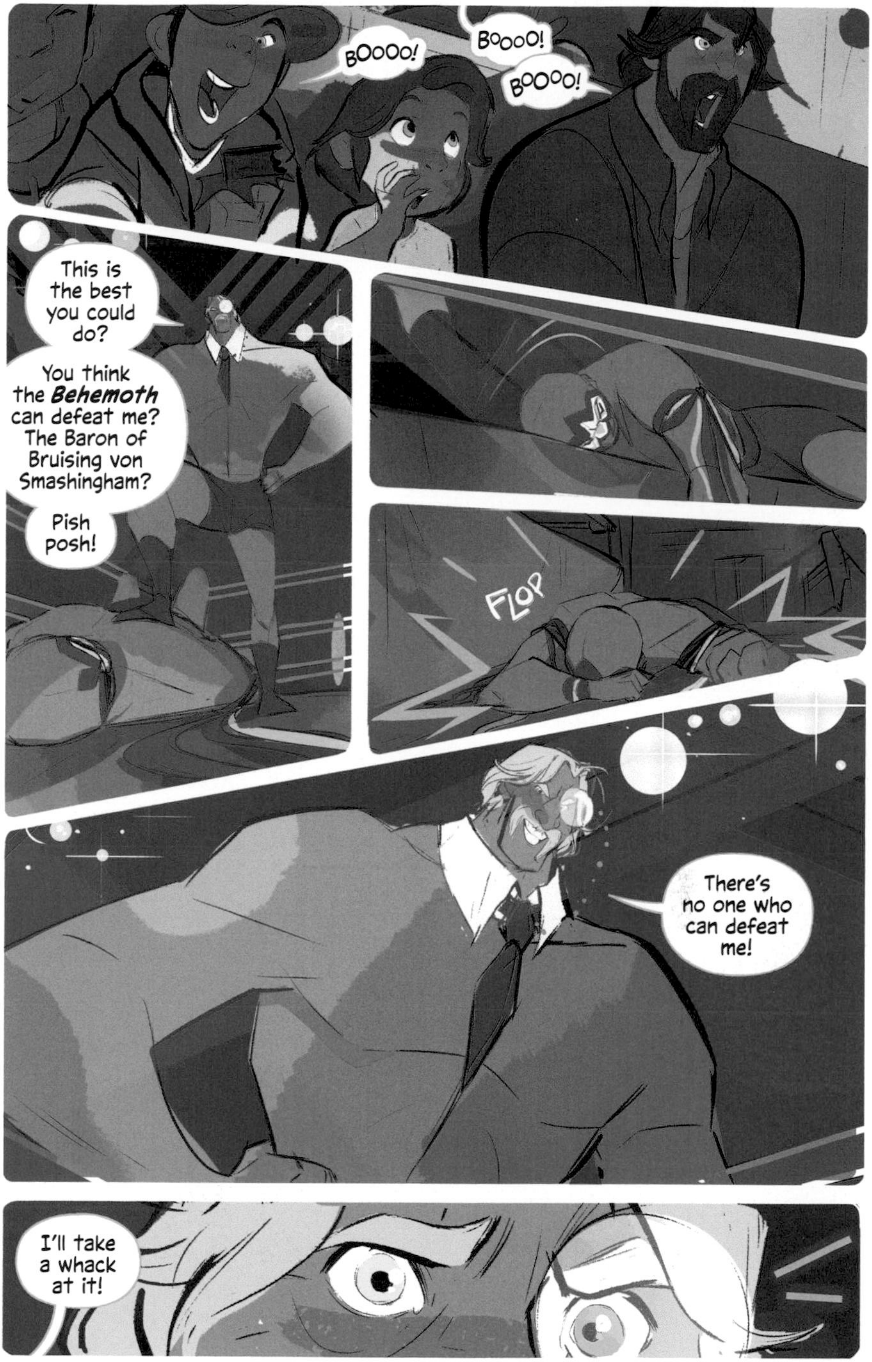
BOOOO!
BOOOO!
BOOOO!
This is the best you could do?
You think the Behemoth can defeat me? The Baron of Bruising von Smashingham?
Pish posh!
FLOP
There's no one who can defeat me!
I'll take a whack at it!

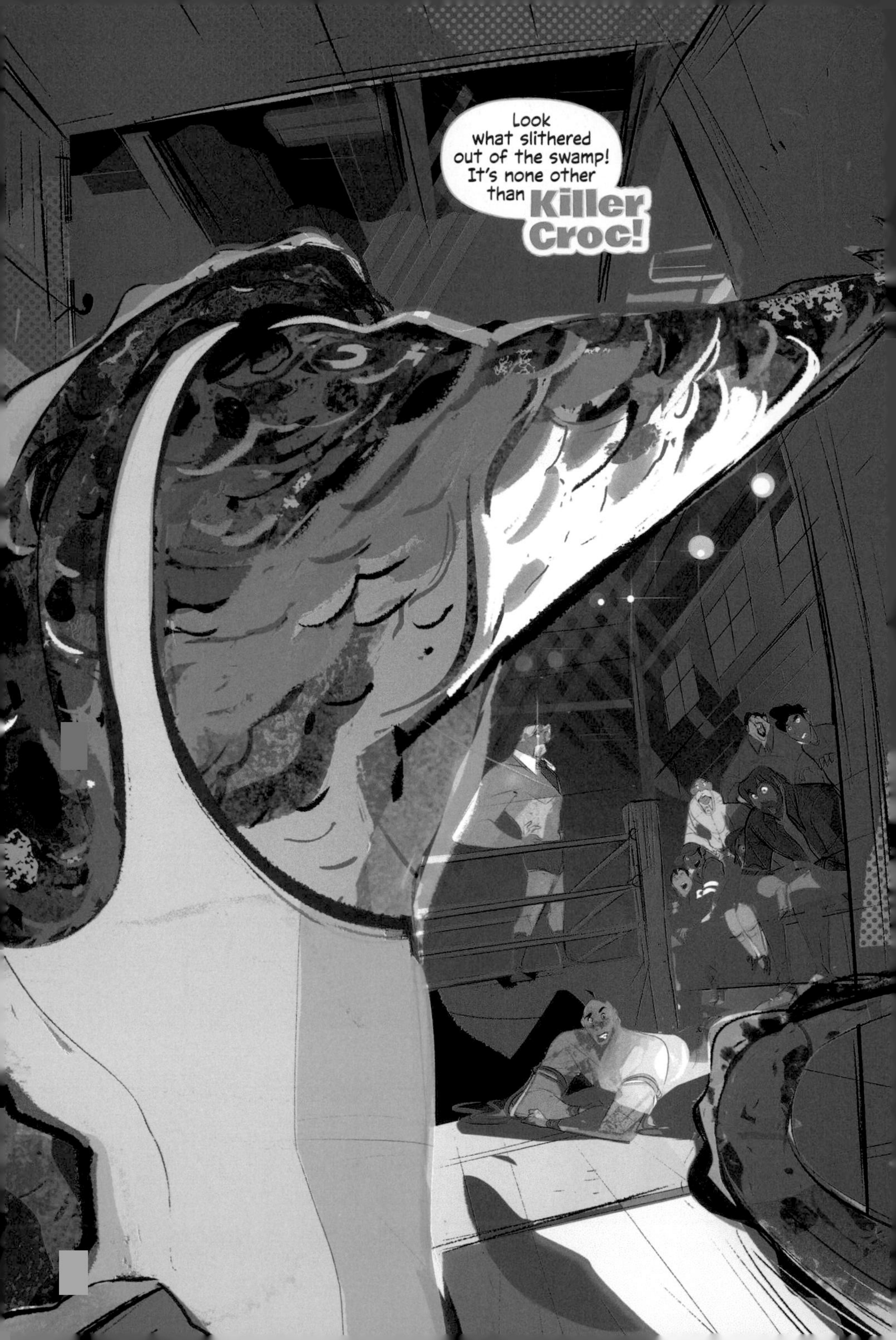
Look what slithered out of the swamp! It's none other than Killer Croc!

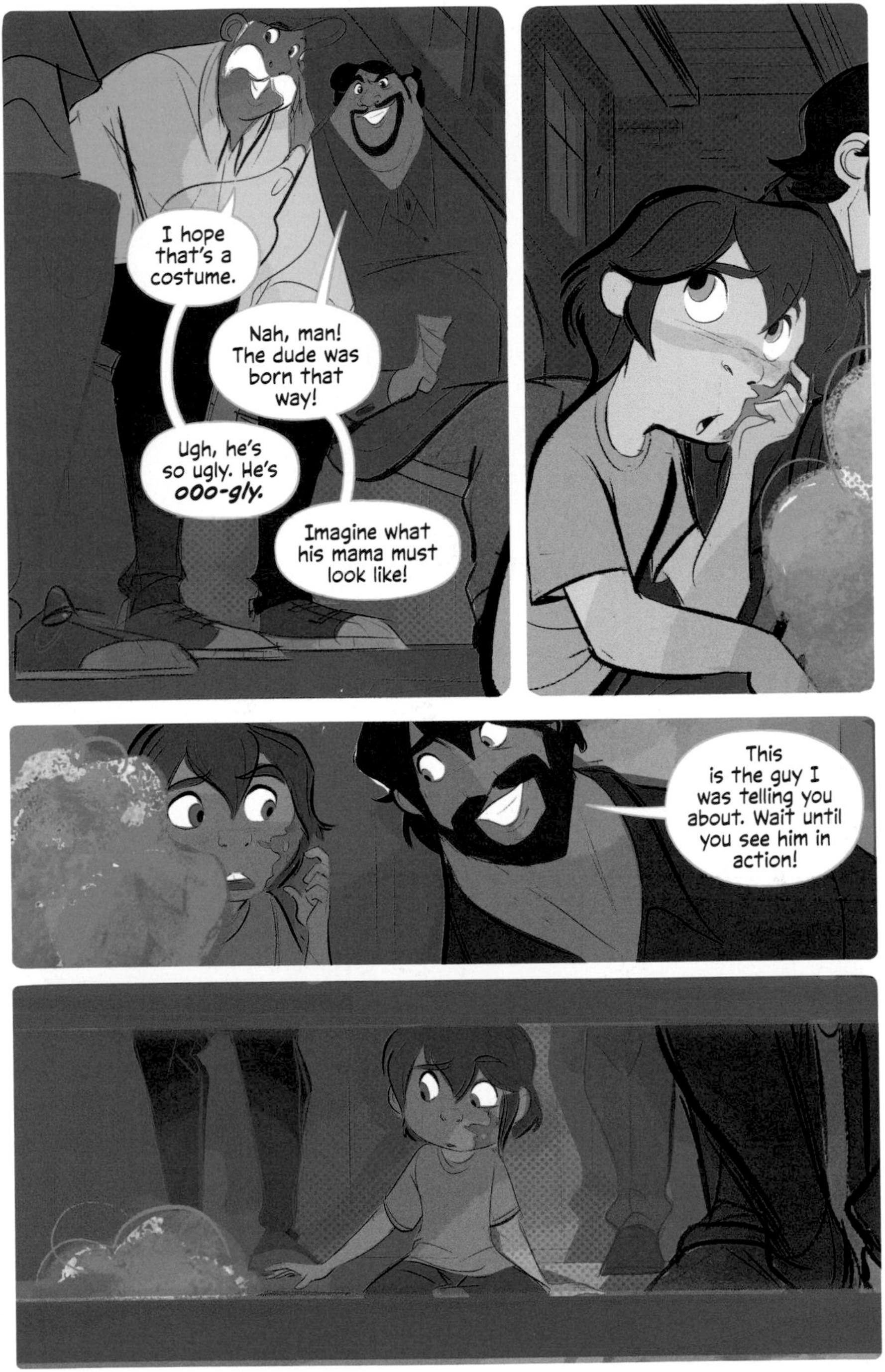
I hope that's a costume.
Nah, man! The dude was born that way!
Ugh, he's so ugly. He's *ooo-gly.*
Imagine what his mama must look like!
This is the guy I was telling you about. Wait until you see him in action!

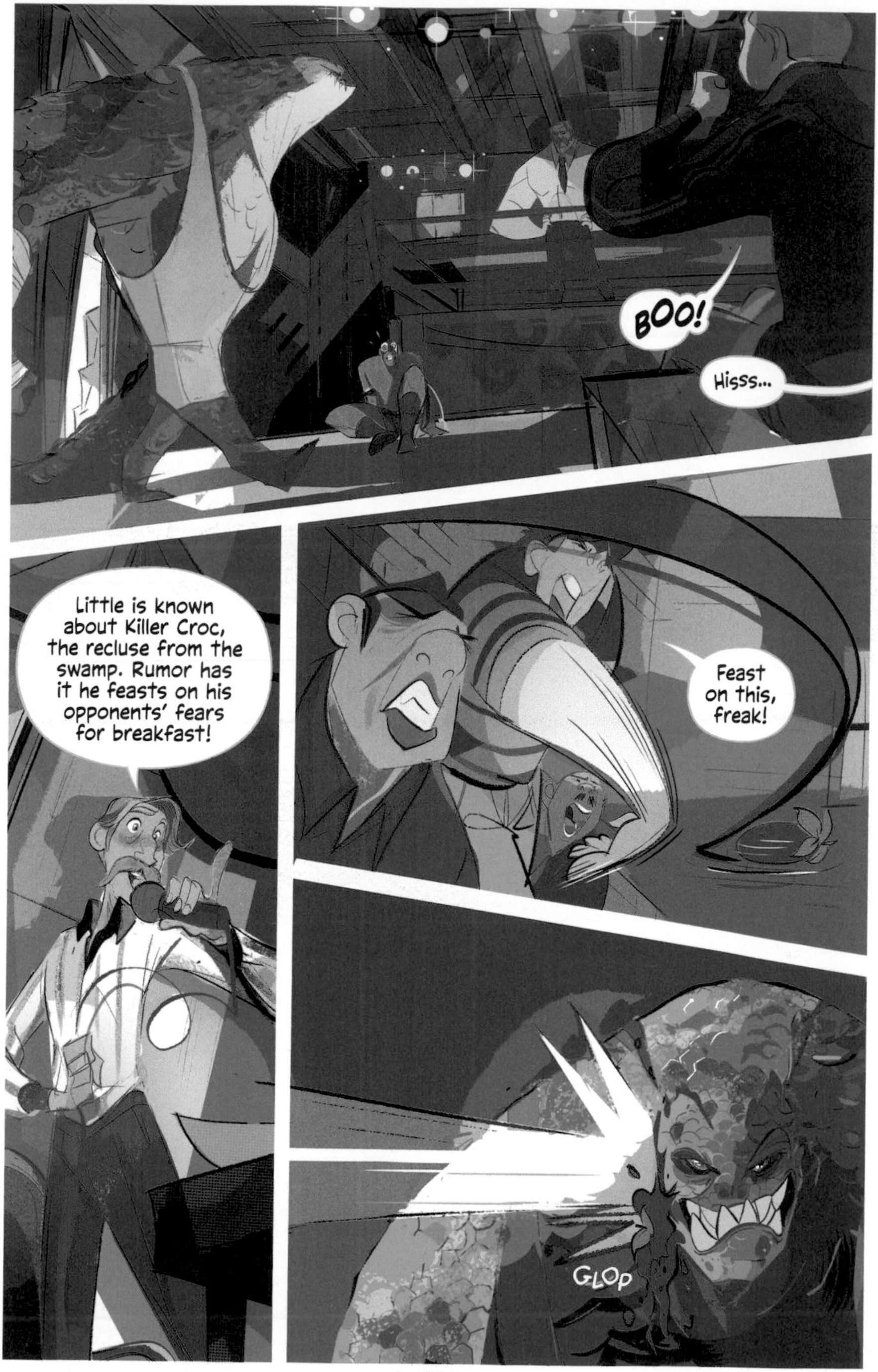
BOO!
Hisss...
Little is known about Killer Croc, the recluse from the swamp. Rumor has it he feasts on his opponents' fears for breakfast!
Feast on this, freak!
GLOP

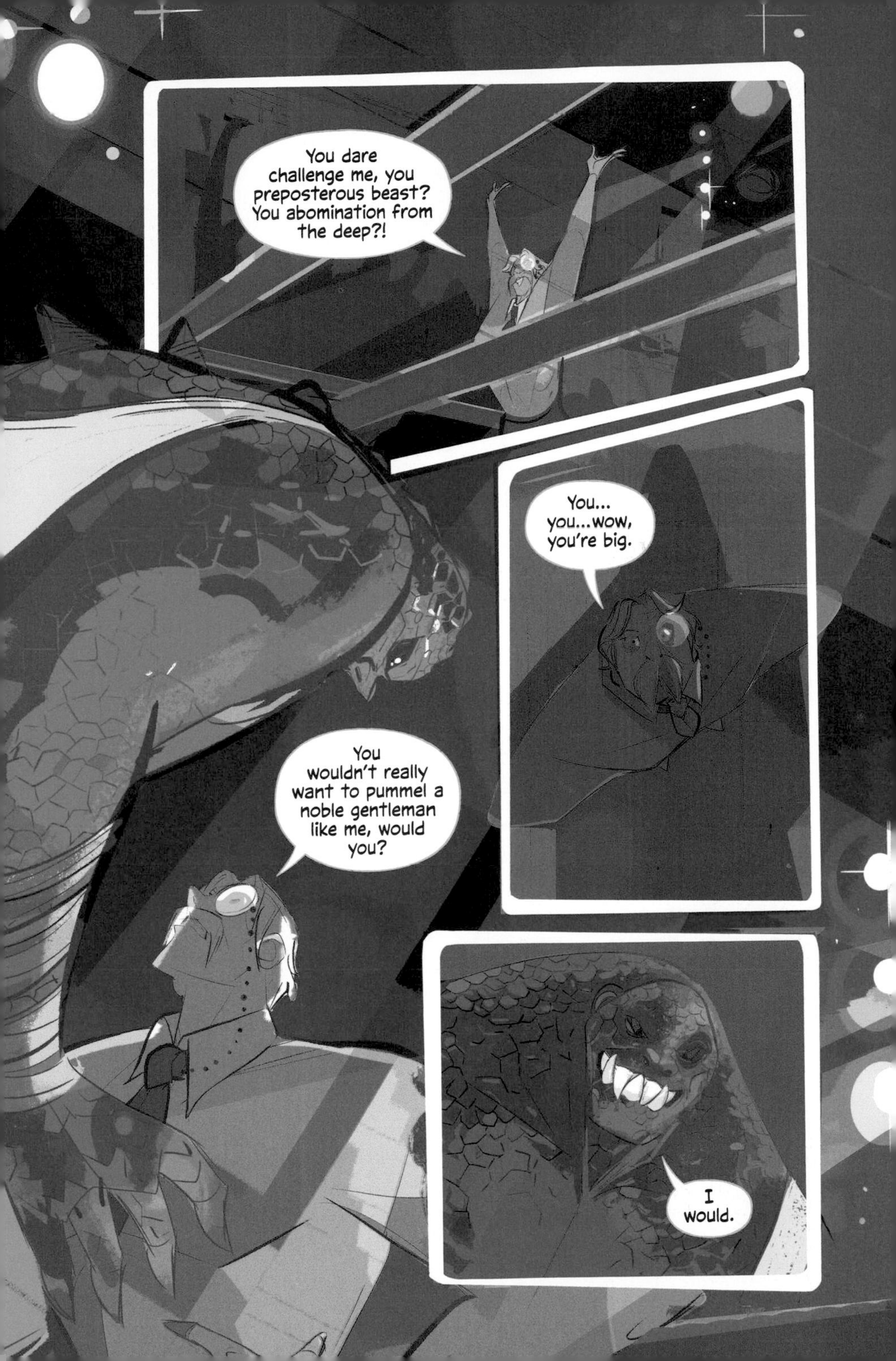
You dare challenge me, you preposterous beast? You abomination from the deep?!
You... you...wow, you're big.
You wouldn't really want to pummel a noble gentleman like me, would you?
I would.

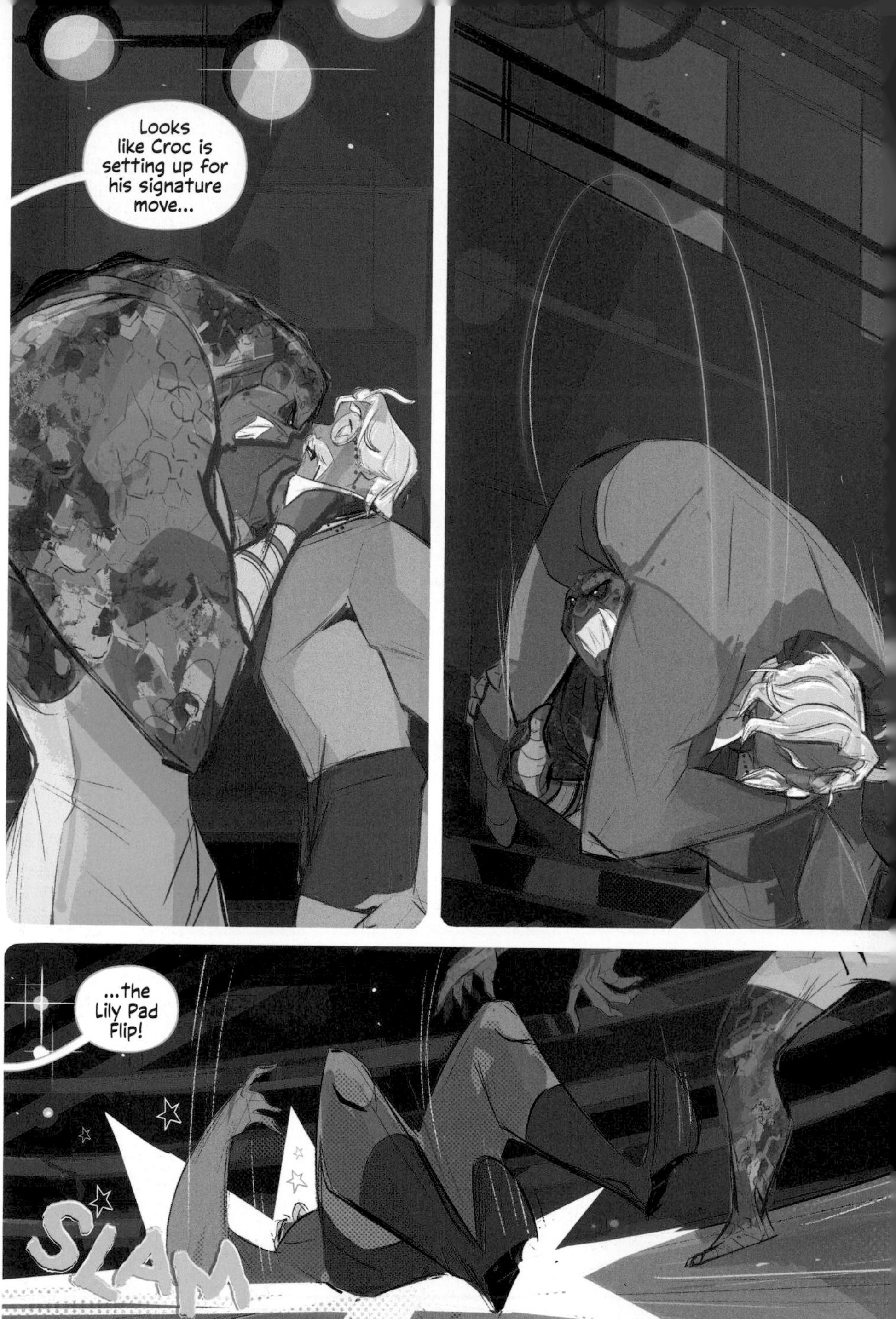
Looks like Croc is setting up for his signature move...
...the Lily Pad Flip!
SLAM

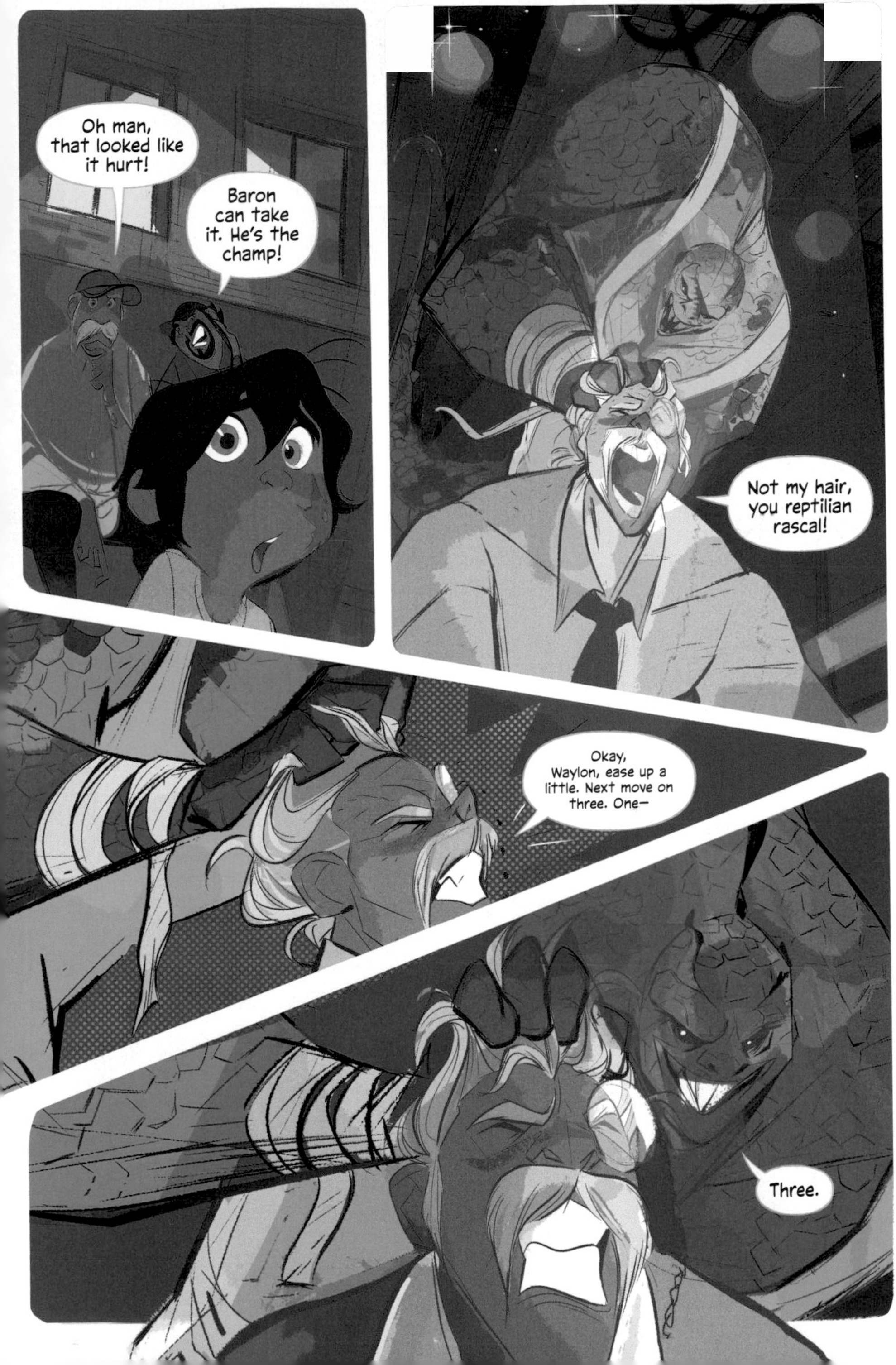

Oh man, that looked like it hurt!
Baron can take it. He's the champ!
Not my hair, you reptilian rascal!
Okay, Waylon, ease up a little. Next move on three. One—
Three.

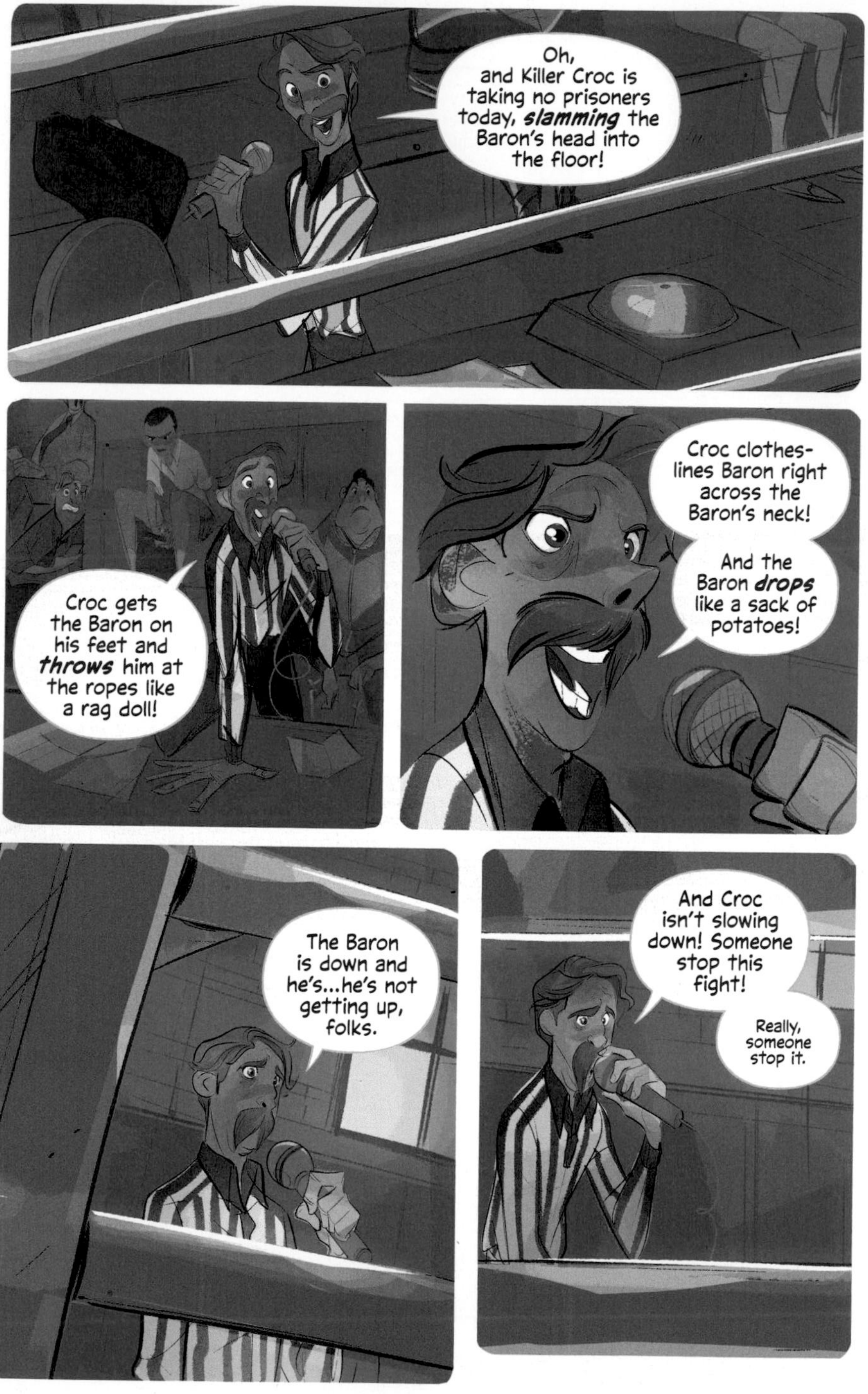
Oh, and Killer Croc is taking no prisoners today, ***slamming*** the Baron's head into the floor!
Croc gets the Baron on his feet and ***throws*** him at the ropes like a rag doll!
Croc clotheslines Baron right across the Baron's neck!
And the Baron ***drops*** like a sack of potatoes!
The Baron is down and he's...he's not getting up, folks.
And Croc isn't slowing down! Someone stop this fight!
Really, someone stop it.

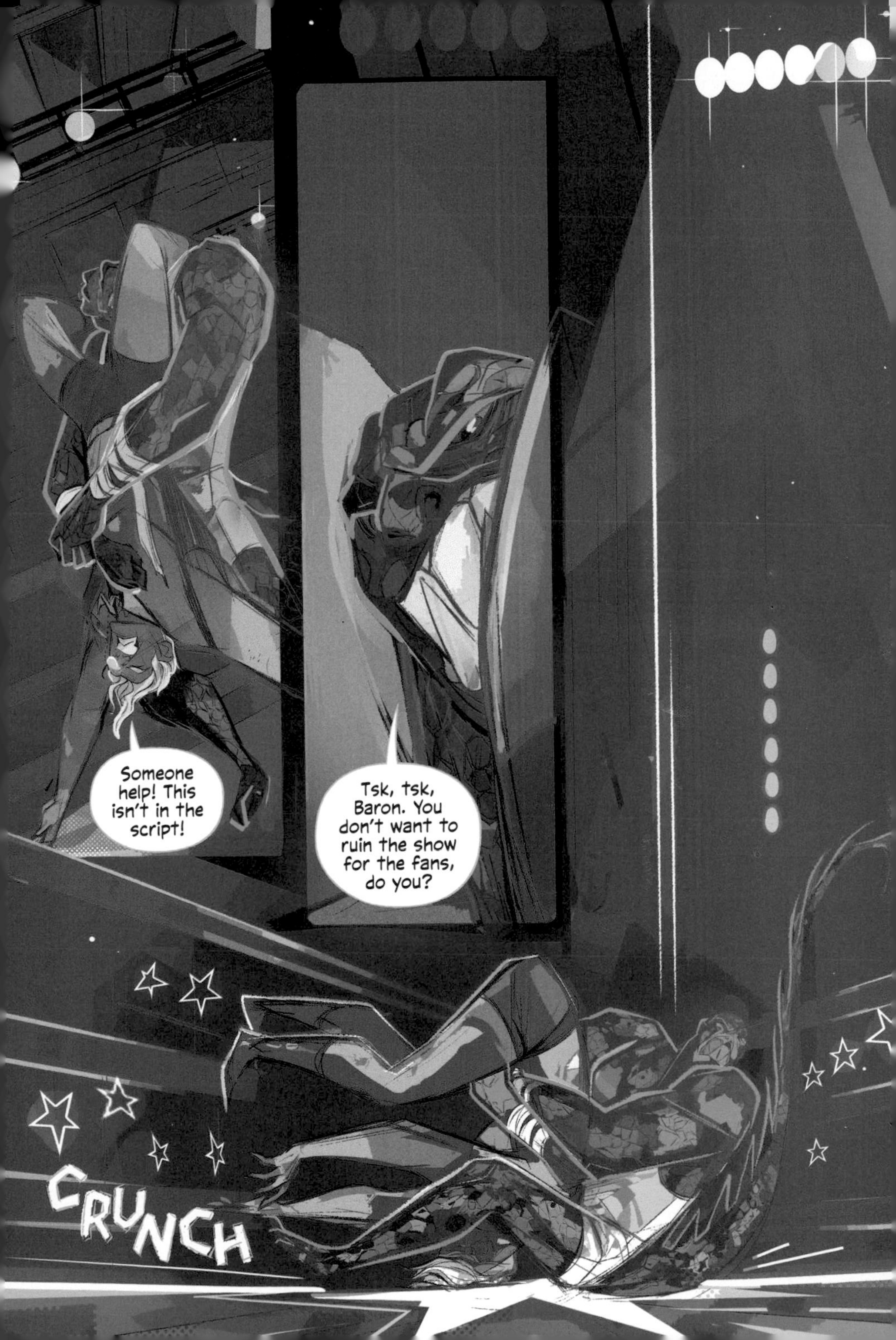
Someone help! This isn't in the script!
Tsk, tsk, Baron. You don't want to ruin the show for the fans, do you?
CRUNCH

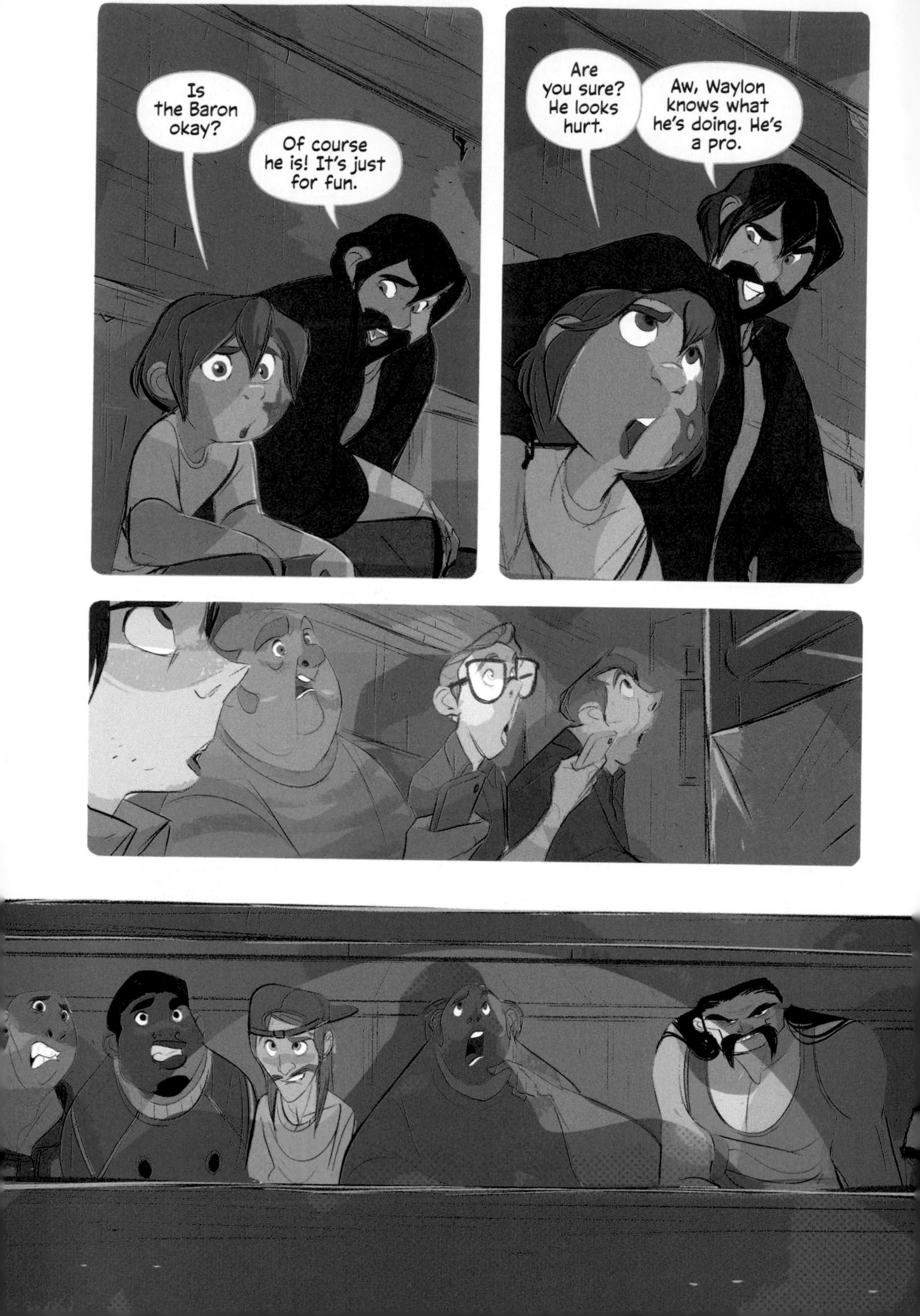
Is the Baron okay?
Of course he is! It's just for fun.
Are you sure? He looks hurt.
Aw, Waylon knows what he's doing. He's a pro.

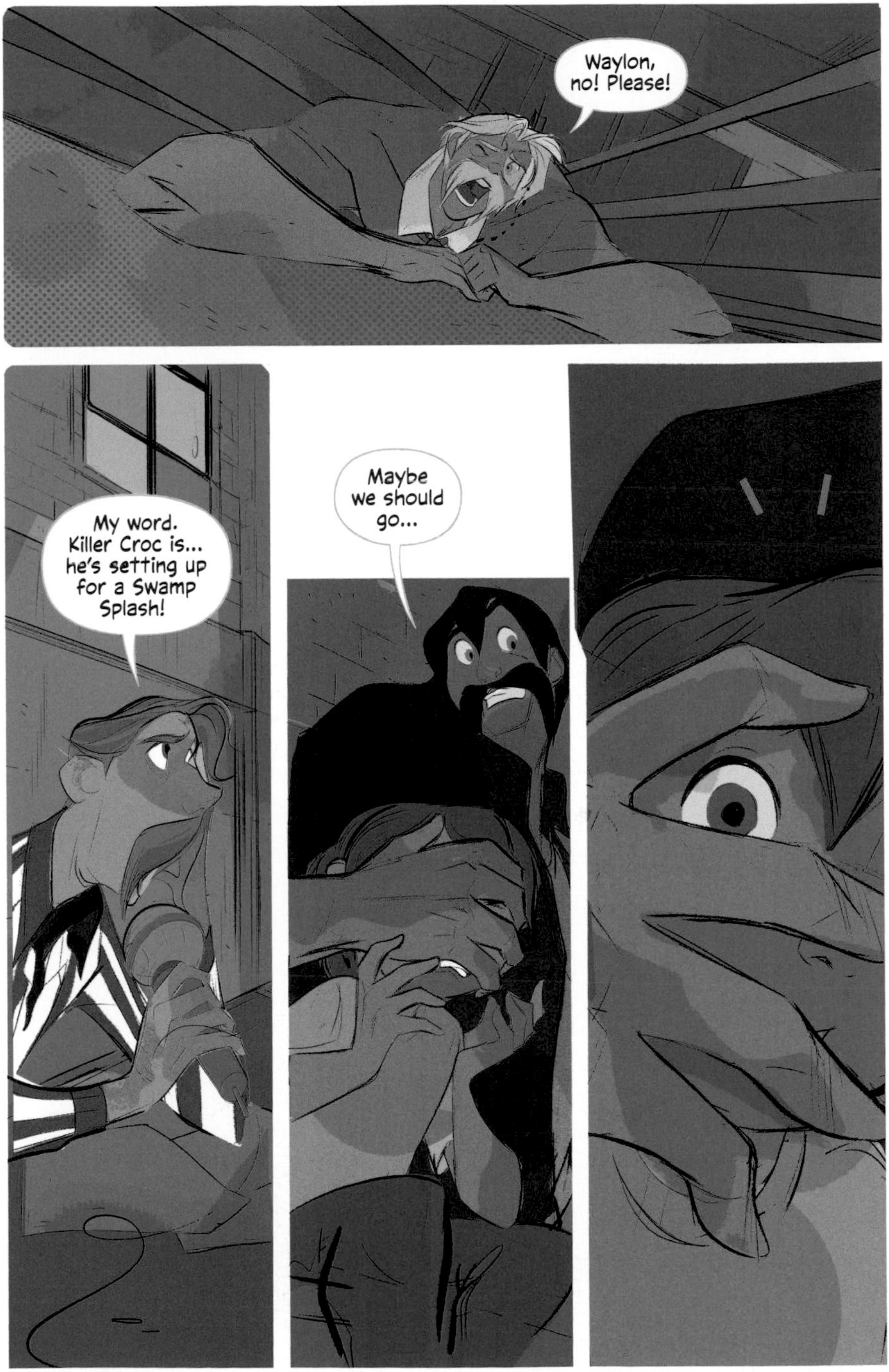
Waylon, no! Please!
My word. Killer Croc is... he's setting up for a Swamp Splash!
Maybe we should go...

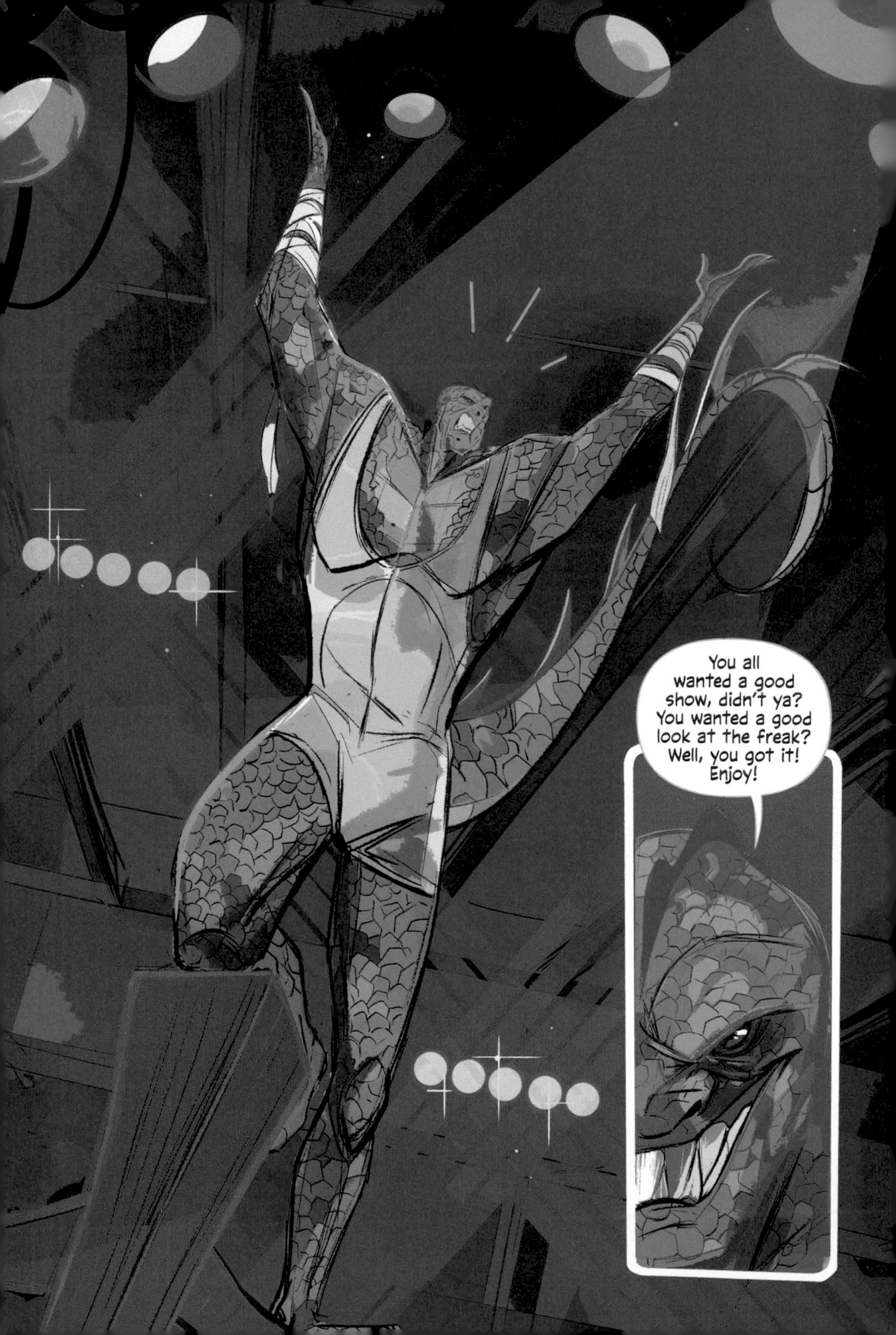
You all wanted a good show, didn't ya? You wanted a good look at the freak? Well, you got it! Enjoy!

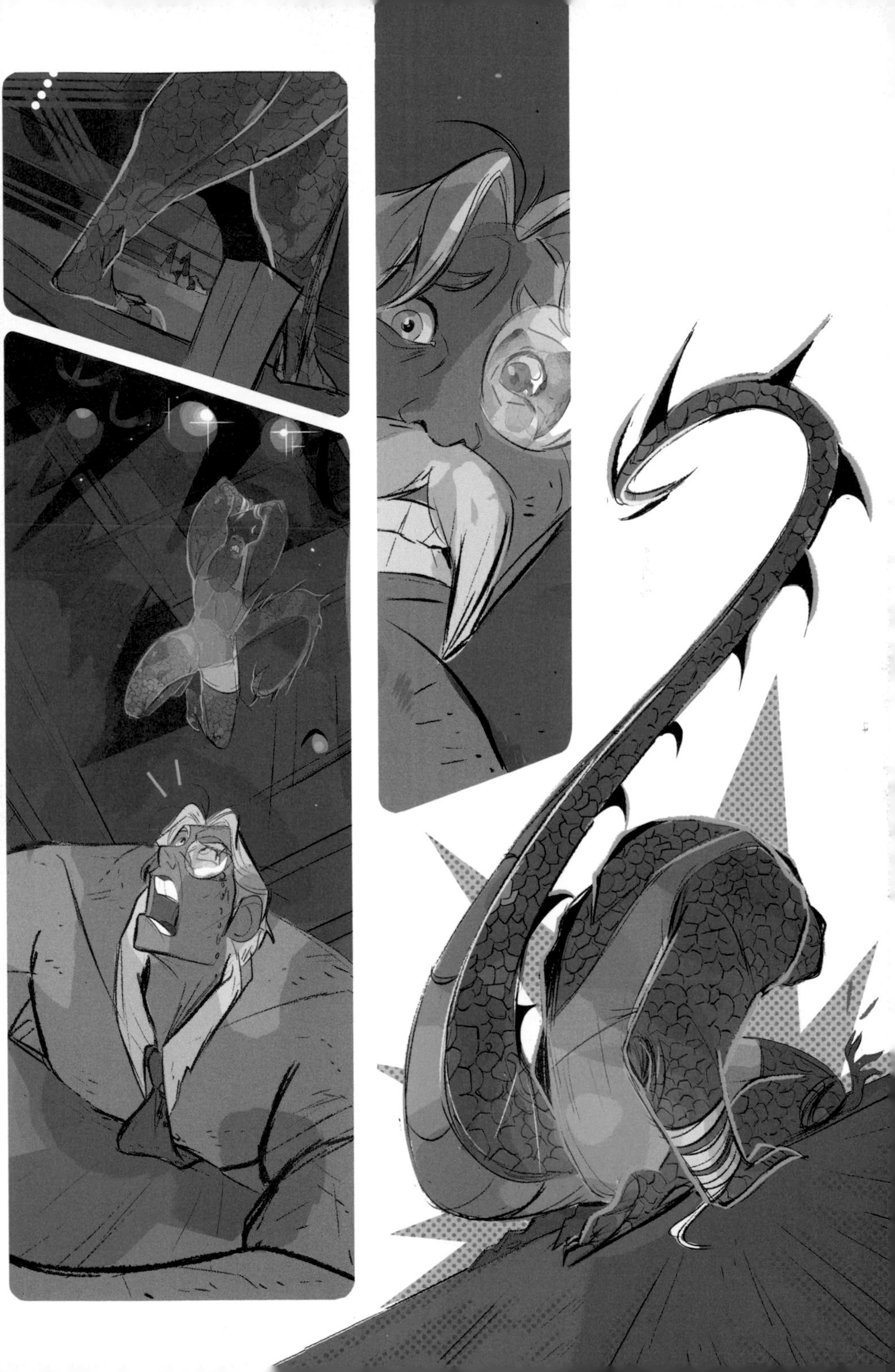

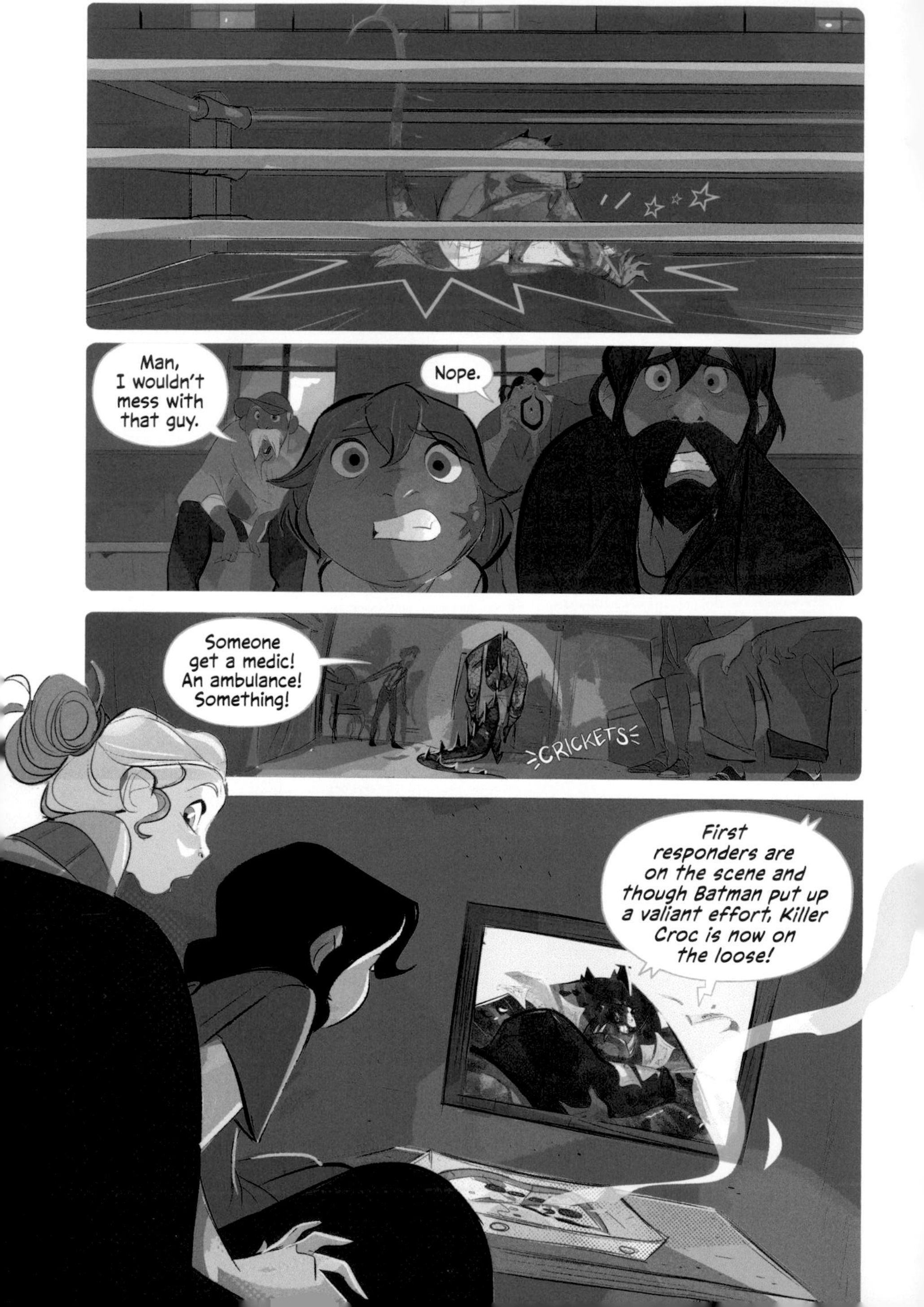
Man, I wouldn't mess with that guy.
Nope.
Someone get a medic! An ambulance! Something!
CRICKETS
First responders are on the scene and though Batman put up a valiant effort, Killer Croc is now on the loose!

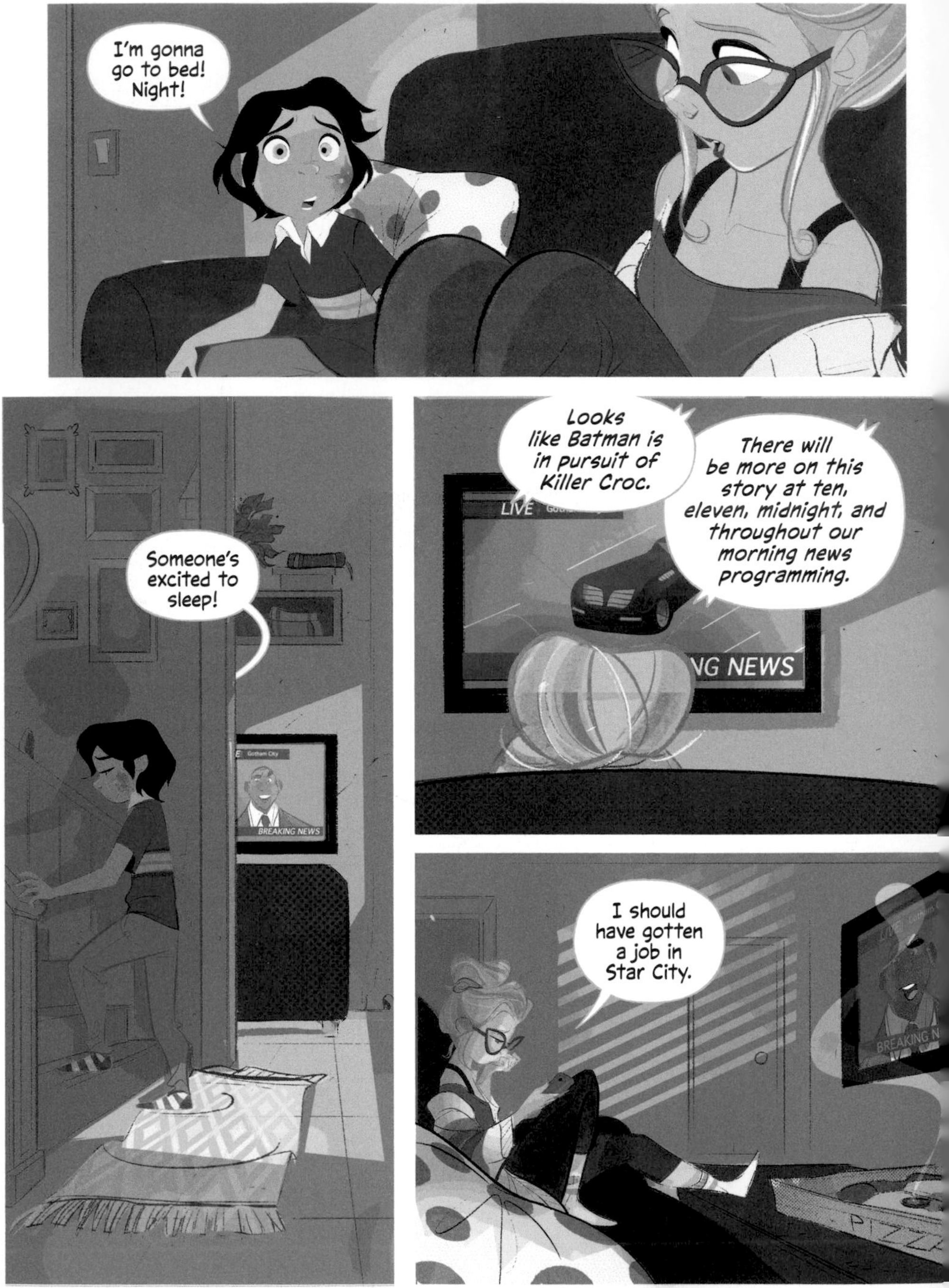
I'm gonna go to bed! Night!
Someone's excited to sleep!
Looks like Batman is in pursuit of Killer Croc.
There will be more on this story at ten, eleven, midnight, and throughout our morning news programming.
LIVE
NG NEWS
BREAKING NEWS
I should have gotten a job in Star City.

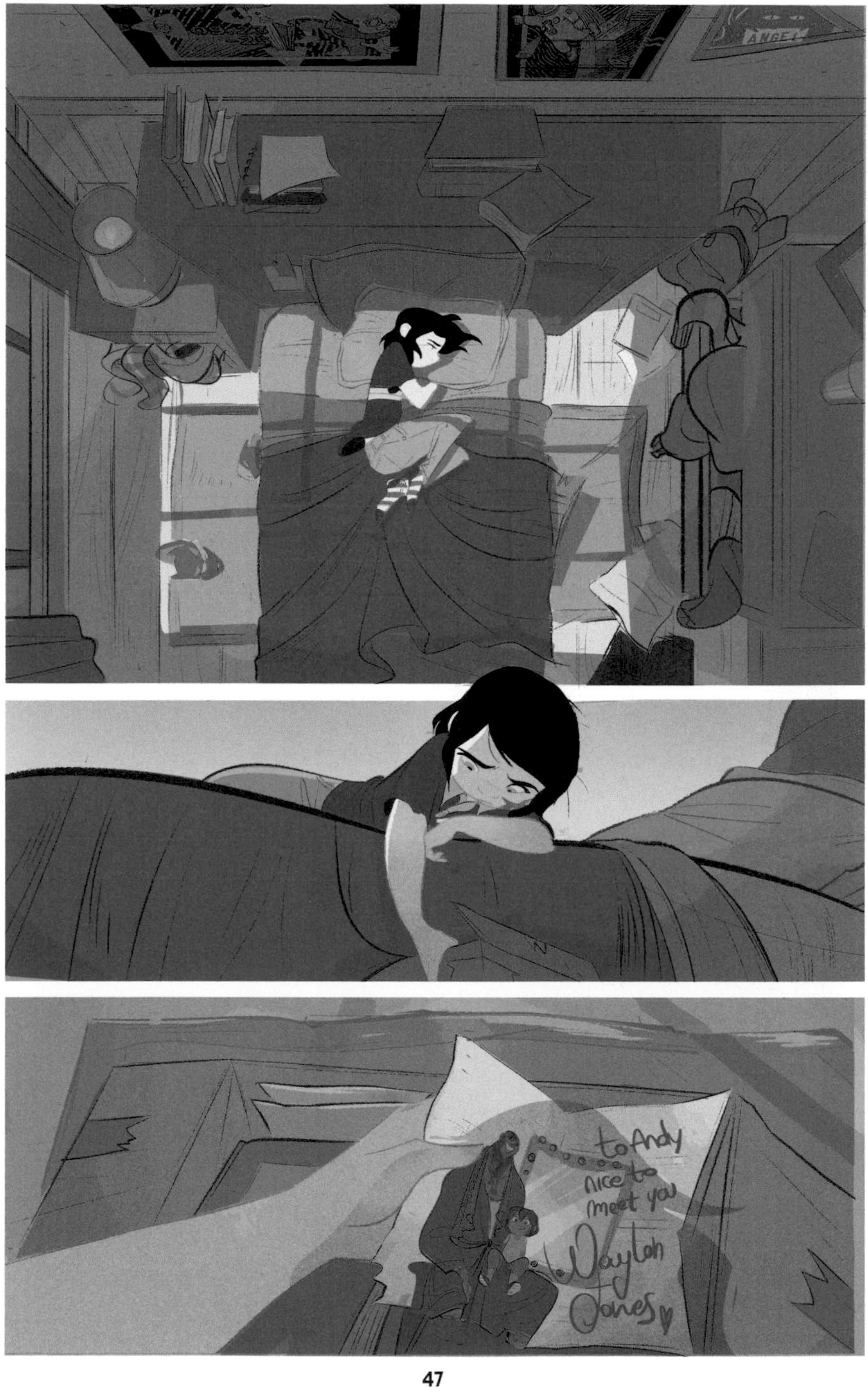
to Andy
nice to
meet you
Dayton
Jones

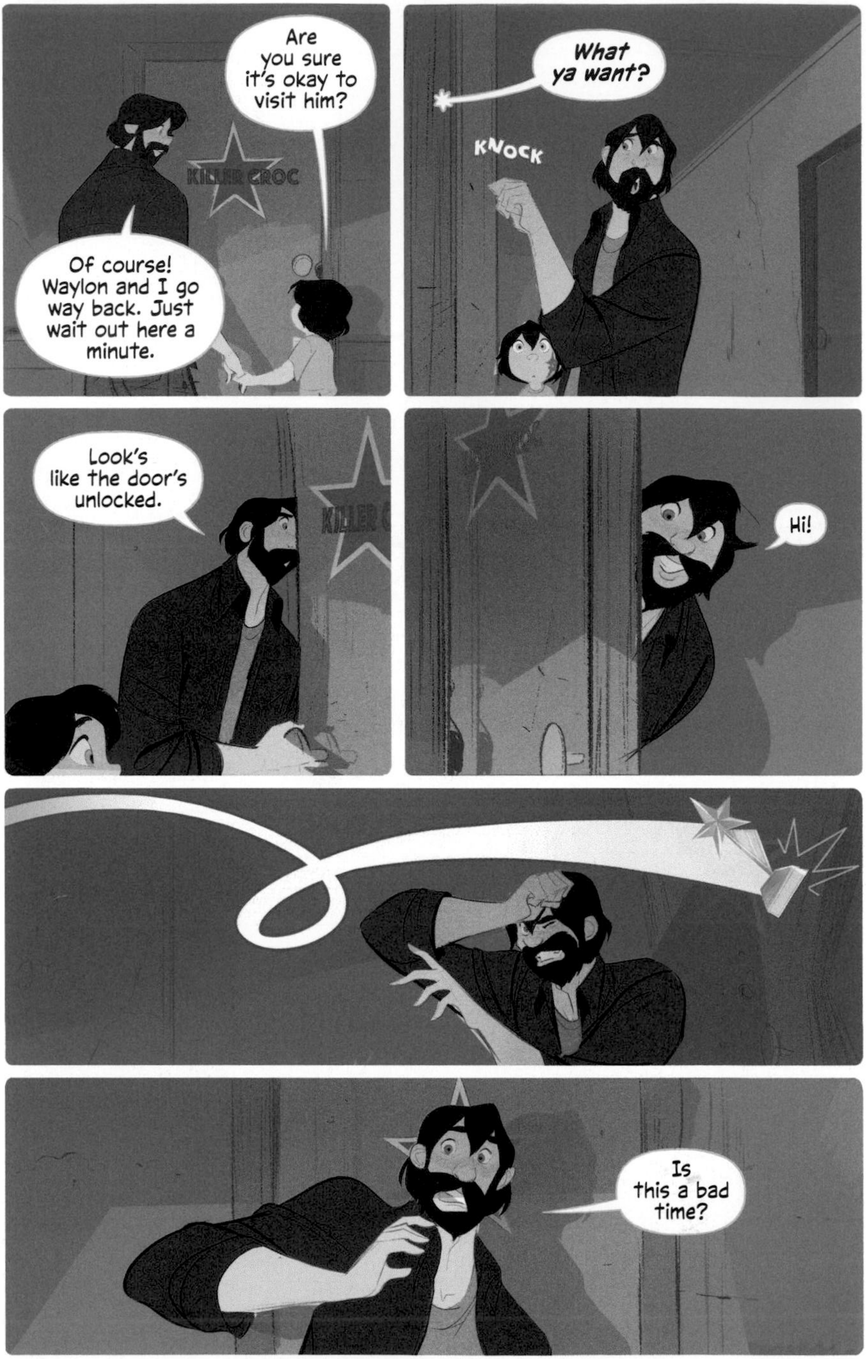
Are you sure it's okay to visit him?
KILLER CROC
Of course! Waylon and I go way back. Just wait out here a minute.
What ya want?
KNOCK
Look's like the door's unlocked.
KILLER C
Hi!
Is this a bad time?

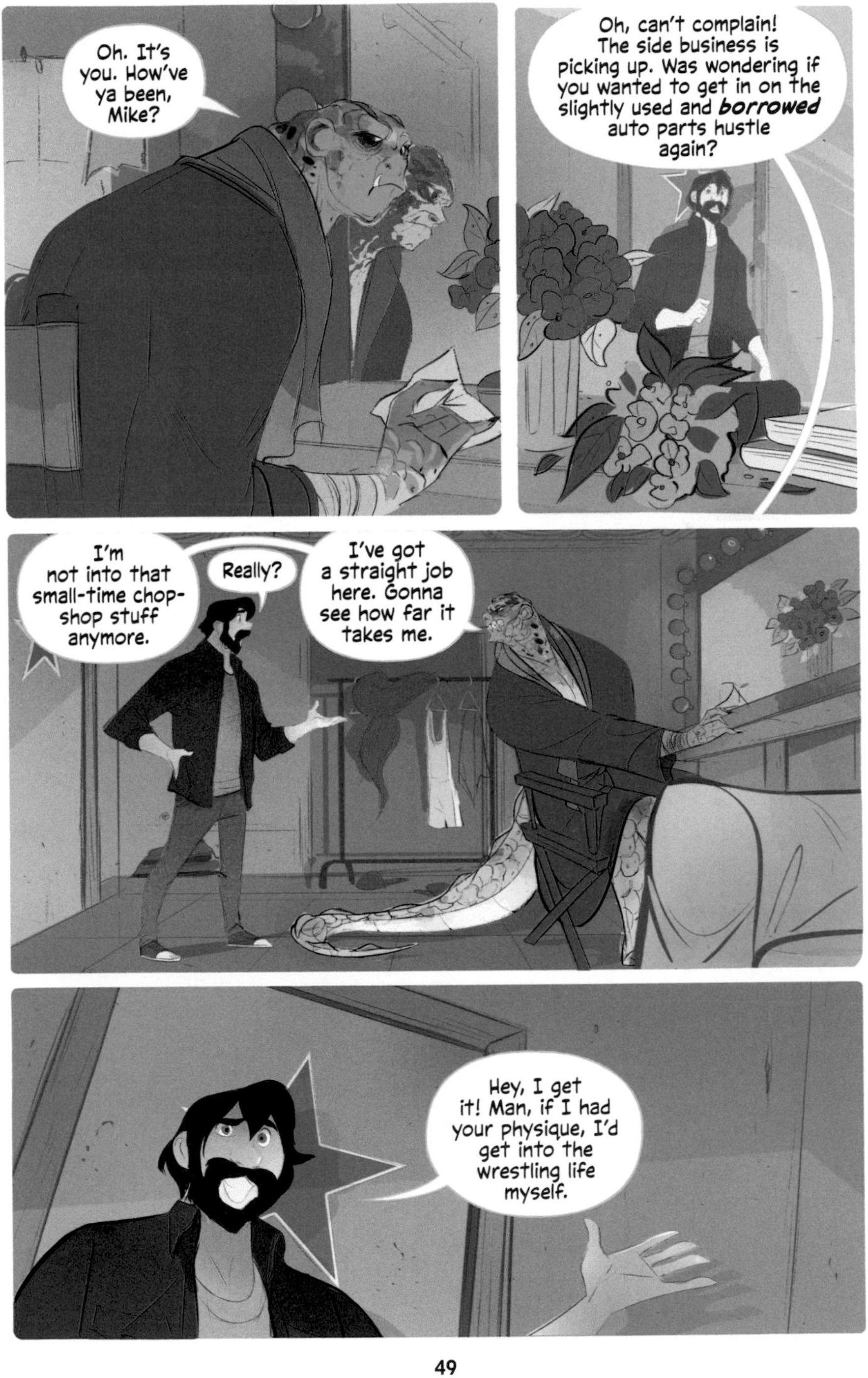
Oh. It's you. How've ya been, Mike?
Oh, can't complain! The side business is picking up. Was wondering if you wanted to get in on the slightly used and ***borrowed*** auto parts hustle again?
I'm not into that small-time chop-shop stuff anymore.
Really?
I've got a straight job here. Gonna see how far it takes me.
Hey, I get it! Man, if I had your physique, I'd get into the wrestling life myself.

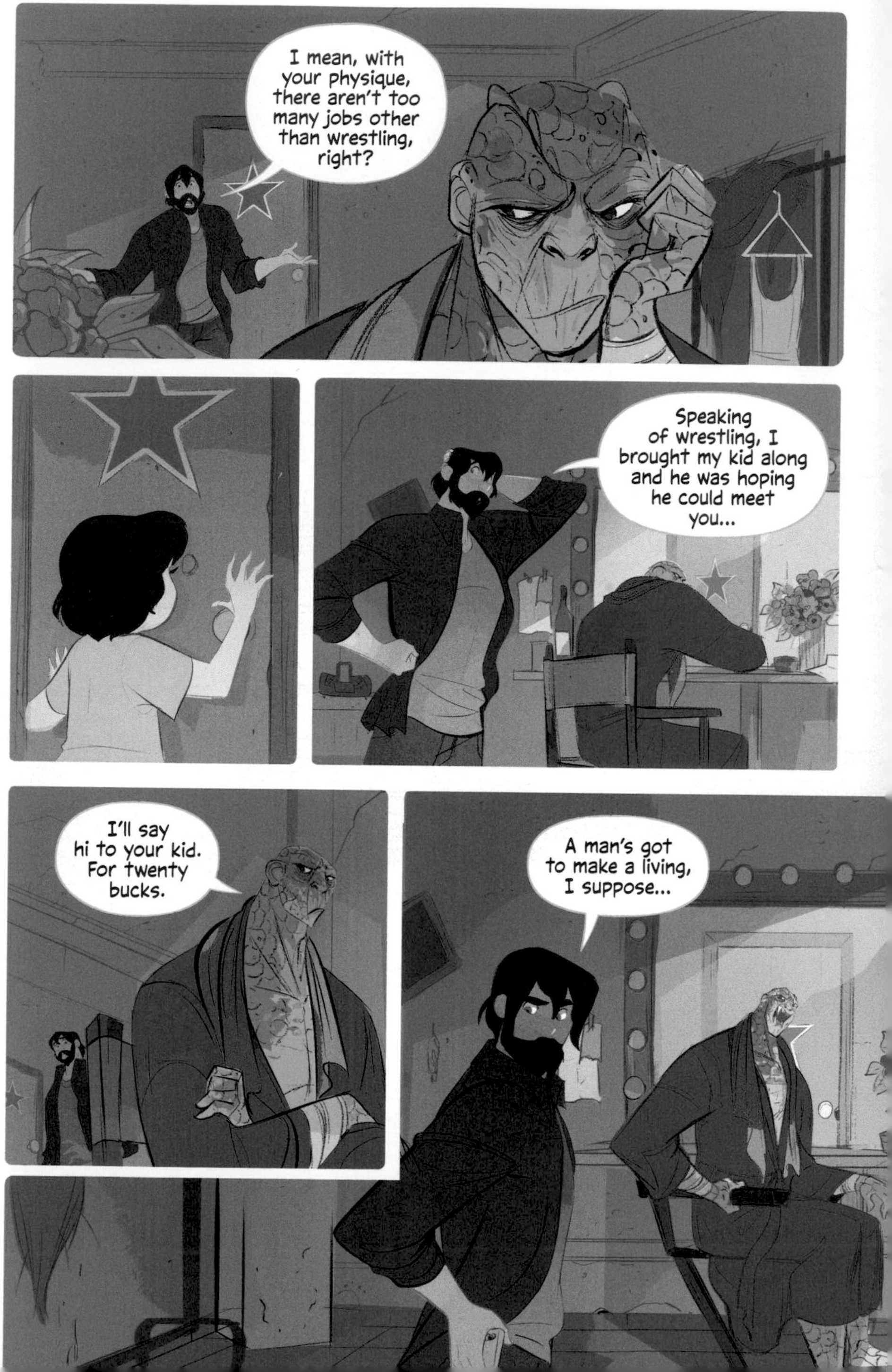
I mean, with your physique, there aren't too many jobs other than wrestling, right?
Speaking of wrestling, I brought my kid along and he was hoping he could meet you...
I'll say hi to your kid. For twenty bucks.
A man's got to make a living, I suppose...

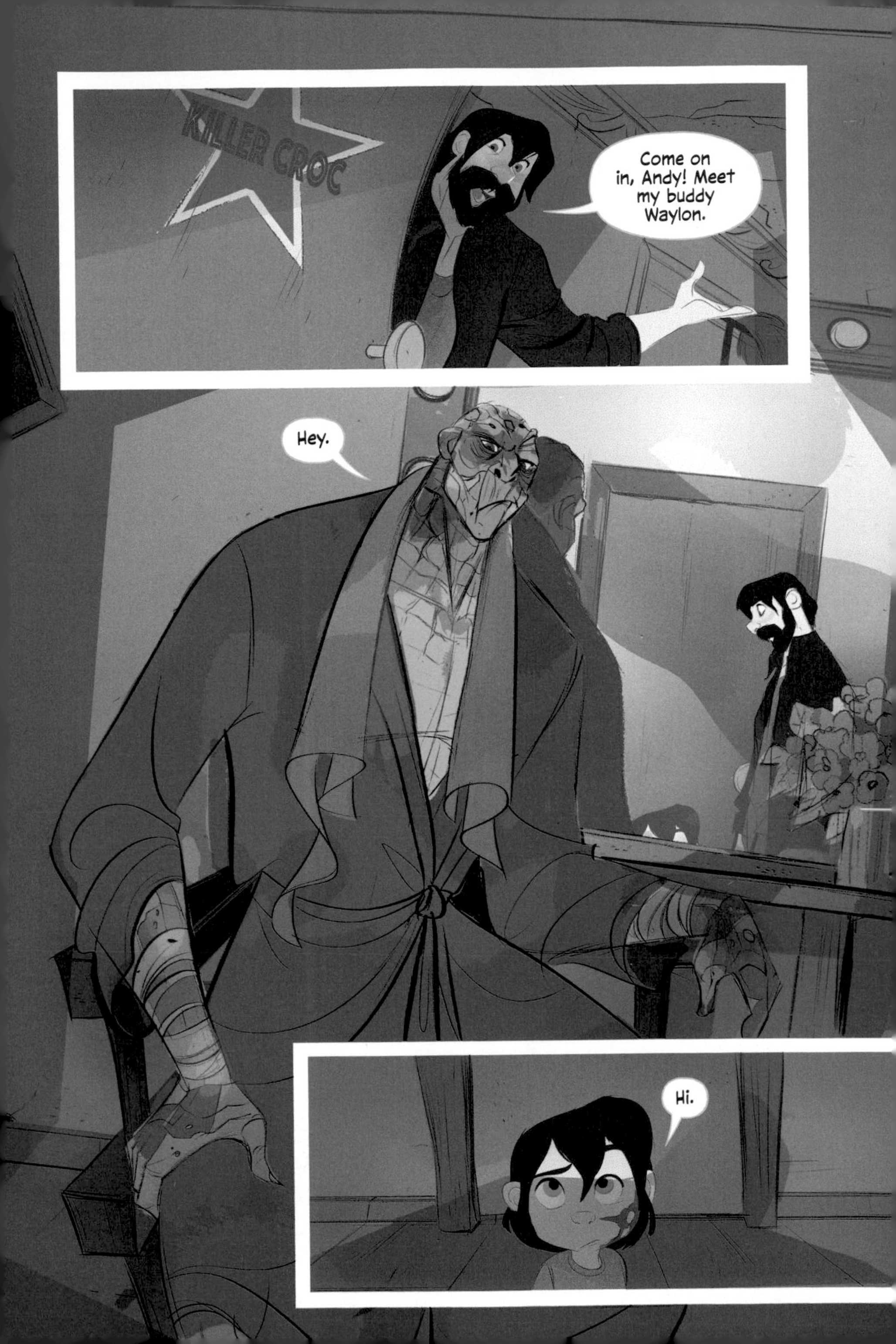
KILLER CROC
Come on in, Andy! Meet my buddy Waylon.
Hey.
Hi.

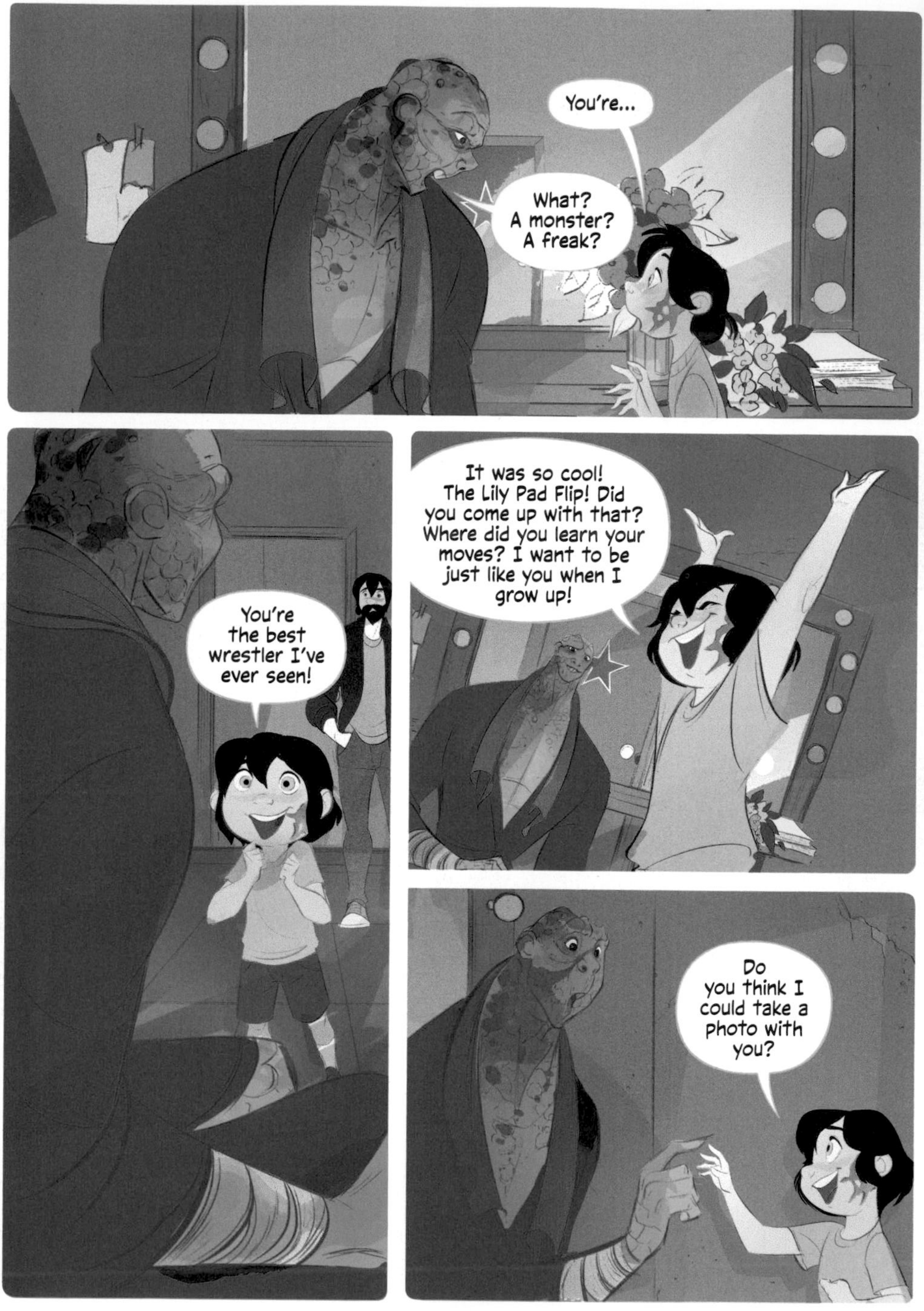
You're...
What?
A monster?
A freak?
You're the best wrestler I've ever seen!
It was so cool! The Lily Pad Flip! Did you come up with that? Where did you learn your moves? I want to be just like you when I grow up!
Do you think I could take a photo with you?

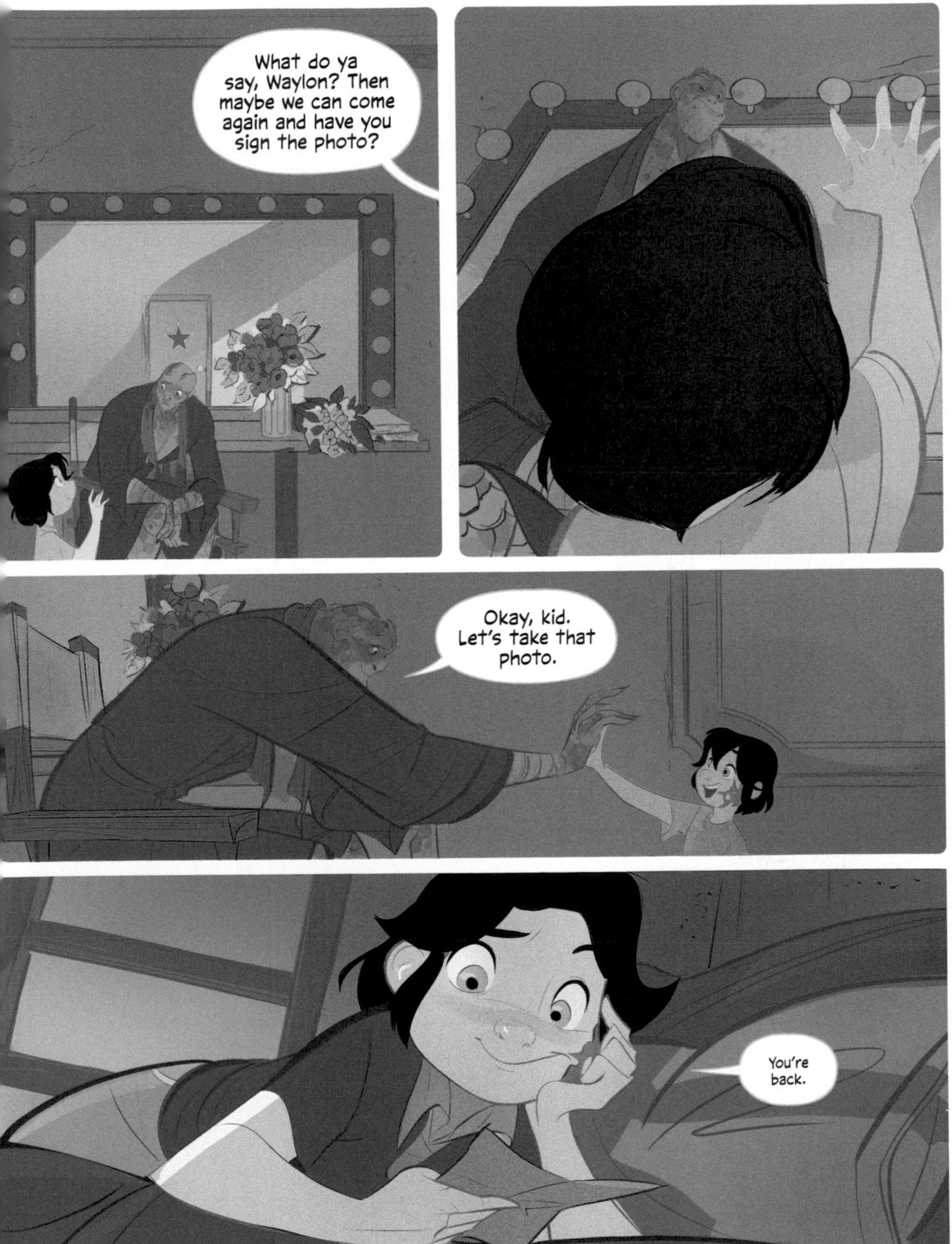
What do ya say, Waylon? Then maybe we can come again and have you sign the photo?
Okay, kid. Let's take that photo.
You're back.

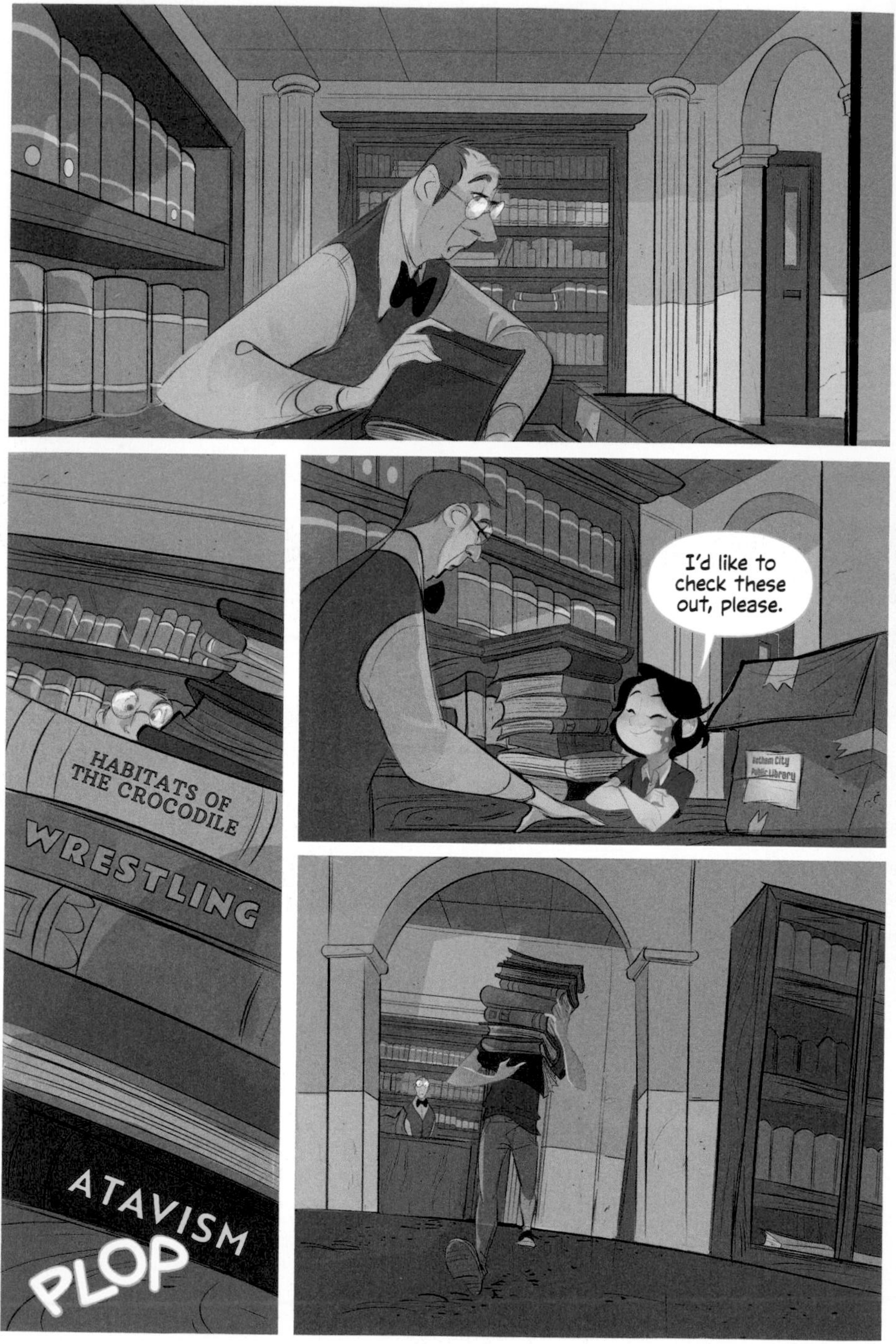
HABITATS OF THE CROCODILE
WRESTLING
ATAVISM
PLOP
I'd like to check these out, please.

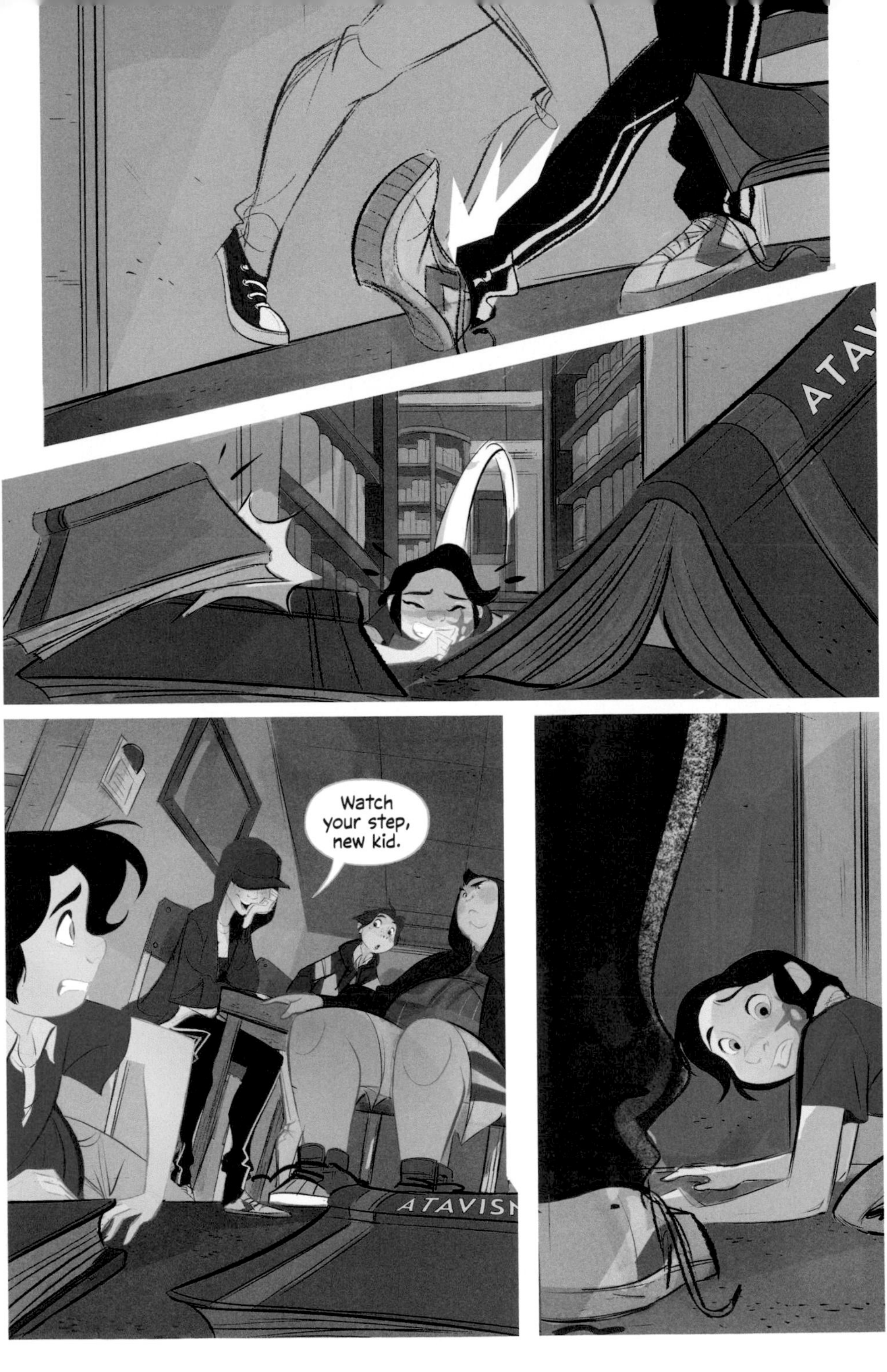
ATAV
Watch your step, new kid.
ATAVISM

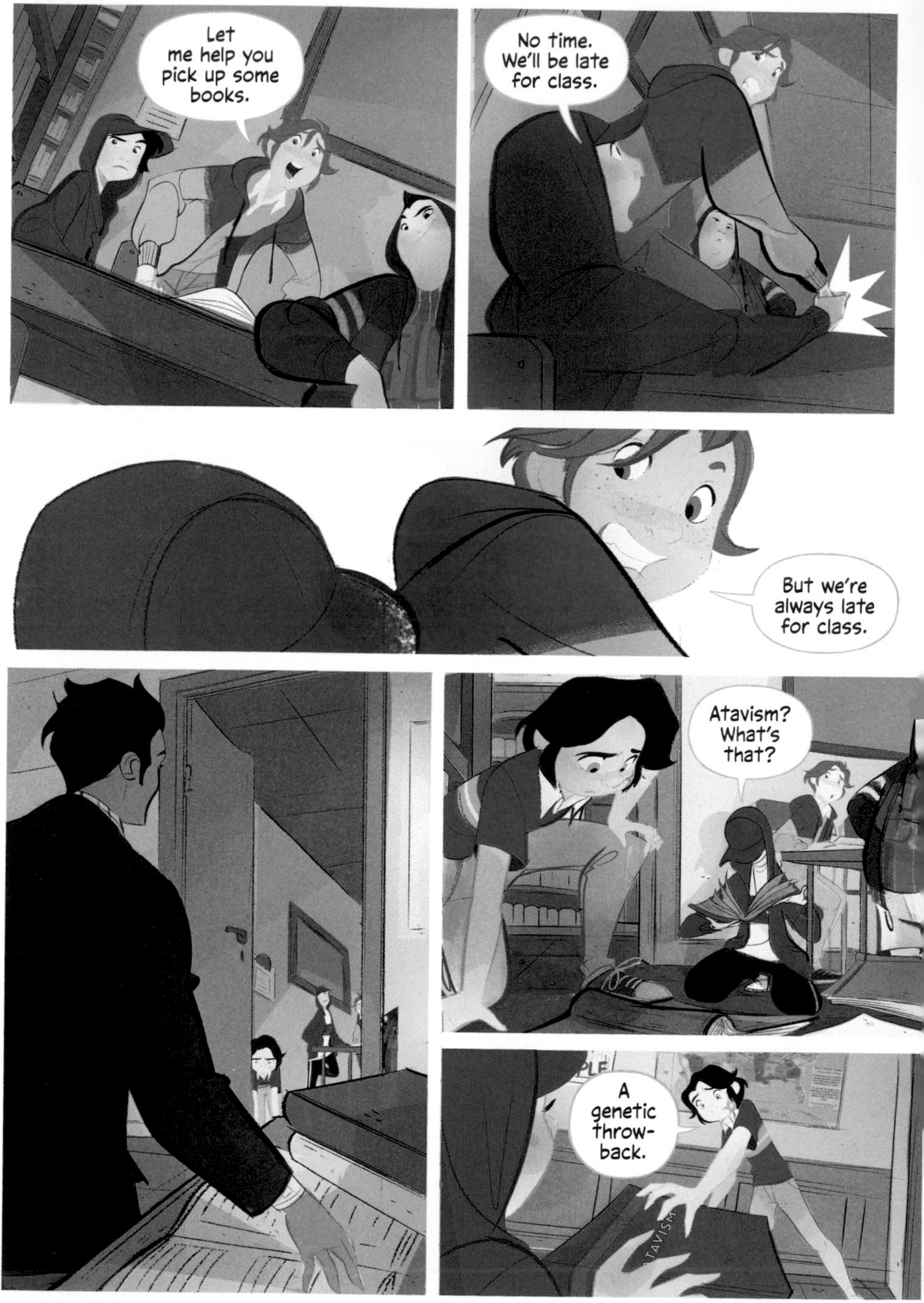
Let me help you pick up some books.
No time. We'll be late for class.
But we're always late for class.
Atavism? What's that?
A genetic throw-back.
ATAVISM

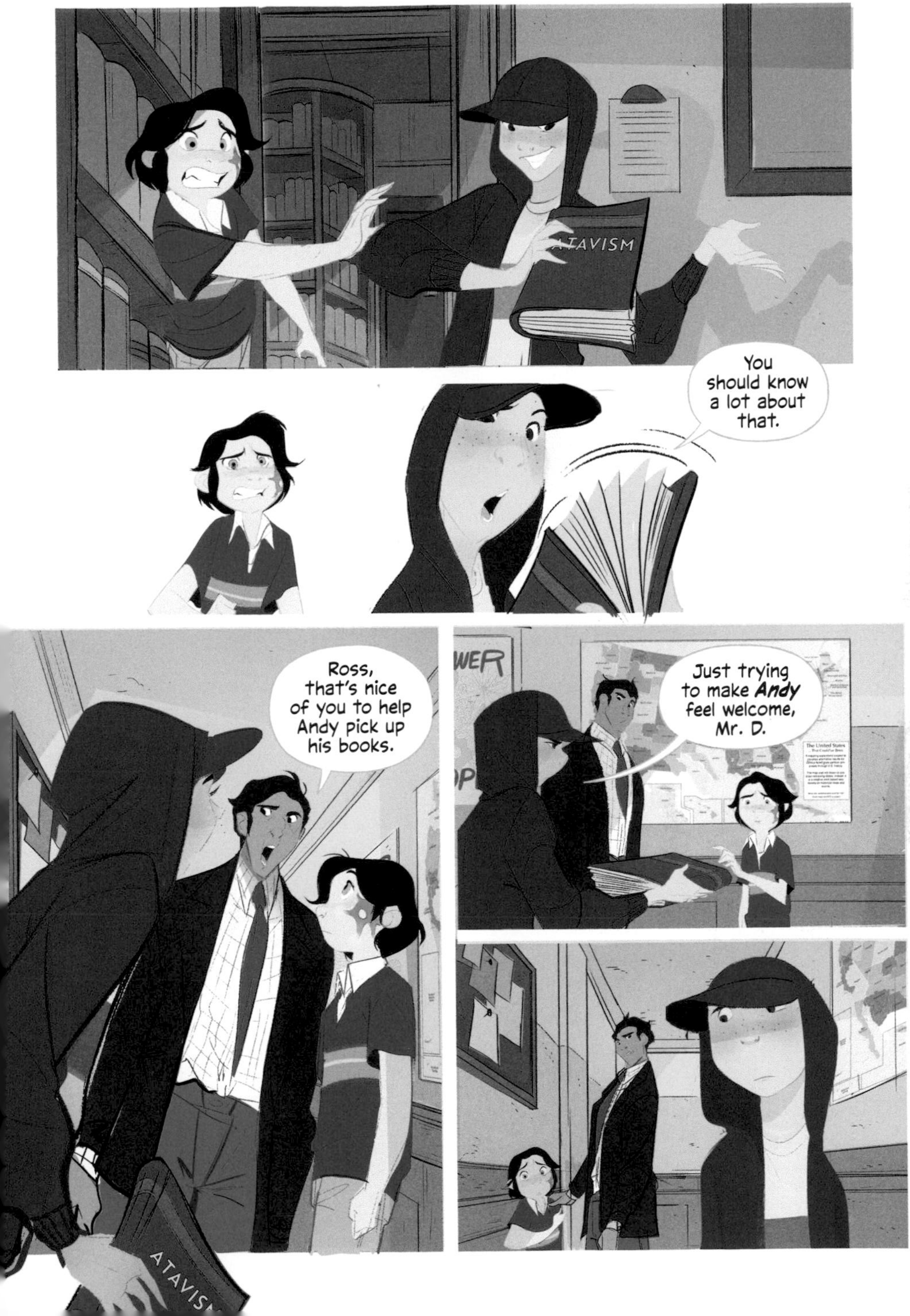
ATAVISM
You should know a lot about that.
Ross, that's nice of you to help Andy pick up his books.
Just trying to make Andy feel welcome, Mr. D.
ATAVISM

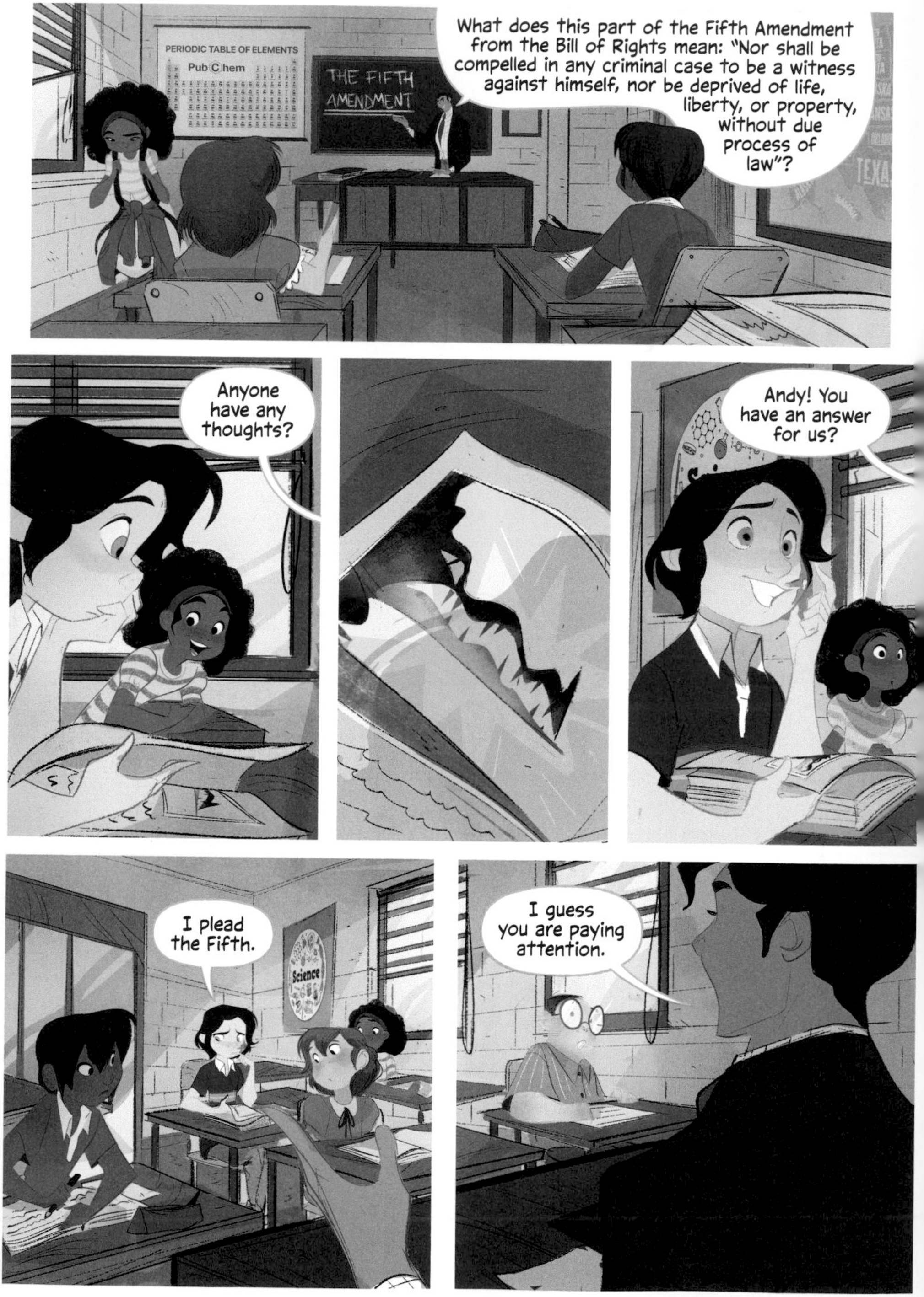
THE FIFTH AMENDMENT
PERIODIC TABLE OF ELEMENTS
PubChem
What does this part of the Fifth Amendment from the Bill of Rights mean: "Nor shall be compelled in any criminal case to be a witness against himself, nor be deprived of life, liberty, or property, without due process of law"?
Anyone have any thoughts?
Andy! You have an answer for us?
I plead the Fifth.
Science
I guess you are paying attention.

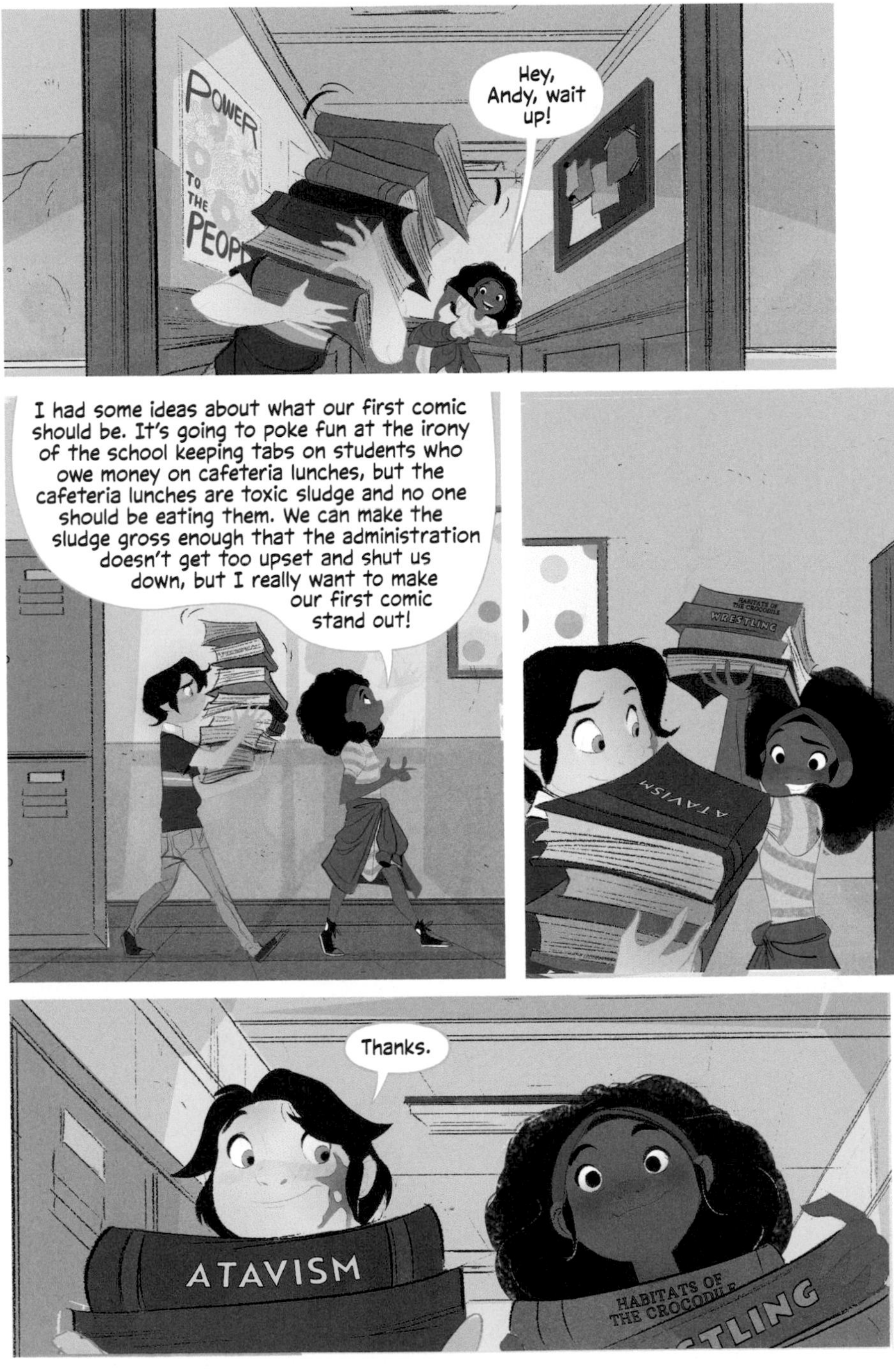
POWER TO THE
Hey, Andy, wait up!
I had some ideas about what our first comic should be. It's going to poke fun at the irony of the school keeping tabs on students who owe money on cafeteria lunches, but the cafeteria lunches are toxic sludge and no one should be eating them. We can make the sludge gross enough that the administration doesn't get too upset and shut us down, but I really want to make our first comic stand out!
HABITATS OF THE CROCODILE
WRESTLING
ATAVISM
Thanks.
ATAVISM
HABITATS OF THE CROCODILE

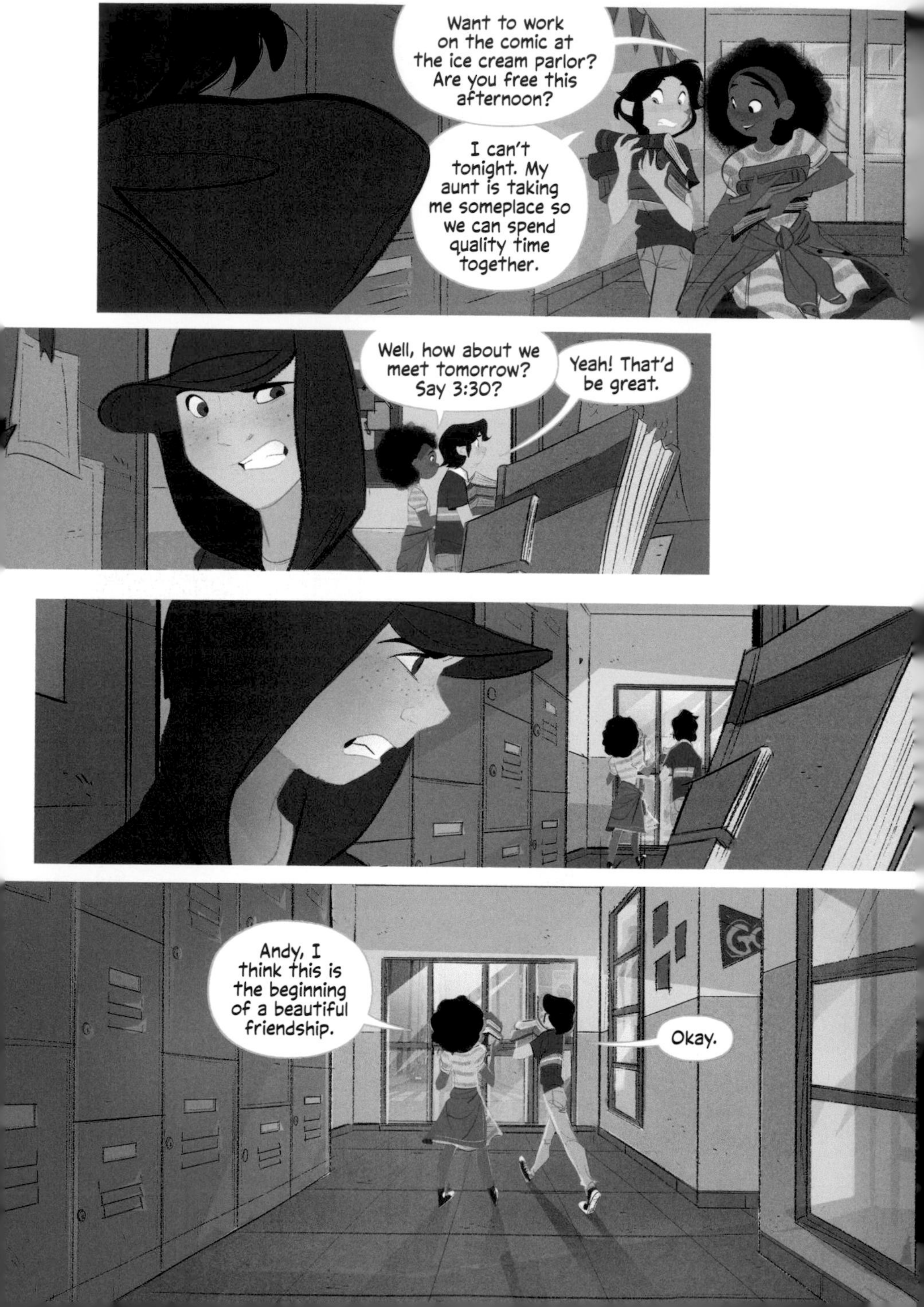

Want to work on the comic at the ice cream parlor? Are you free this afternoon?
I can't tonight. My aunt is taking me someplace so we can spend quality time together.
Well, how about we meet tomorrow? Say 3:30?
Yeah! That'd be great.
Andy, I think this is the beginning of a beautiful friendship.
Okay.

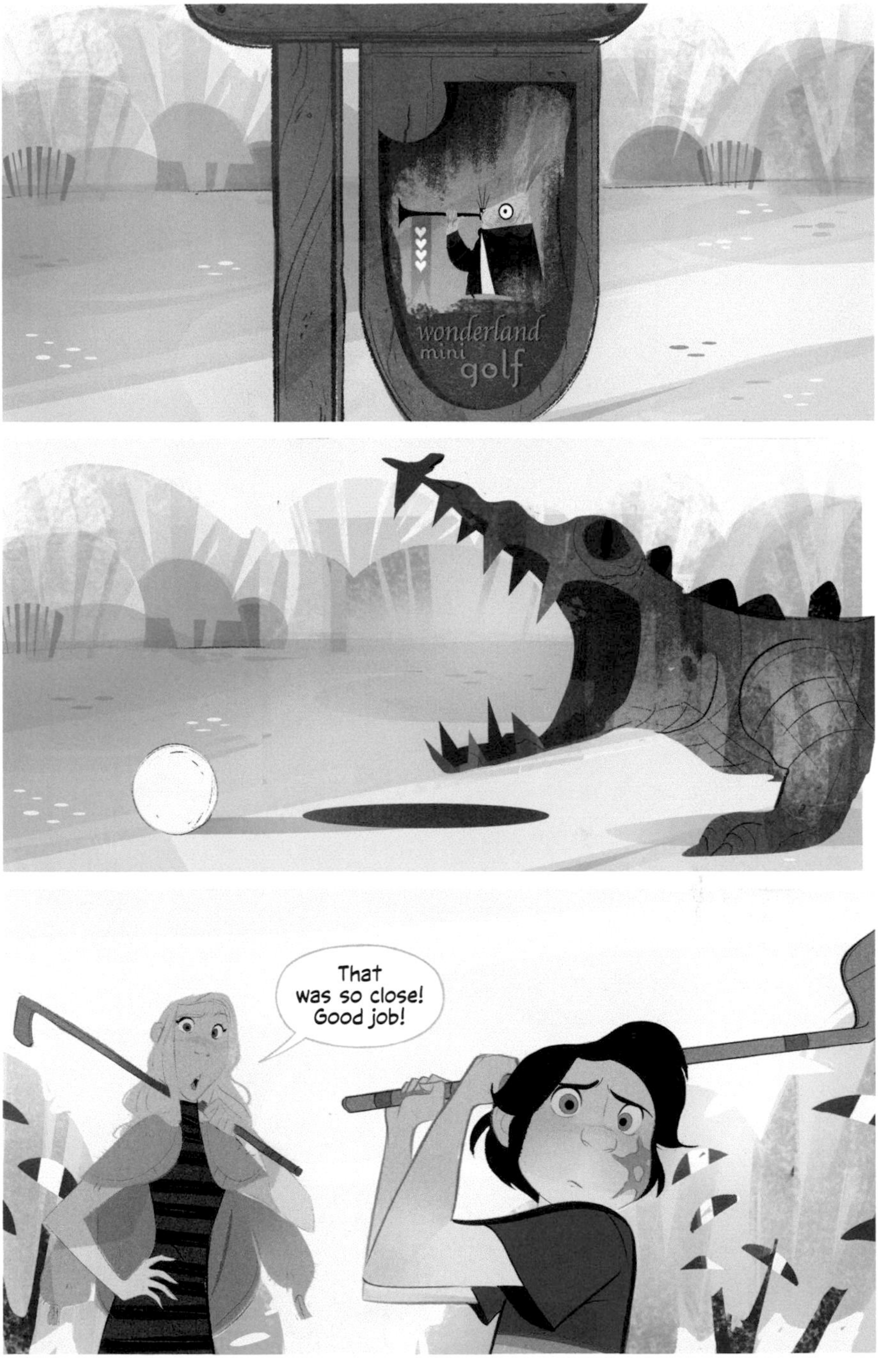
wonderland mini golf
That was so close! Good job!

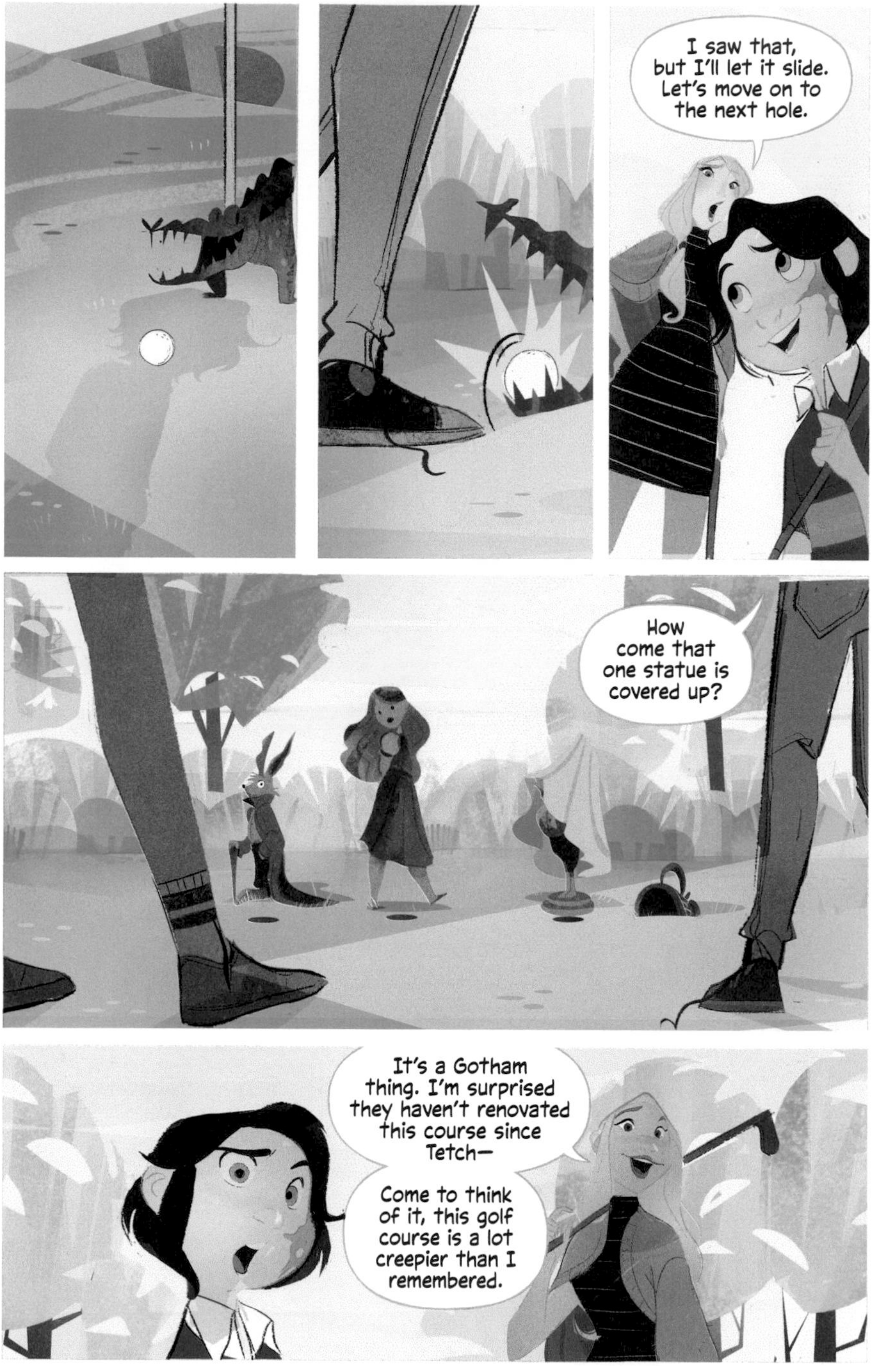
I saw that, but I'll let it slide. Let's move on to the next hole.
How come that one statue is covered up?
It's a Gotham thing. I'm surprised they haven't renovated this course since Tetch—
Come to think of it, this golf course is a lot creepier than I remembered.

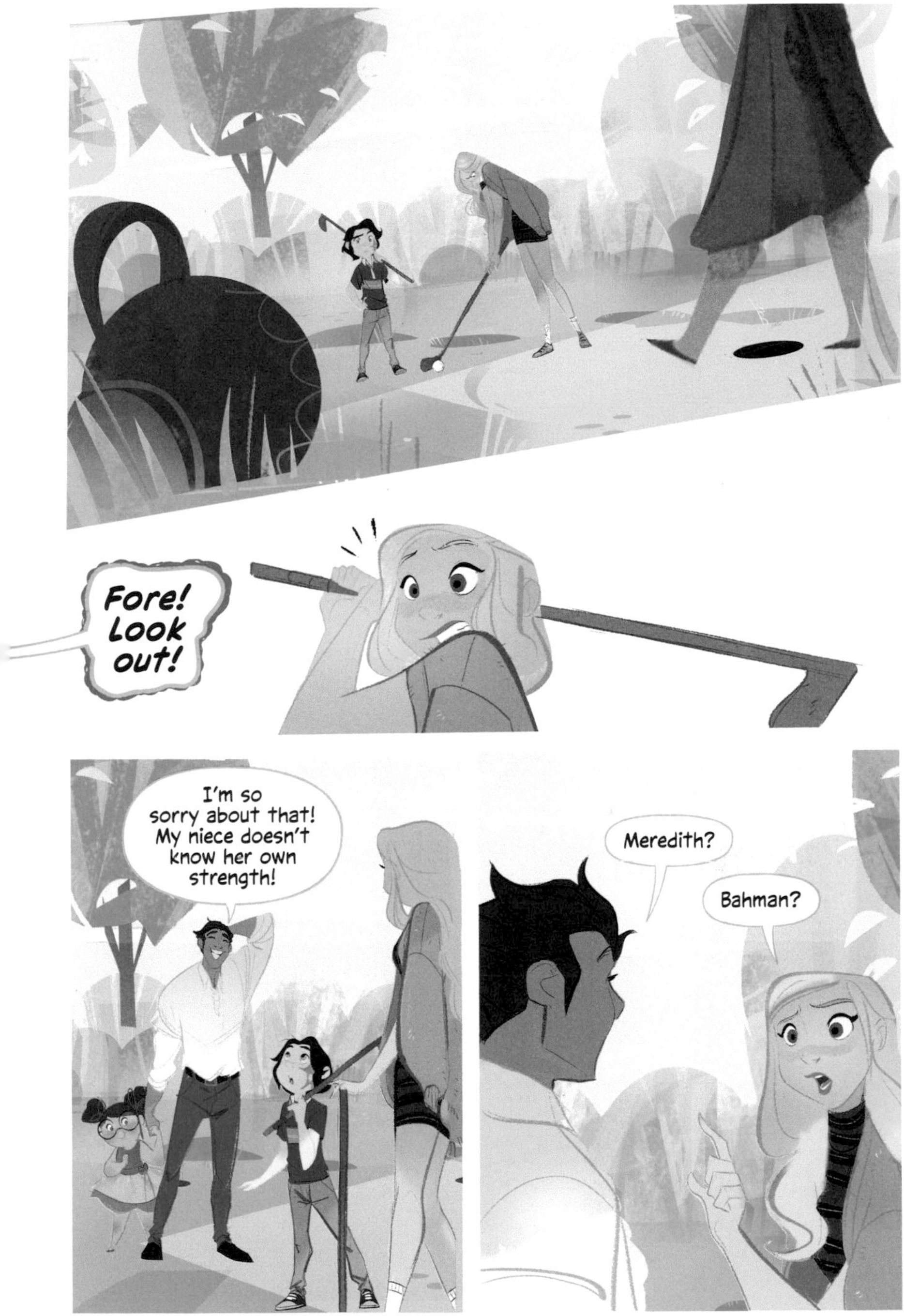

Fore! Look out!
I'm so sorry about that! My niece doesn't know her own strength!
Meredith?
Bahman?

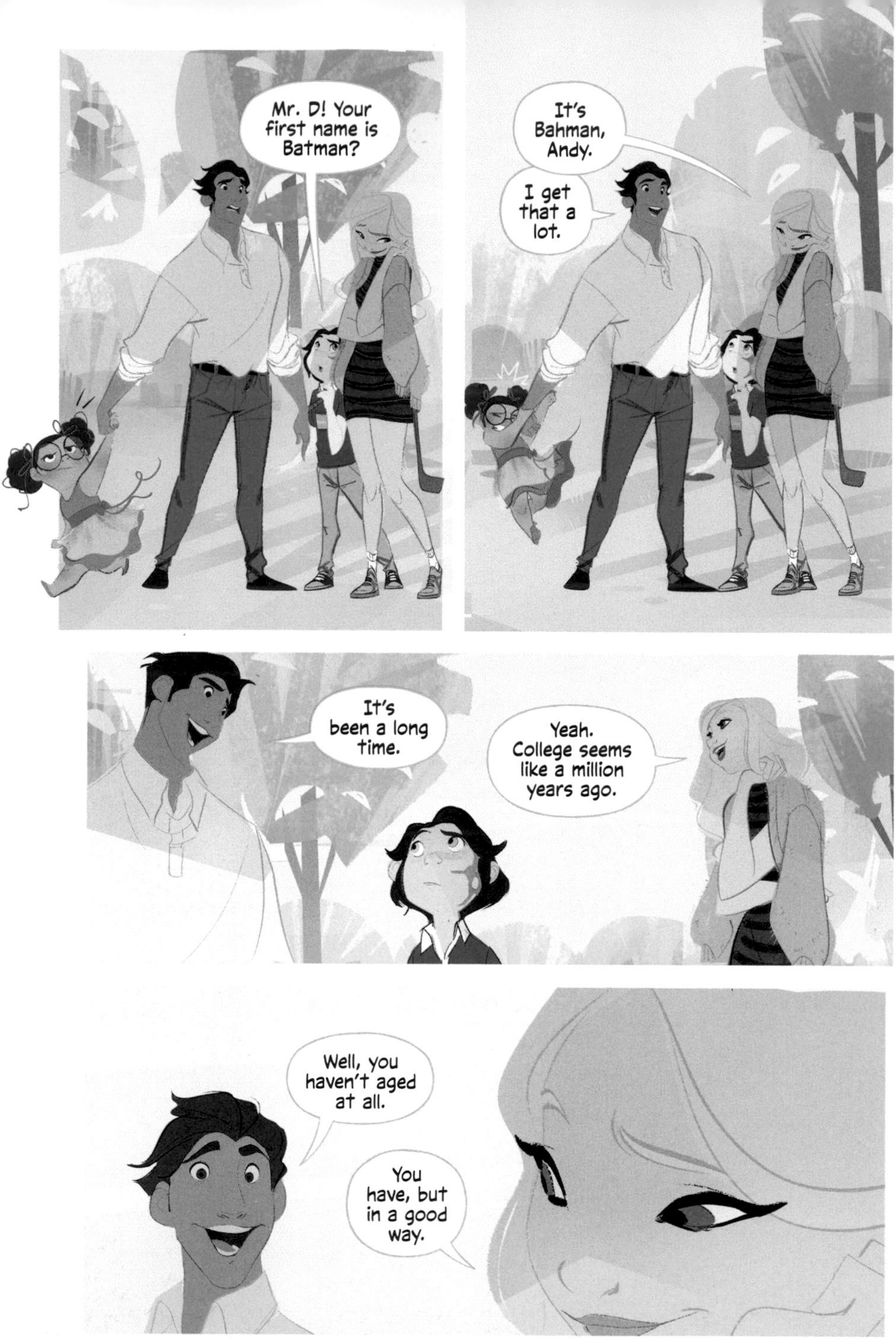
Mr. D! Your first name is Batman?
It's Bahman, Andy.
I get that a lot.
It's been a long time.
Yeah. College seems like a million years ago.
Well, you haven't aged at all.
You have, but in a good way.

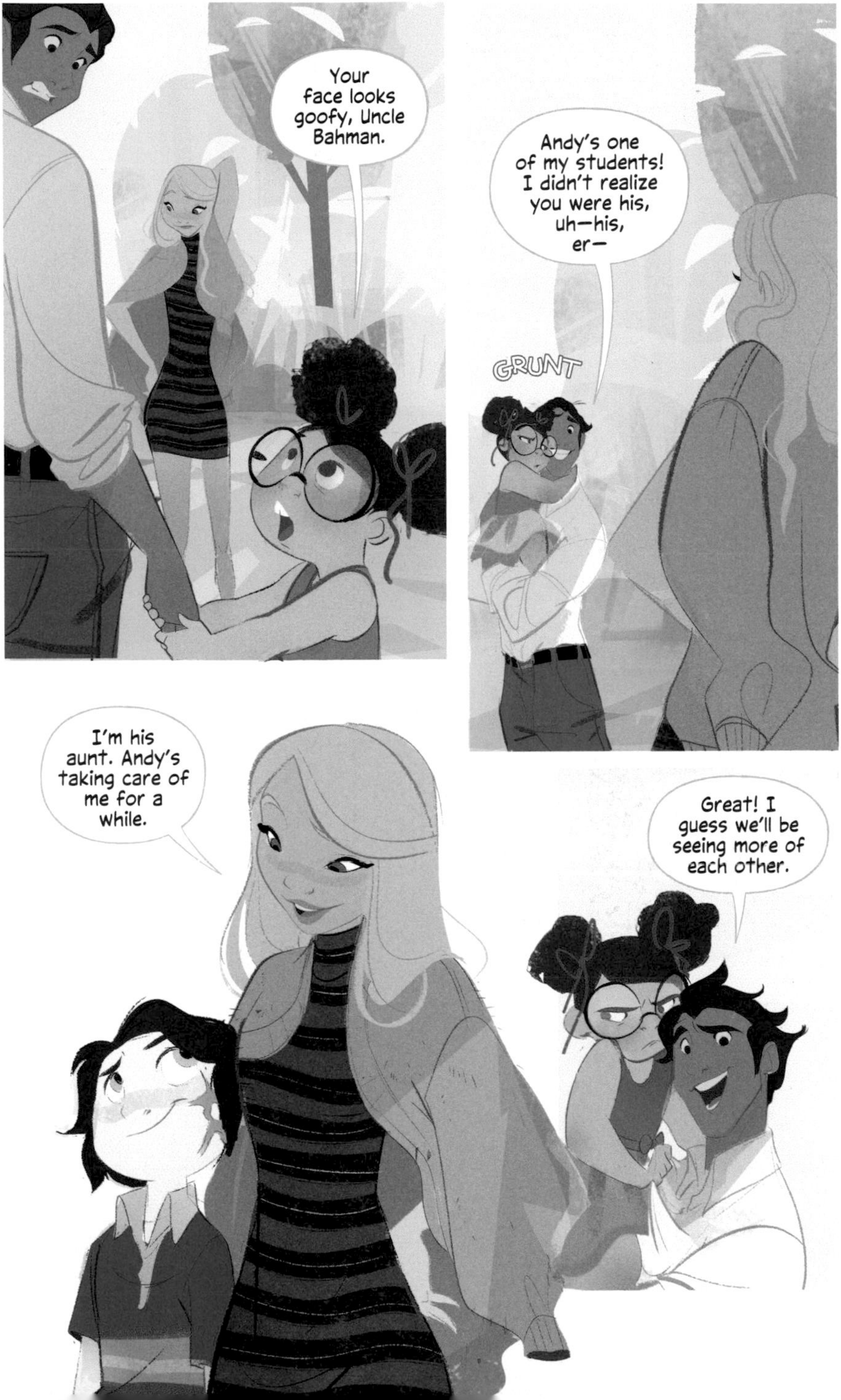
Your face looks goofy, Uncle Bahman.
Andy's one of my students! I didn't realize you were his, uh—his, er—
GRUNT
I'm his aunt. Andy's taking care of me for a while.
Great! I guess we'll be seeing more of each other.

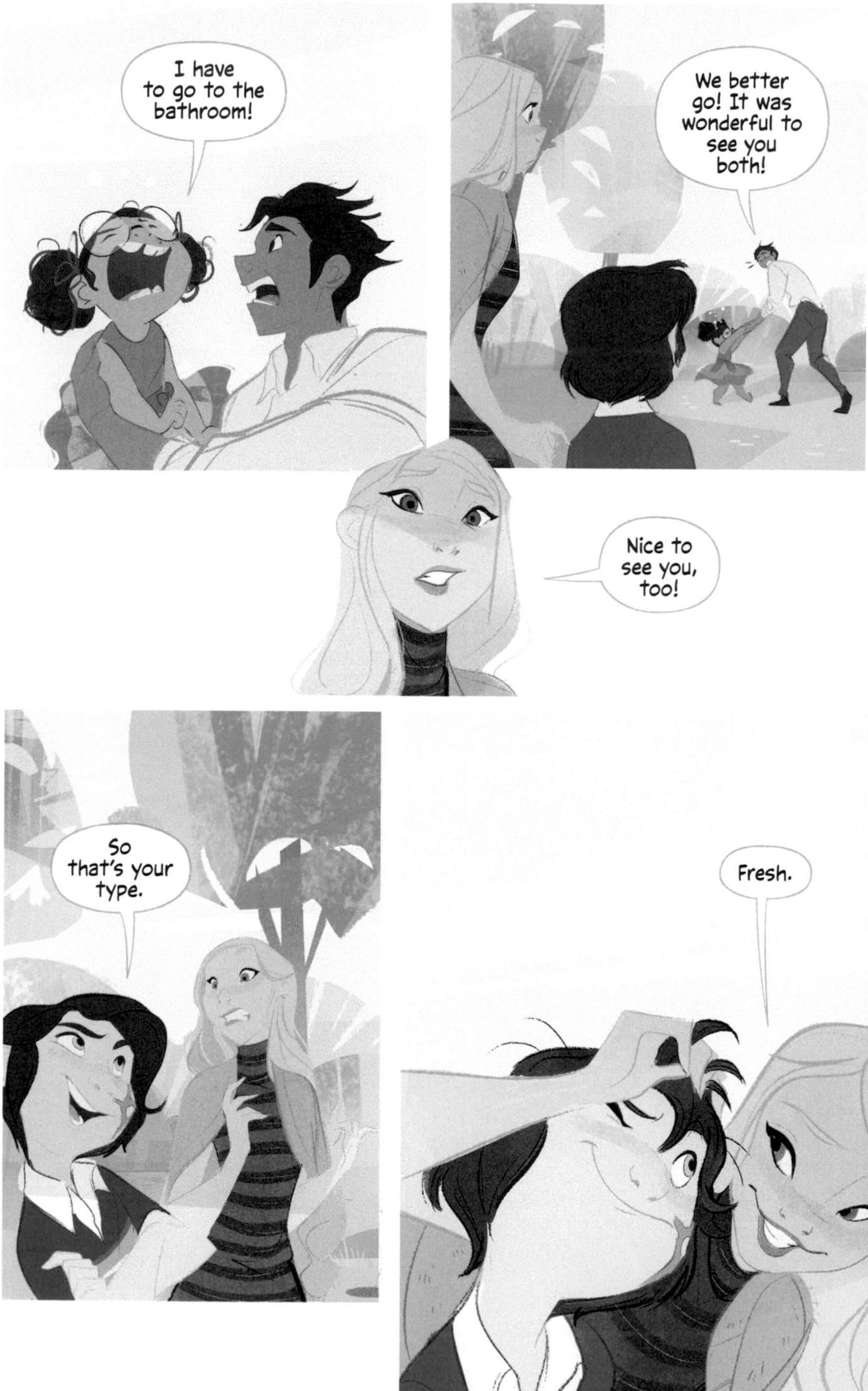
I have to go to the bathroom!
We better go! It was wonderful to see you both!
Nice to see you, too!
So that's your type.
Fresh.

CHAPTER FOUR

67

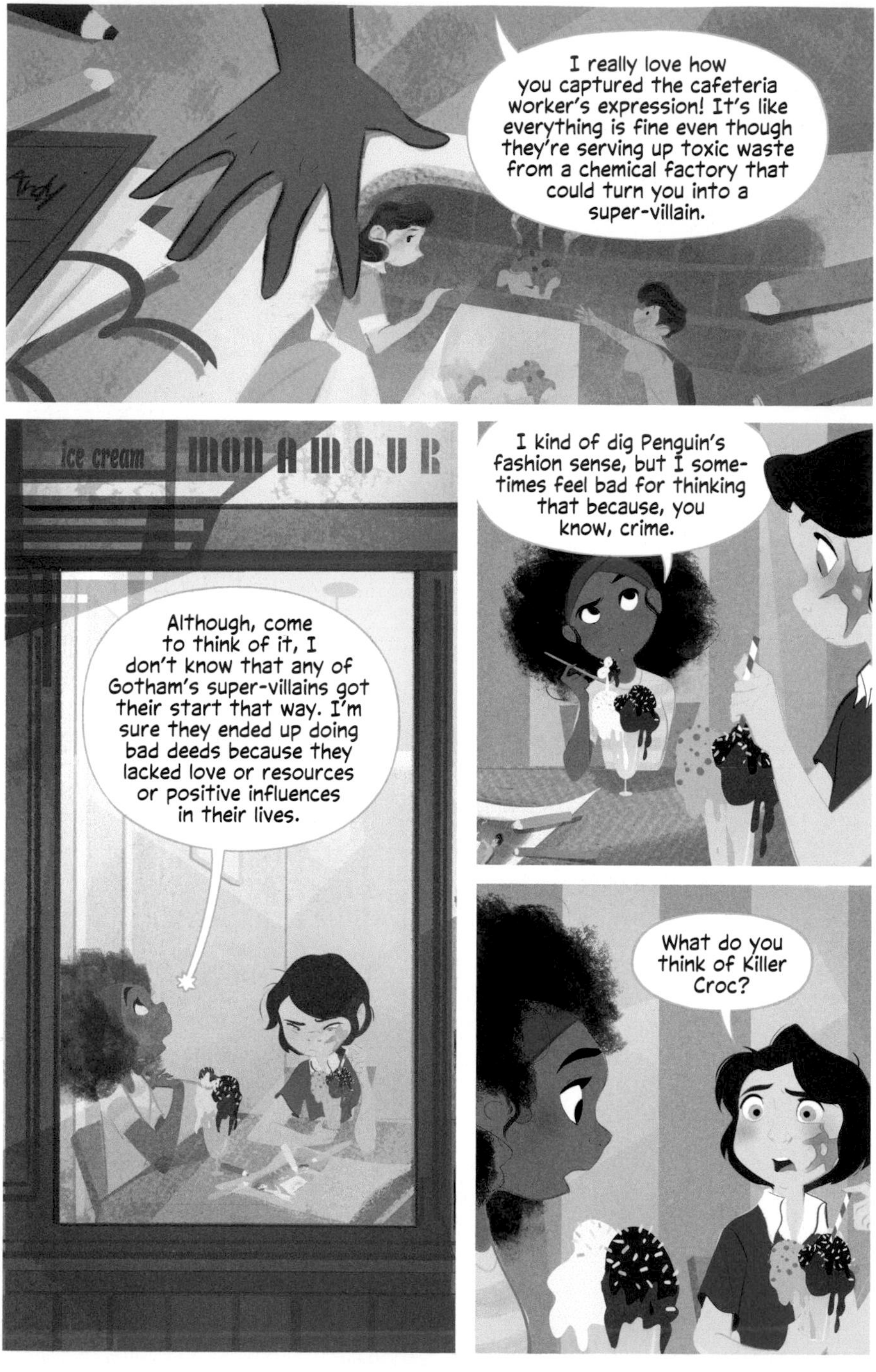
I really love how you captured the cafeteria worker's expression! It's like everything is fine even though they're serving up toxic waste from a chemical factory that could turn you into a super-villain.
ice cream
MON AMOUR
Although, come to think of it, I don't know that any of Gotham's super-villains got their start that way. I'm sure they ended up doing bad deeds because they lacked love or resources or positive influences in their lives.
I kind of dig Penguin's fashion sense, but I sometimes feel bad for thinking that because, you know, crime.
What do you think of Killer Croc?

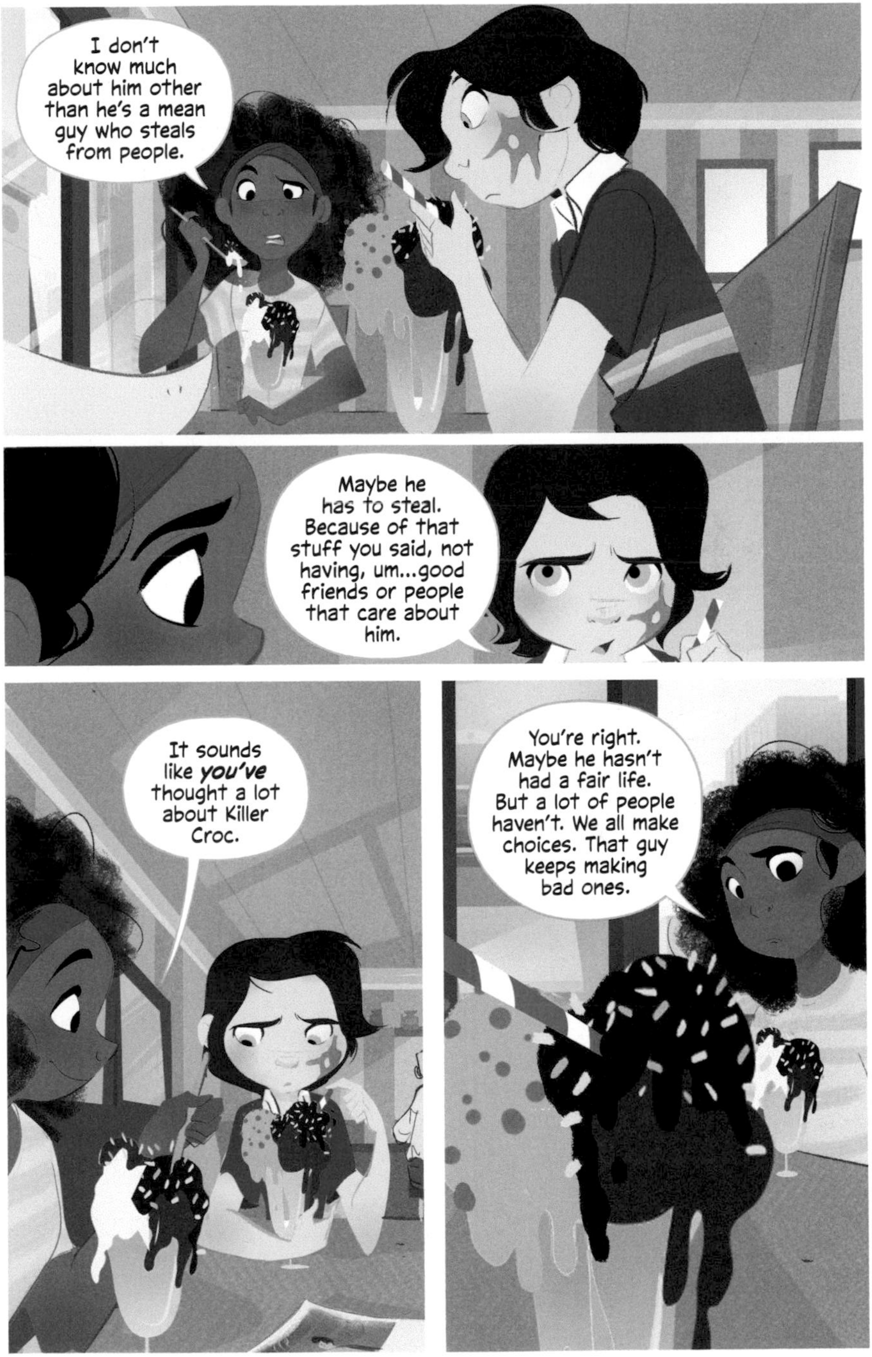
I don't know much about him other than he's a mean guy who steals from people.
Maybe he has to steal. Because of that stuff you said, not having, um...good friends or people that care about him.
It sounds like ***you've*** thought a lot about Killer Croc.
You're right. Maybe he hasn't had a fair life. But a lot of people haven't. We all make choices. That guy keeps making bad ones.

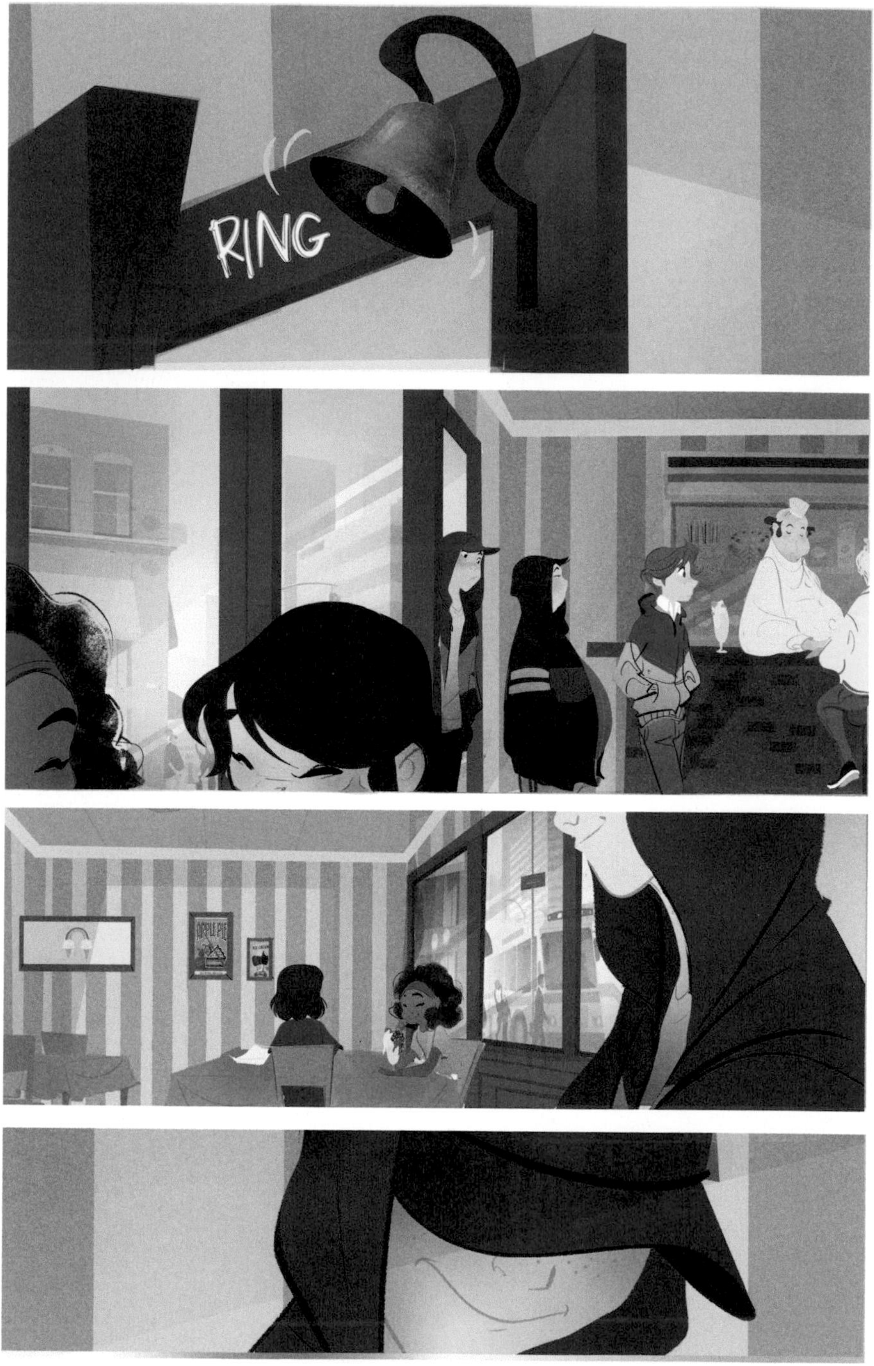
RING
APPLE PIE

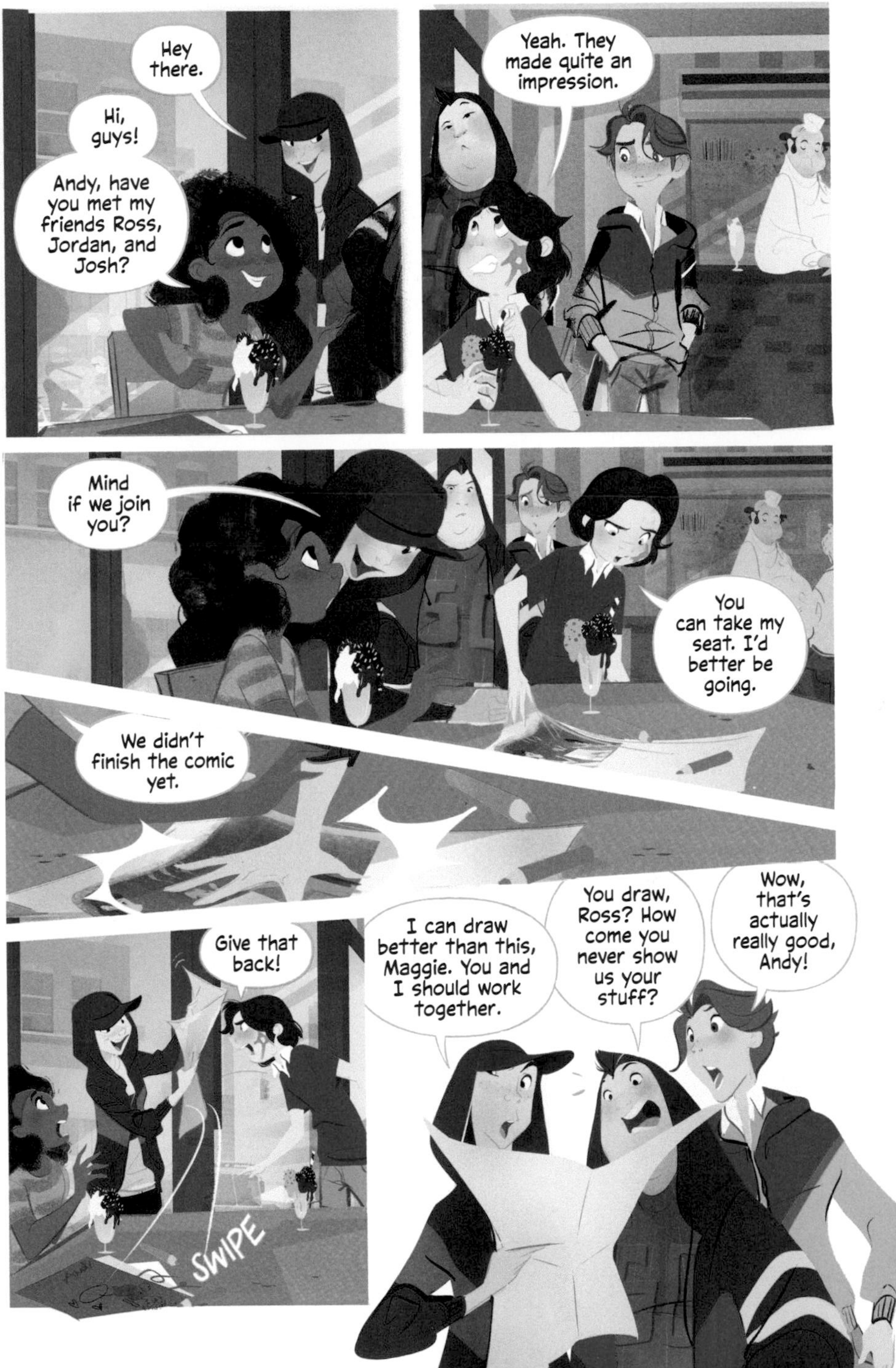
Hey there.
Hi, guys!
Andy, have you met my friends Ross, Jordan, and Josh?
Yeah. They made quite an impression.
Mind if we join you?
You can take my seat. I'd better be going.
We didn't finish the comic yet.
Give that back!
SWIPE
I can draw better than this, Maggie. You and I should work together.
You draw, Ross? How come you never show us your stuff?
Wow, that's actually really good, Andy!

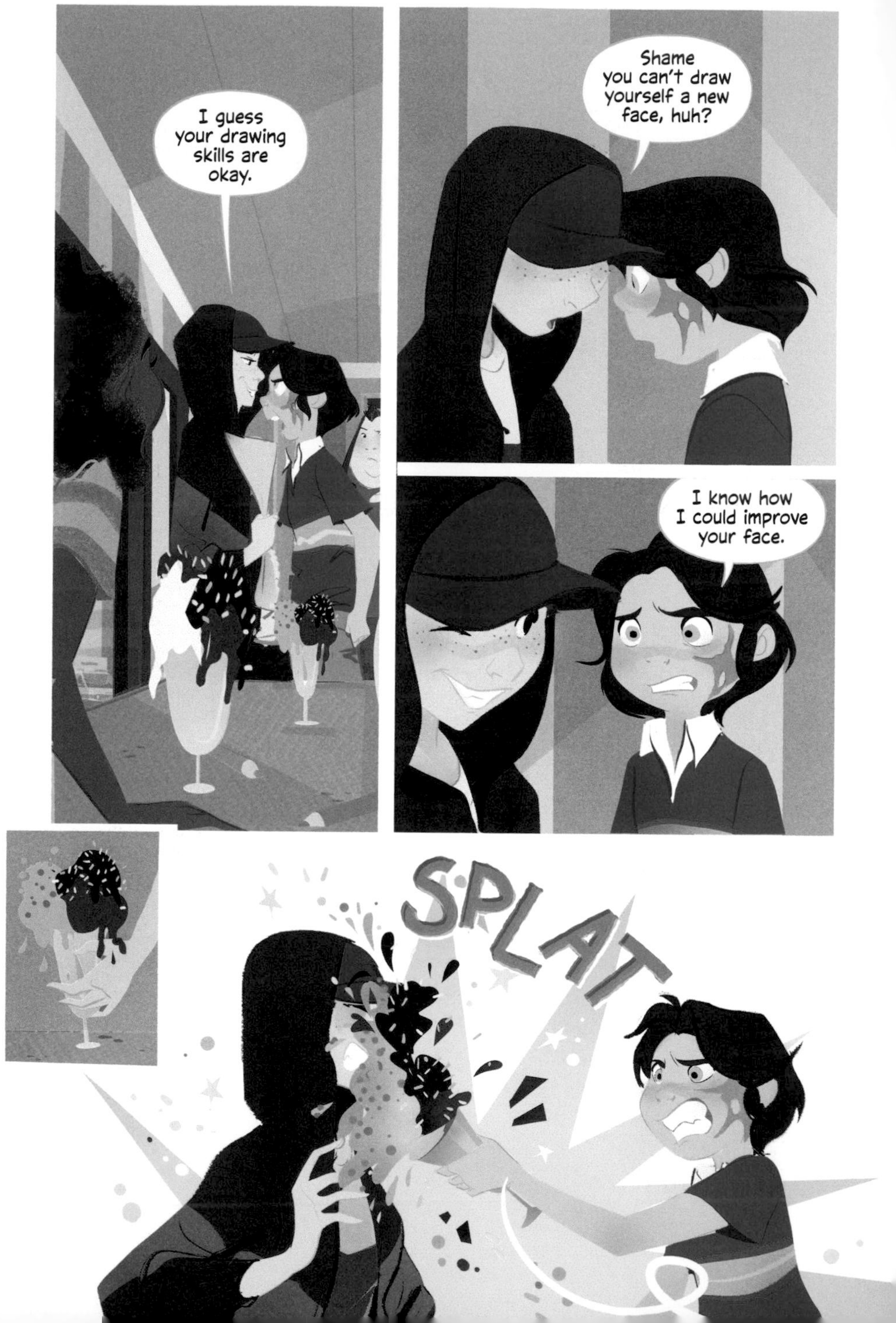
I guess your drawing skills are okay.
Shame you can't draw yourself a new face, huh?
I know how I could improve your face.
SPLAT

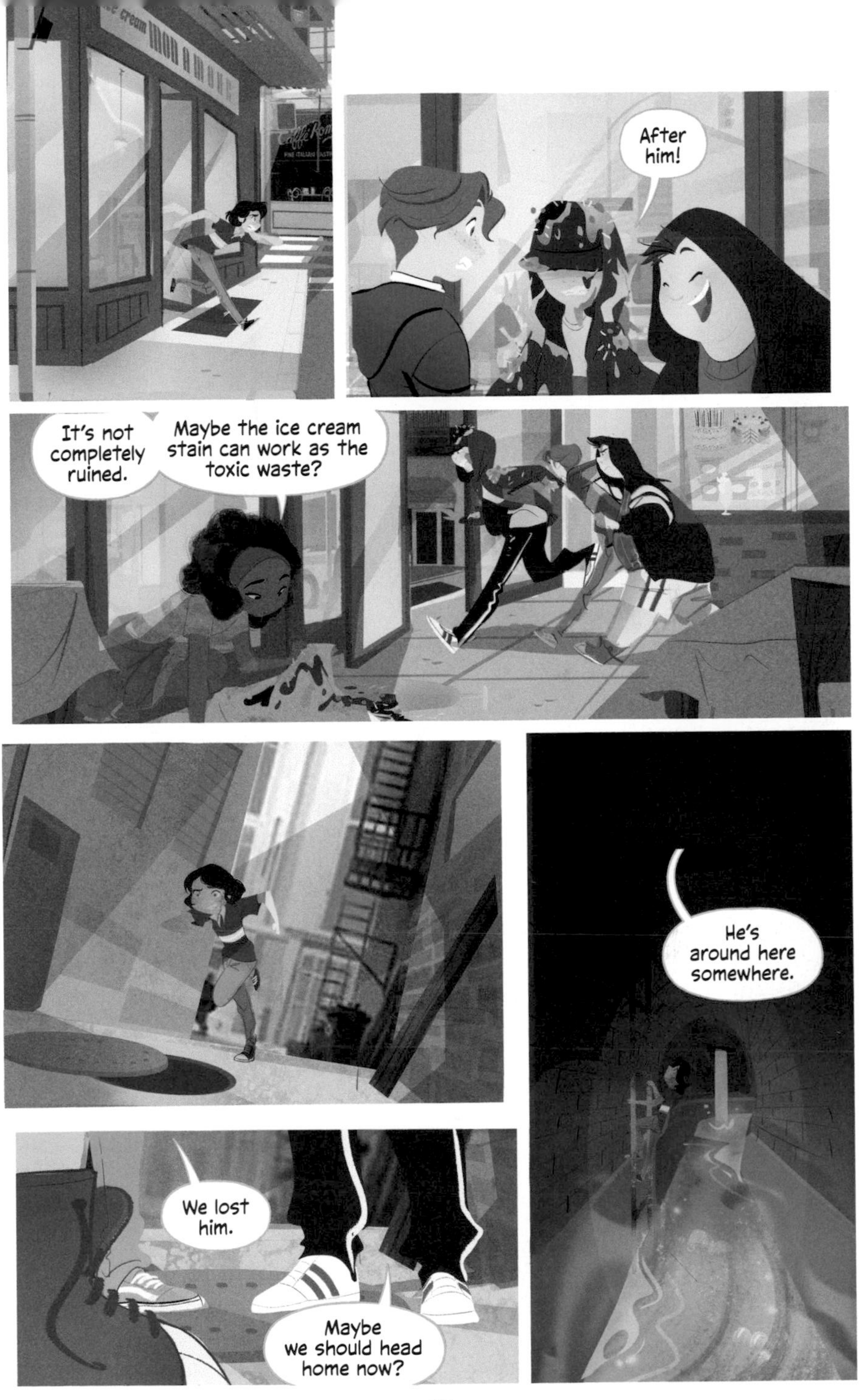
After him!
It's not completely ruined.
Maybe the ice cream stain can work as the toxic waste?
He's around here somewhere.
We lost him.
Maybe we should head home now?

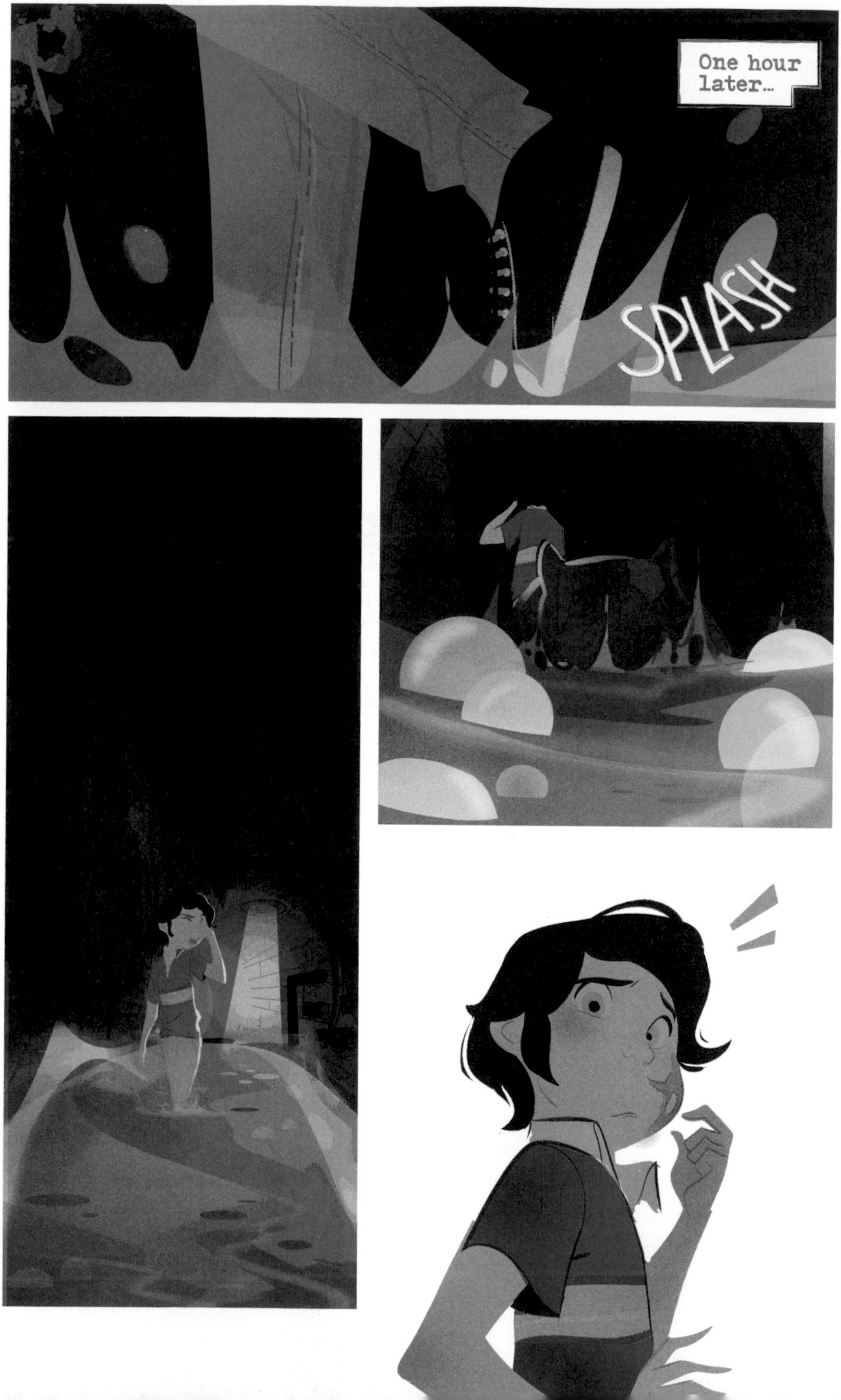
One hour later...
SPLASH

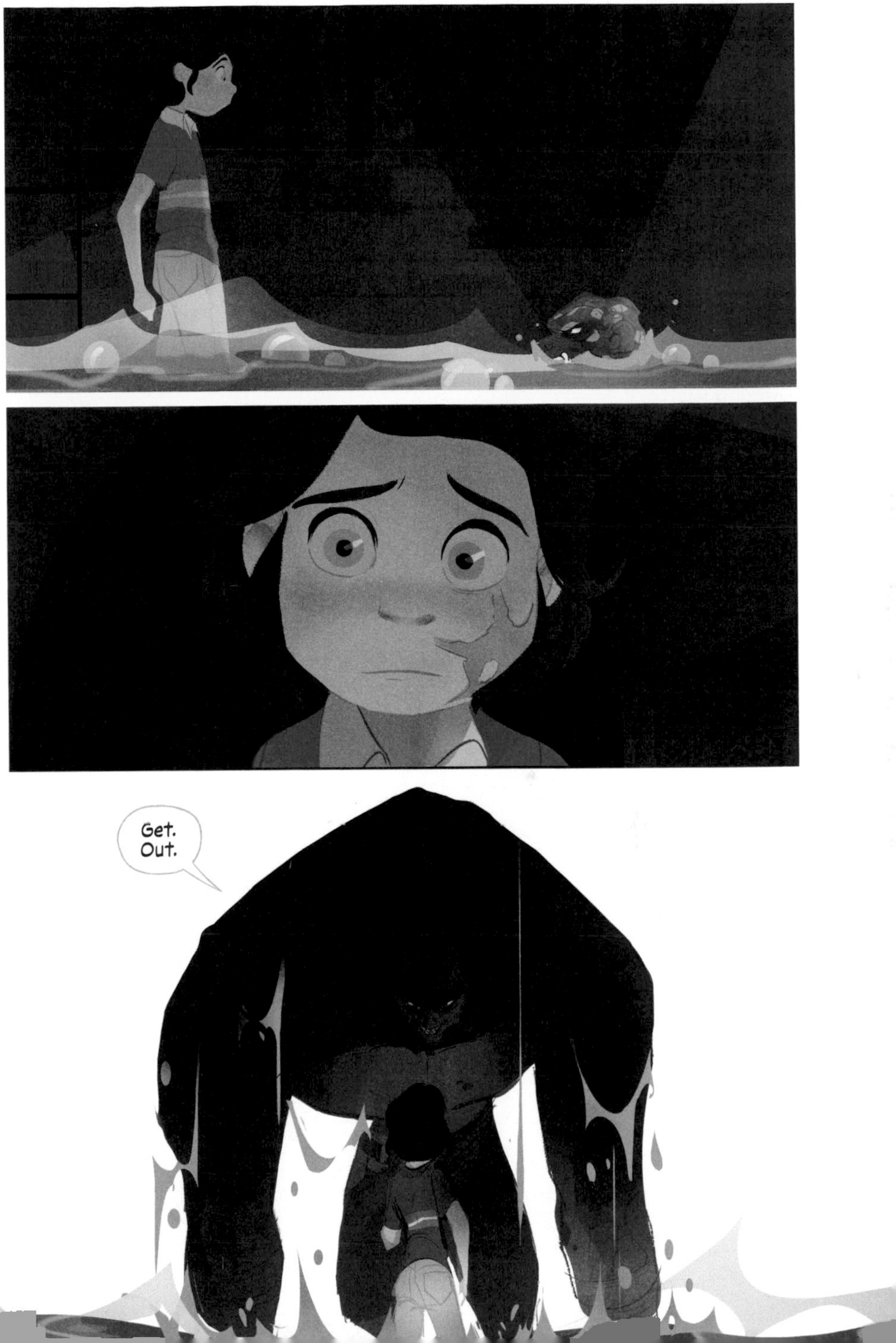
Get. Out.

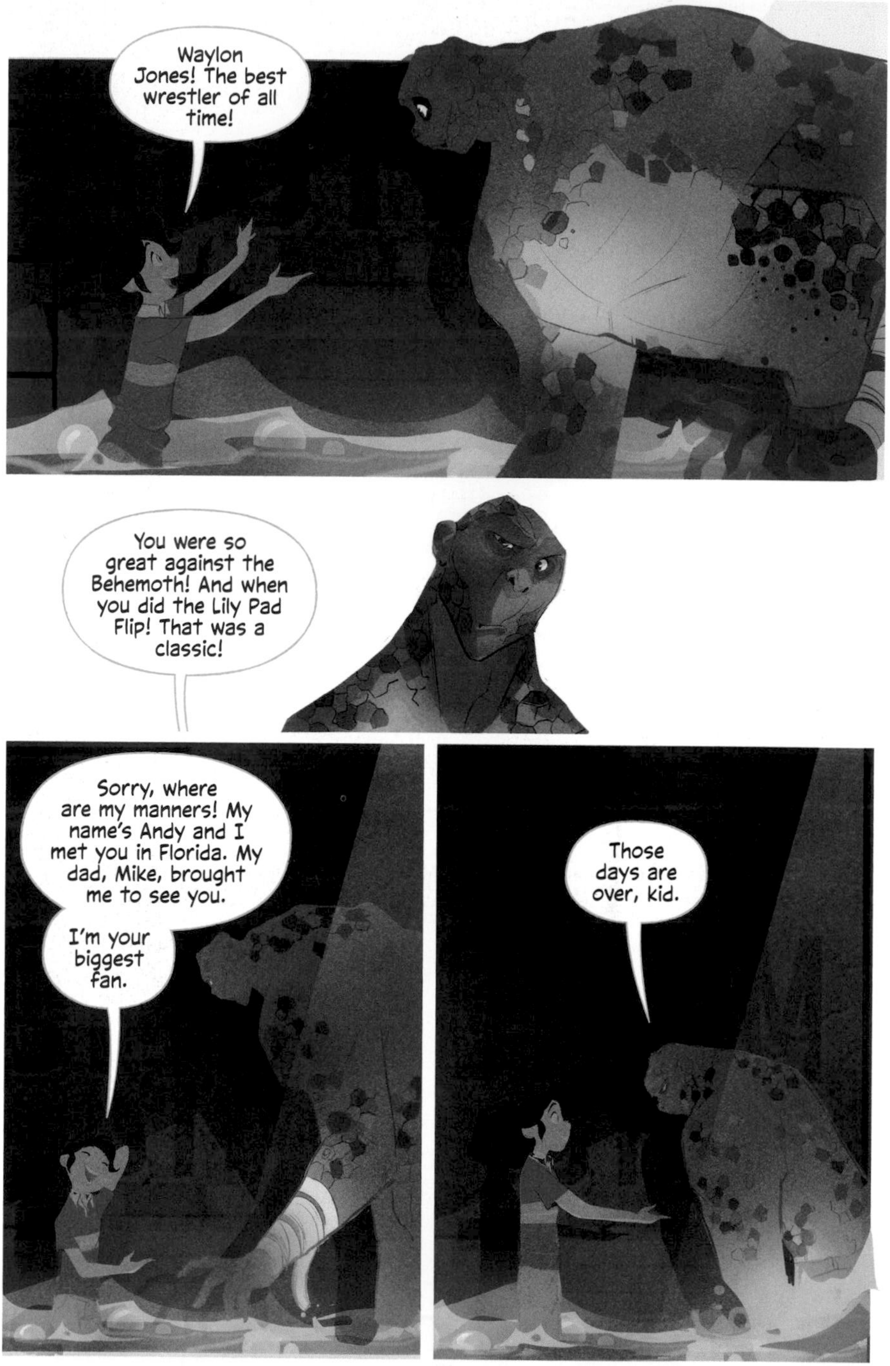
Waylon Jones! The best wrestler of all time!
You were so great against the Behemoth! And when you did the Lily Pad Flip! That was a classic!
Sorry, where are my manners! My name's Andy and I met you in Florida. My dad, Mike, brought me to see you.
I'm your biggest fan.
Those days are over, kid.

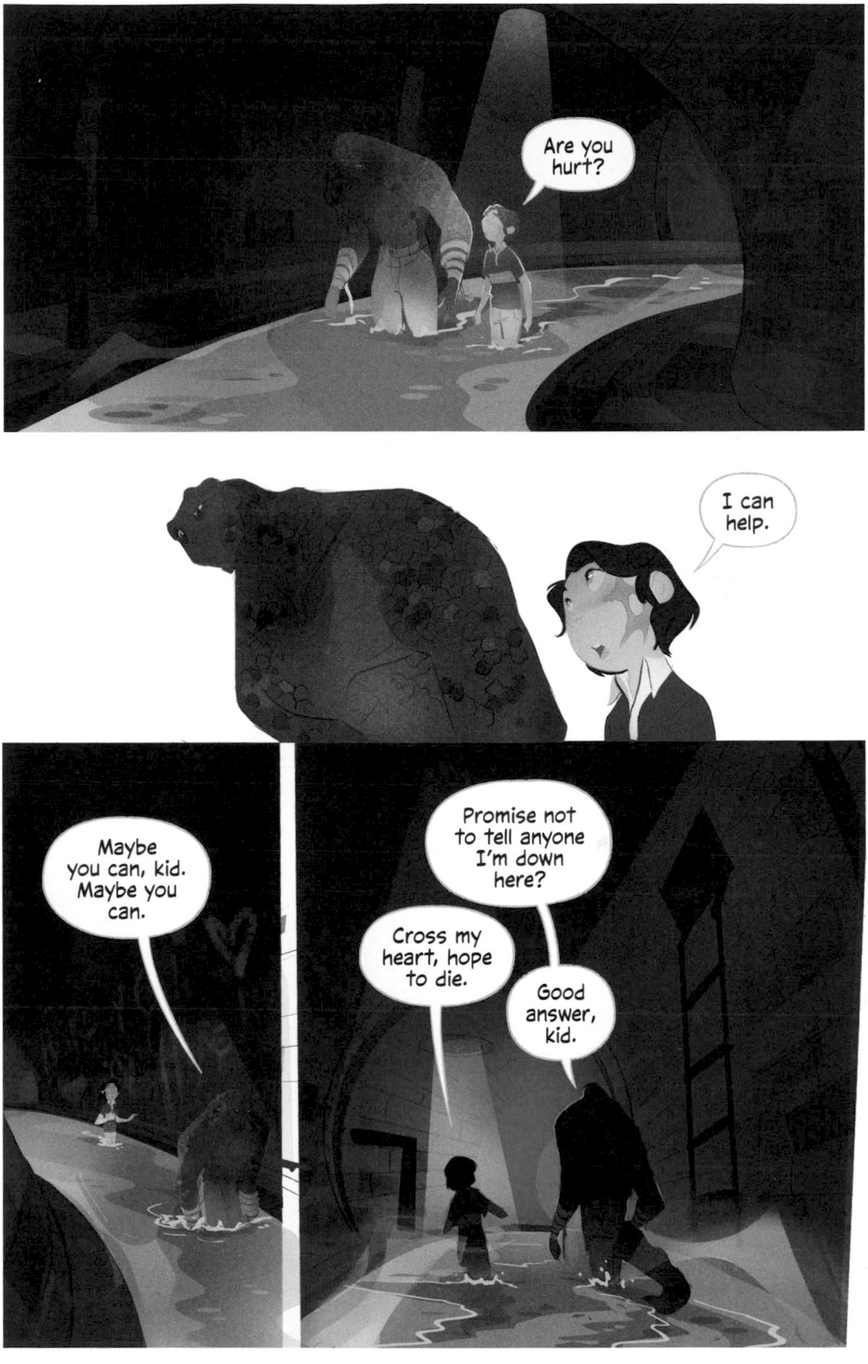
Are you hurt?
I can help.
Maybe you can, kid. Maybe you can.
Promise not to tell anyone I'm down here?
Cross my heart, hope to die.
Good answer, kid.

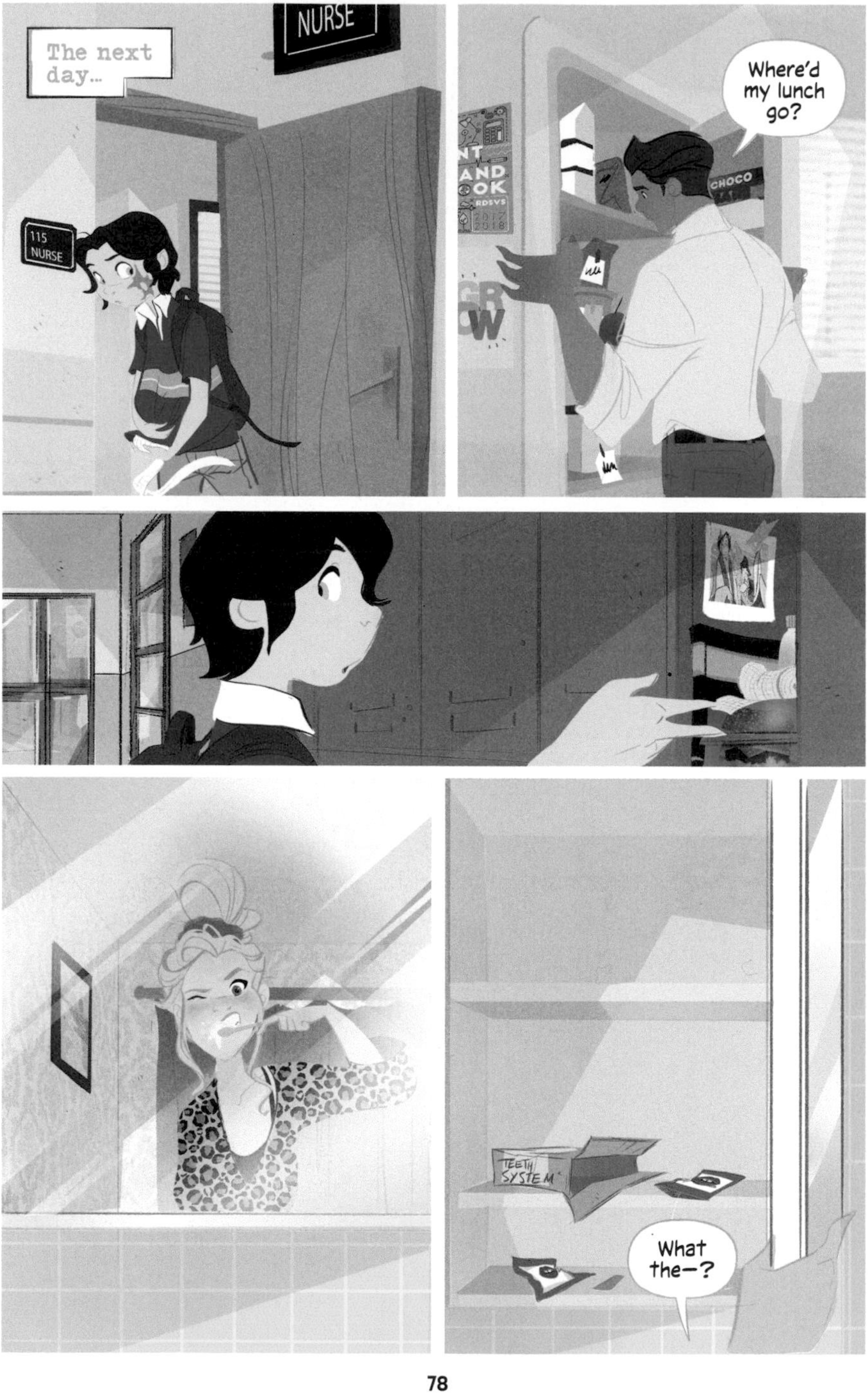
The next day...
NURSE
115
NURSE
Where'd my lunch go?
CHOCO
TEETH SYSTEM
What the—?

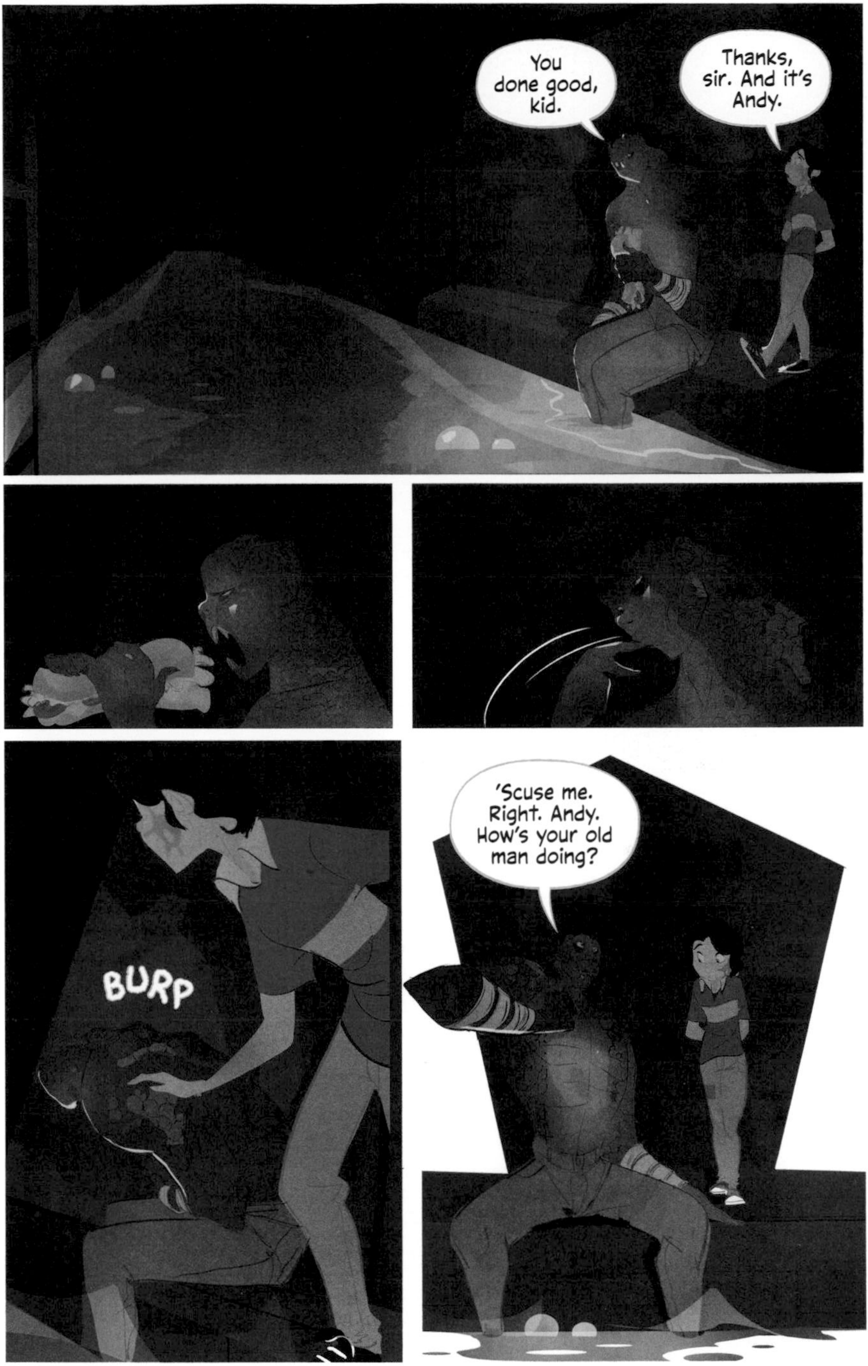
You done good, kid.
Thanks, sir. And it's Andy.
BURP
'Scuse me. Right. Andy. How's your old man doing?

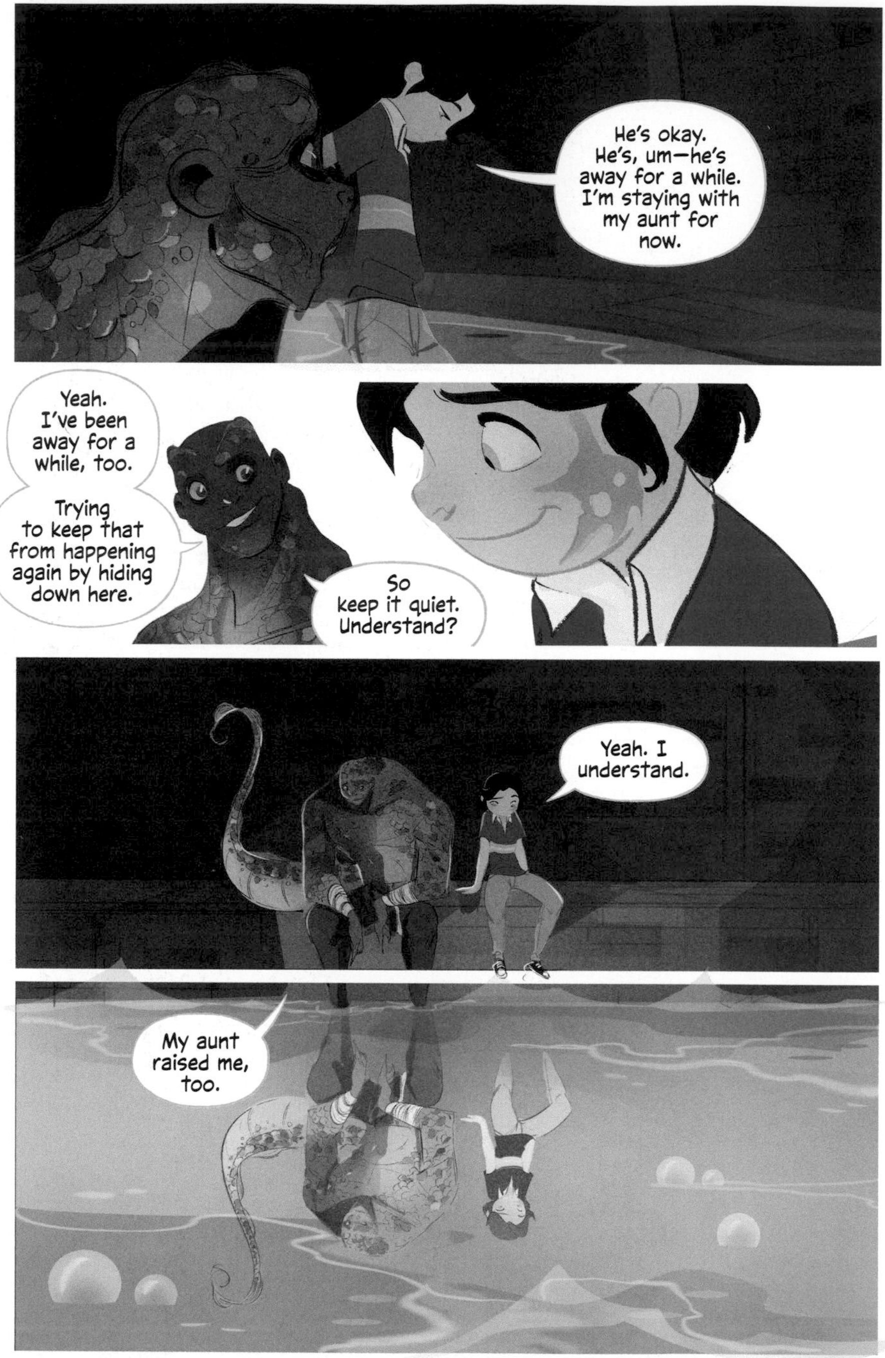
He's okay. He's, um—he's away for a while. I'm staying with my aunt for now.
Yeah. I've been away for a while, too.
Trying to keep that from happening again by hiding down here.
So keep it quiet. Understand?
Yeah. I understand.
My aunt raised me, too.

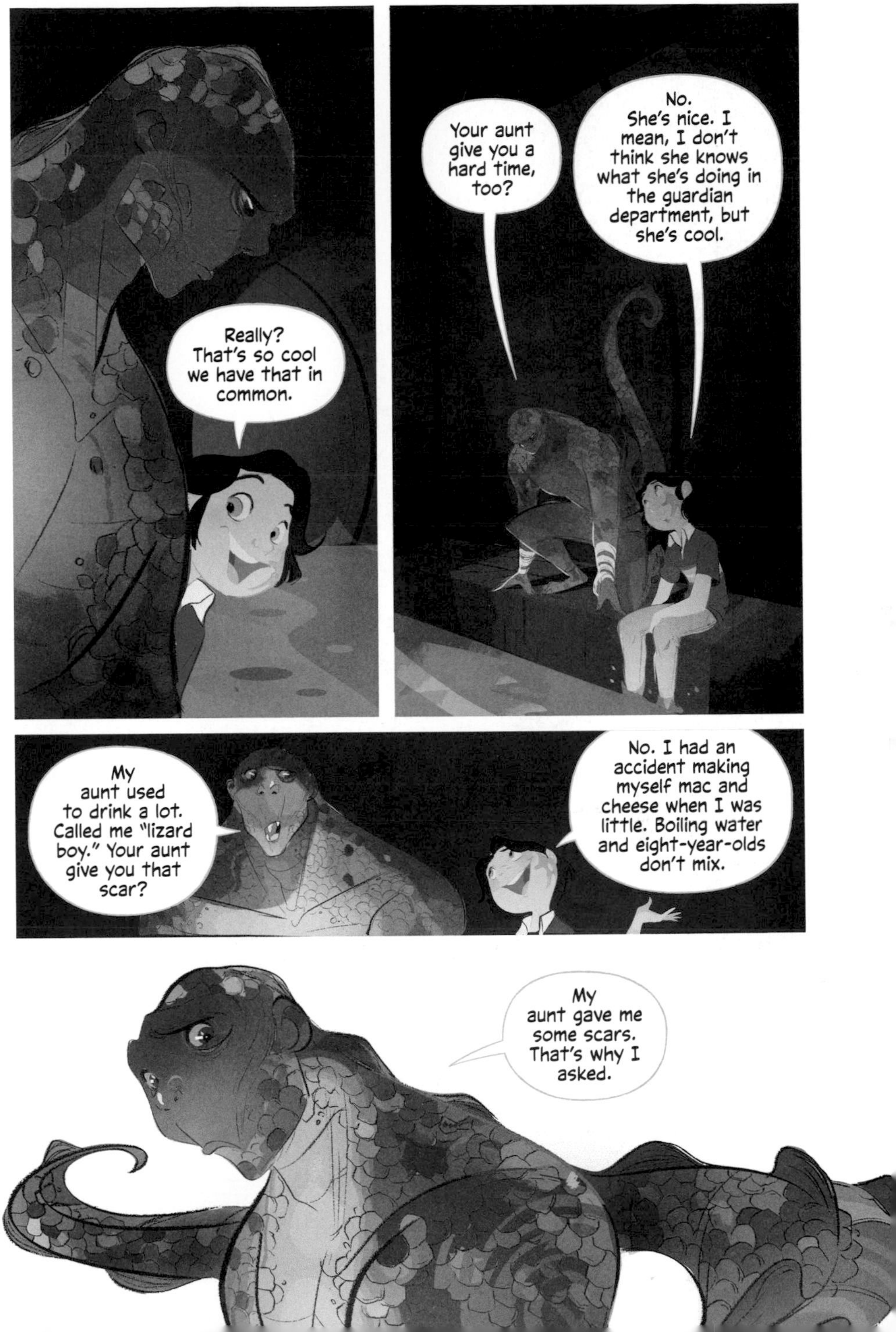
Really? That's so cool we have that in common.
Your aunt give you a hard time, too?
No. She's nice. I mean, I don't think she knows what she's doing in the guardian department, but she's cool.
My aunt used to drink a lot. Called me "lizard boy." Your aunt give you that scar?
No. I had an accident making myself mac and cheese when I was little. Boiling water and eight-year-olds don't mix.
My aunt gave me some scars. That's why I asked.

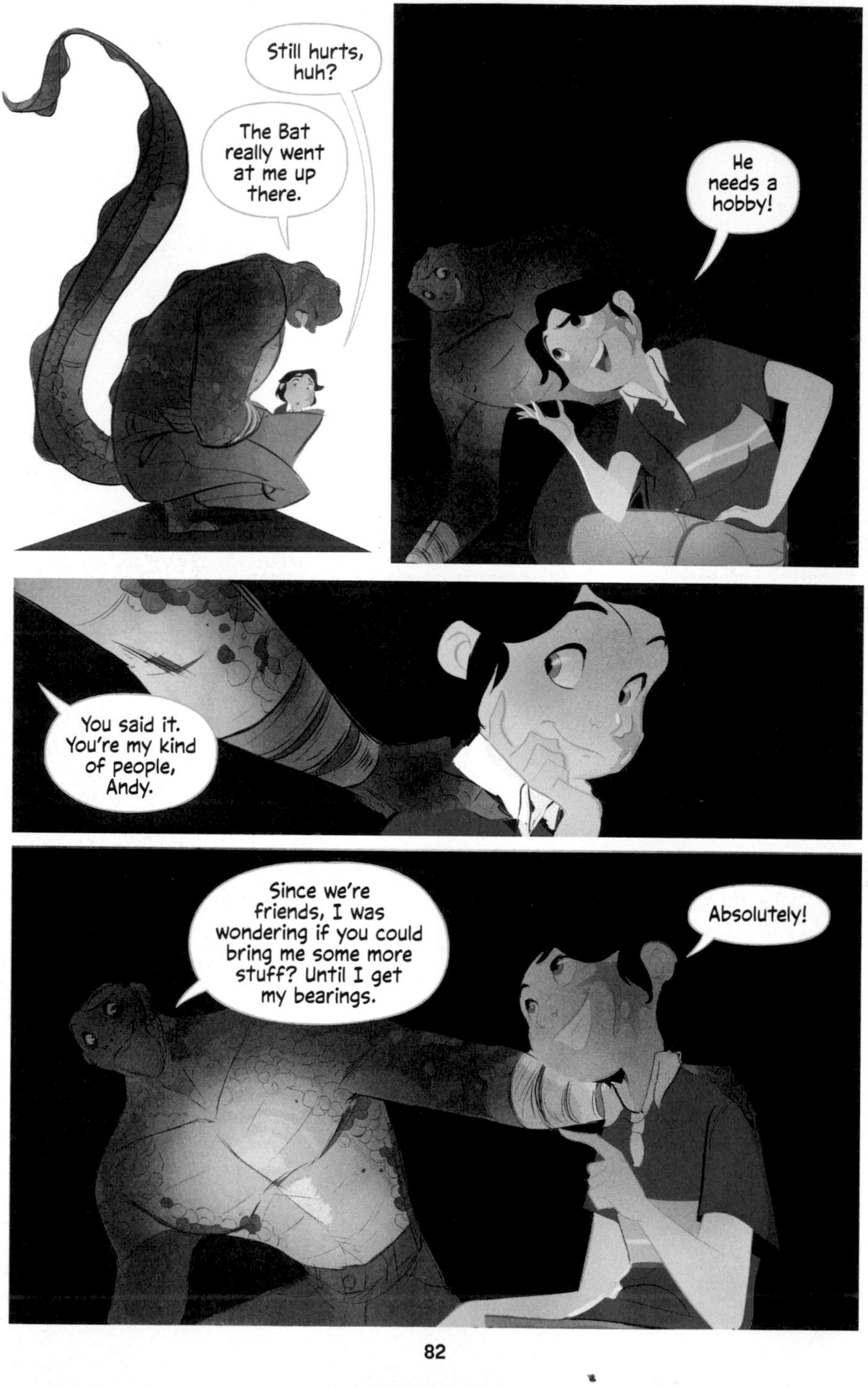
Still hurts, huh?
The Bat really went at me up there.
He needs a hobby!
You said it. You're my kind of people, Andy.
Since we're friends, I was wondering if you could bring me some more stuff? Until I get my bearings.
Absolutely!

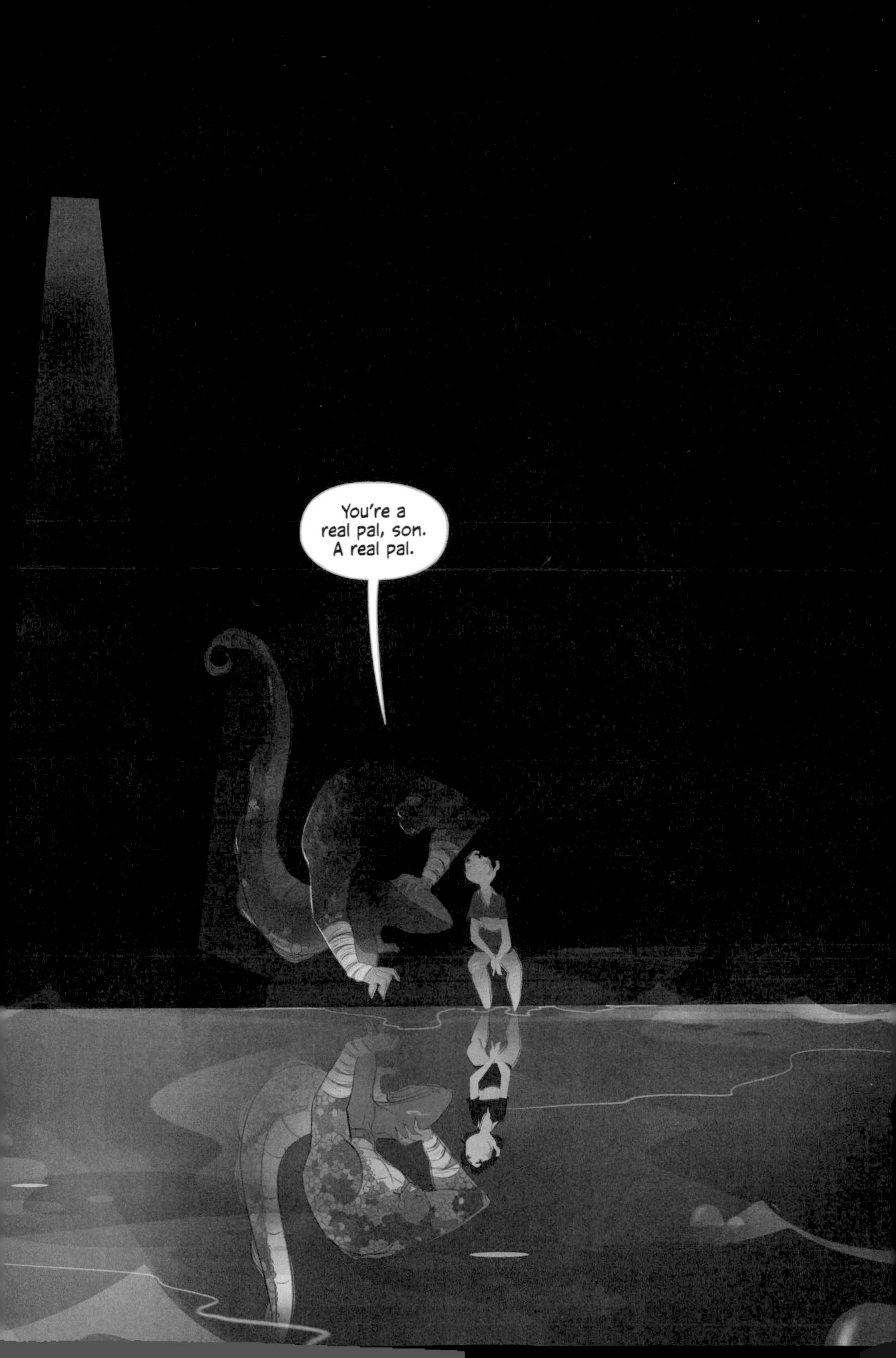
You're a real pal, son. A real pal.

CHAPTER FIVE

84

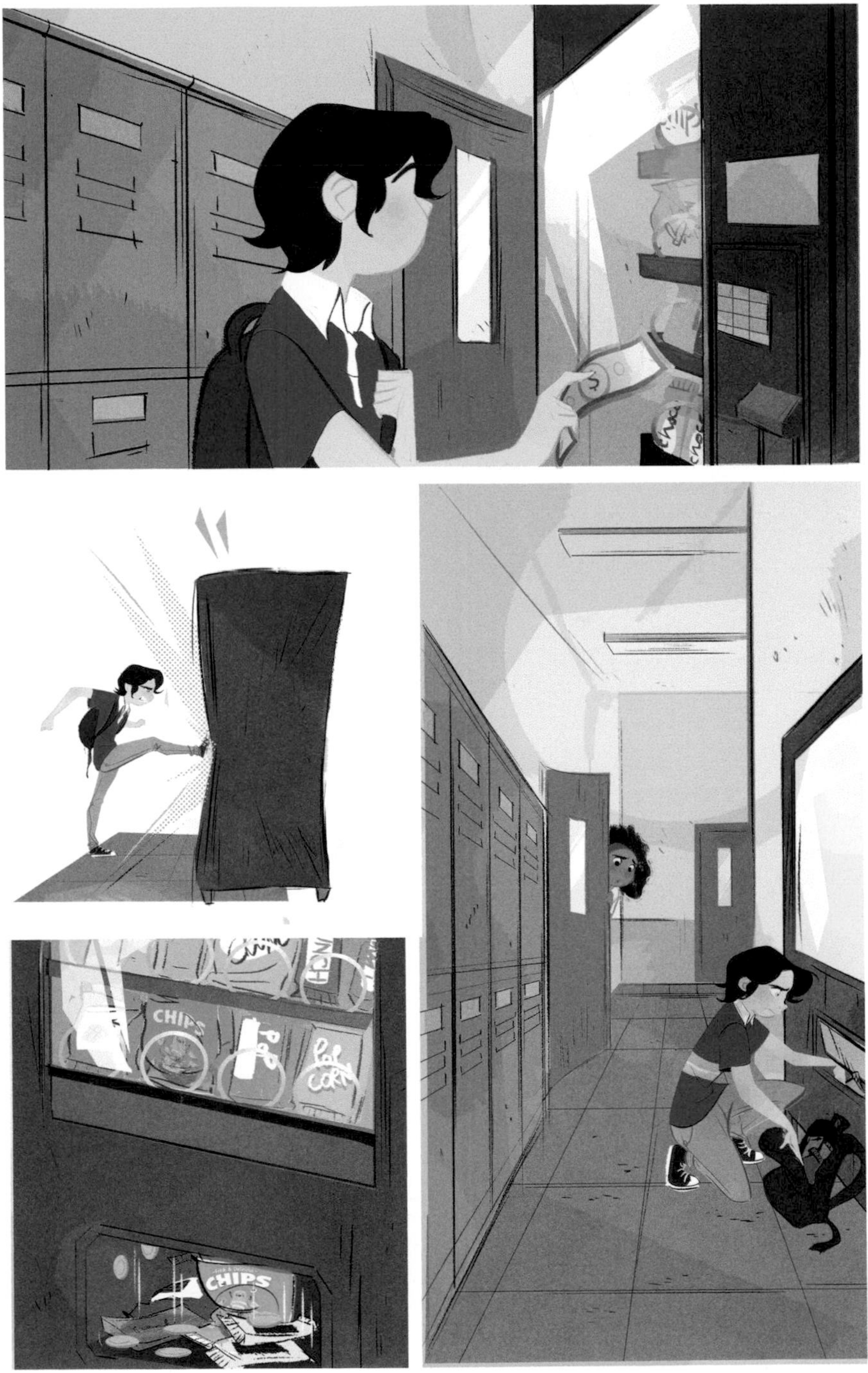
CHIPS
CHIPS

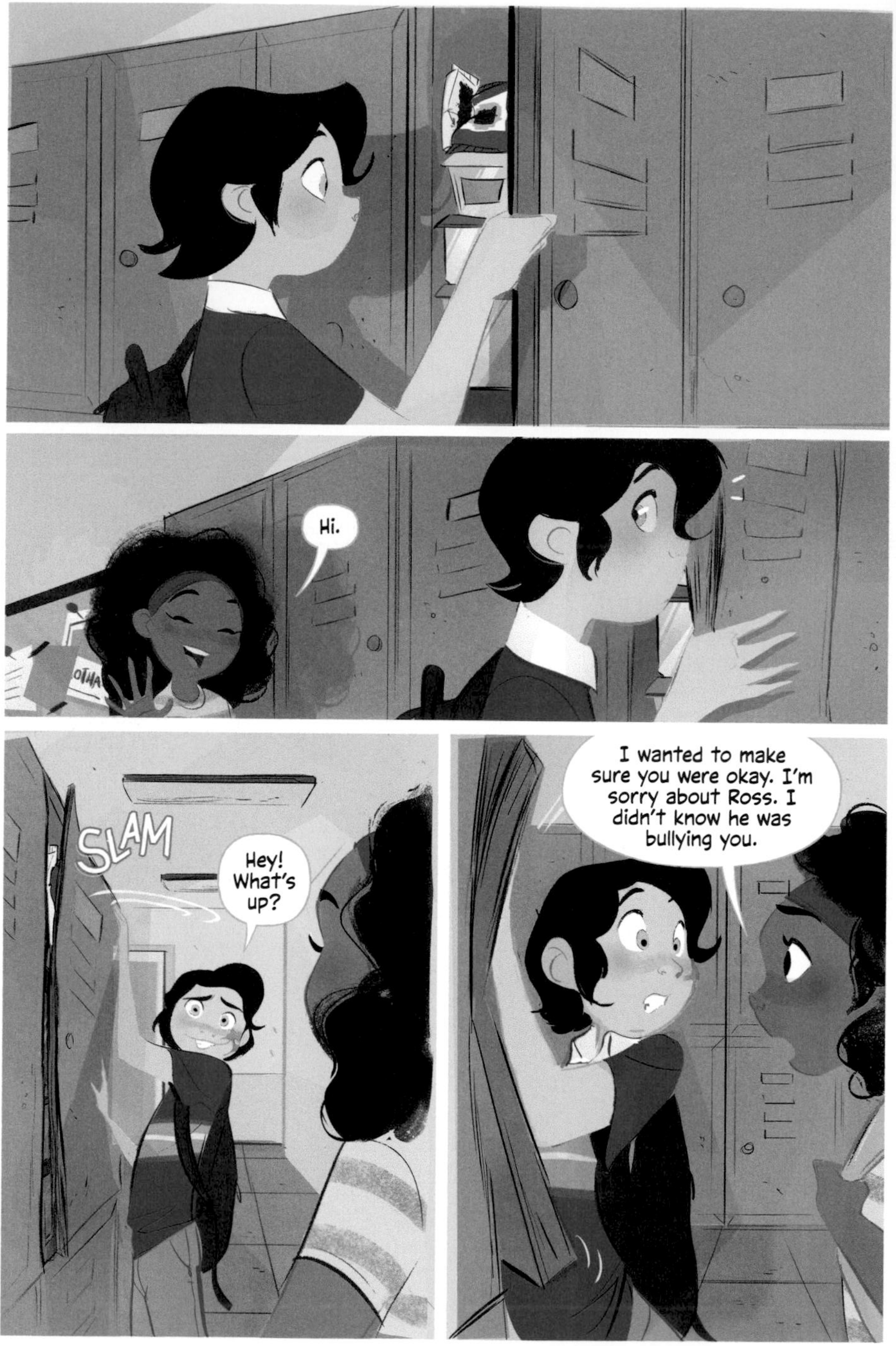
Hi.
SLAM
Hey! What's up?
I wanted to make sure you were okay. I'm sorry about Ross. I didn't know he was bullying you.

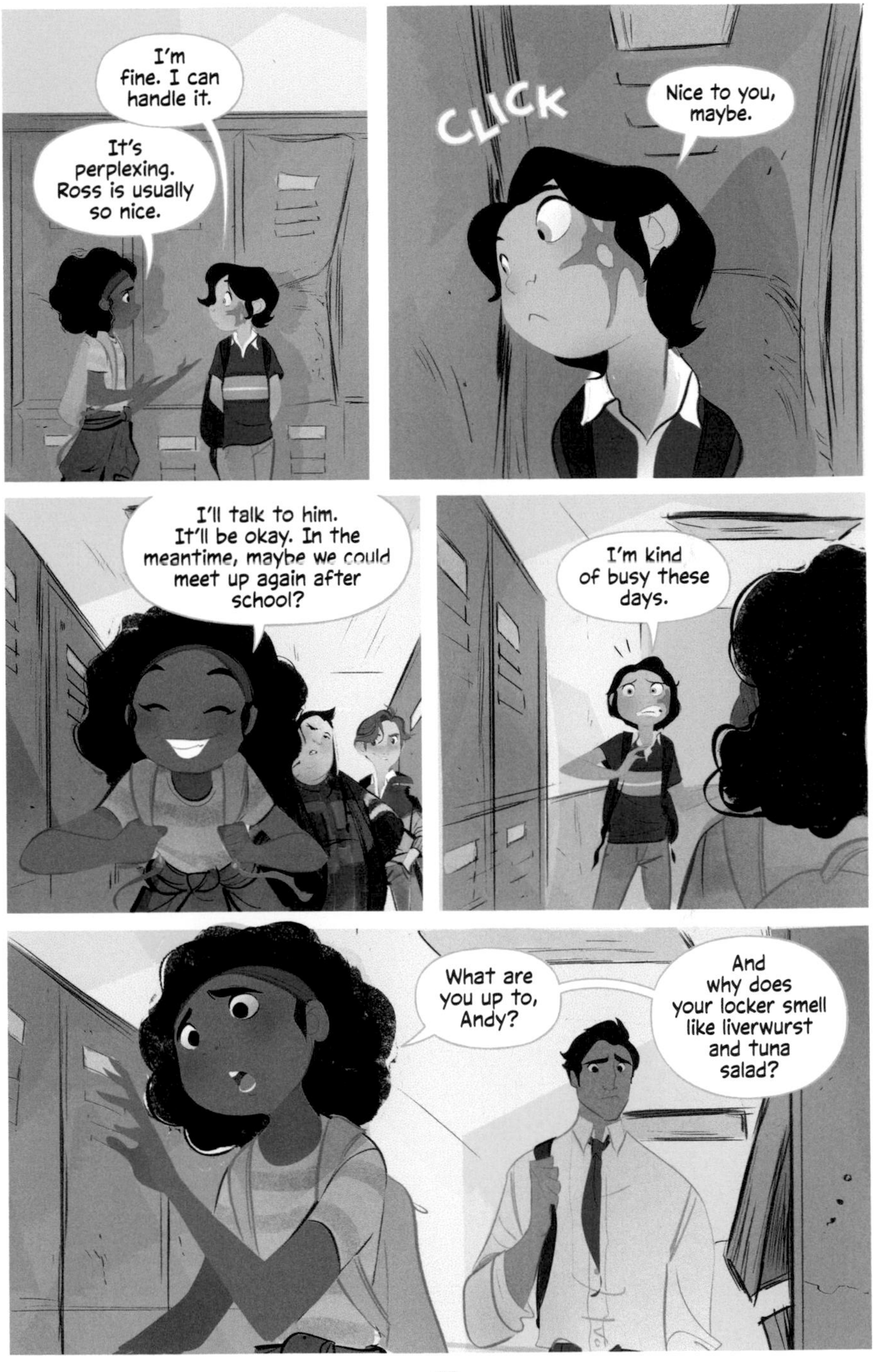
I'm fine. I can handle it.
It's perplexing. Ross is usually so nice.
CLICK
Nice to you, maybe.
I'll talk to him. It'll be okay. In the meantime, maybe we could meet up again after school?
I'm kind of busy these days.
What are you up to, Andy?
And why does your locker smell like liverwurst and tuna salad?

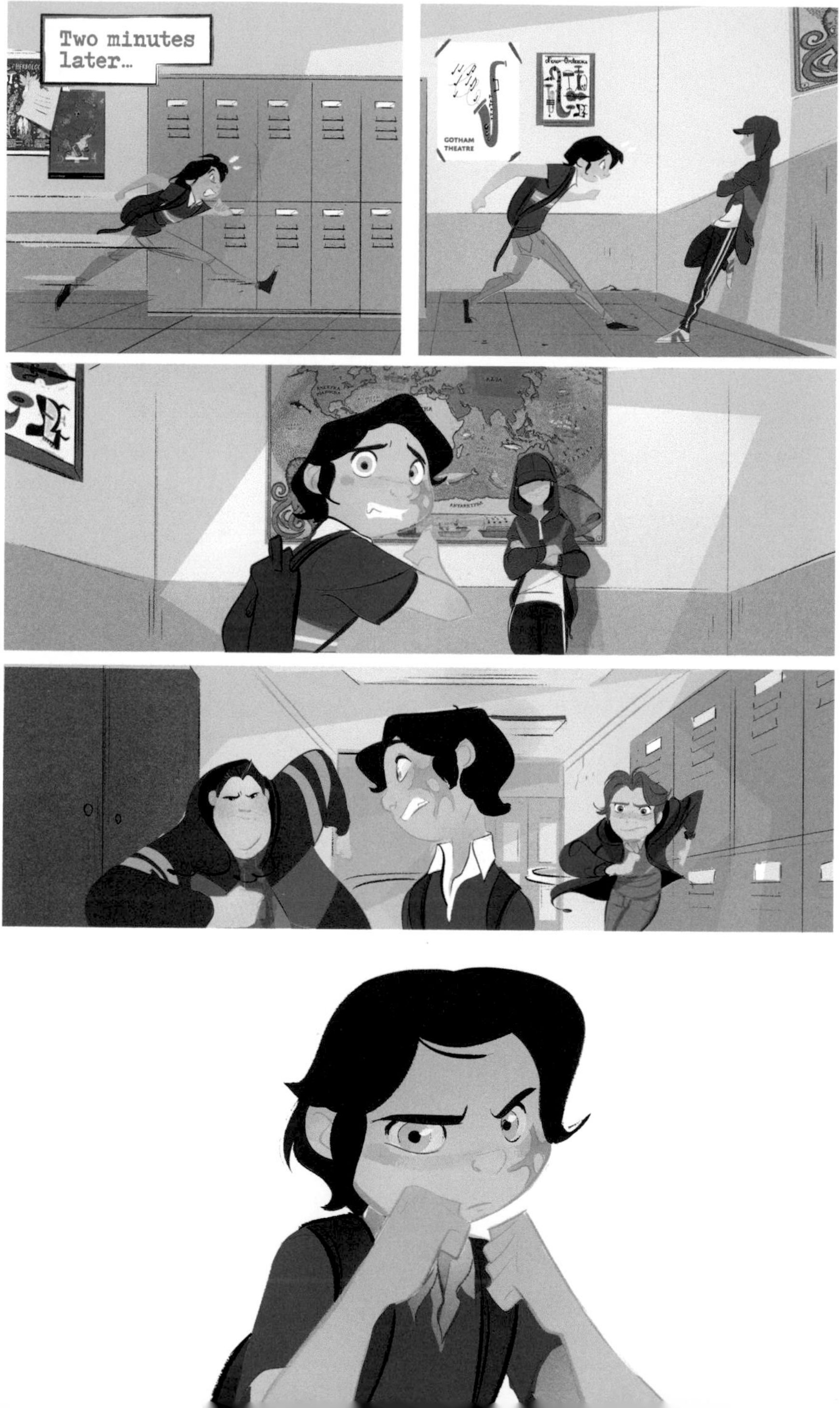
Two minutes later…
GOTHAM THEATRE

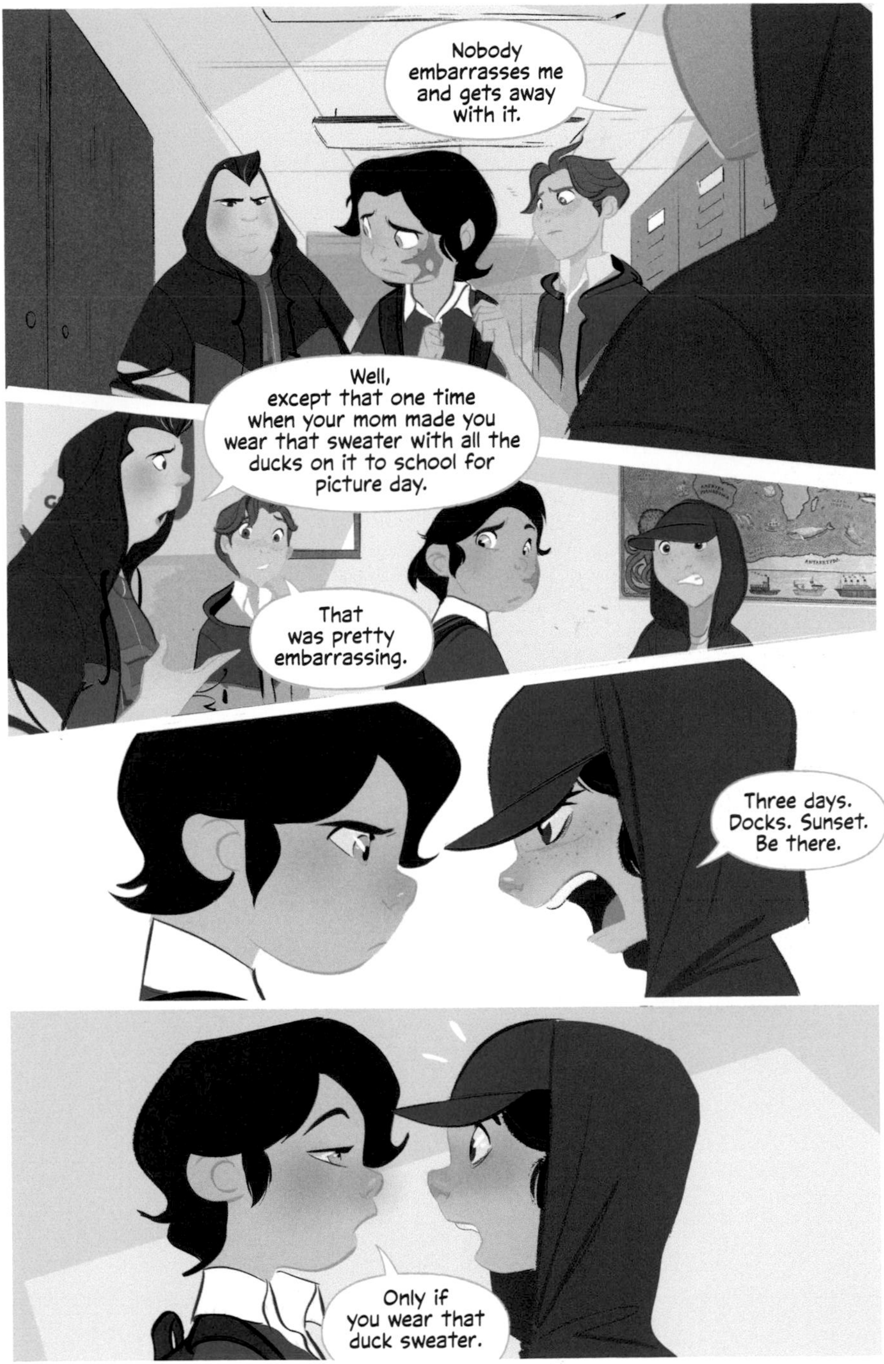
Nobody embarrasses me and gets away with it.
Well, except that one time when your mom made you wear that sweater with all the ducks on it to school for picture day.
That was pretty embarrassing.
Three days. Docks. Sunset. Be there.
Only if you wear that duck sweater.

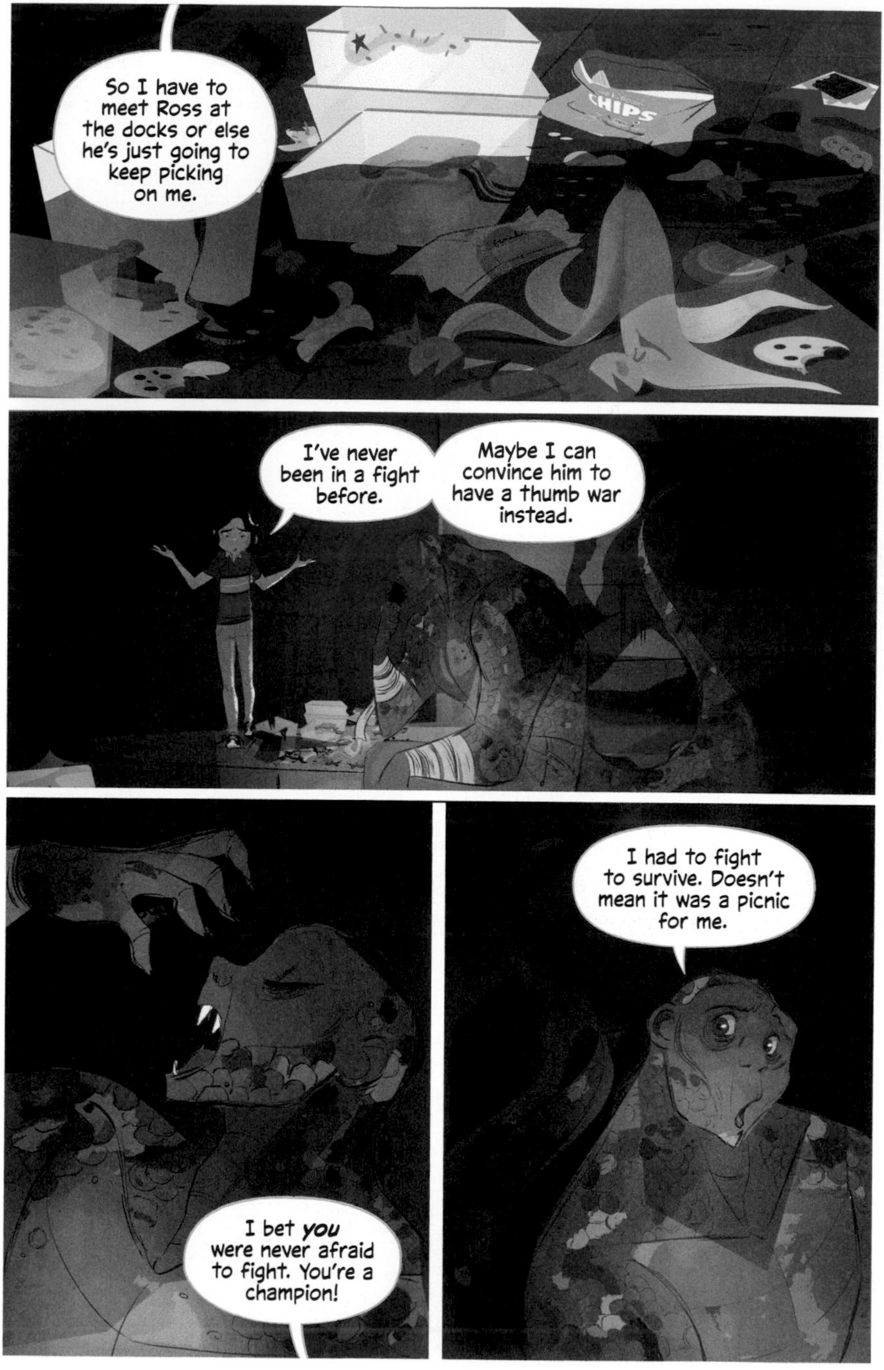
So I have to meet Ross at the docks or else he's just going to keep picking on me.
I've never been in a fight before.
Maybe I can convince him to have a thumb war instead.
I bet *you* were never afraid to fight. You're a champion!
I had to fight to survive. Doesn't mean it was a picnic for me.

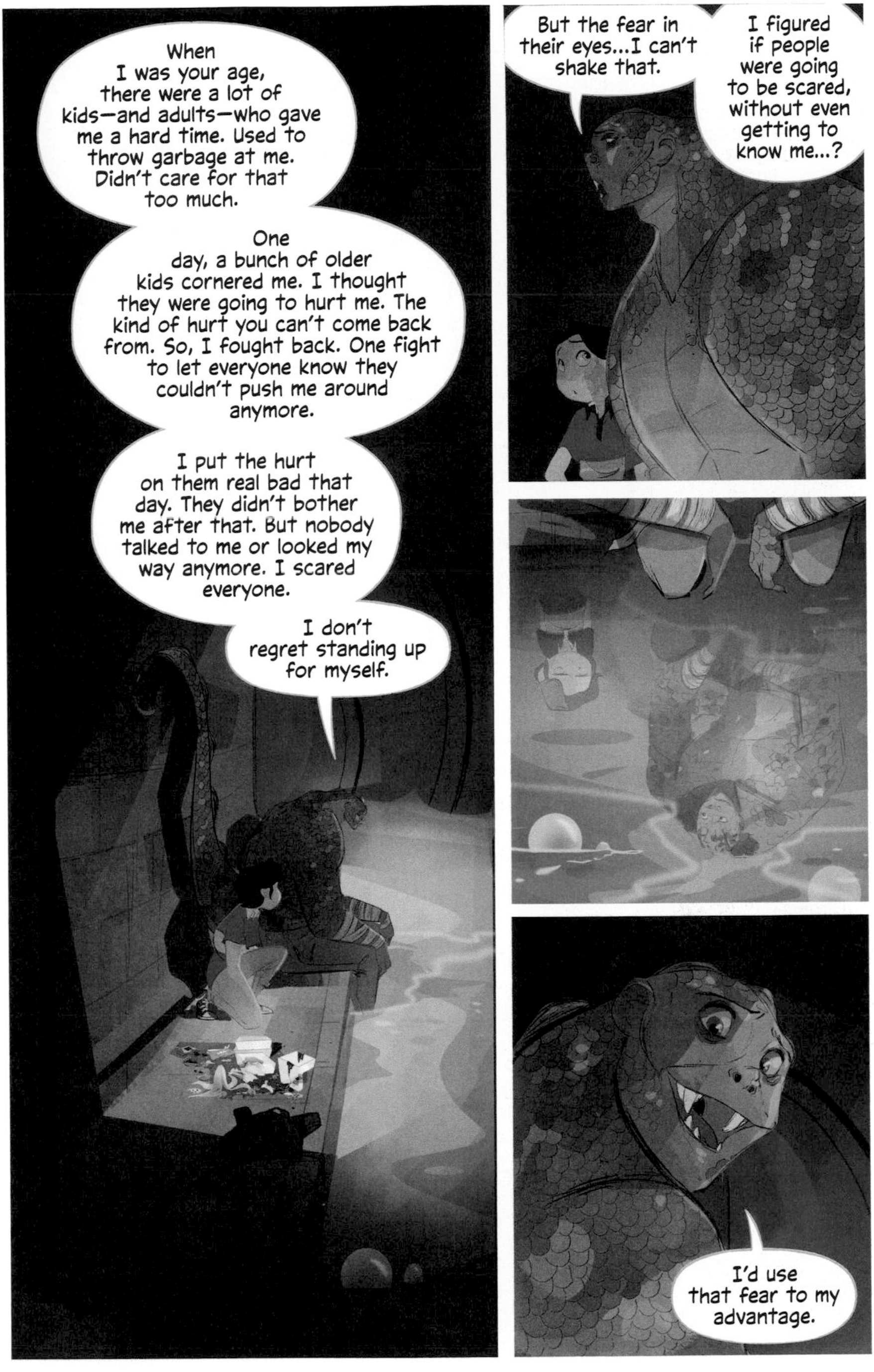
When I was your age, there were a lot of kids—and adults—who gave me a hard time. Used to throw garbage at me. Didn't care for that too much.
One day, a bunch of older kids cornered me. I thought they were going to hurt me. The kind of hurt you can't come back from. So, I fought back. One fight to let everyone know they couldn't push me around anymore.
I put the hurt on them real bad that day. They didn't bother me after that. But nobody talked to me or looked my way anymore. I scared everyone.
I don't regret standing up for myself.
But the fear in their eyes...I can't shake that.
I figured if people were going to be scared, without even getting to know me...?
I'd use that fear to my advantage.

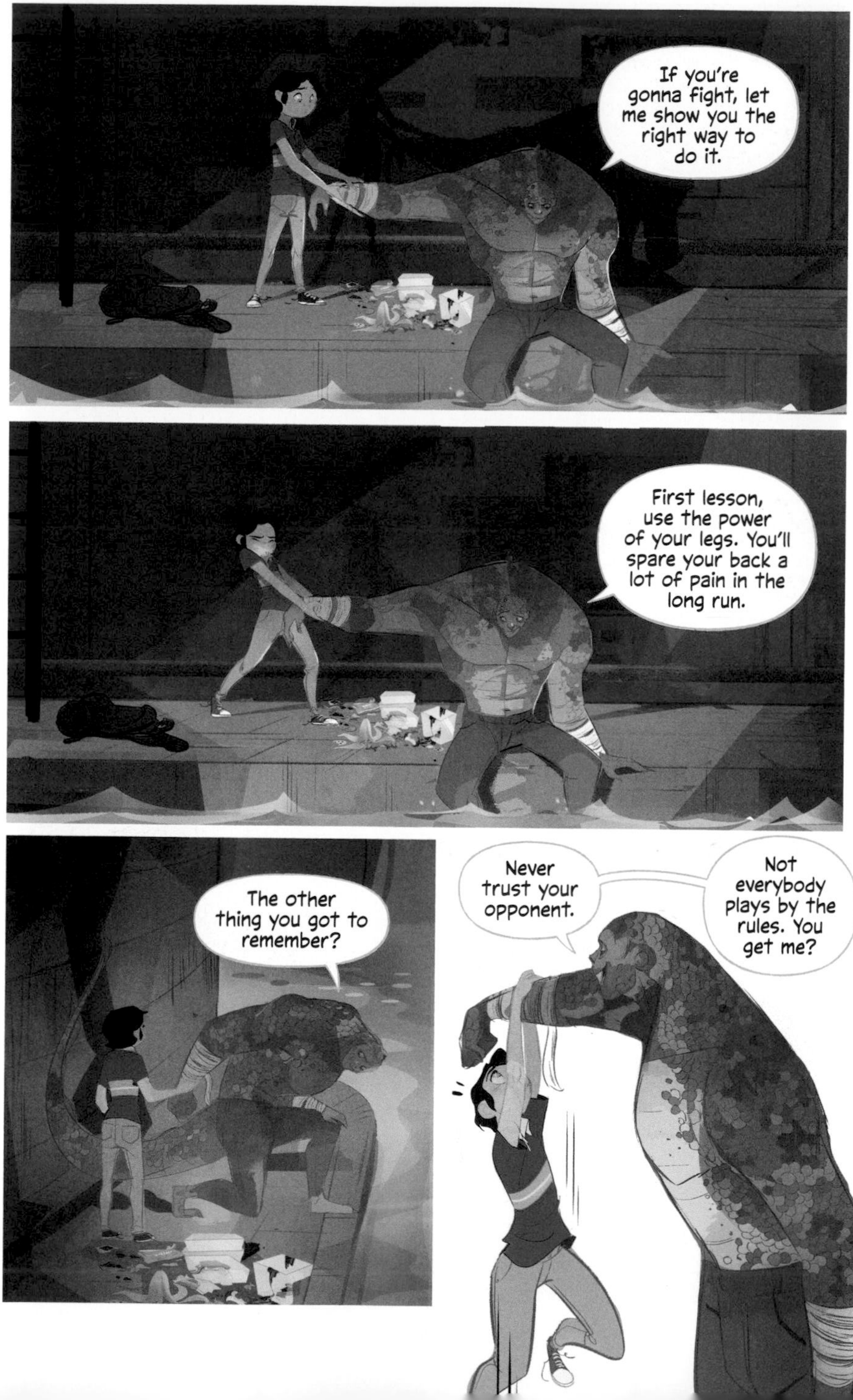
If you're gonna fight, let me show you the right way to do it.
First lesson, use the power of your legs. You'll spare your back a lot of pain in the long run.
The other thing you got to remember?
Never trust your opponent.
Not everybody plays by the rules. You get me?

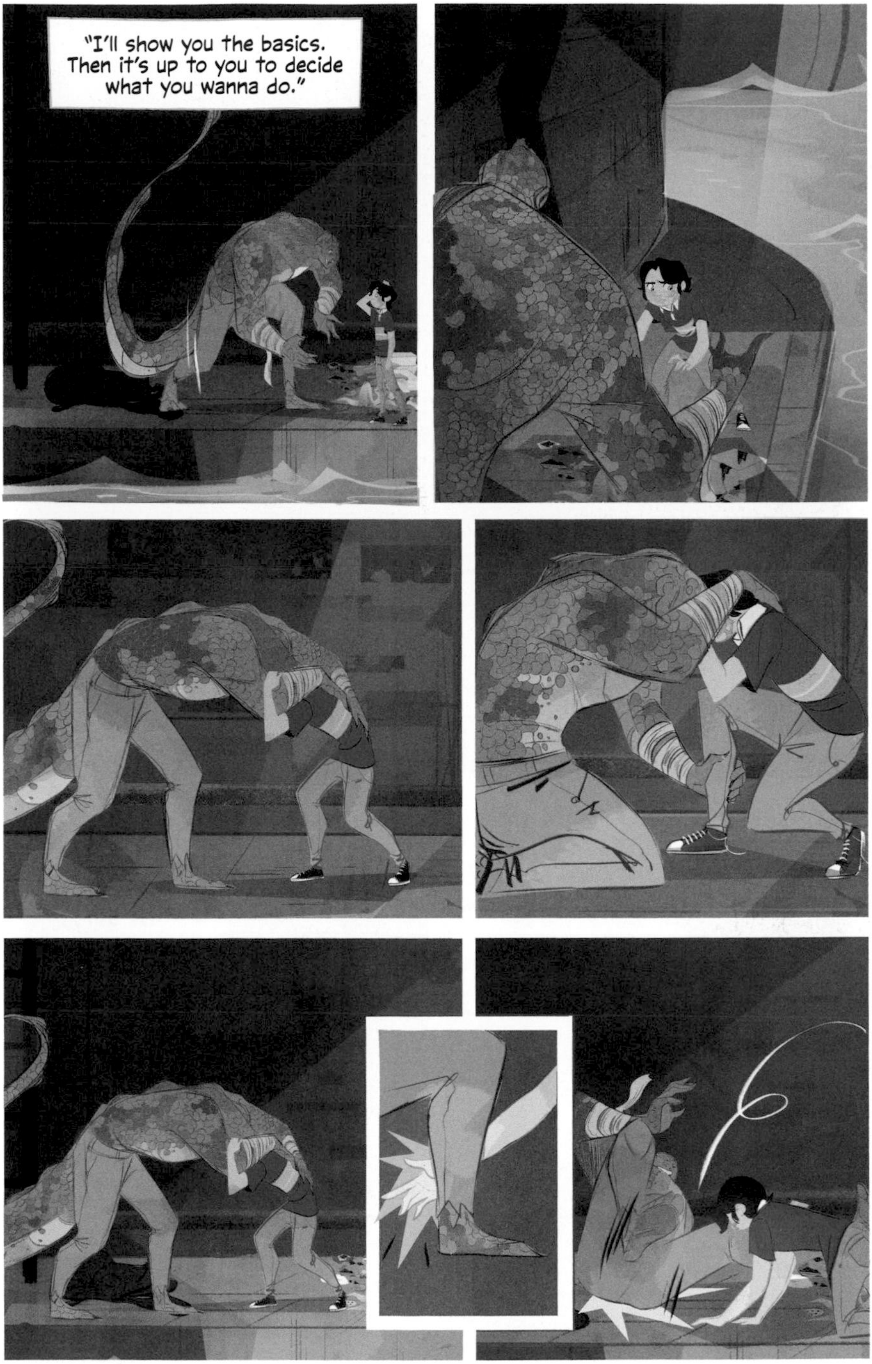
"I'll show you the basics.
Then it's up to you to decide
what you wanna do."

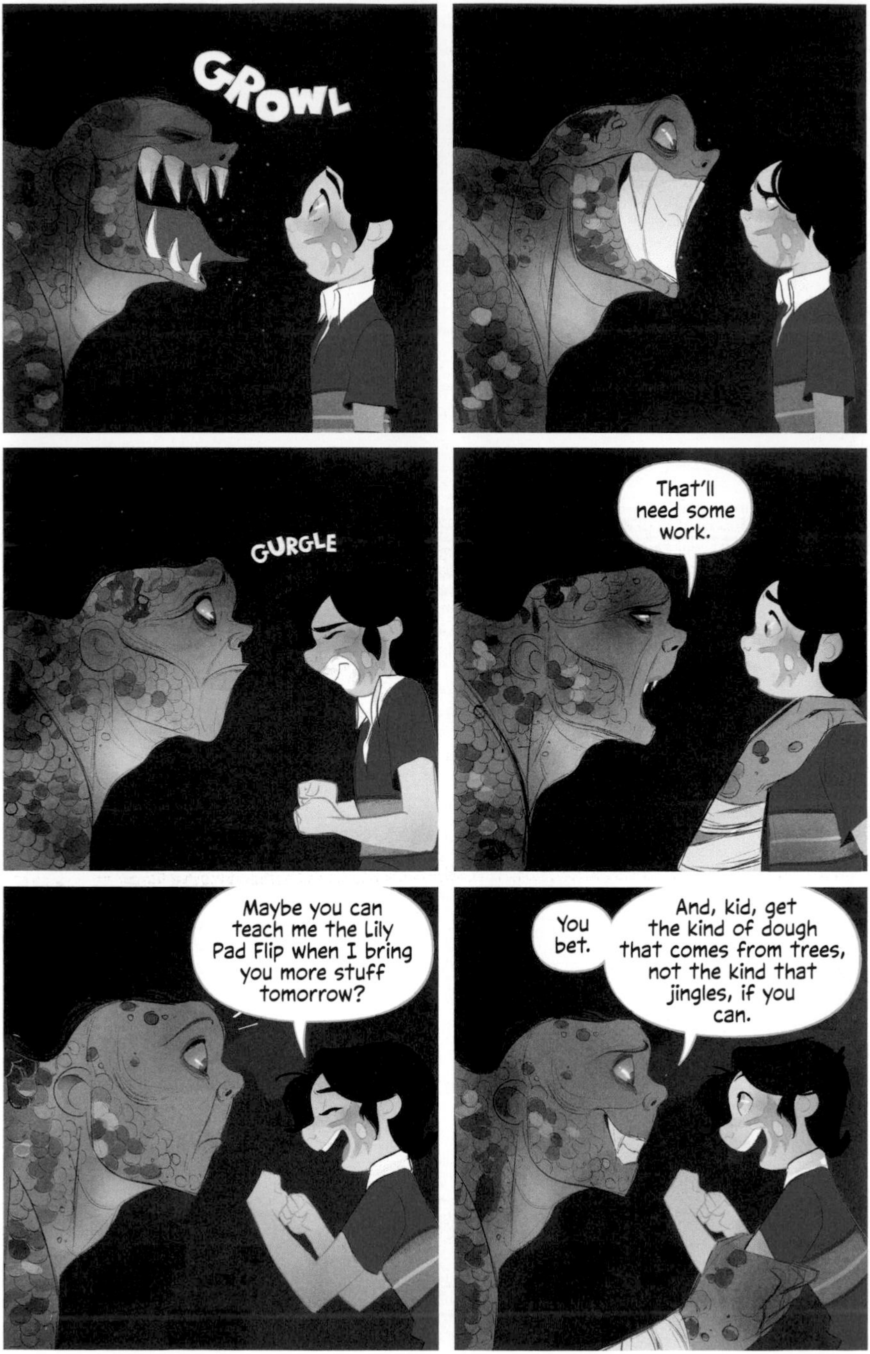
GROWL
GURGLE
That'll need some work.
Maybe you can teach me the Lily Pad Flip when I bring you more stuff tomorrow?
You bet.
And, kid, get the kind of dough that comes from trees, not the kind that jingles, if you can.

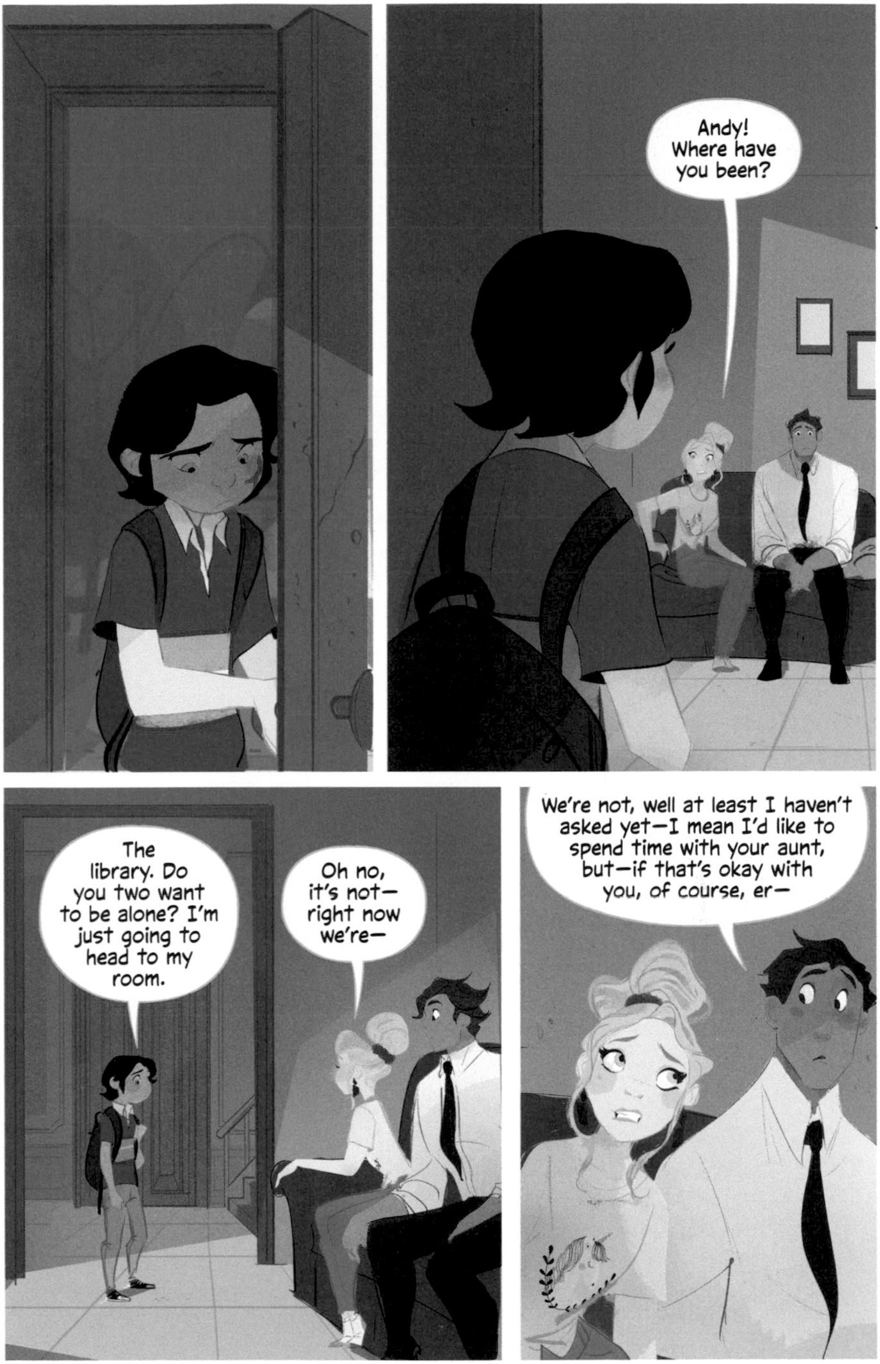
Andy! Where have you been?
The library. Do you two want to be alone? I'm just going to head to my room.
Oh no, it's not— right now we're—
We're not, well at least I haven't asked yet—I mean I'd like to spend time with your aunt, but—if that's okay with you, of course, er—

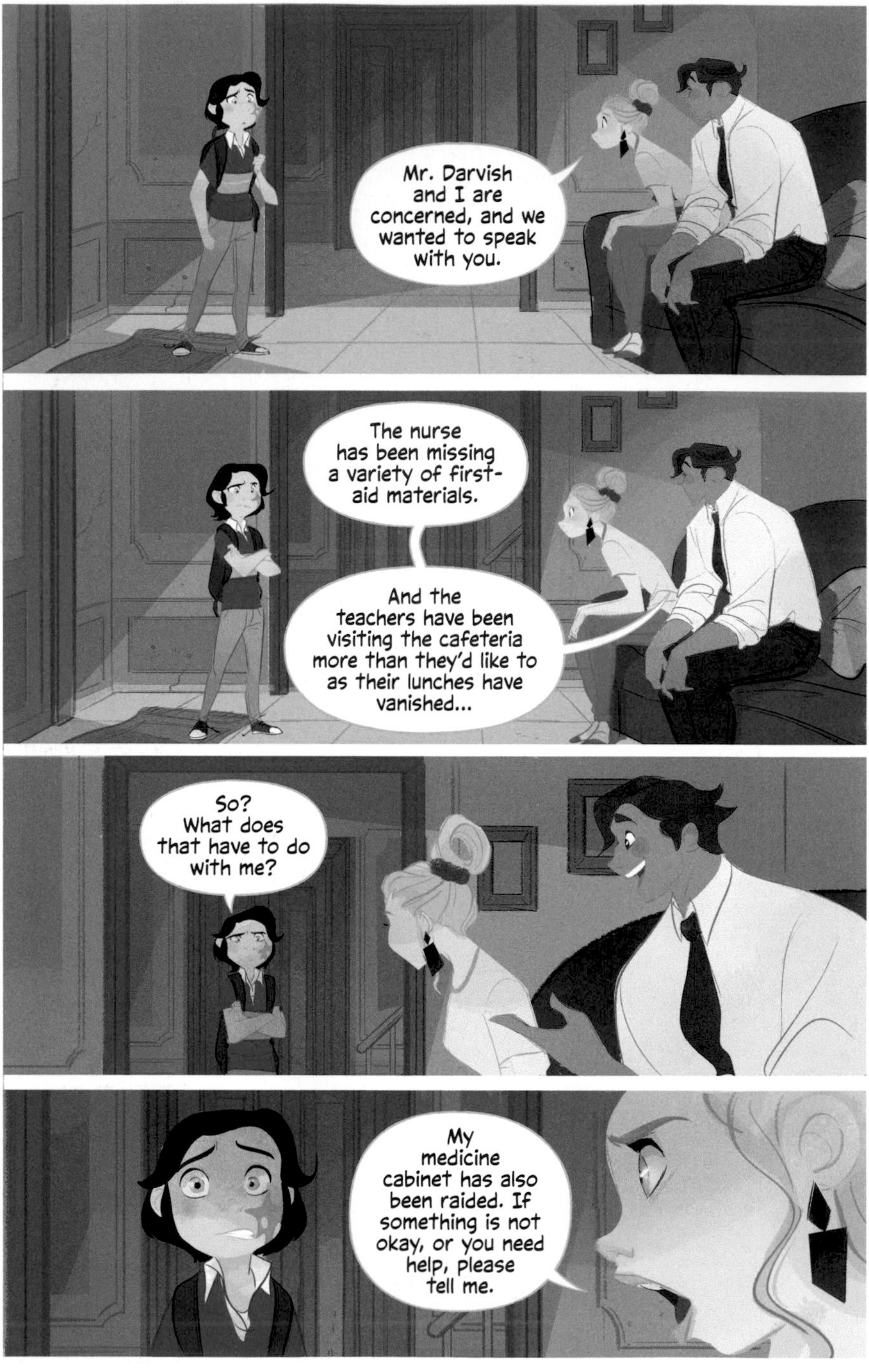
Mr. Darvish and I are concerned, and we wanted to speak with you.
The nurse has been missing a variety of first-aid materials.
And the teachers have been visiting the cafeteria more than they'd like to as their lunches have vanished...
So? What does that have to do with me?
My medicine cabinet has also been raided. If something is not okay, or you need help, please tell me.

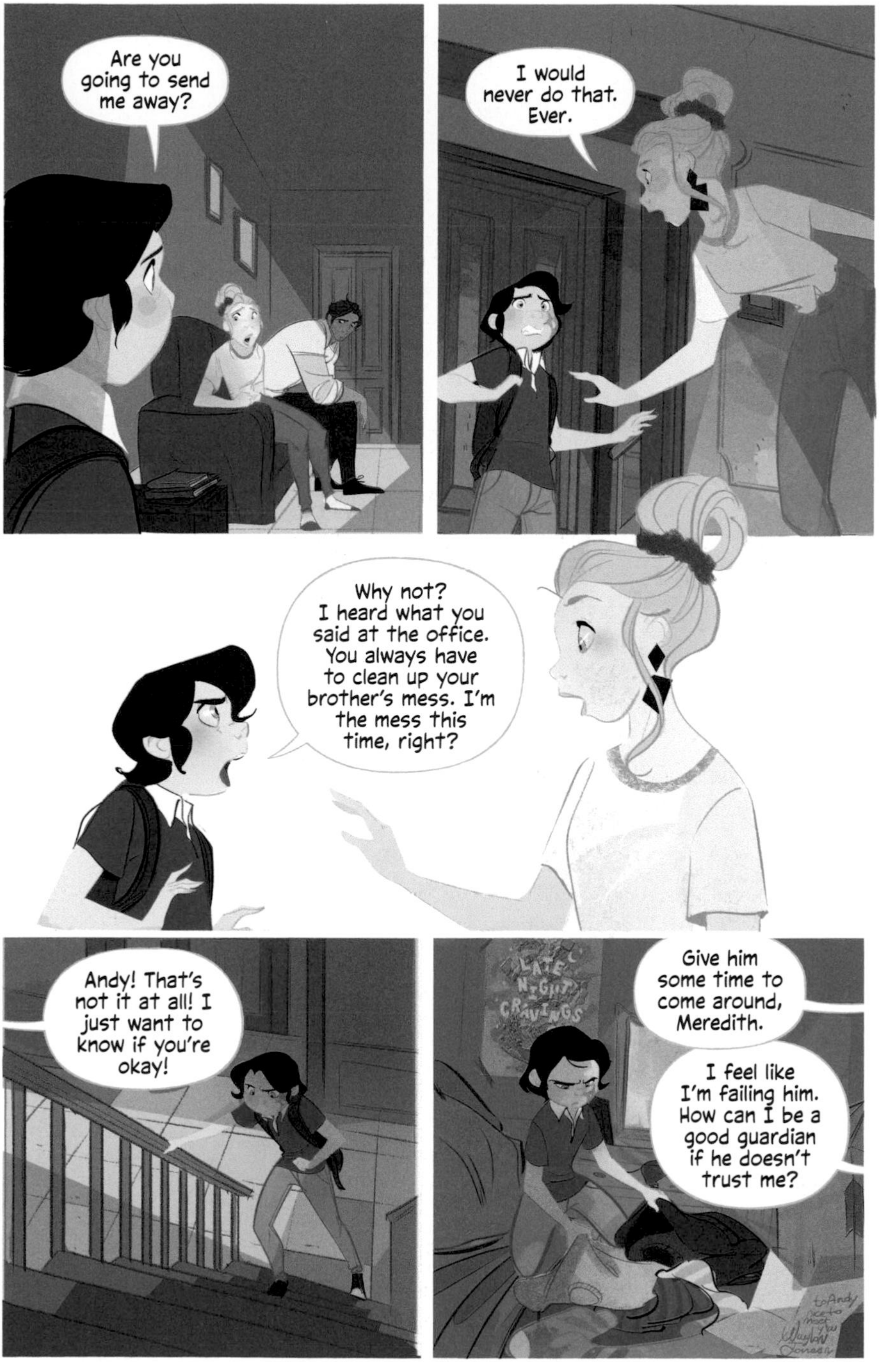
Are you going to send me away?
I would never do that. Ever.
Why not? I heard what you said at the office. You always have to clean up your brother's mess. I'm the mess this time, right?
Andy! That's not it at all! I just want to know if you're okay!
LATE NIGHT CRAVINGS
Give him some time to come around, Meredith.
I feel like I'm failing him. How can I be a good guardian if he doesn't trust me?

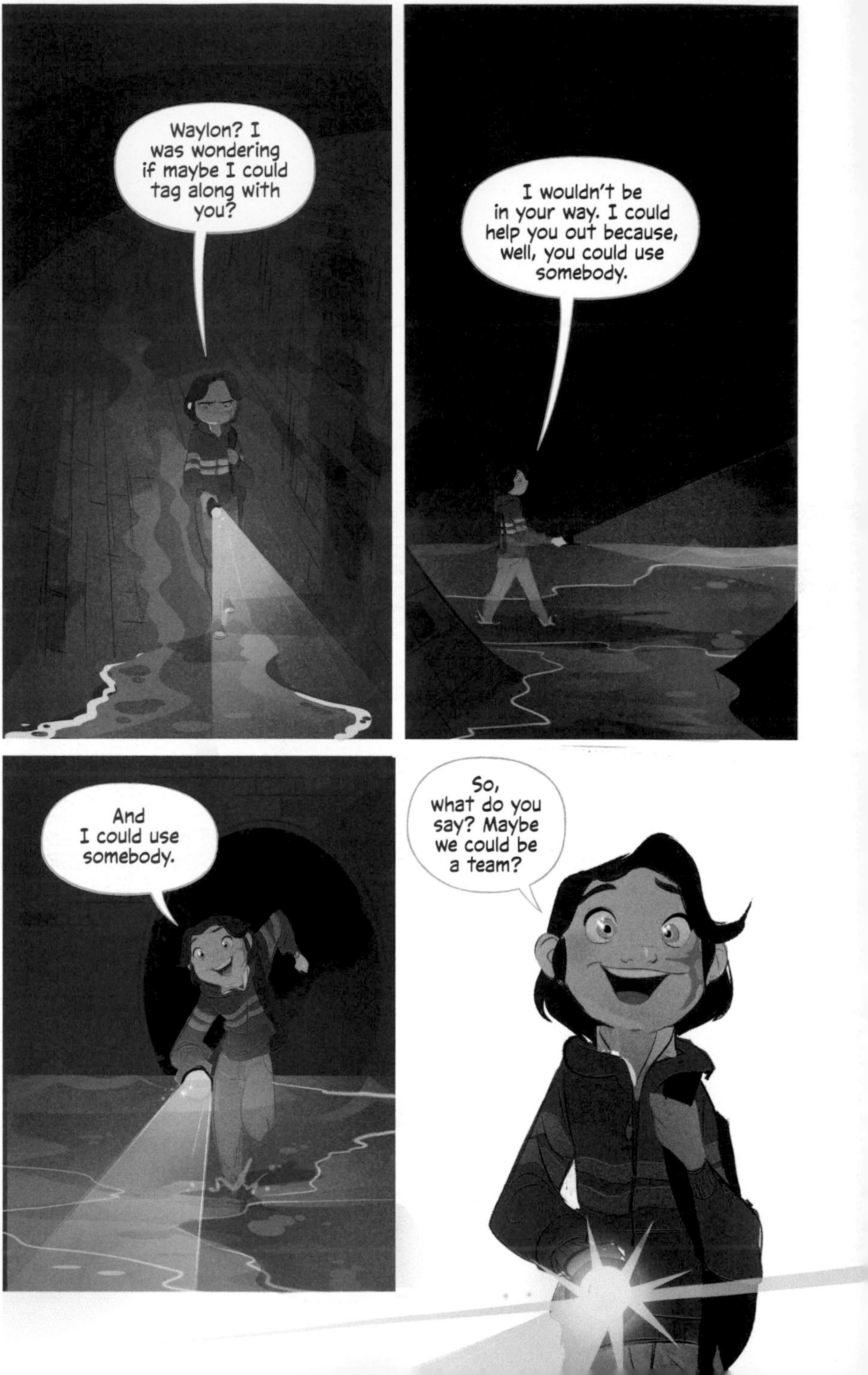
Waylon? I was wondering if maybe I could tag along with you?
I wouldn't be in your way. I could help you out because, well, you could use somebody.
And I could use somebody.
So, what do you say? Maybe we could be a team?

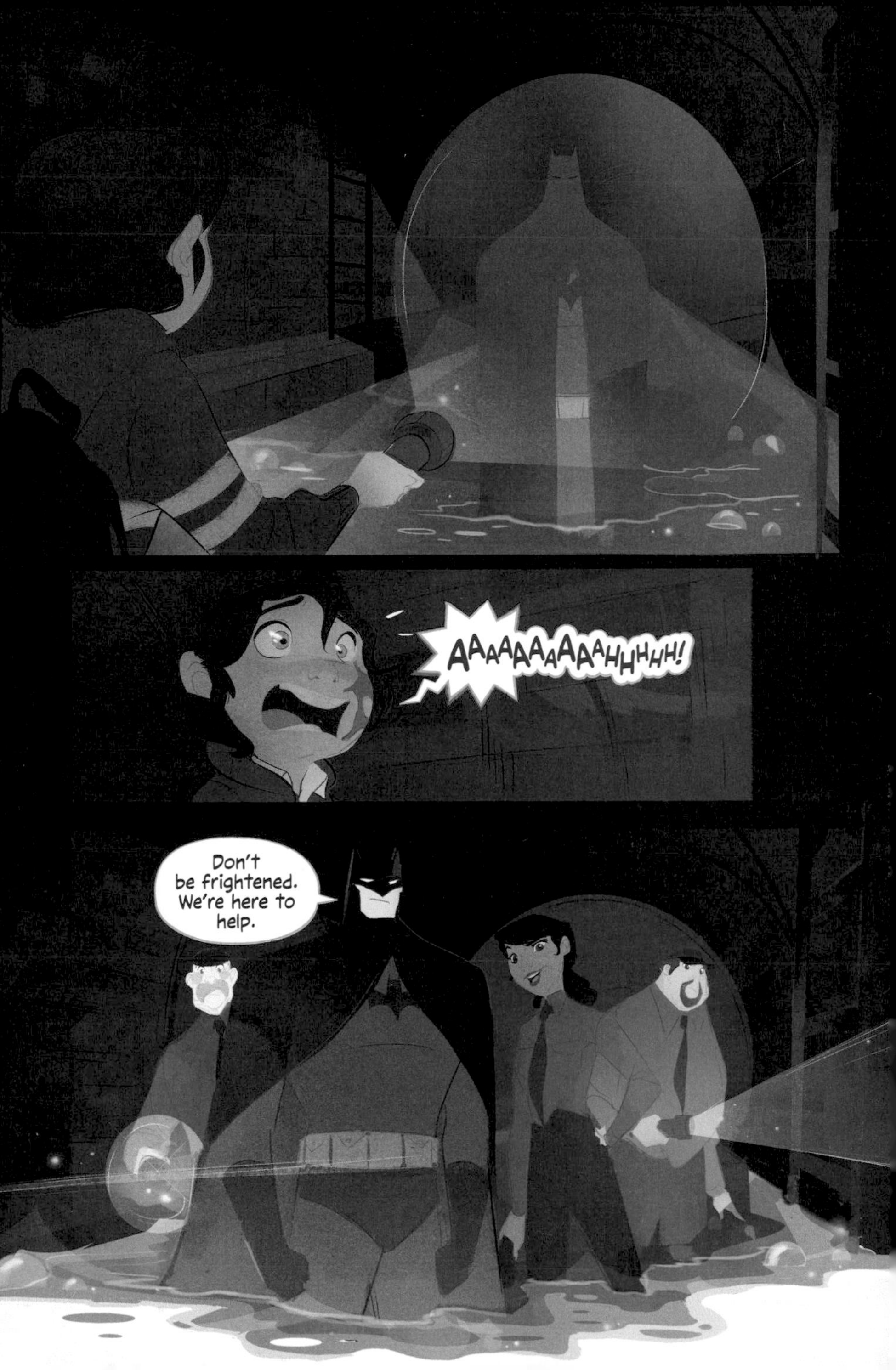
AAAAAAAAAAHHHHH!
Don't be frightened. We're here to help.

CHAPTER SIX
100

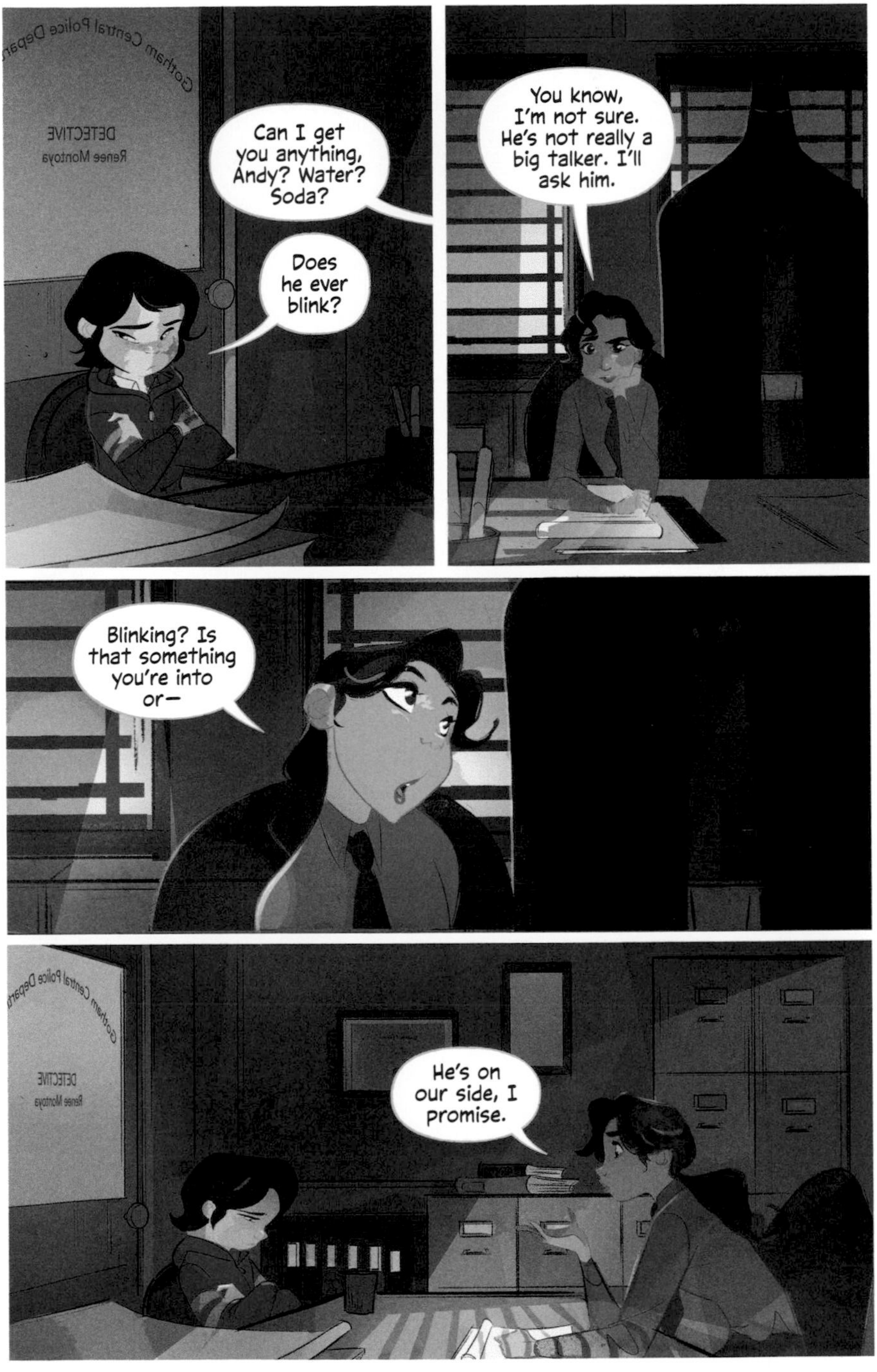
Can I get you anything, Andy? Water? Soda?
Does he ever blink?
You know, I'm not sure. He's not really a big talker. I'll ask him.
Blinking? Is that something you're into or—
He's on our side, I promise.

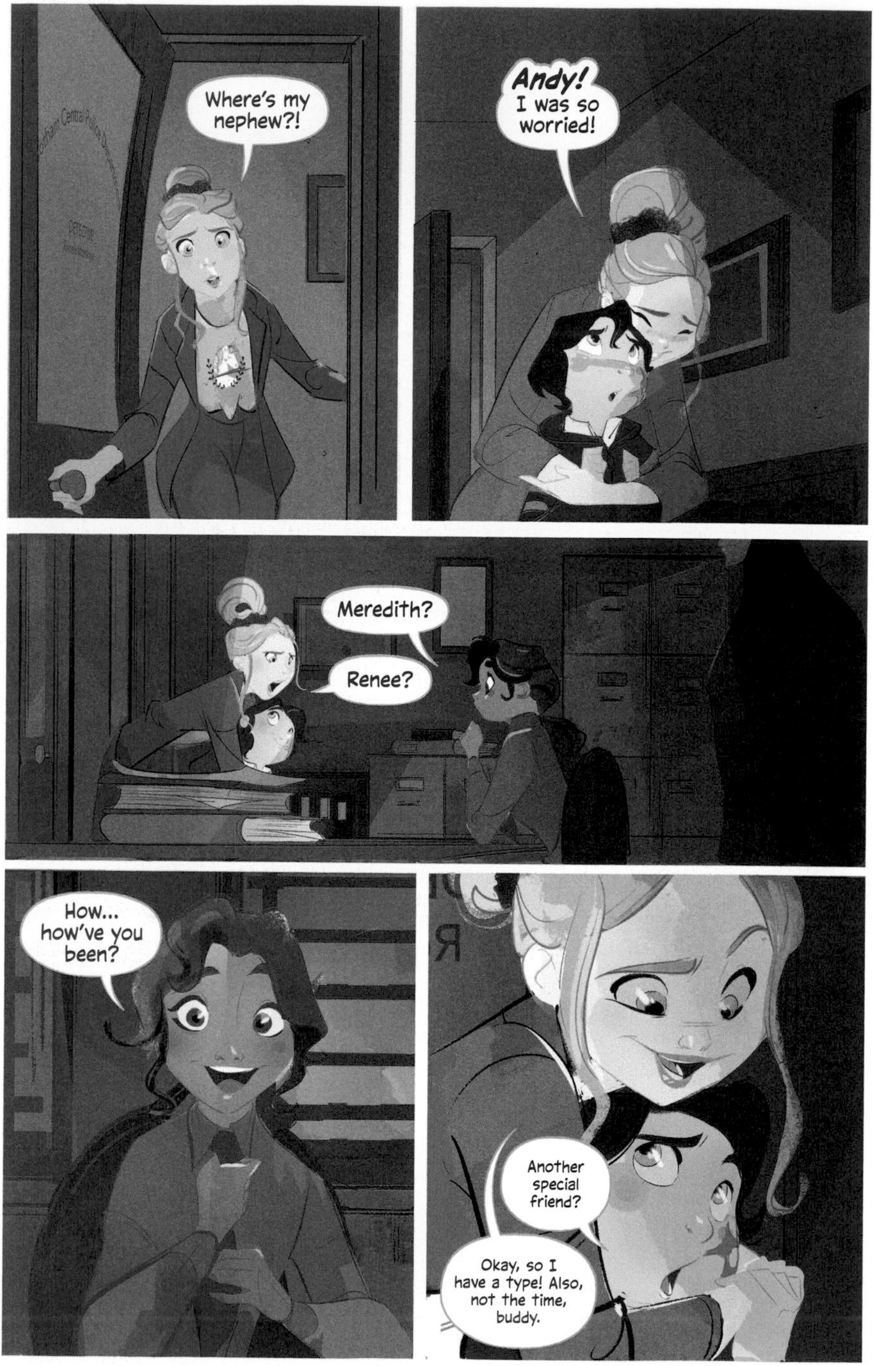
Where's my nephew?!
Andy! I was so worried!
Meredith?
Renee?
How... how've you been?
Another special friend?
Okay, so I have a type! Also, not the time, buddy.

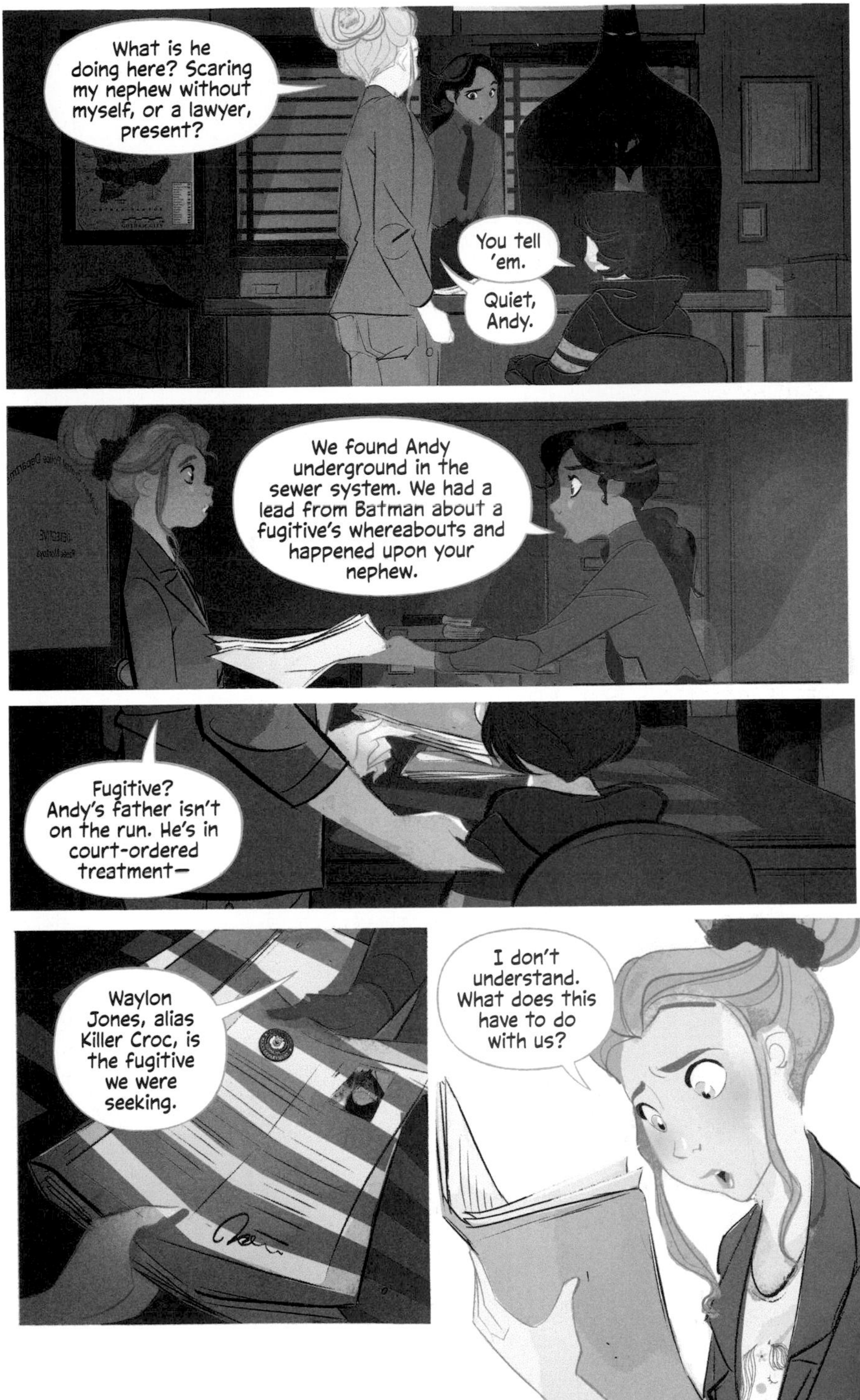
What is he doing here? Scaring my nephew without myself, or a lawyer, present?
You tell 'em.
Quiet, Andy.
We found Andy underground in the sewer system. We had a lead from Batman about a fugitive's whereabouts and happened upon your nephew.
Fugitive? Andy's father isn't on the run. He's in court-ordered treatment—
Waylon Jones, alias Killer Croc, is the fugitive we were seeking.
I don't understand. What does this have to do with us?

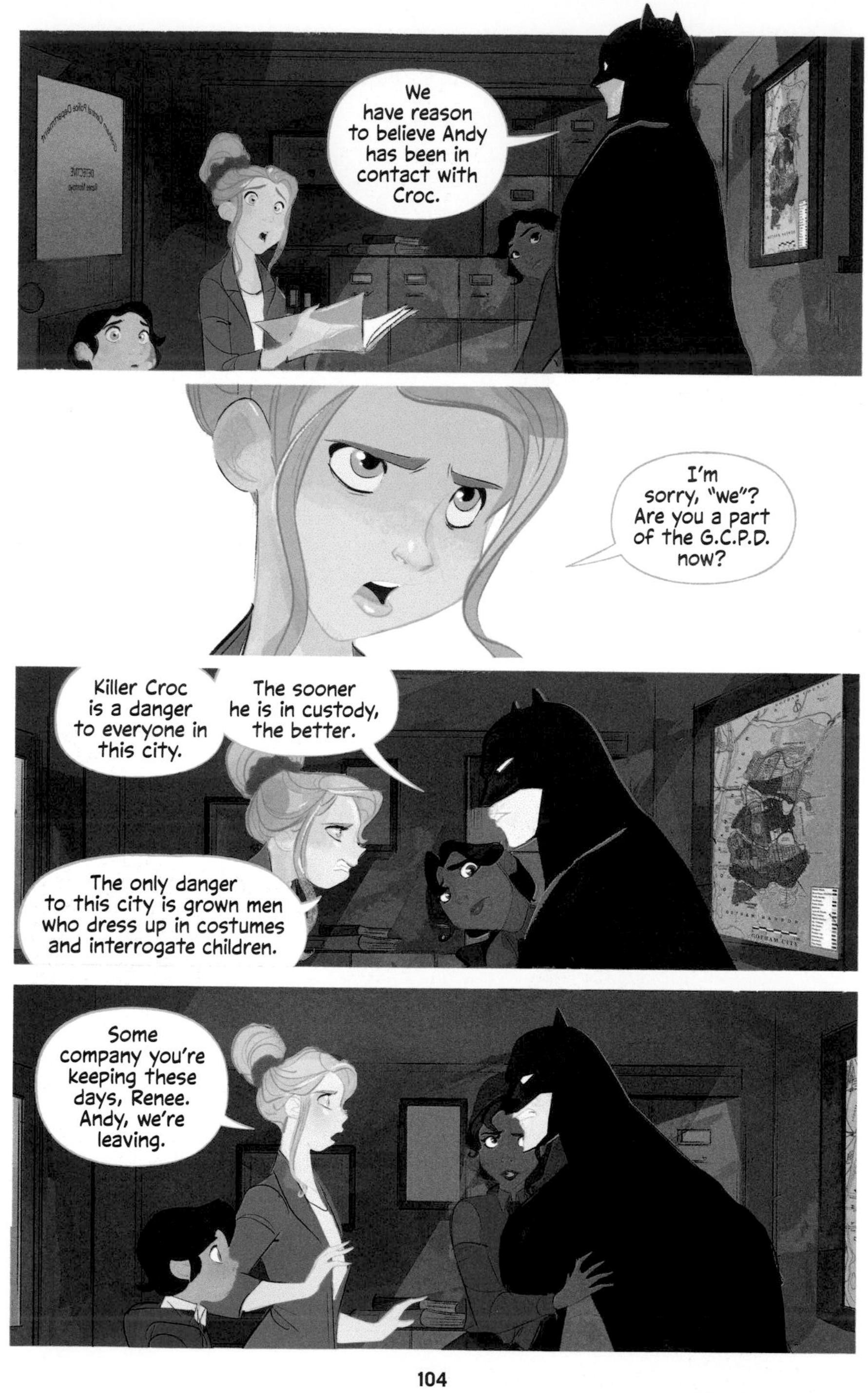
We have reason to believe Andy has been in contact with Croc.
I'm sorry, "we"? Are you a part of the G.C.P.D. now?
Killer Croc is a danger to everyone in this city.
The sooner he is in custody, the better.
The only danger to this city is grown men who dress up in costumes and interrogate children.
Some company you're keeping these days, Renee. Andy, we're leaving.

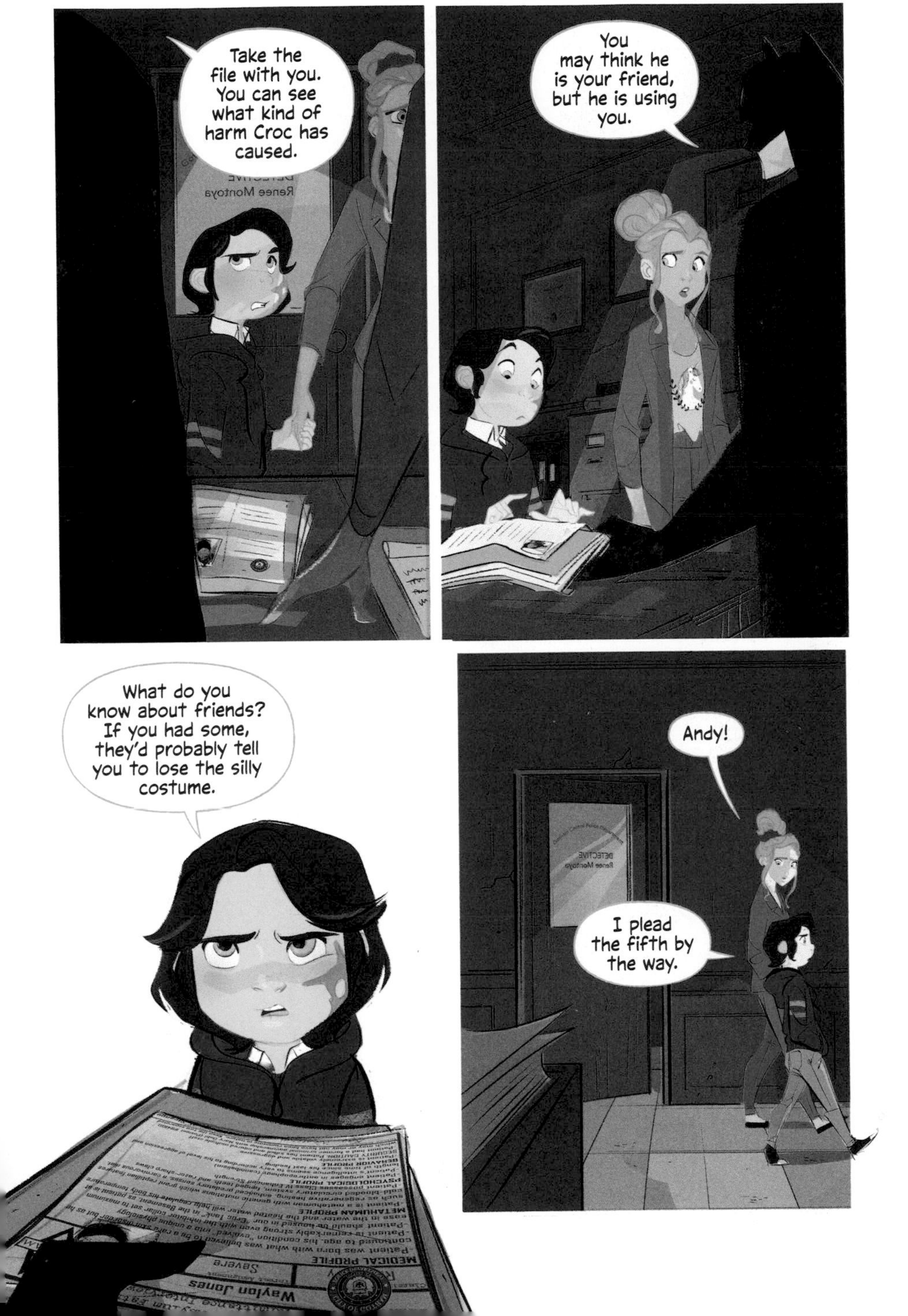
Take the file with you. You can see what kind of harm Croc has caused.
You may think he is your friend, but he is using you.
What do you know about friends? If you had some, they'd probably tell you to lose the silly costume.
Andy!
I plead the fifth by the way.

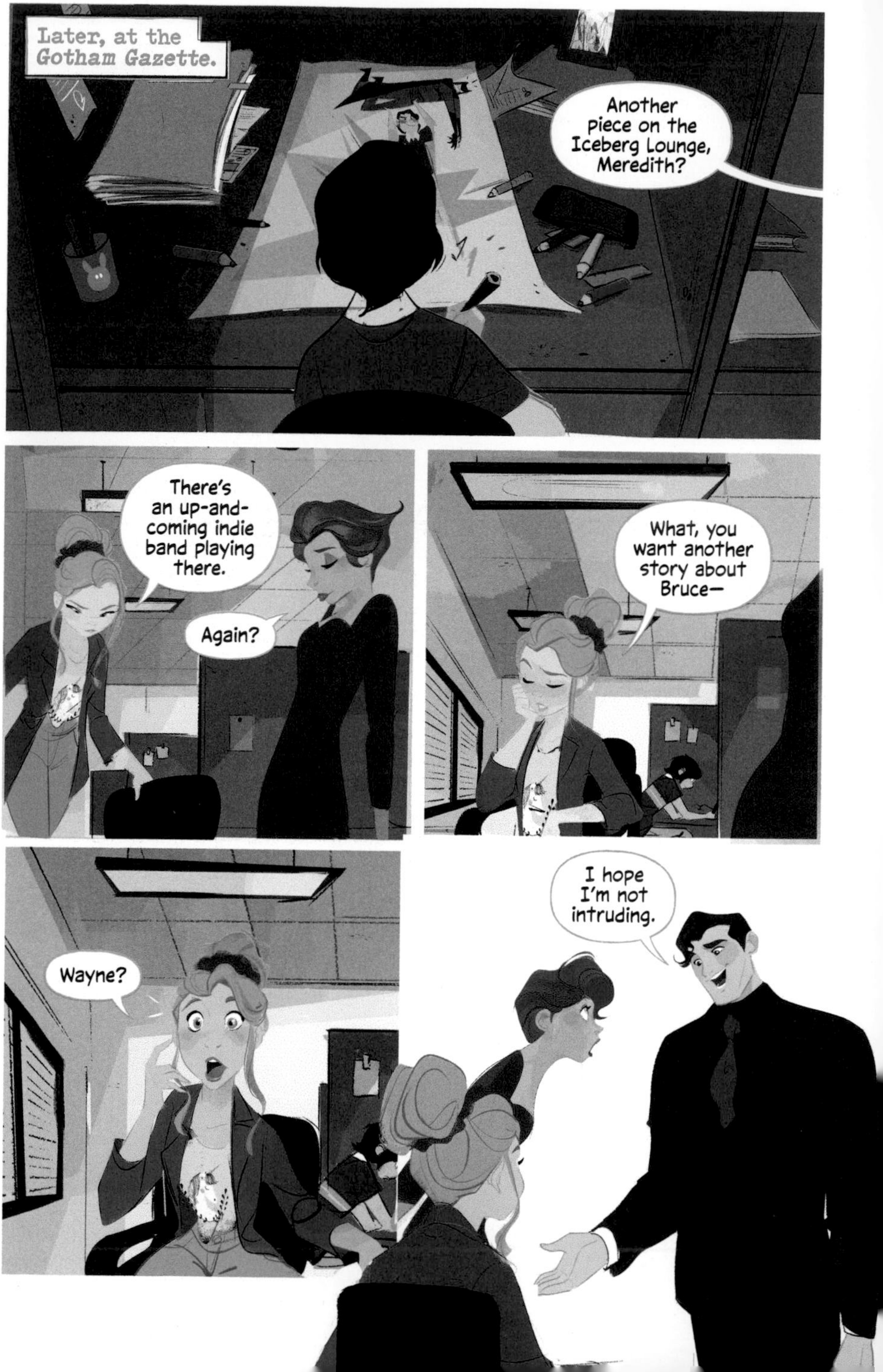
Later, at the Gotham Gazette.
Another piece on the Iceberg Lounge, Meredith?
There's an up-and-coming indie band playing there.
Again?
What, you want another story about Bruce—
Wayne?
I hope I'm not intruding.

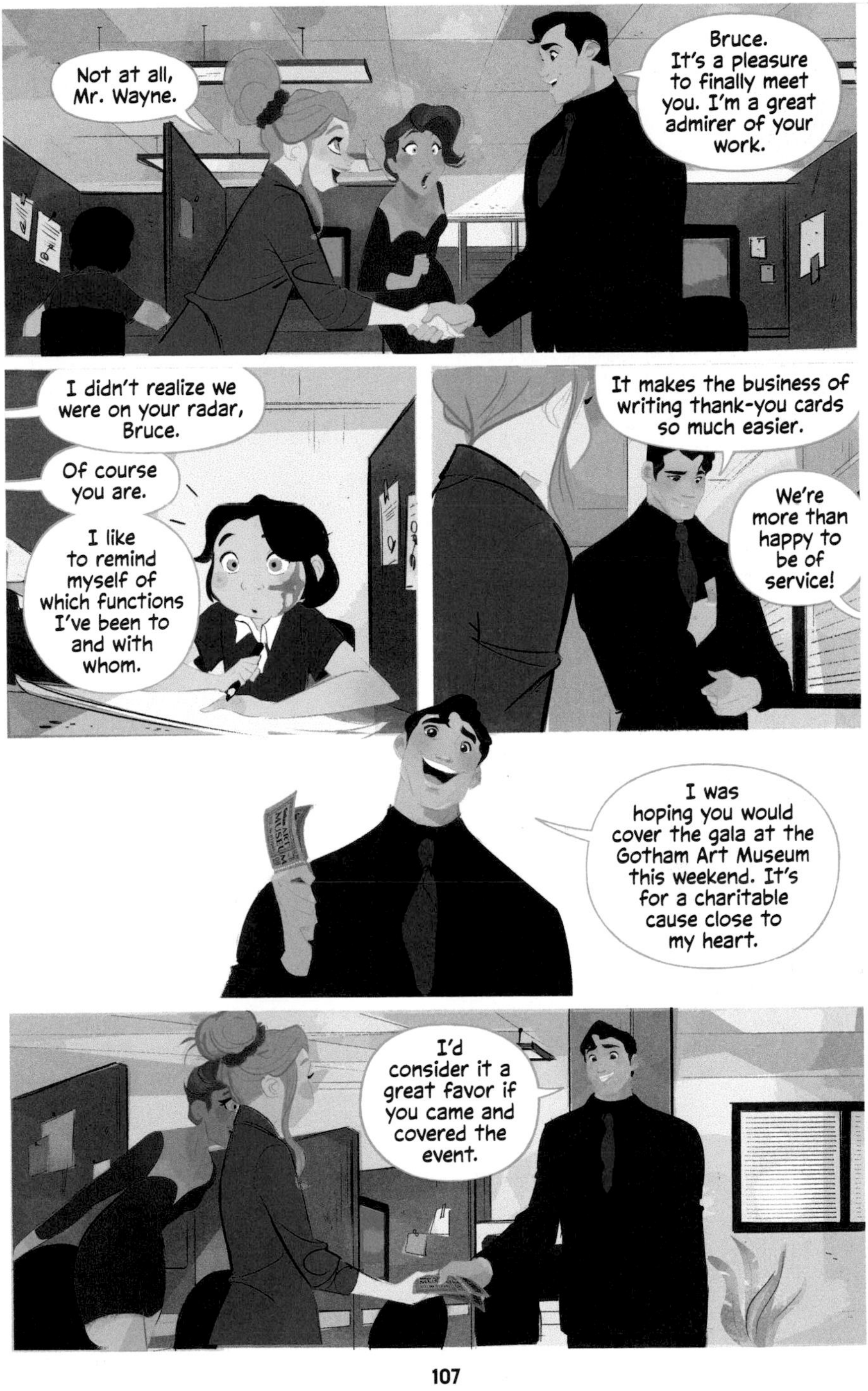
Not at all, Mr. Wayne.
Bruce. It's a pleasure to finally meet you. I'm a great admirer of your work.
I didn't realize we were on your radar, Bruce.
Of course you are.
I like to remind myself of which functions I've been to and with whom.
It makes the business of writing thank-you cards so much easier.
We're more than happy to be of service!
I was hoping you would cover the gala at the Gotham Art Museum this weekend. It's for a charitable cause close to my heart.
I'd consider it a great favor if you came and covered the event.

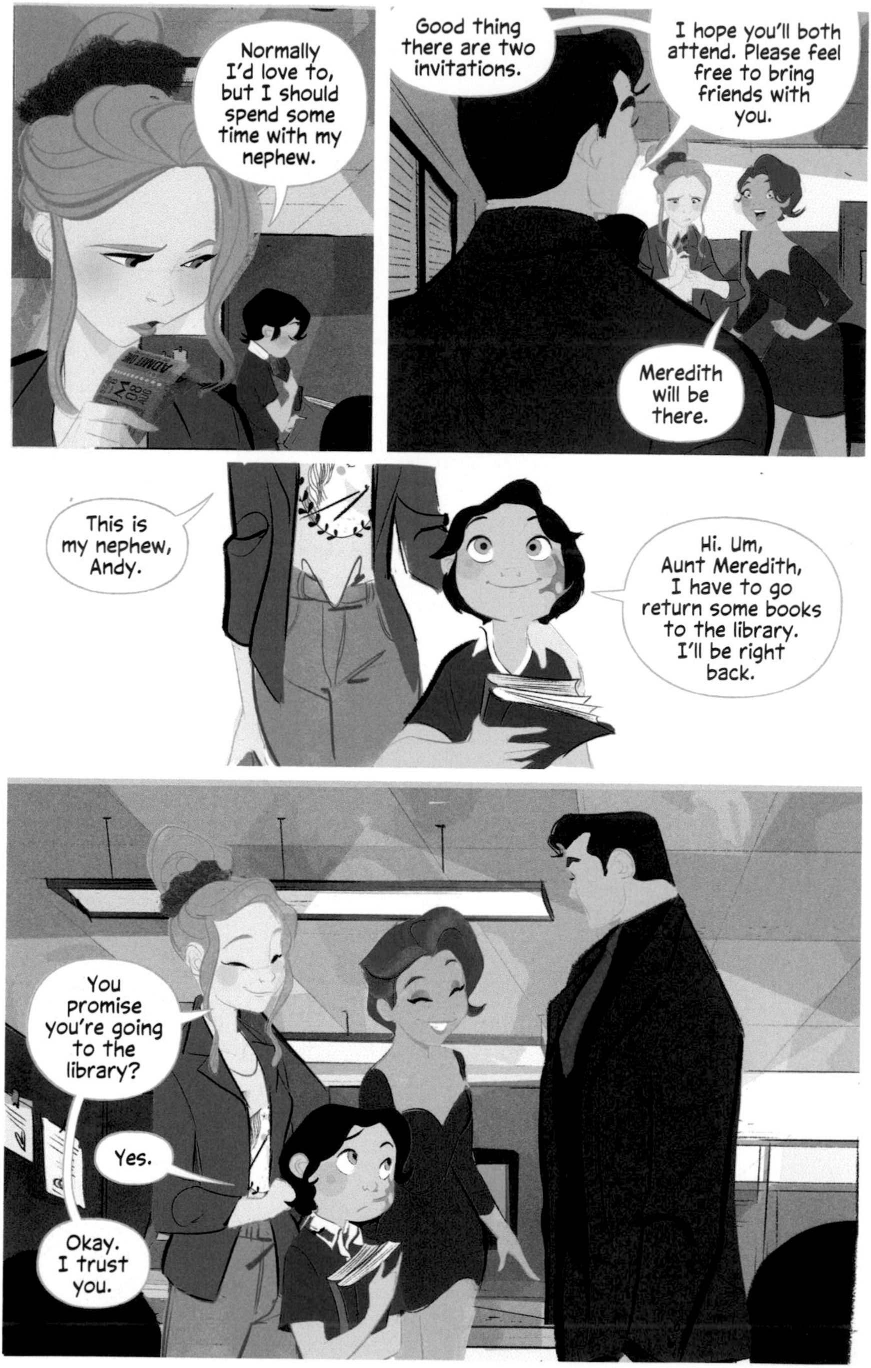
Normally I'd love to, but I should spend some time with my nephew.
Good thing there are two invitations.
I hope you'll both attend. Please feel free to bring friends with you.
Meredith will be there.
This is my nephew, Andy.
Hi. Um, Aunt Meredith, I have to go return some books to the library. I'll be right back.
You promise you're going to the library?
Yes.
Okay. I trust you.

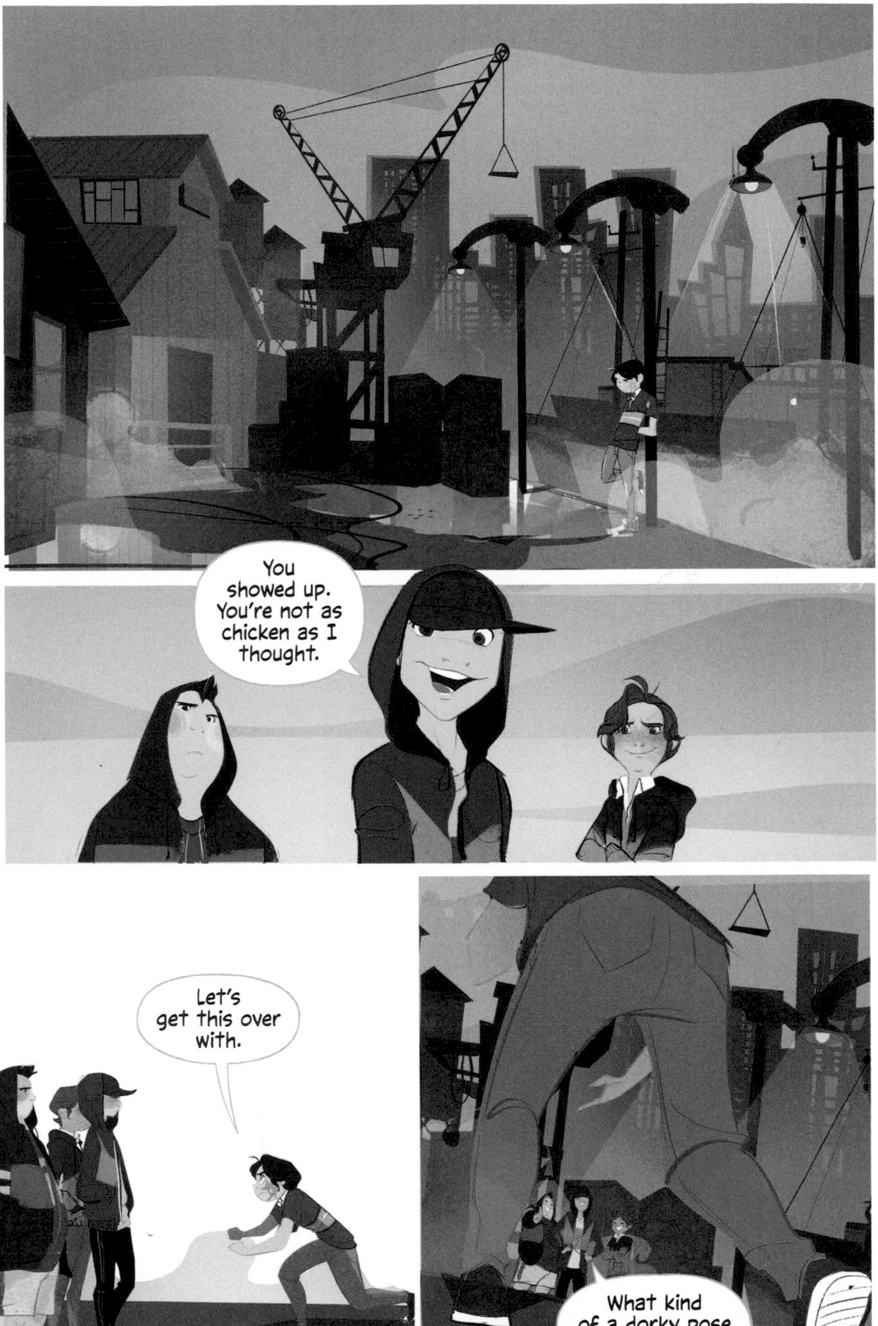
You showed up. You're not as chicken as I thought.
Let's get this over with.
What kind of a dorky pose is that?

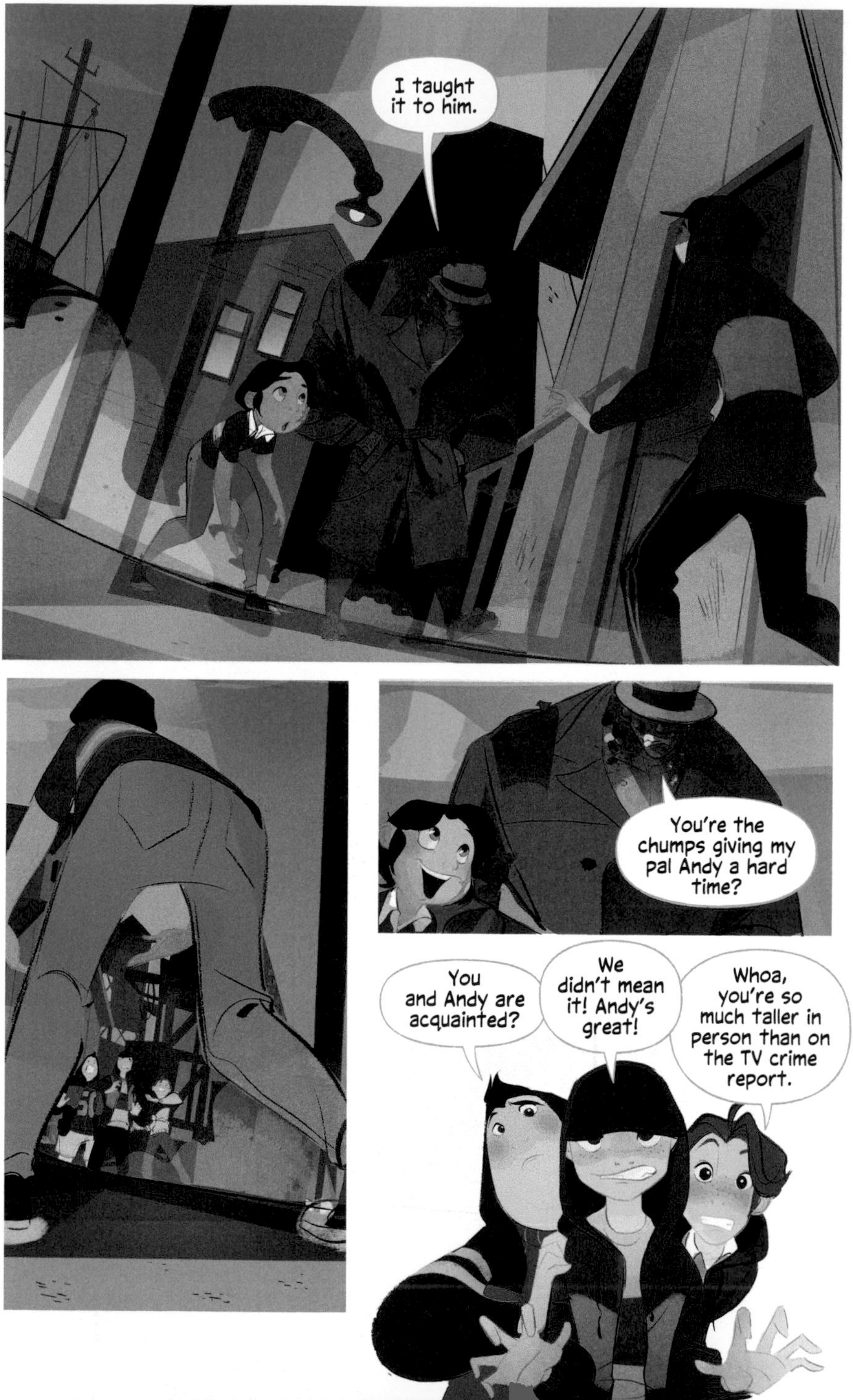

I taught it to him.
You're the chumps giving my pal Andy a hard time?
You and Andy are acquainted?
We didn't mean it! Andy's great!
Whoa, you're so much taller in person than on the TV crime report.

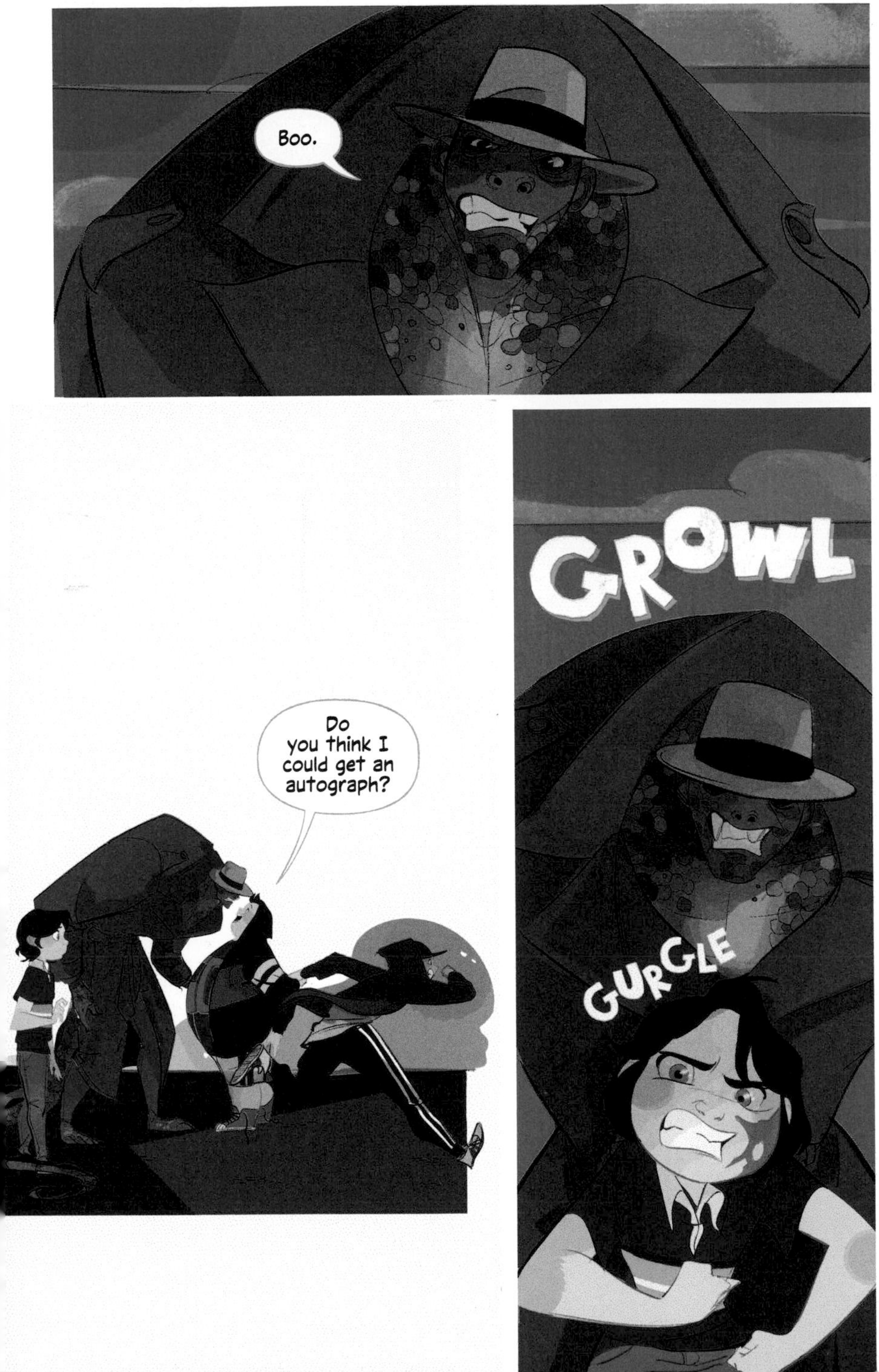
Boo.
Do you think I could get an autograph?
GROWL
GURGLE

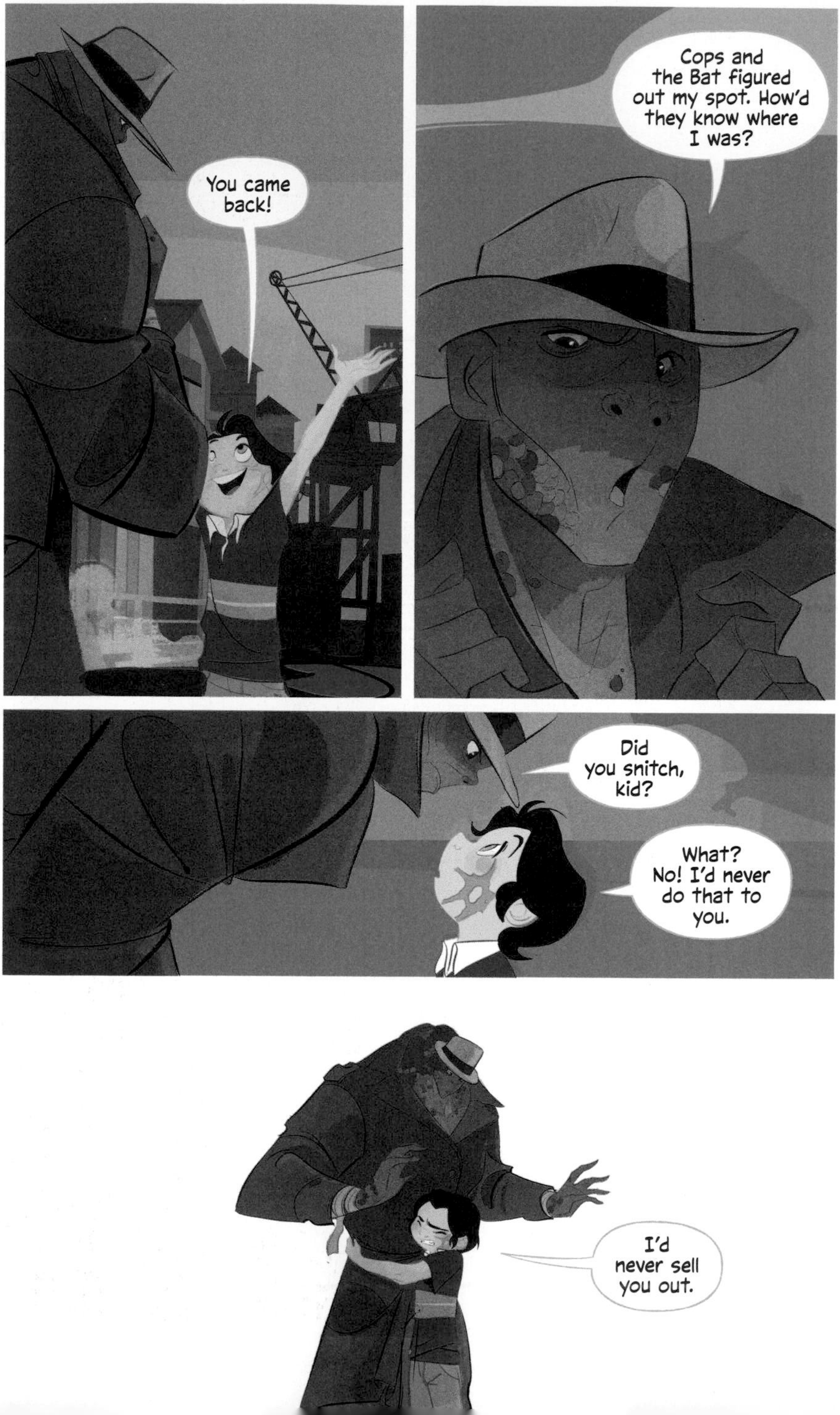

You came back!
Cops and the Bat figured out my spot. How'd they know where I was?
Did you snitch, kid?
What? No! I'd never do that to you.
I'd never sell you out.

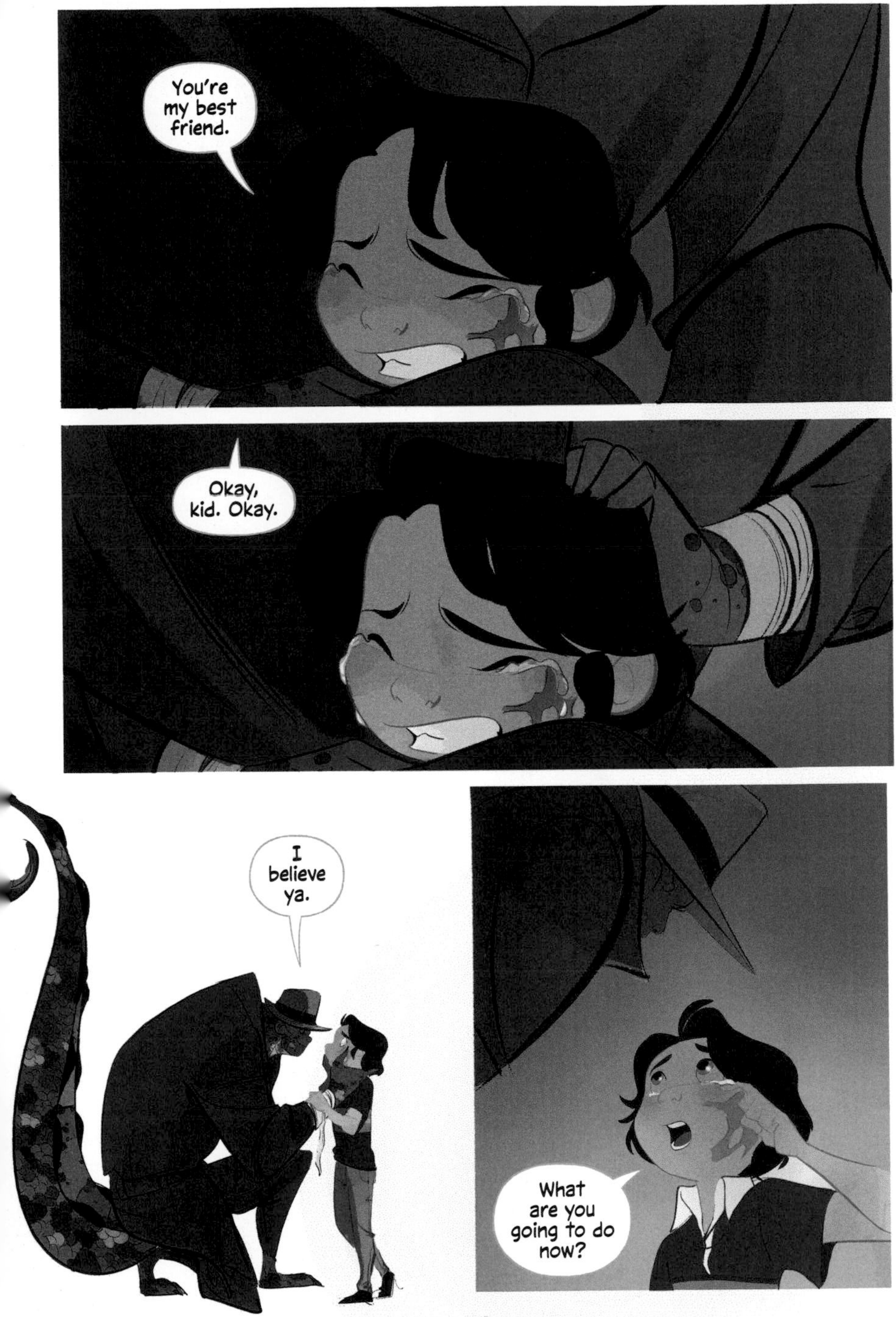
You're my best friend.
Okay, kid. Okay.
I believe ya.
What are you going to do now?

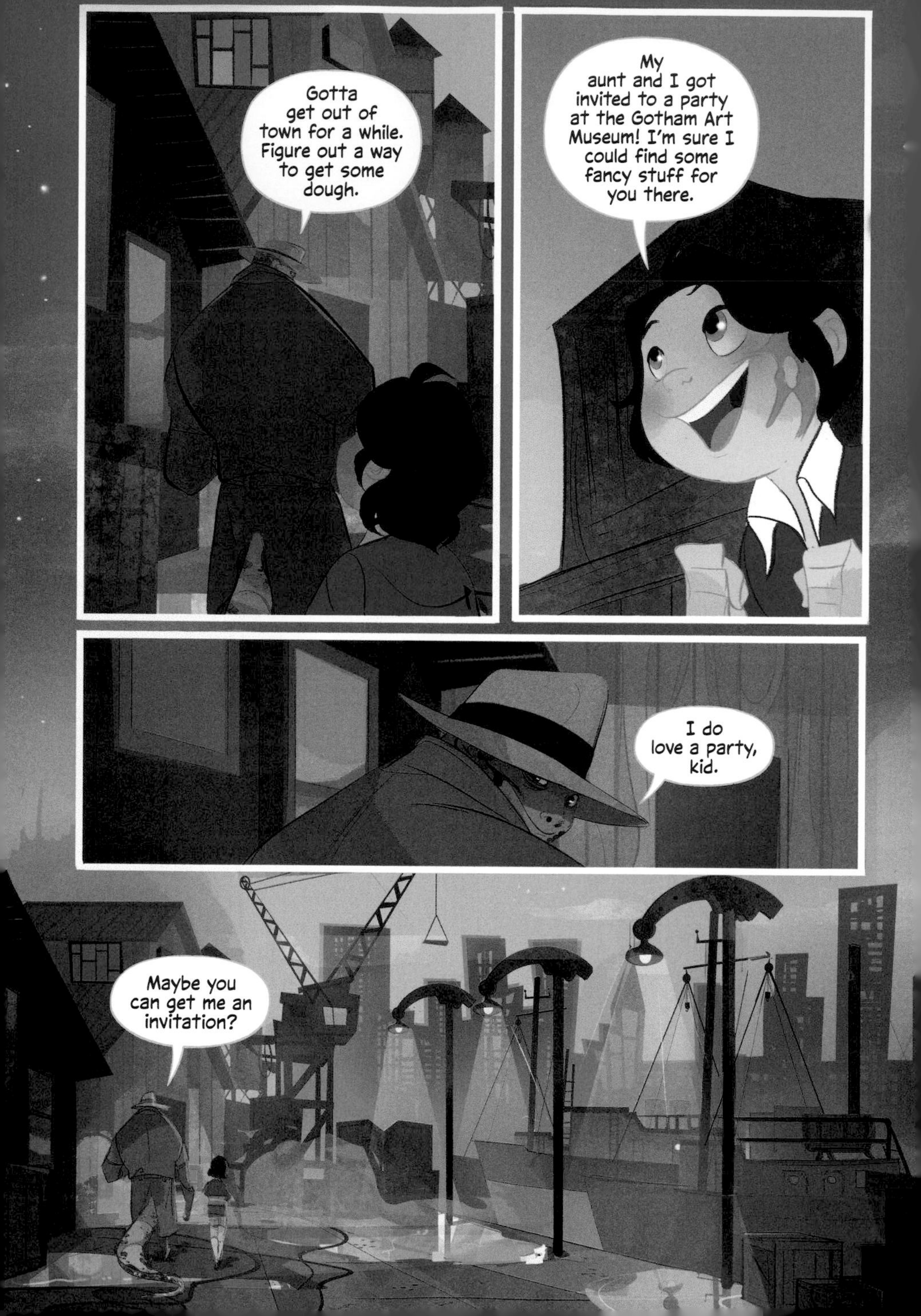
Gotta get out of town for a while. Figure out a way to get some dough.
My aunt and I got invited to a party at the Gotham Art Museum! I'm sure I could find some fancy stuff for you there.
I do love a party, kid.
Maybe you can get me an invitation?

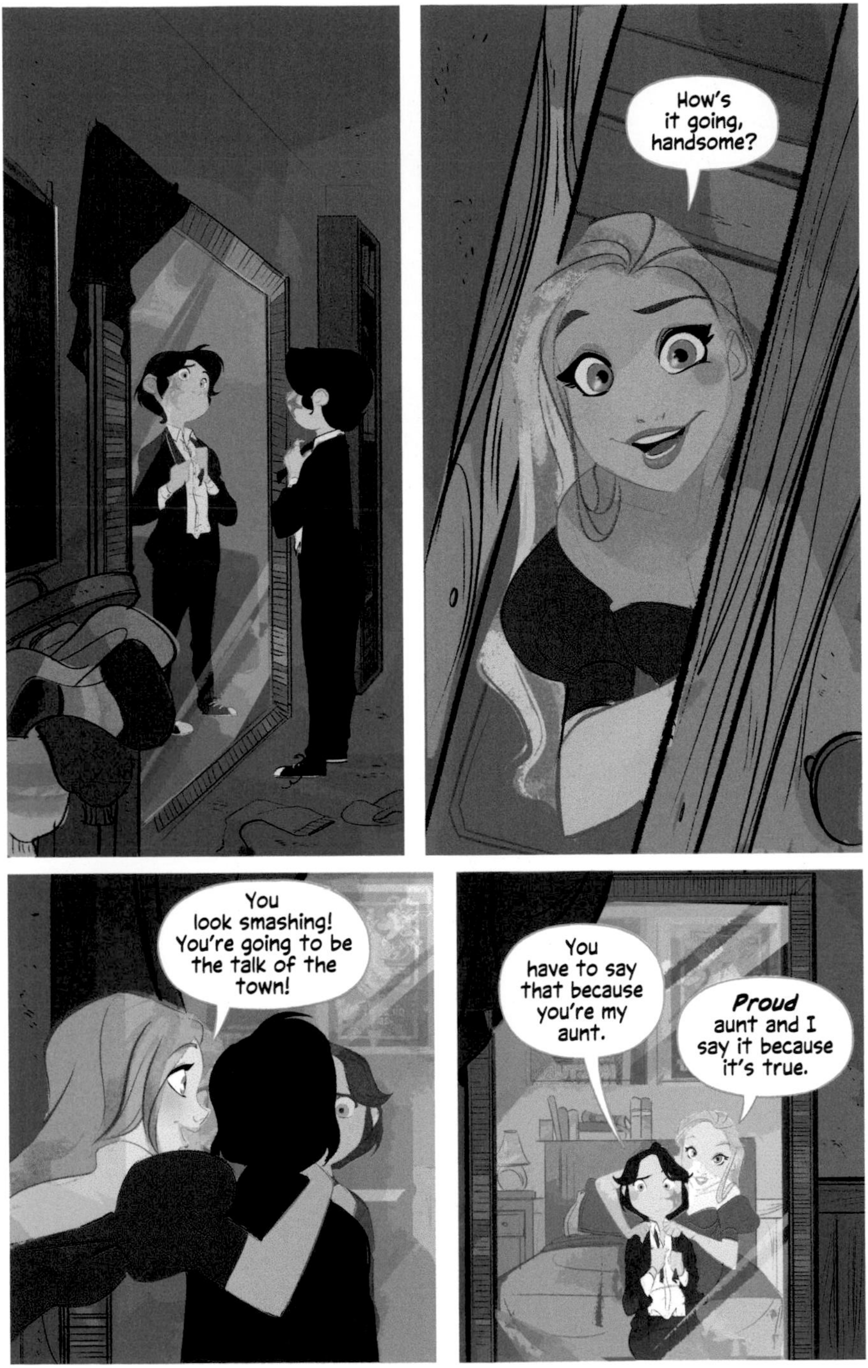
How's it going, handsome?
You look smashing! You're going to be the talk of the town!
You have to say that because you're my aunt.
Proud aunt and I say it because it's true.

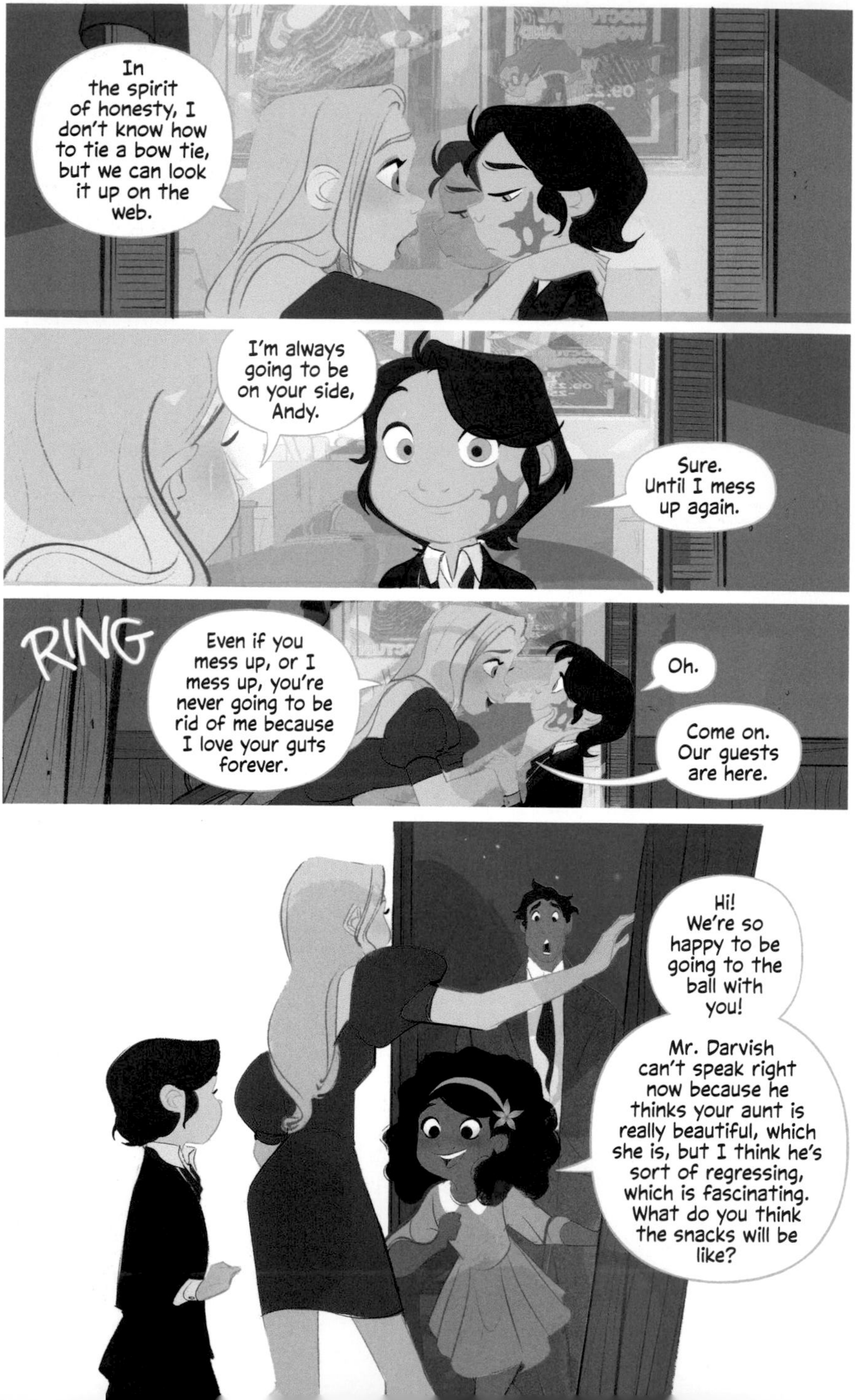
In the spirit of honesty, I don't know how to tie a bow tie, but we can look it up on the web.
I'm always going to be on your side, Andy.
Sure. Until I mess up again.
RING
Even if you mess up, or I mess up, you're never going to be rid of me because I love your guts forever.
Oh.
Come on. Our guests are here.
Hi! We're so happy to be going to the ball with you!
Mr. Darvish can't speak right now because he thinks your aunt is really beautiful, which she is, but I think he's sort of regressing, which is fascinating. What do you think the snacks will be like?

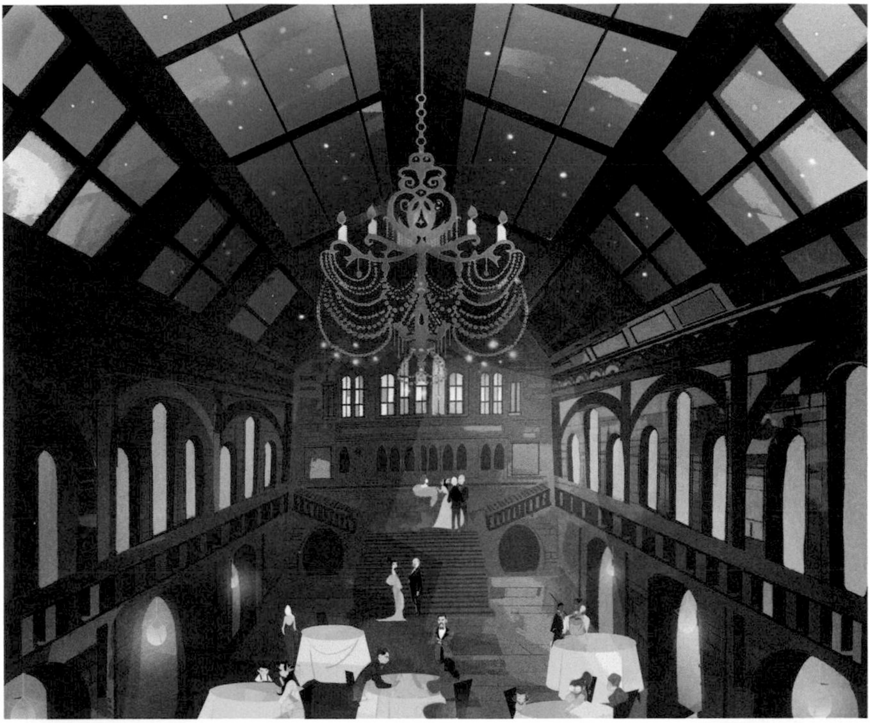

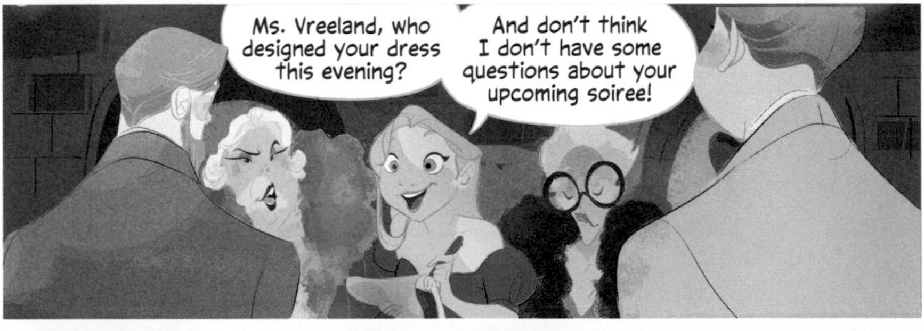
Ms. Vreeland, who designed your dress this evening?
And don't think I don't have some questions about your upcoming soiree!

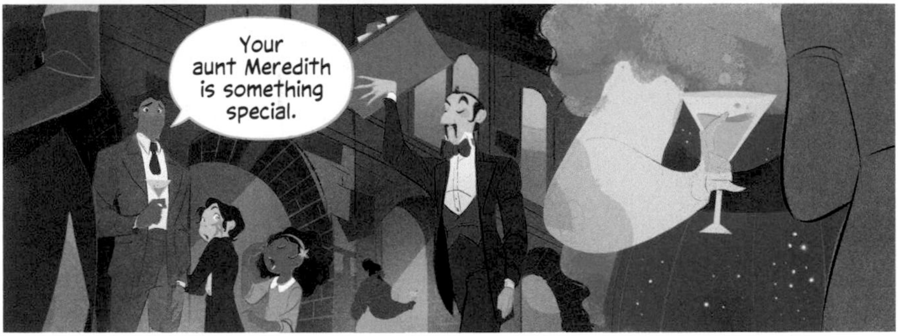
Your aunt Meredith is something special.

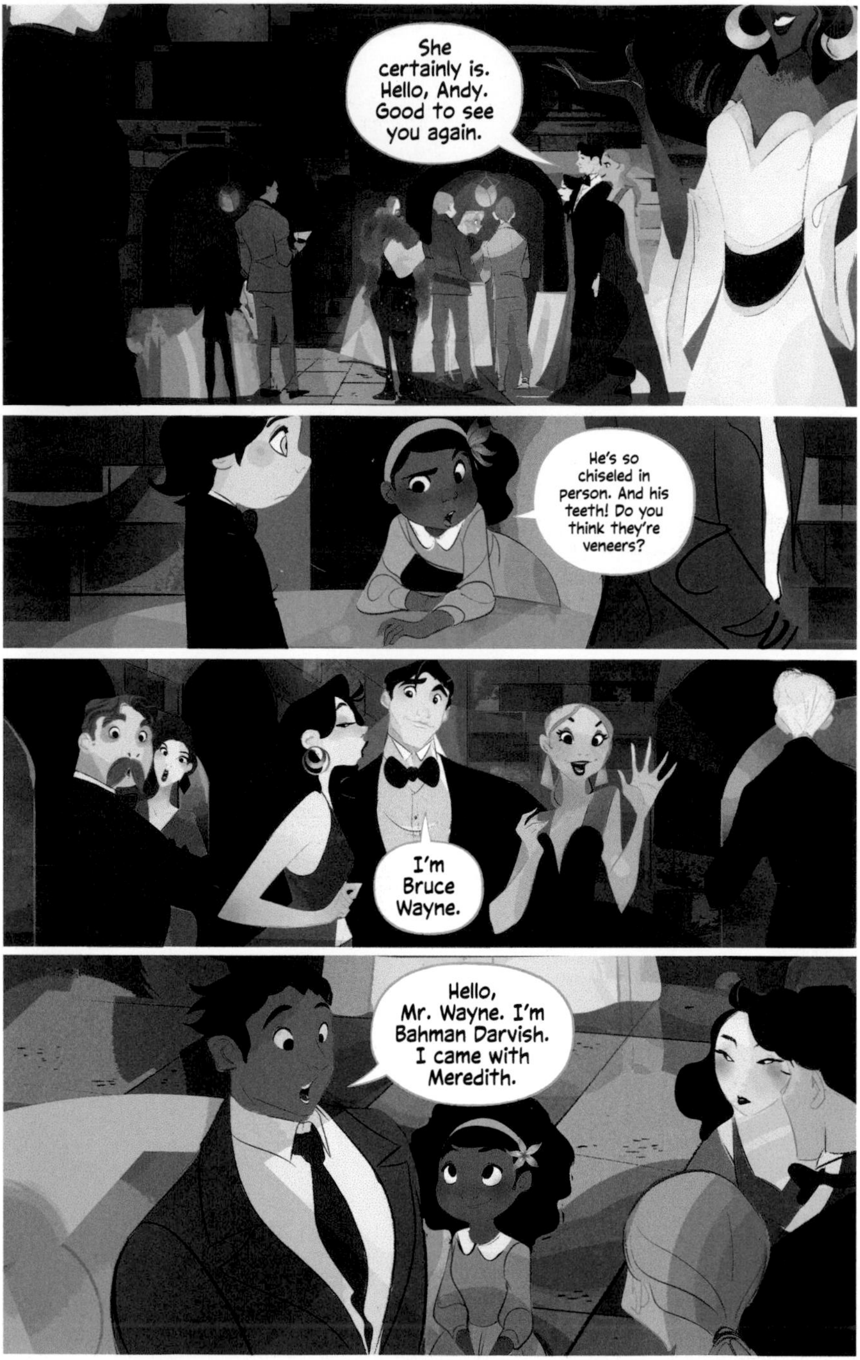
She certainly is. Hello, Andy. Good to see you again.
He's so chiseled in person. And his teeth! Do you think they're veneers?
I'm Bruce Wayne.
Hello, Mr. Wayne. I'm Bahman Darvish. I came with Meredith.

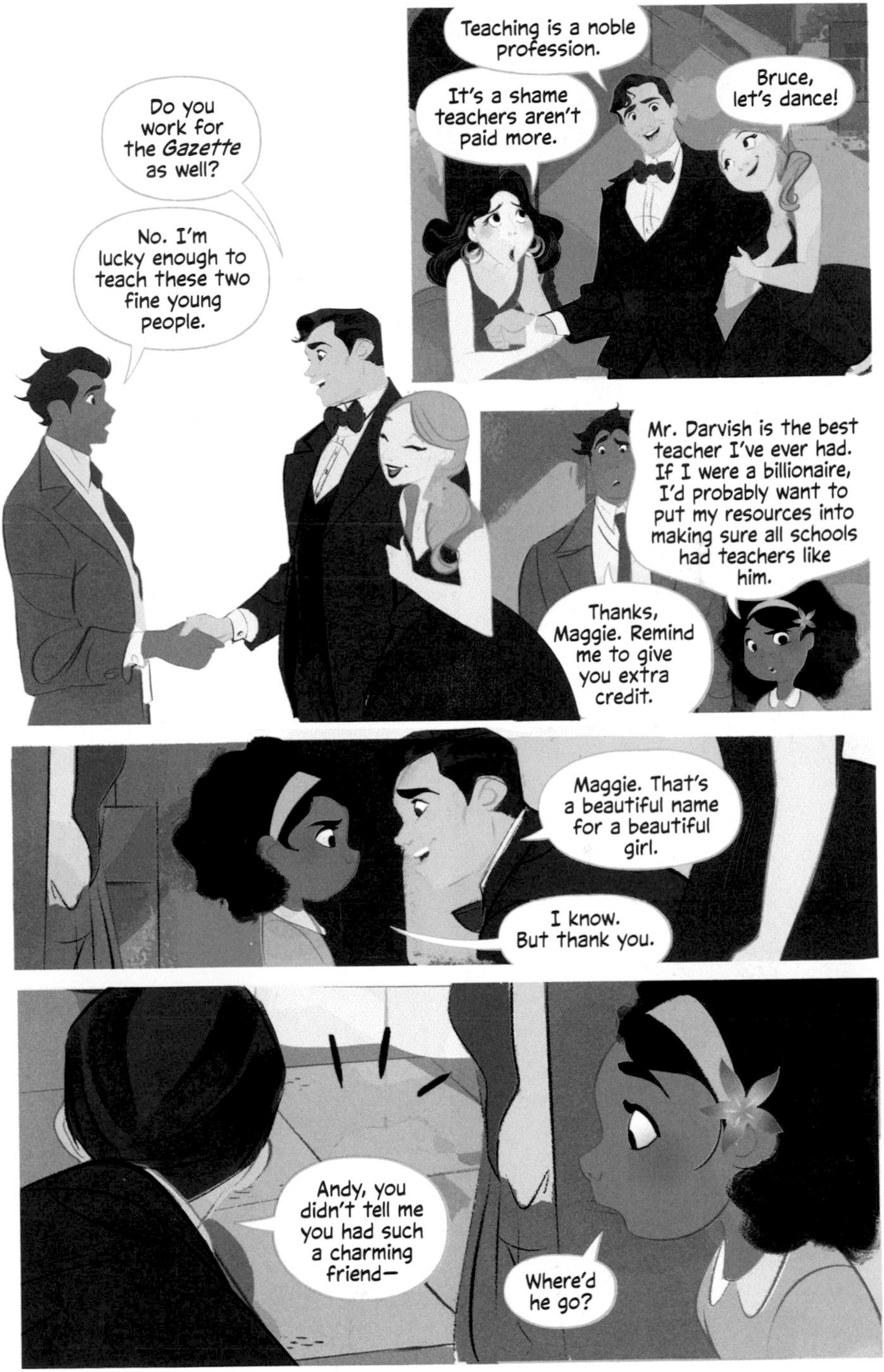
Do you work for the *Gazette* as well?
No. I'm lucky enough to teach these two fine young people.
Teaching is a noble profession.
It's a shame teachers aren't paid more.
Bruce, let's dance!
Mr. Darvish is the best teacher I've ever had. If I were a billionaire, I'd probably want to put my resources into making sure all schools had teachers like him.
Thanks, Maggie. Remind me to give you extra credit.
Maggie. That's a beautiful name for a beautiful girl.
I know. But thank you.
Andy, you didn't tell me you had such a charming friend—
Where'd he go?

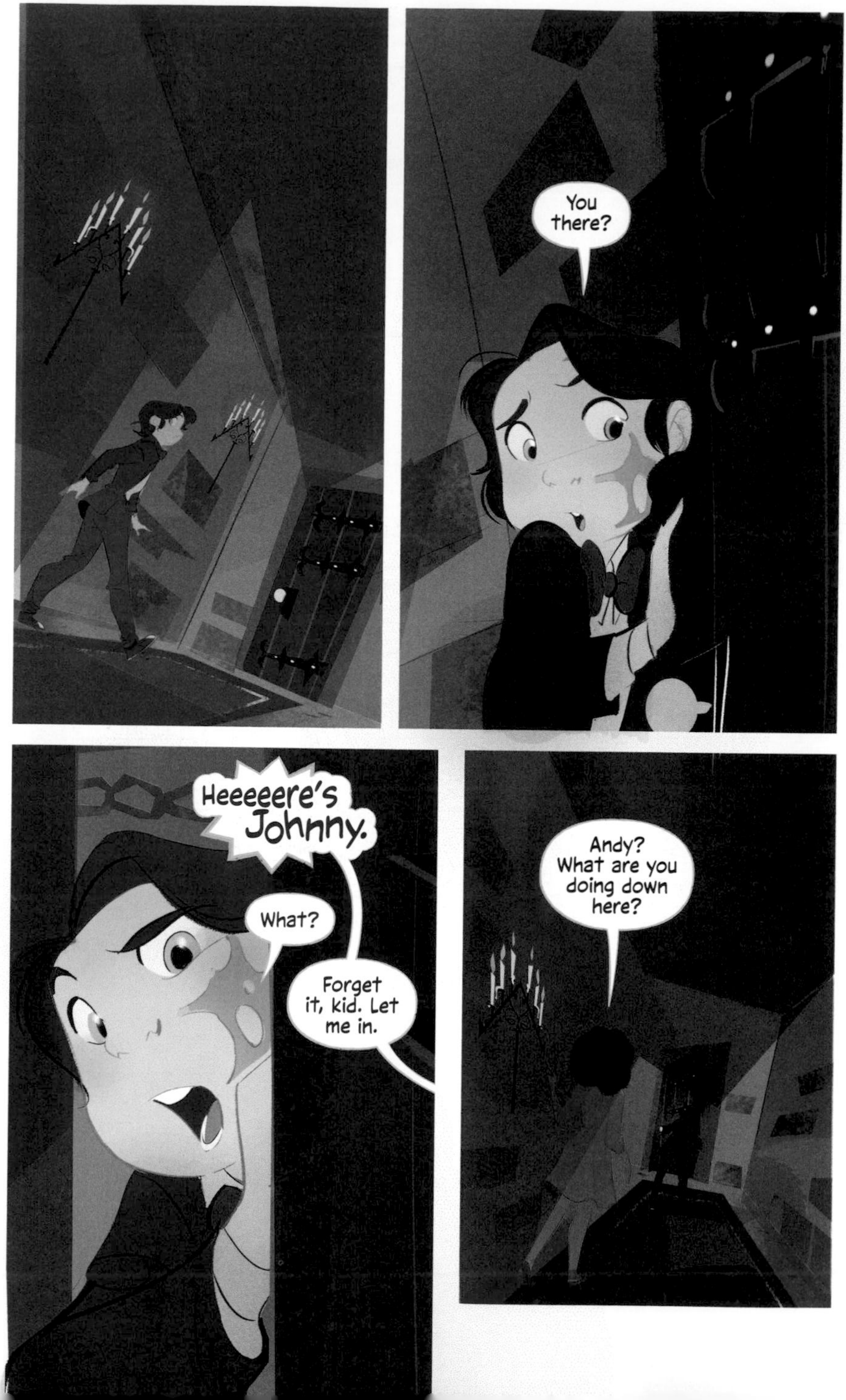
You there?
Heeeeere's Johnny.
What?
Forget it, kid. Let me in.
Andy? What are you doing down here?

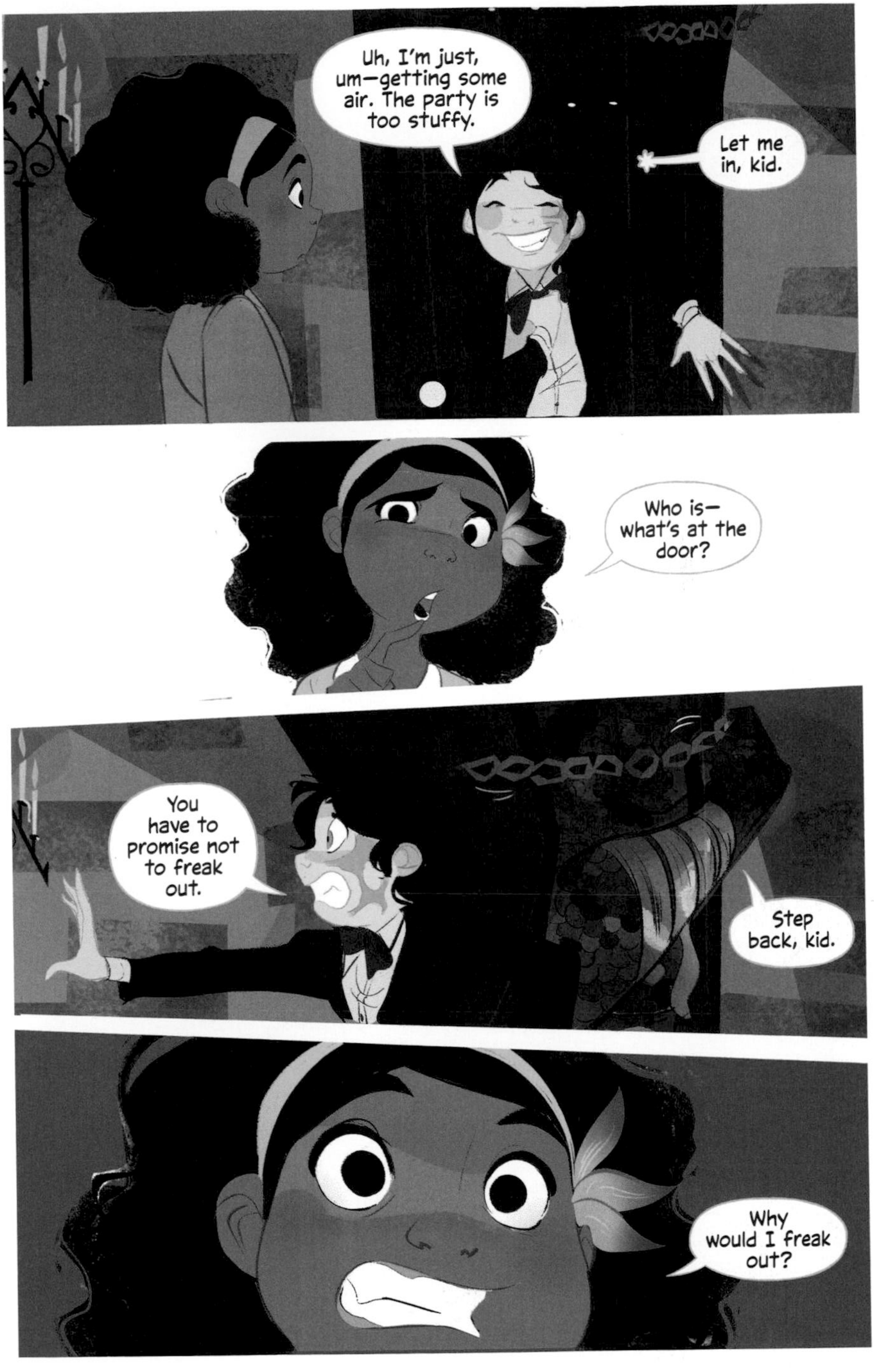
Uh, I'm just, um—getting some air. The party is too stuffy.
Let me in, kid.
Who is— what's at the door?
You have to promise not to freak out.
Step back, kid.
Why would I freak out?

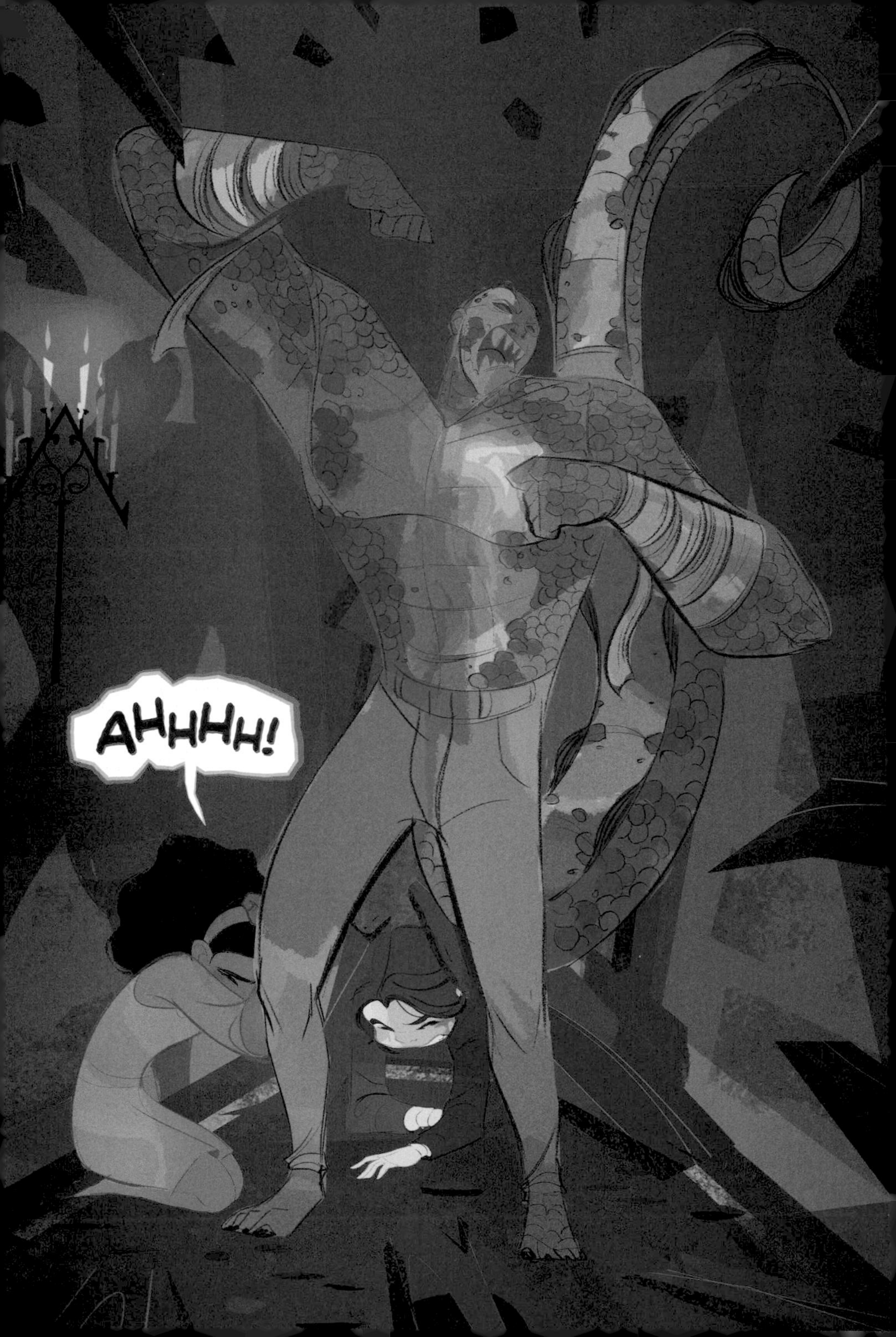
AHHHH!

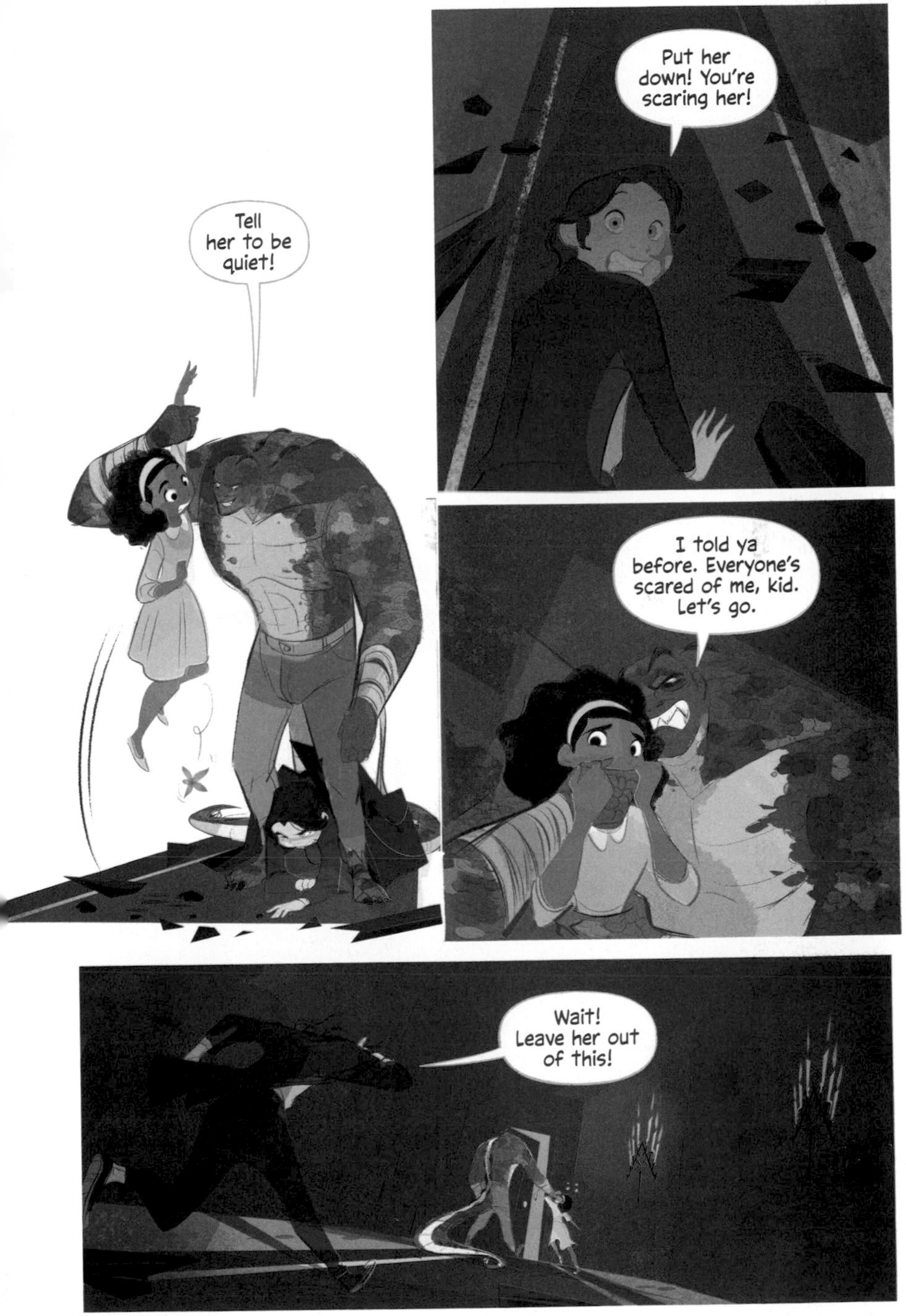

Tell her to be quiet!
Put her down! You're scaring her!
I told ya before. Everyone's scared of me, kid. Let's go.
Wait! Leave her out of this!

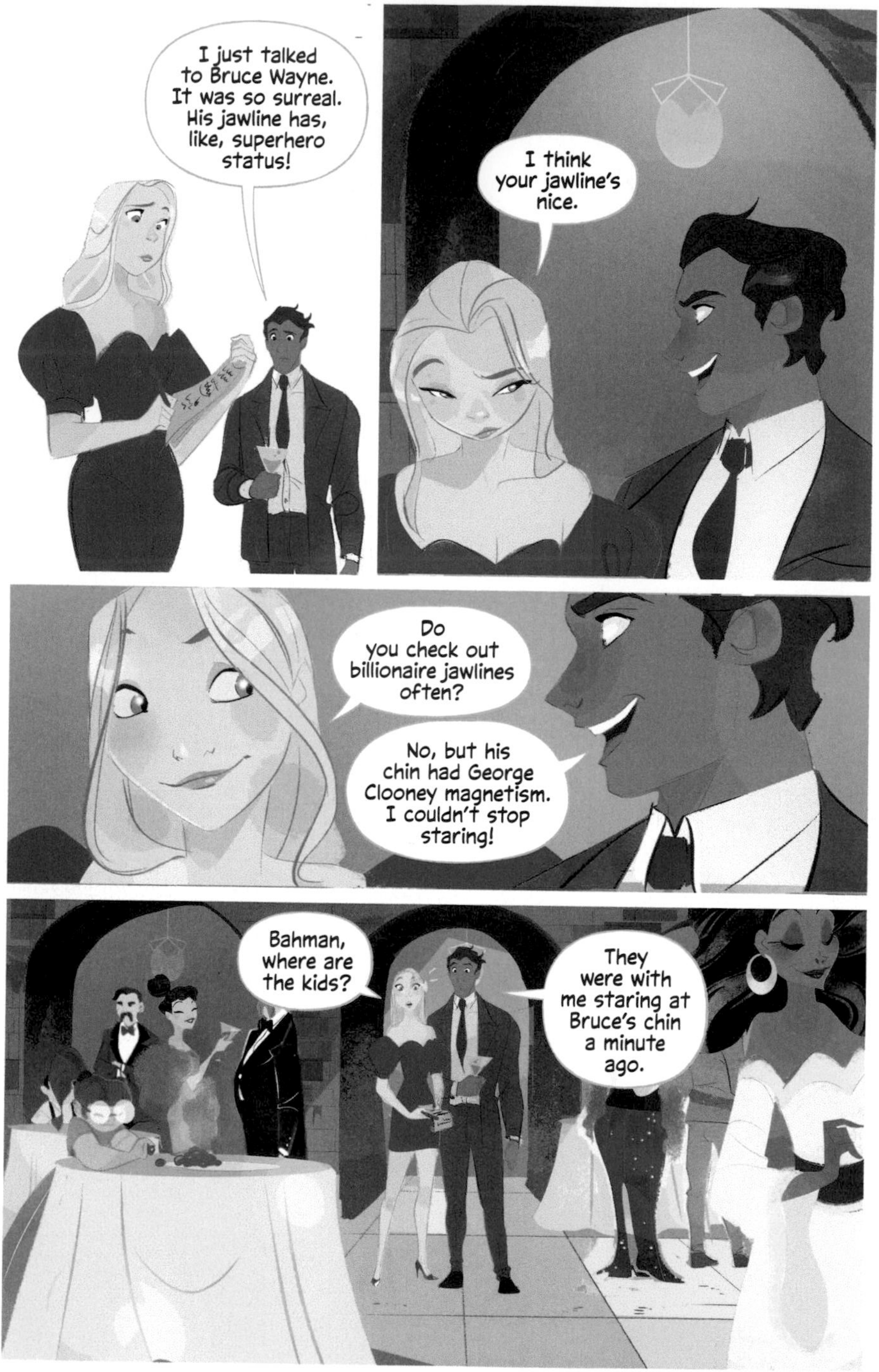
I just talked to Bruce Wayne. It was so surreal. His jawline has, like, superhero status!
I think your jawline's nice.
Do you check out billionaire jawlines often?
No, but his chin had George Clooney magnetism. I couldn't stop staring!
Bahman, where are the kids?
They were with me staring at Bruce's chin a minute ago.

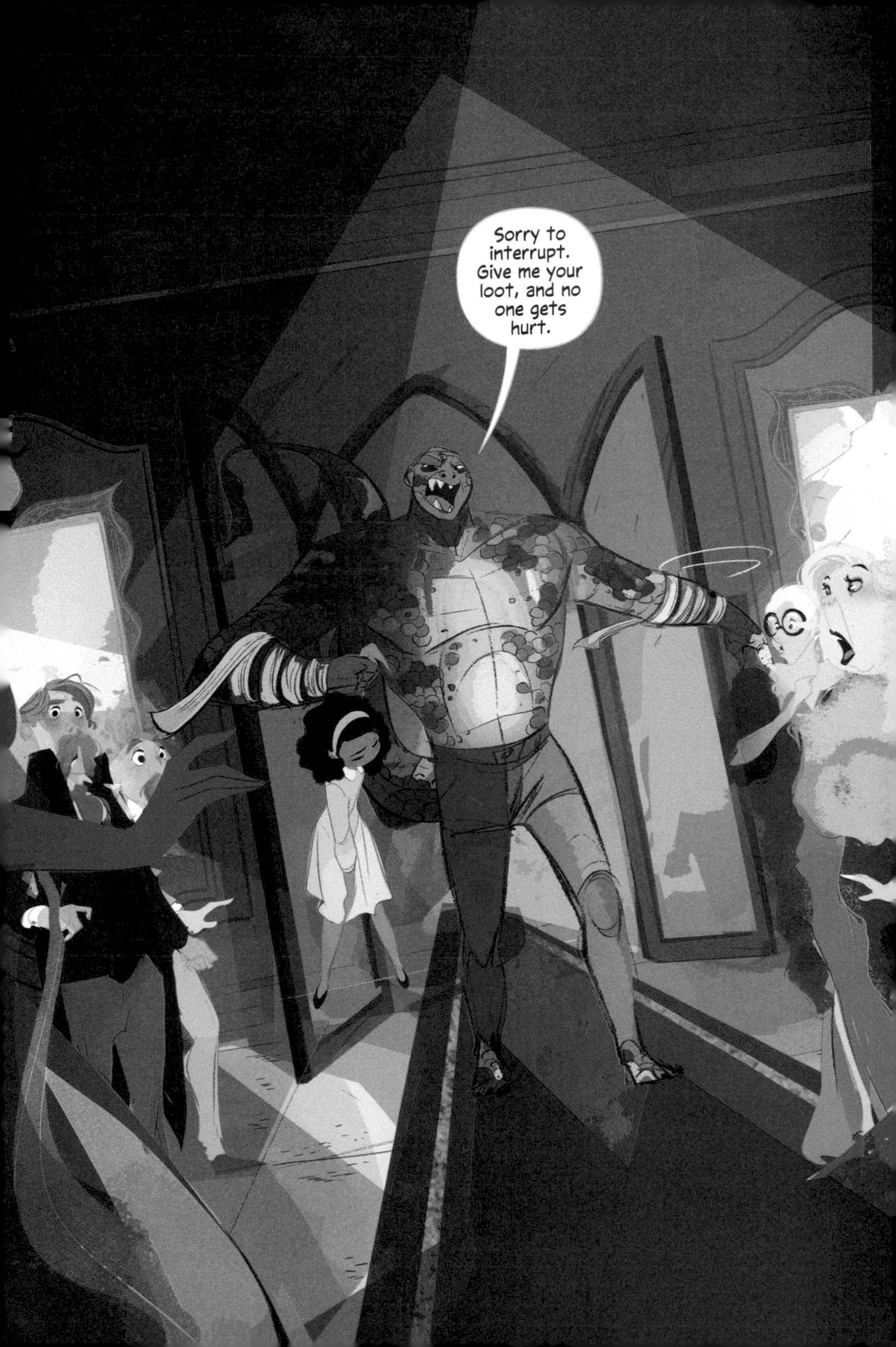
Sorry to interrupt. Give me your loot, and no one gets hurt.

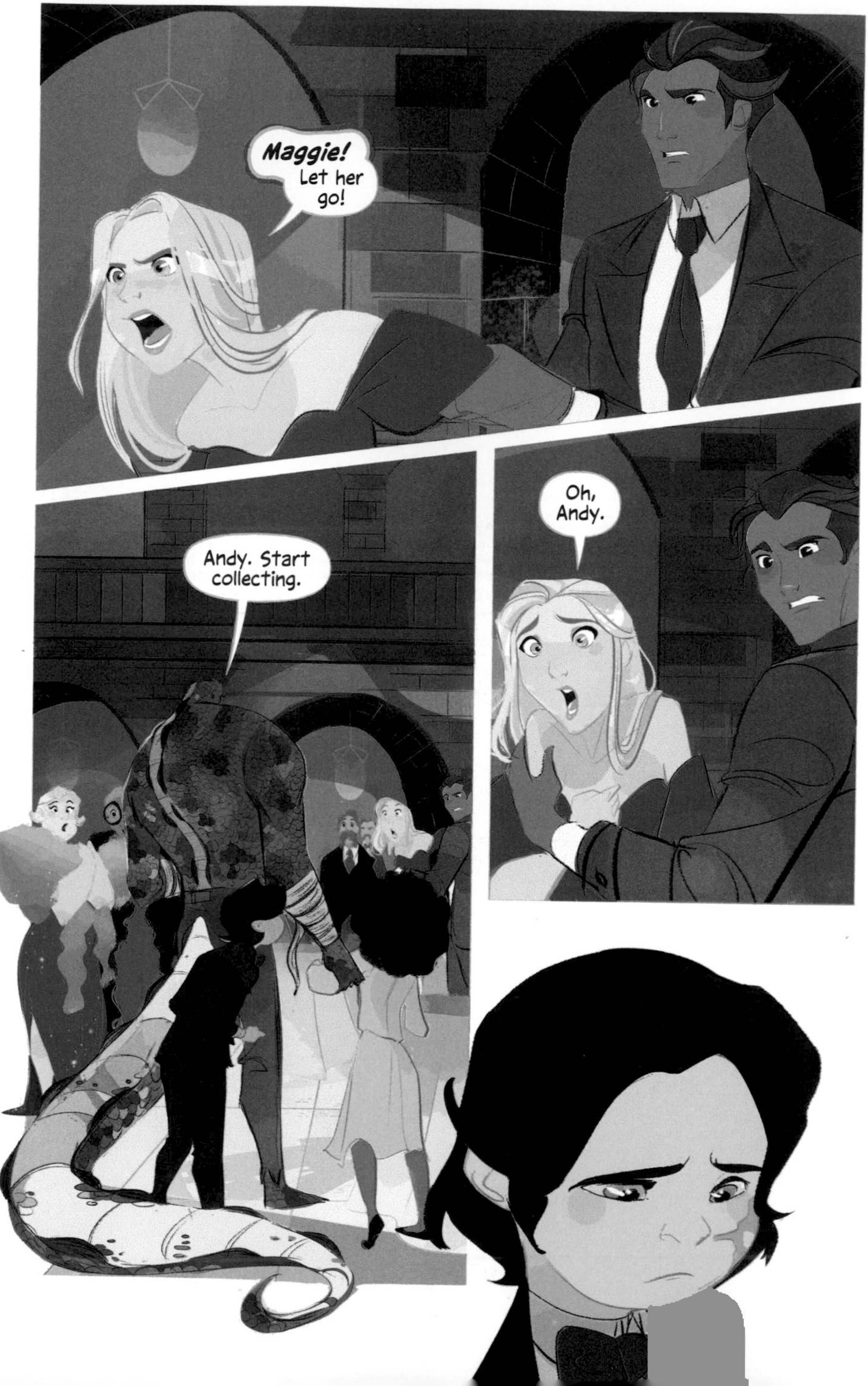
Maggie! Let her go!
Andy. Start collecting.
Oh, Andy.

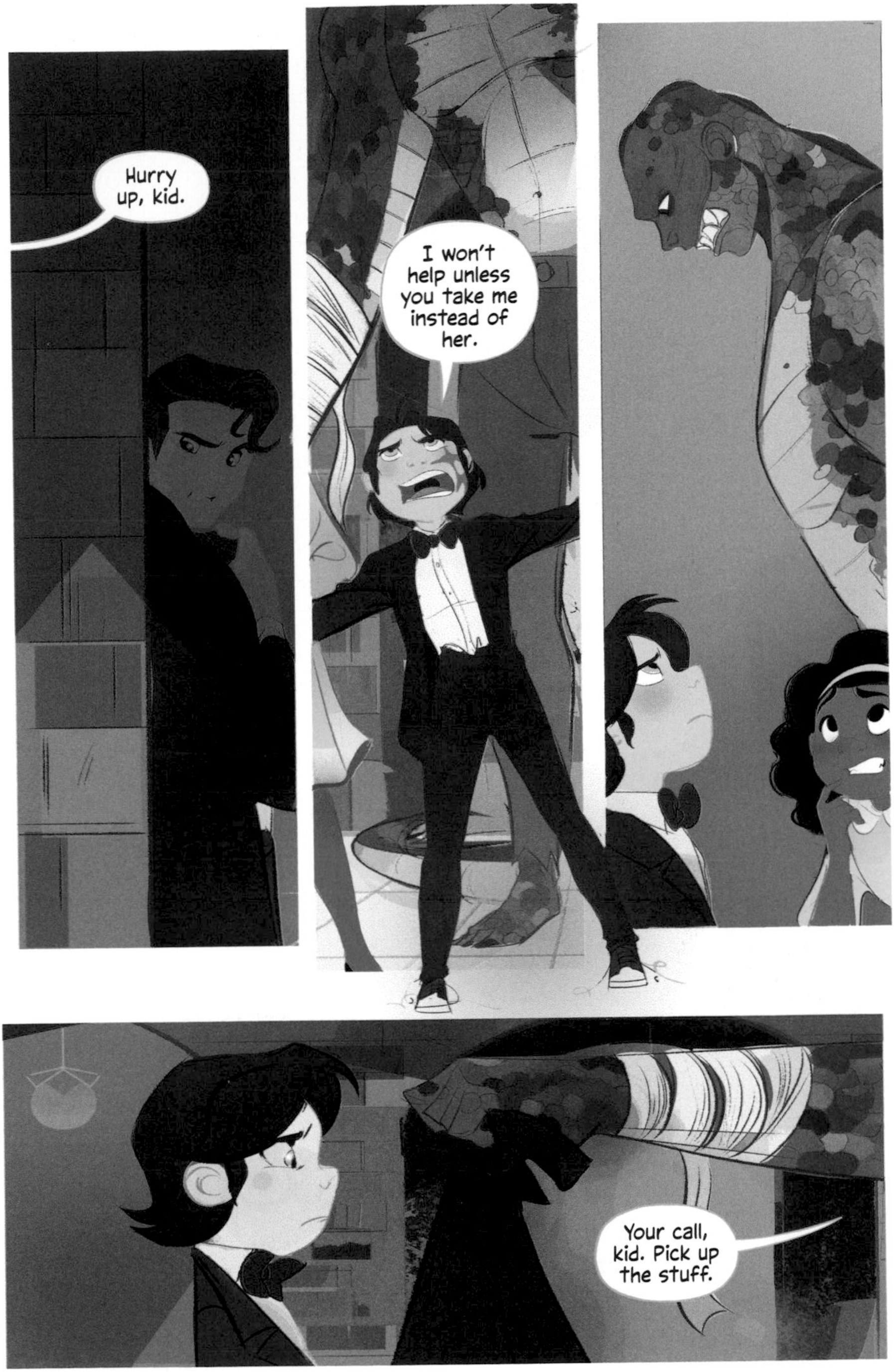
Hurry up, kid.
I won't help unless you take me instead of her.
Your call, kid. Pick up the stuff.

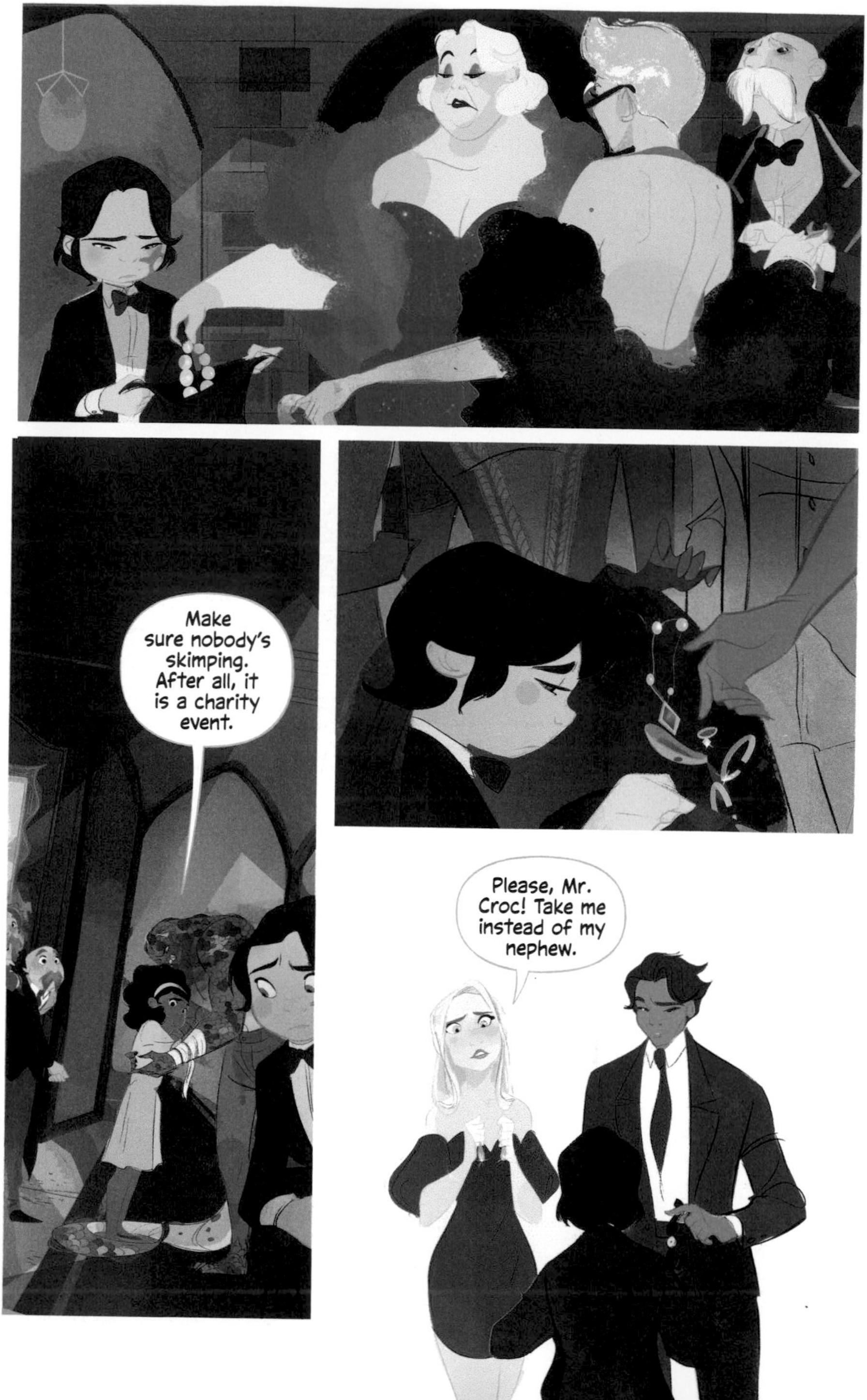
Make sure nobody's skimping. After all, it is a charity event.
Please, Mr. Croc! Take me instead of my nephew.

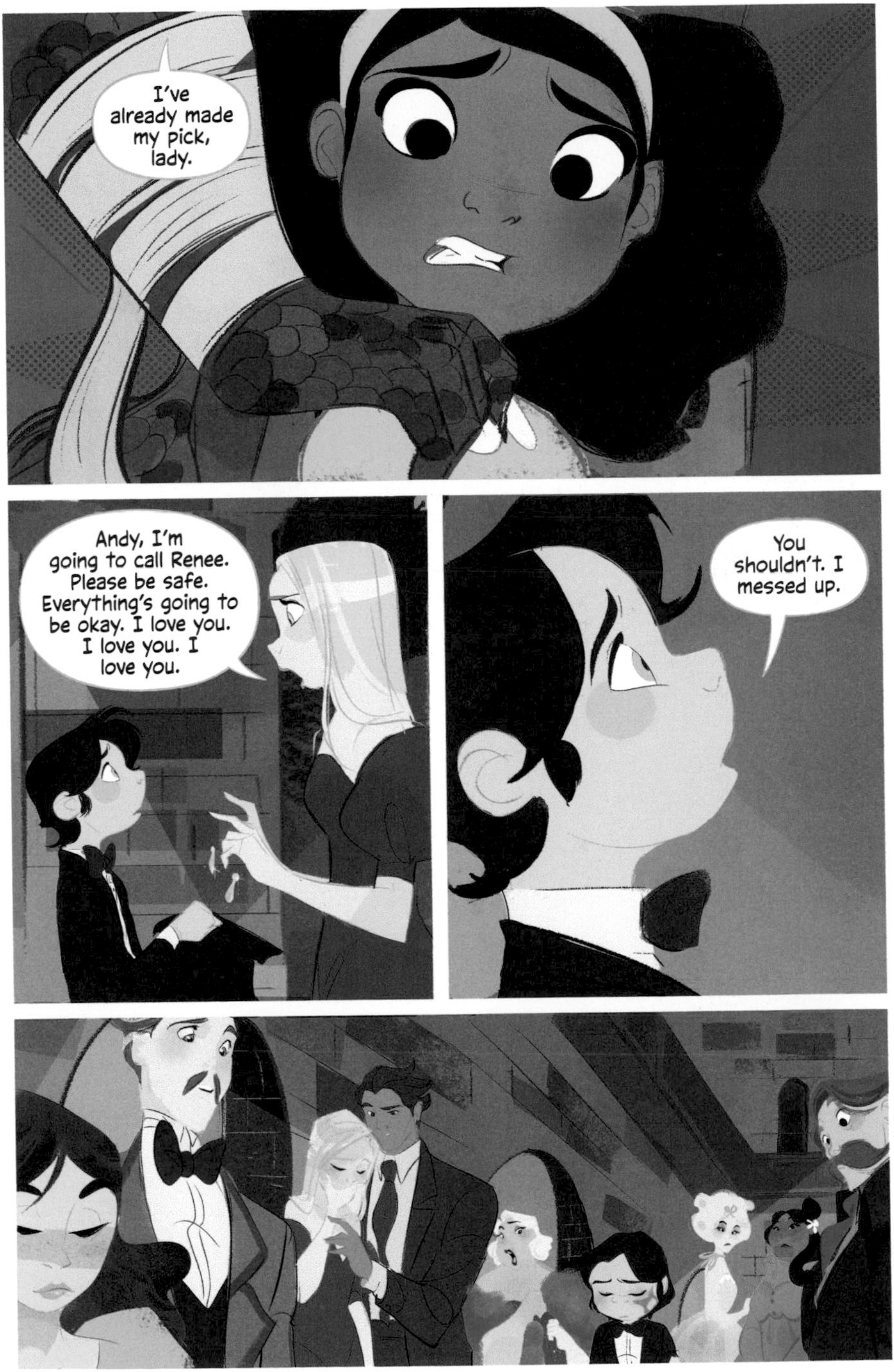
I've already made my pick, lady.
Andy, I'm going to call Renee. Please be safe. Everything's going to be okay. I love you. I love you. I love you.
You shouldn't. I messed up.

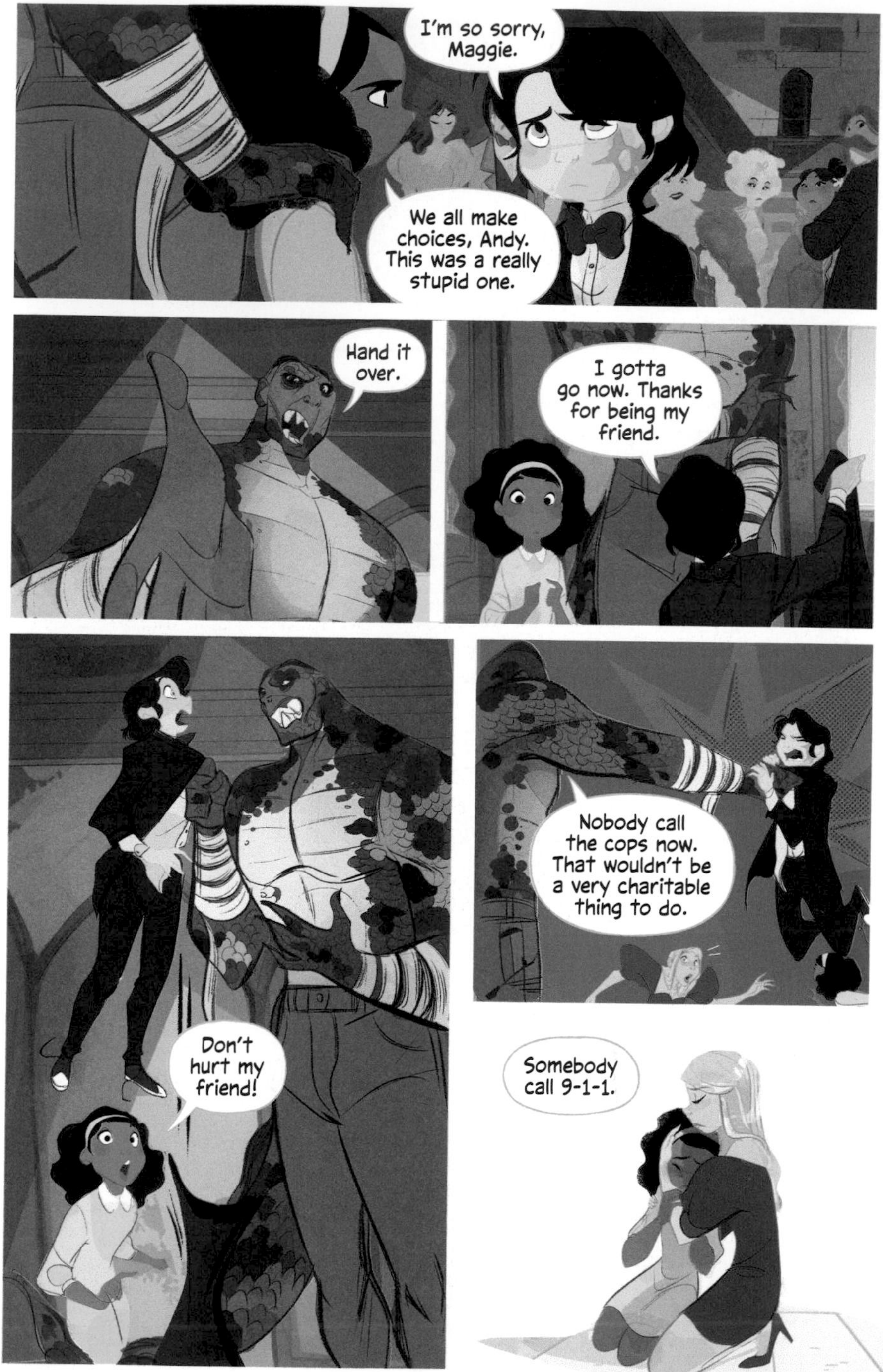
I'm so sorry, Maggie.
We all make choices, Andy. This was a really stupid one.
Hand it over.
I gotta go now. Thanks for being my friend.
Don't hurt my friend!
Nobody call the cops now. That wouldn't be a very charitable thing to do.
Somebody call 9-1-1.

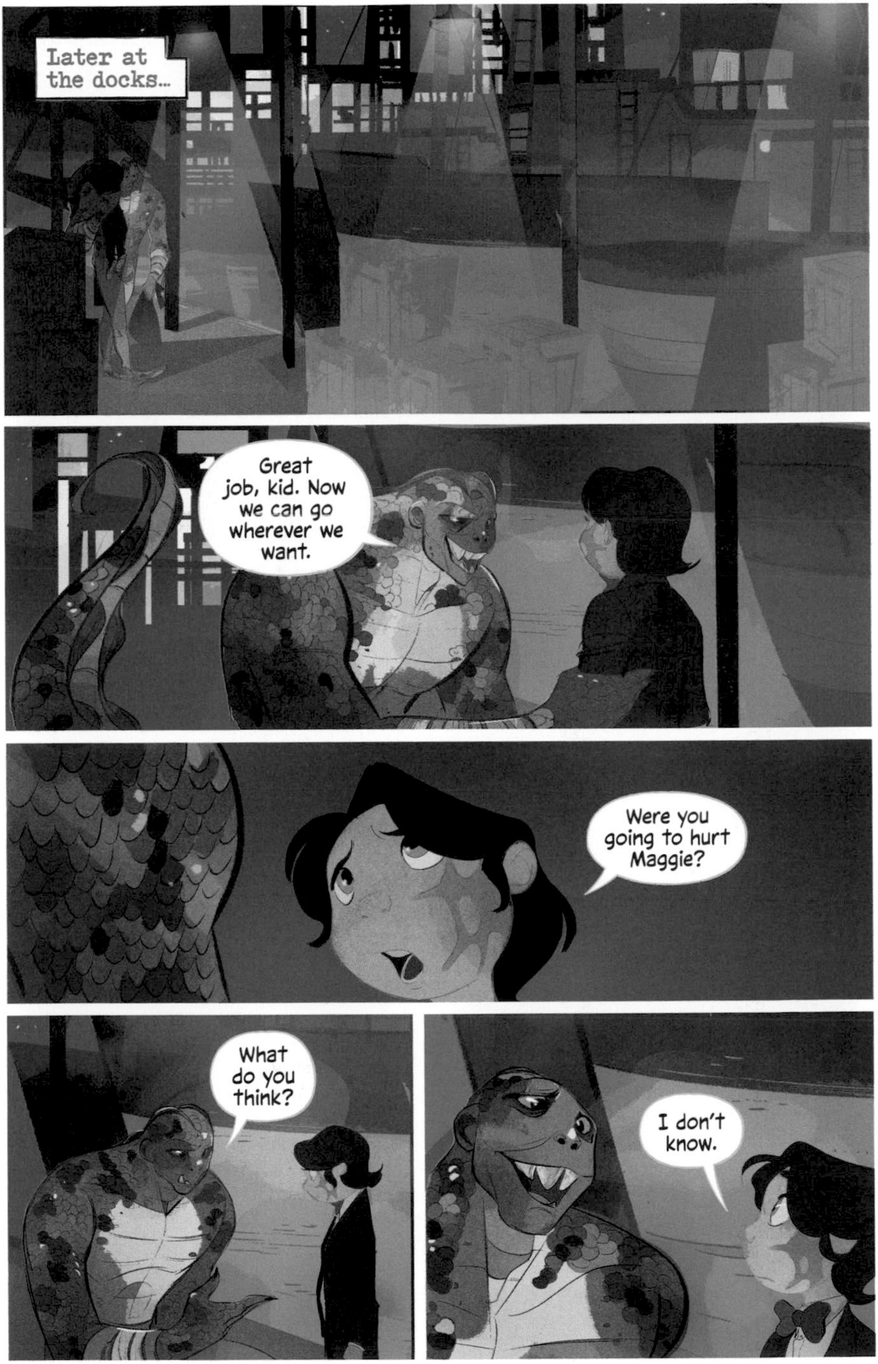
Later at the docks...
Great job, kid. Now we can go wherever we want.
Were you going to hurt Maggie?
What do you think?
I don't know.

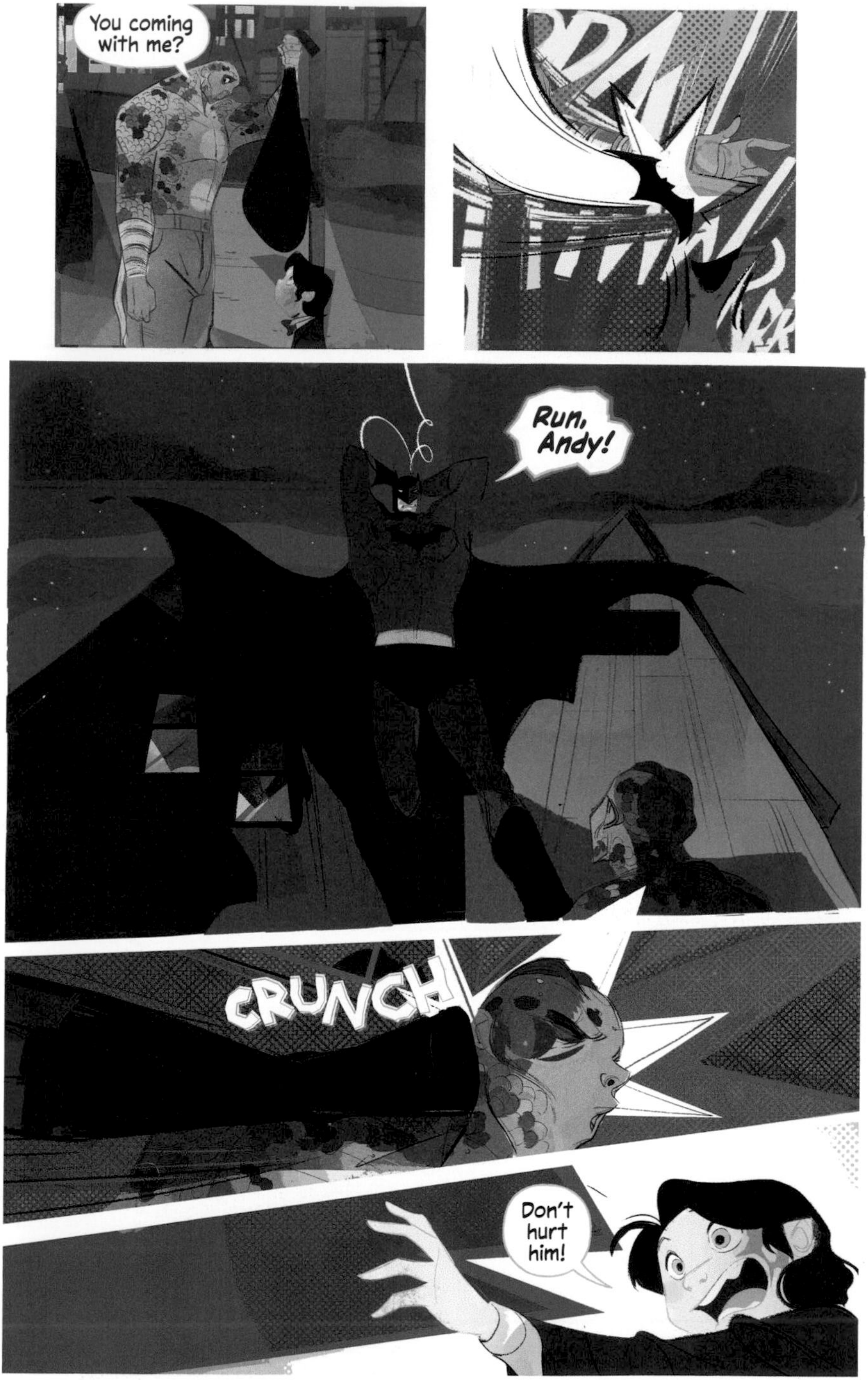
You coming with me?
Run, Andy!
CRUNCH
Don't hurt him!

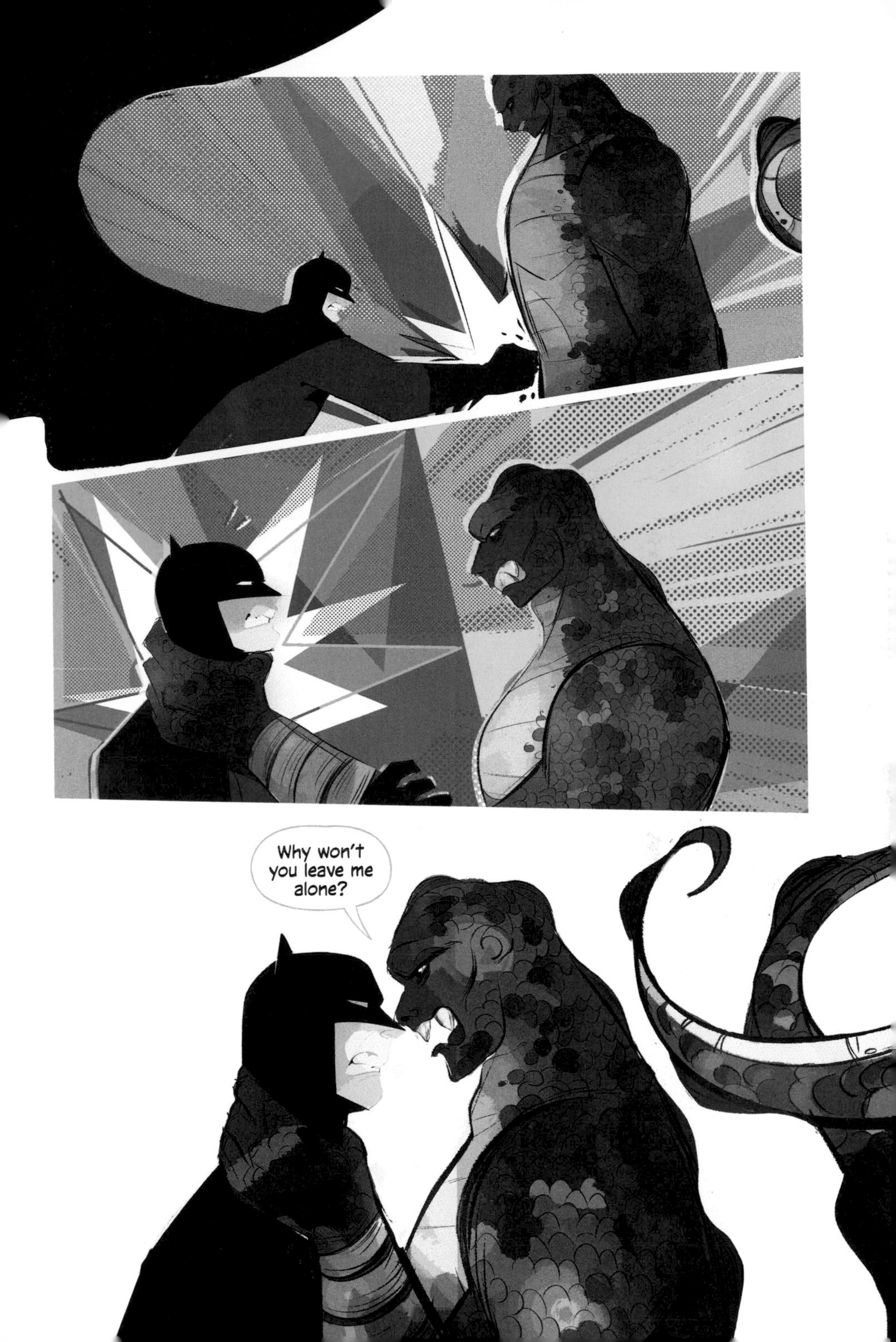
Why won't you leave me alone?

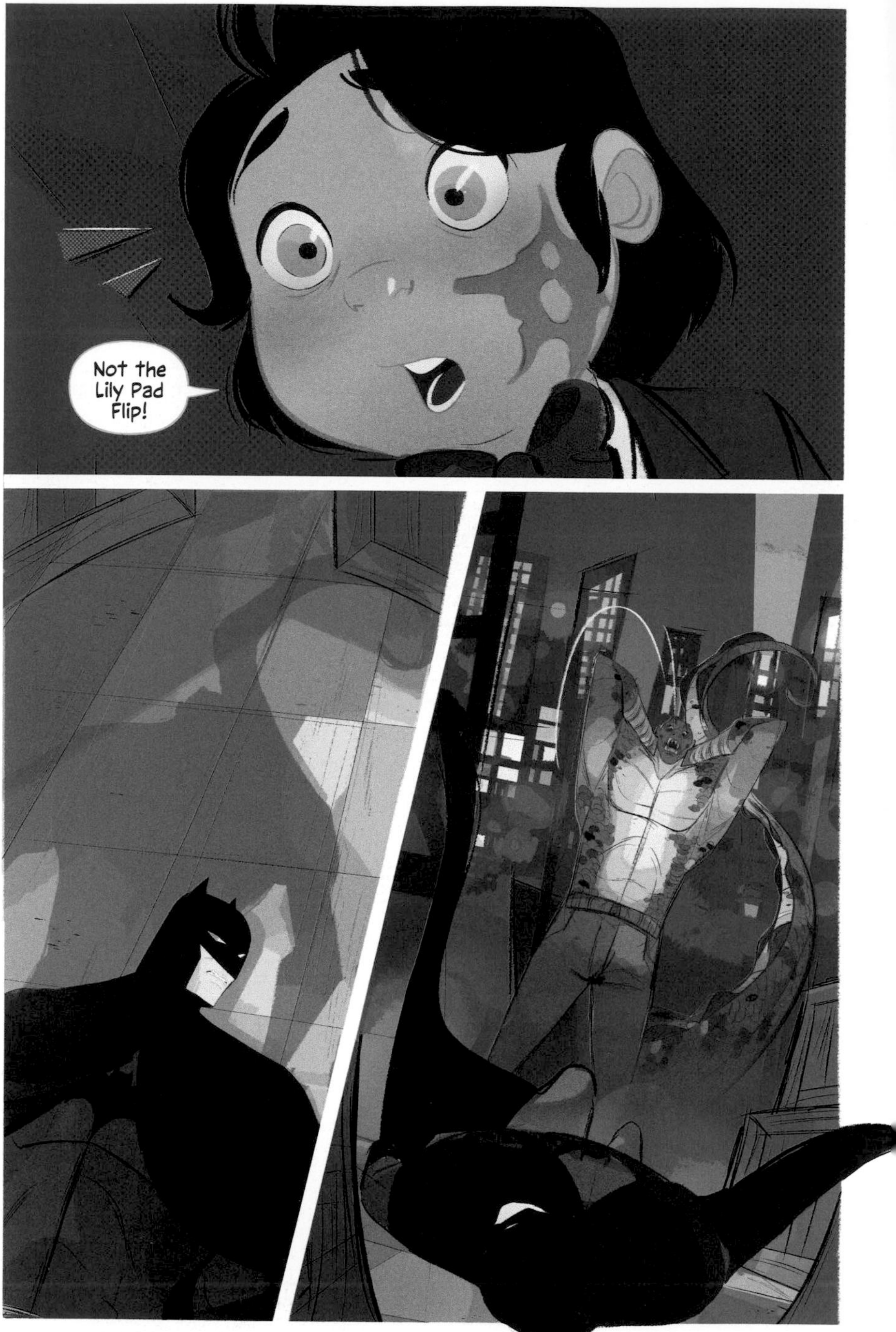
Not the Lily Pad Flip!

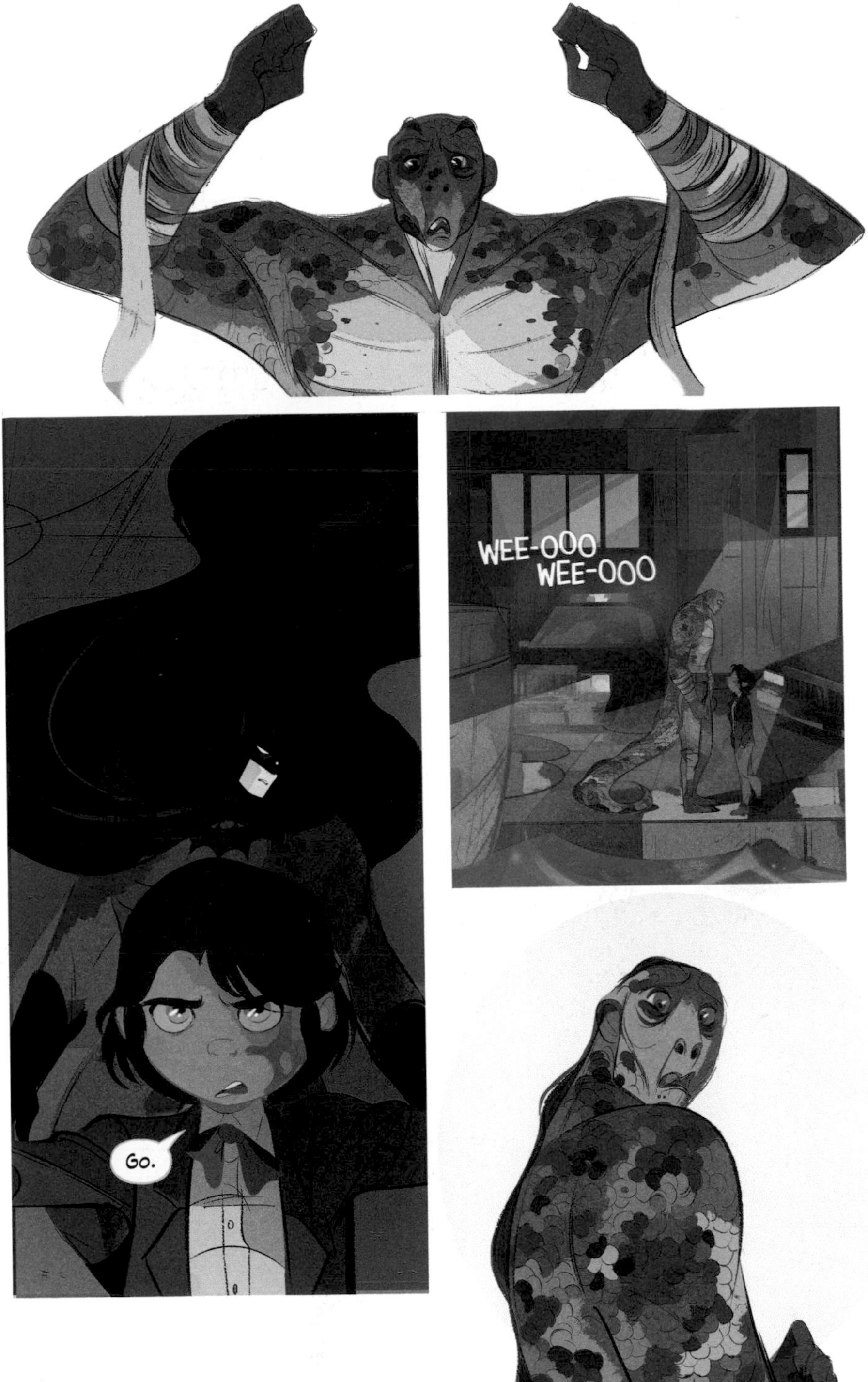
WEE-OOO
WEE-OOO
Go.

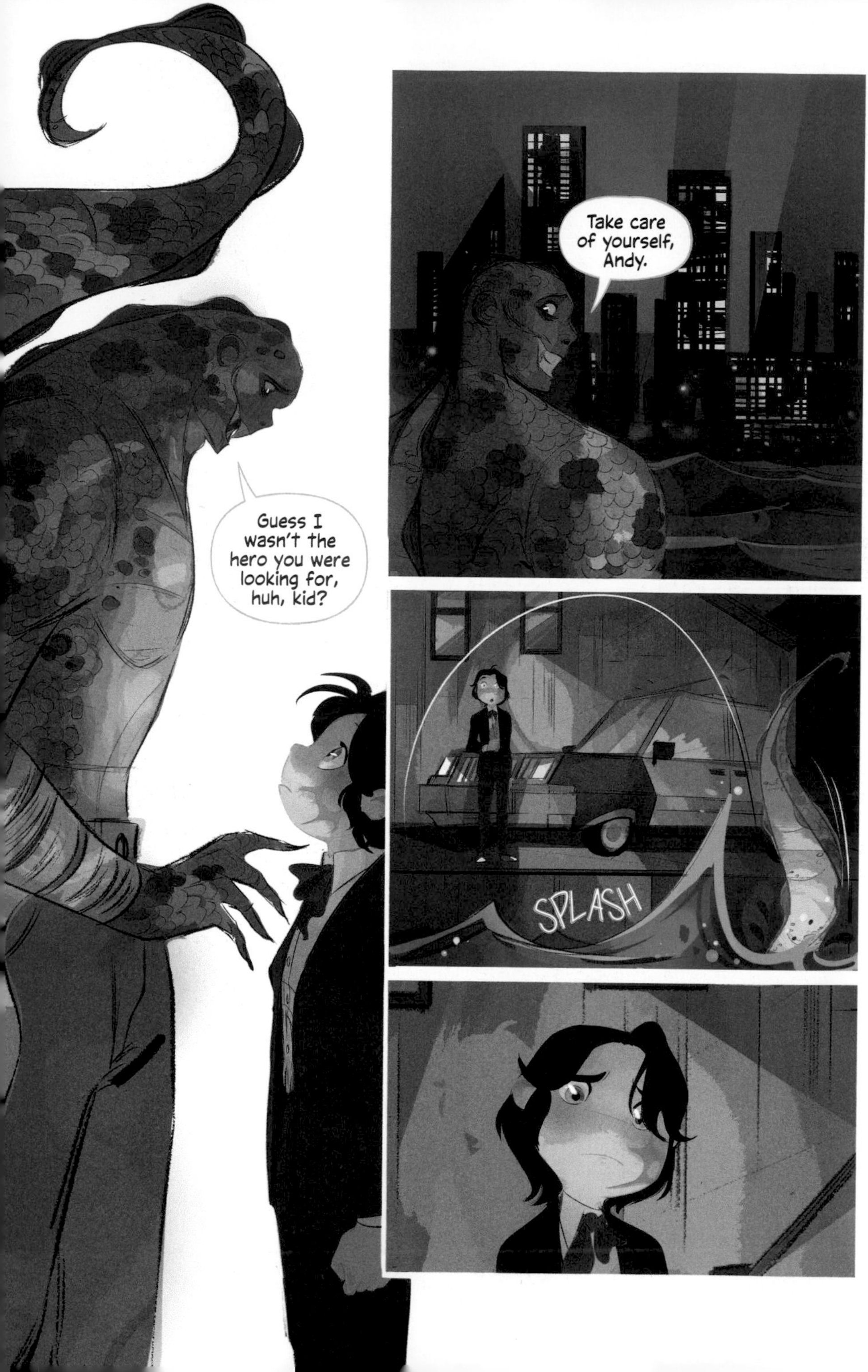
Guess I wasn't the hero you were looking for, huh, kid?
Take care of yourself, Andy.
SPLASH

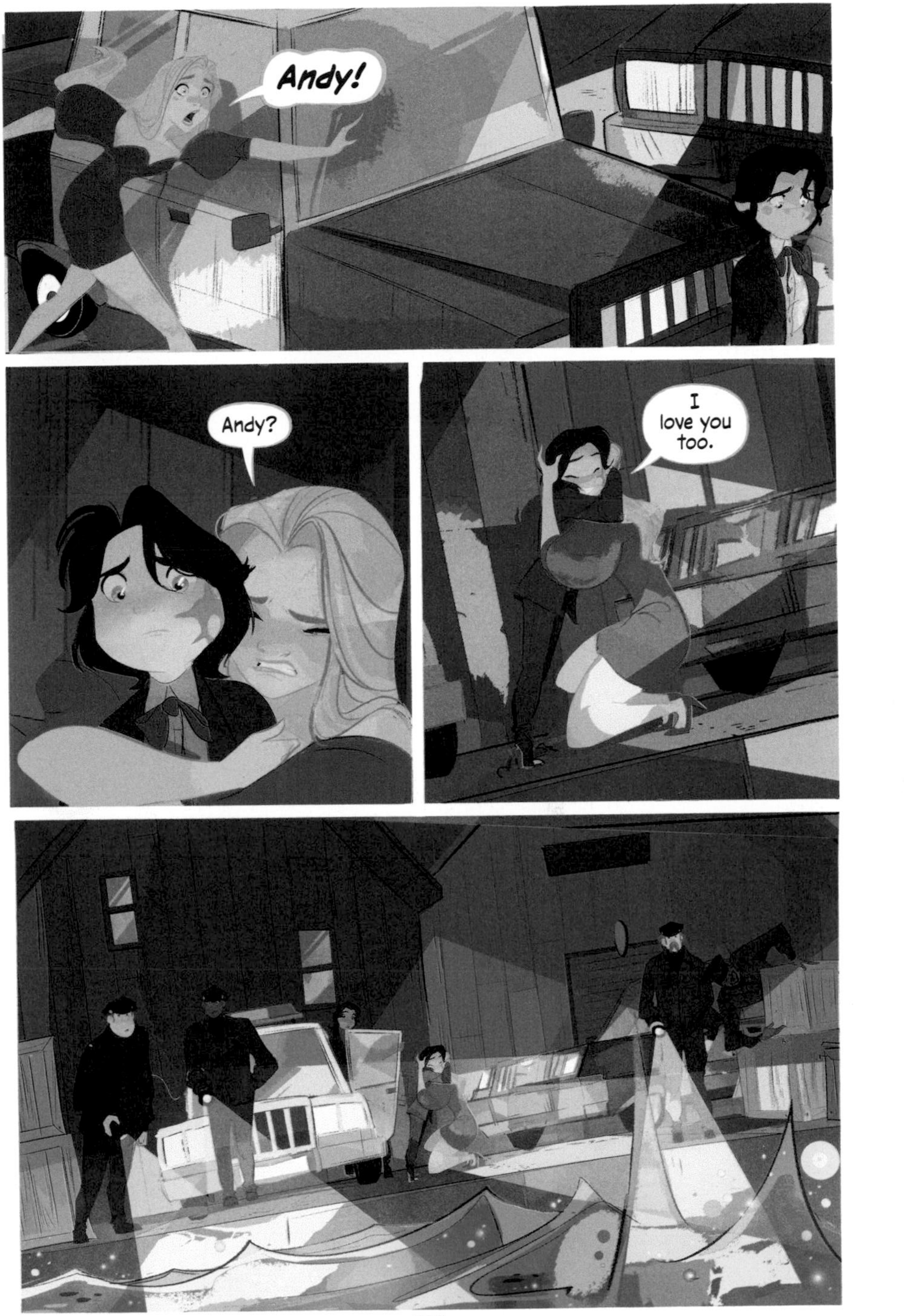
Andy!
Andy?
I love you too.

CHAPTER EIGHT

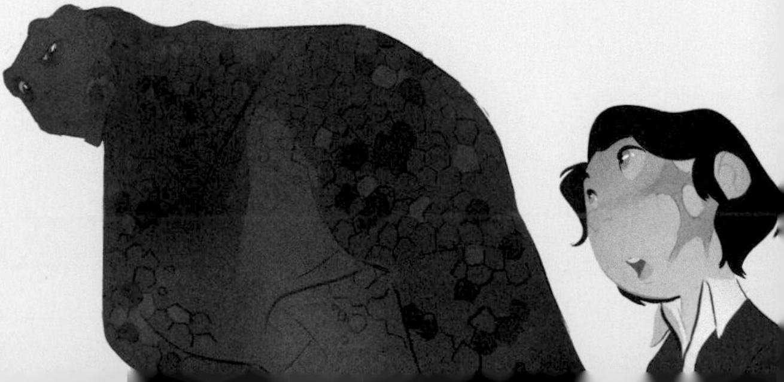

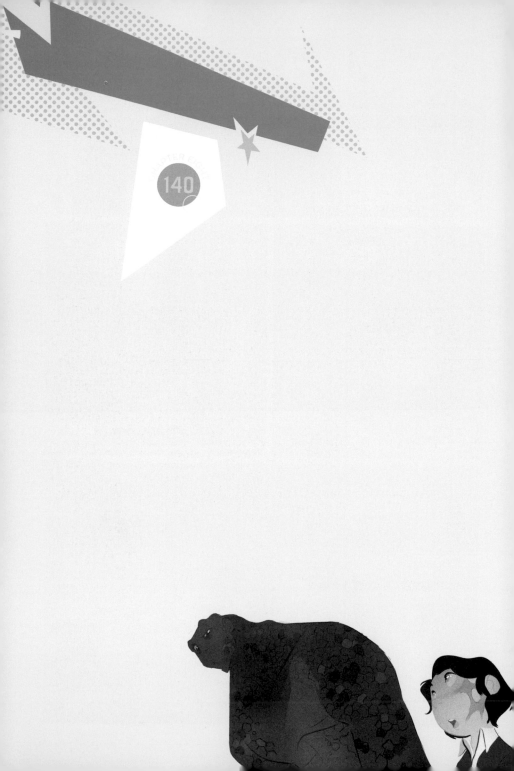

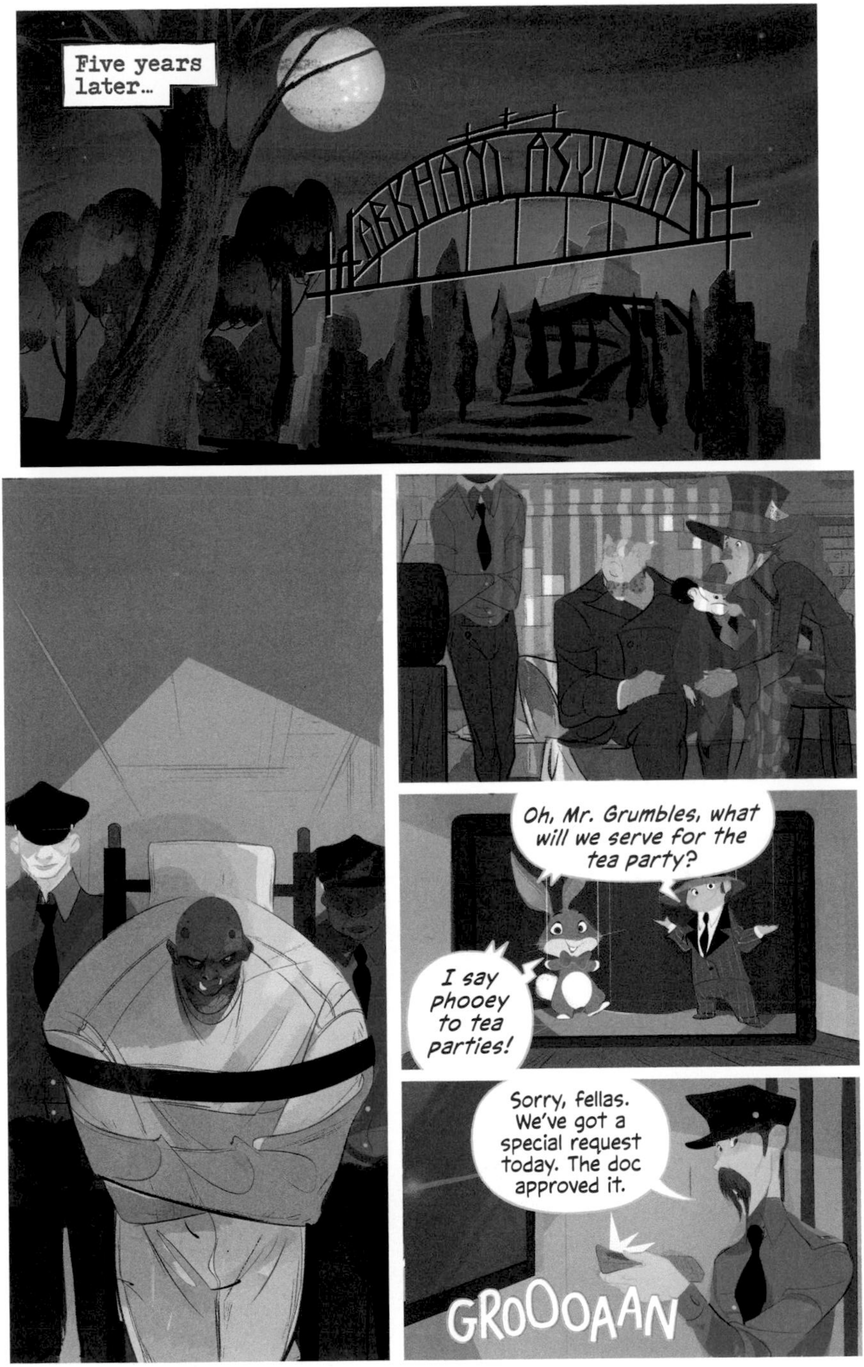

Five years later...
ARKHAM ASYLUM
Oh, Mr. Grumbles, what will we serve for the tea party?
I say phooey to tea parties!
Sorry, fellas. We've got a special request today. The doc approved it.
GROOOAAN

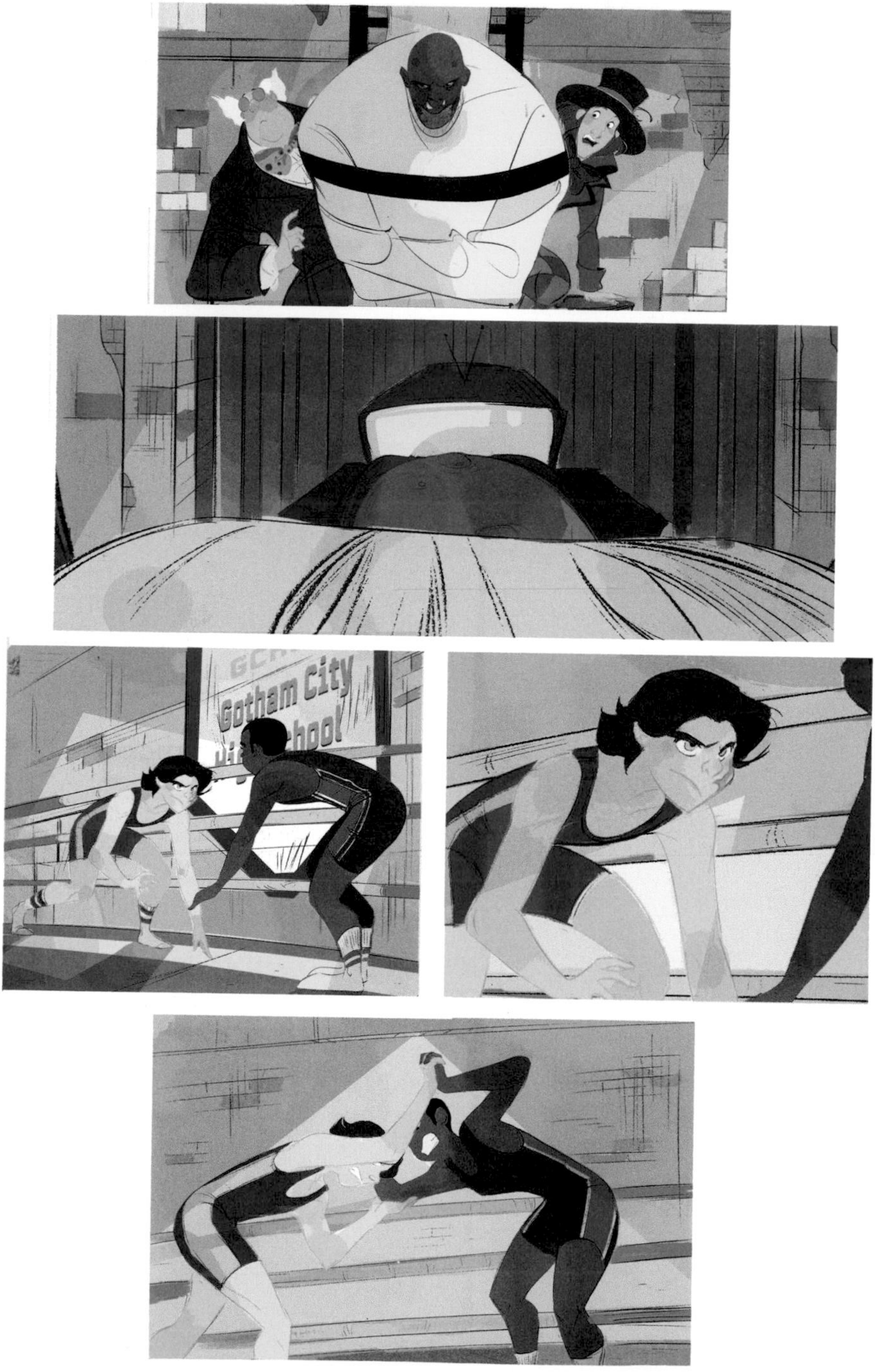
Gotham City

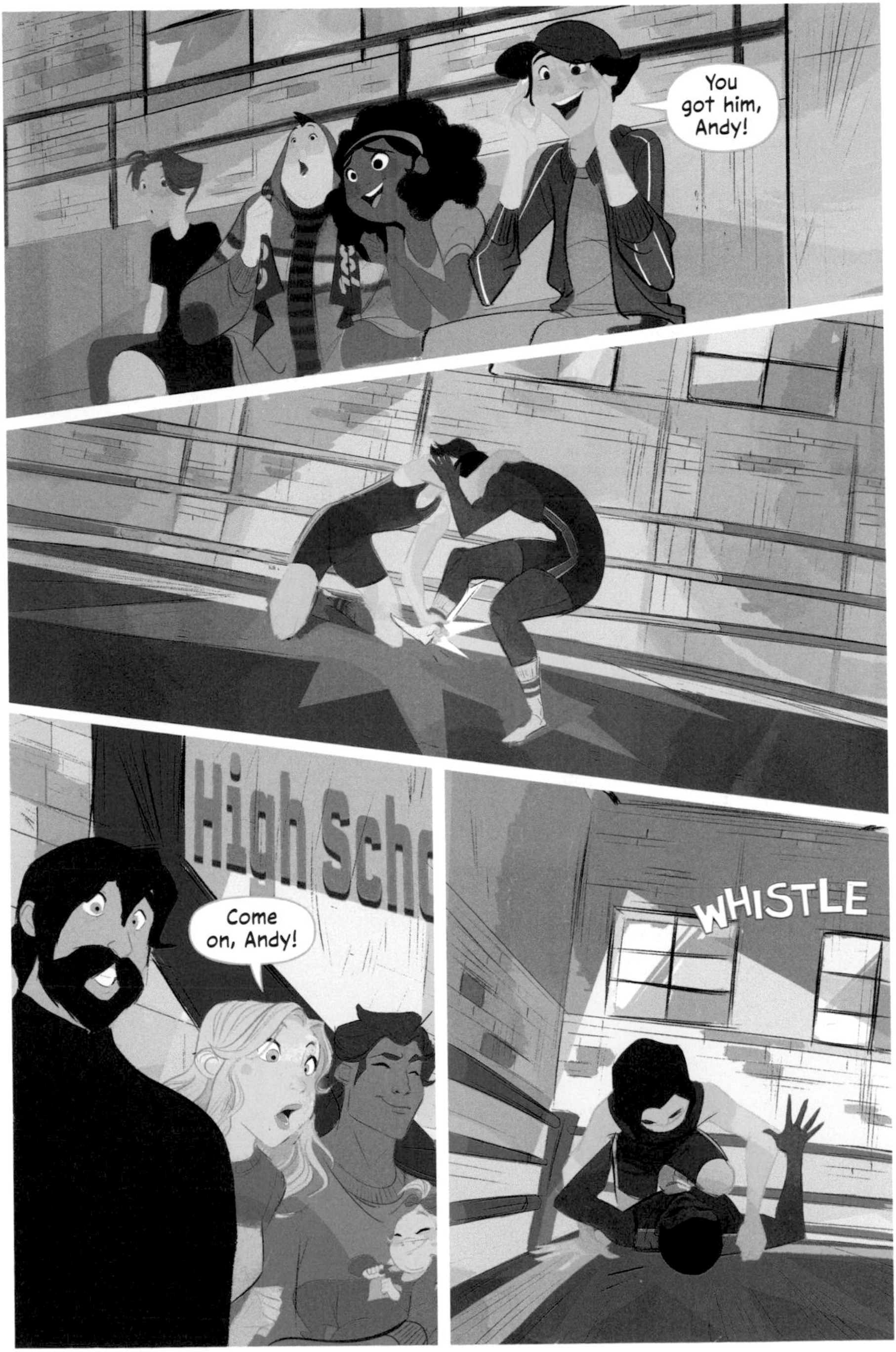
You got him, Andy!
High Scho
Come on, Andy!
WHISTLE

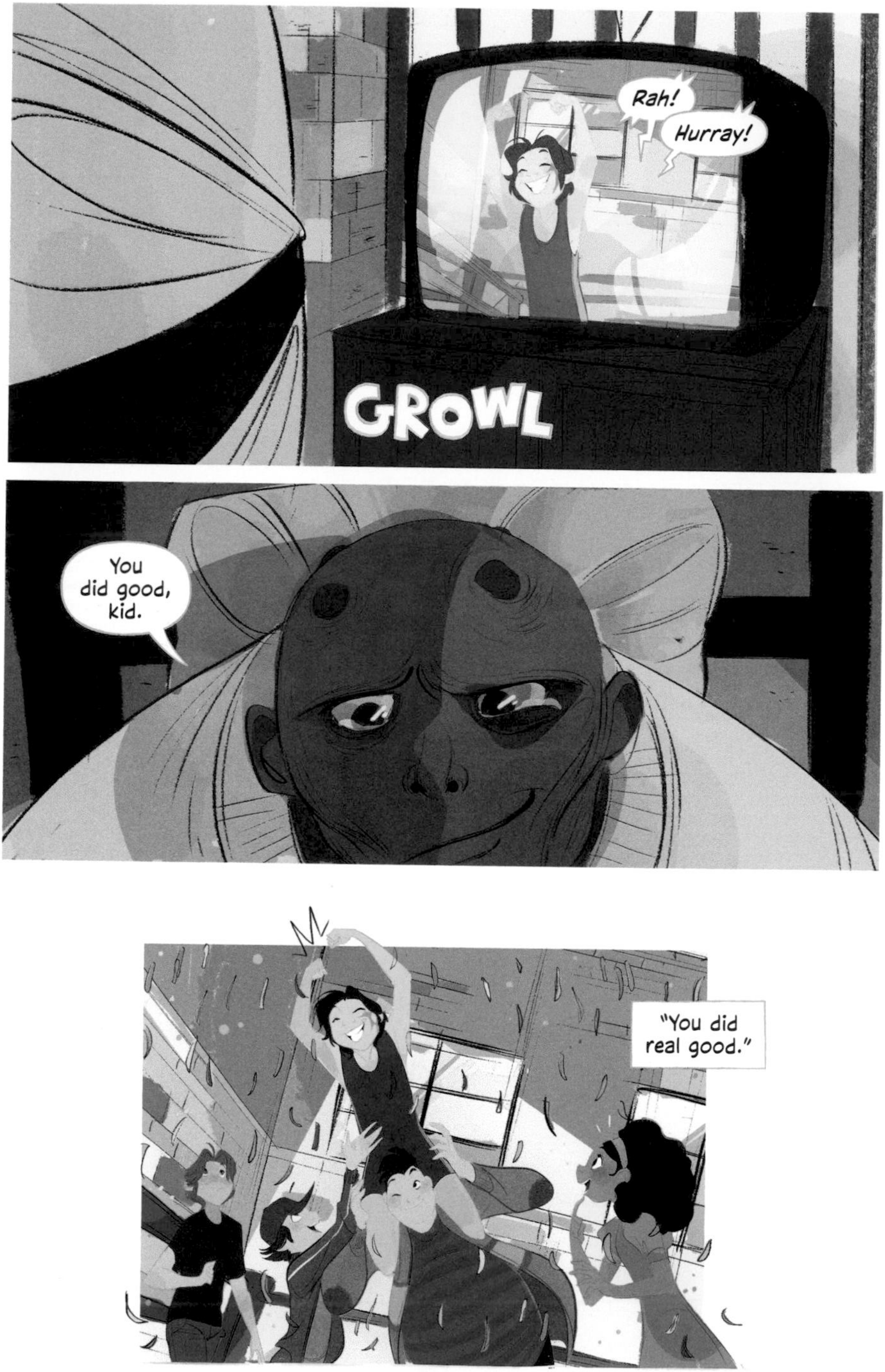
Rah!
Hurray!
GROWL
You did good, kid.
"You did real good."

SARA FARIZAN is the award-winning and critically acclaimed author of the young adult novels *Here to Stay*, *Tell Me Again How a Crush Should Feel*, and *If You Could Be Mine*. She also has short stories in the anthologies *Fresh Ink*, *All Out*, *The Radical Element*, *Hungry Hearts*, and *Come On In*. She has a comic book collection from childhood that continues to grow, and writing this story is a dream come true.

NiCOLETTA BALDARi is a cartoonist and character designer who has worked with Disney, DC Comics, Hasbro, Konami, Dark Horse, IDW, and Lucasfilm. She's drawn cool princesses, Jedis, and everything you can imagine! Nicoletta is an avid french fry eater whose home is in the west wing of Wayne Manor (which everybody knows is on the south side of Rome), where she lives with her husband, son, and two sweet kittens, who are always playing with her hair.

BECCA CAREY is a graphic designer and letterer who has worked on books like *Redlands*, *Vampirella/Red Sonja*, *Buffy the Vampire Slayer*, and more super-secret fun projects to watch out for. She loves terrible horror movies and having conversations with her dog and has proudly read *War and Peace*, but couldn't tell you a thing about it.

Ever had the feeling that you were being watched? Or taken a dark shortcut on the way home? Wondered just what might be living under your bed? Well, **Deadman** knows... has always known...and he's here to shed some light on those spine-tingling adventures and things that go bump in the night.

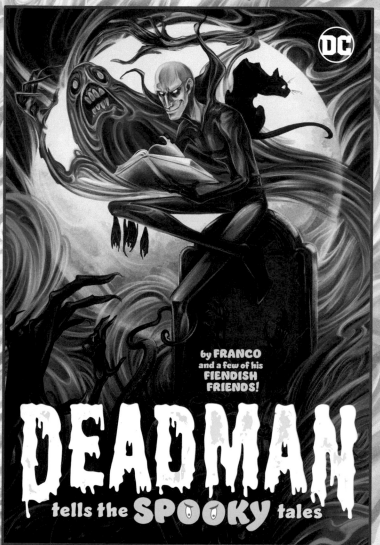

by FRANCO
and a few of his
FIENDISH
FRIENDS!

DEADMAN

tells the SPOOKY tales

Check out this sneak peek written by *New York Times* bestselling and Eisner Award-winning writer **Franco** and featuring art by some of DC Comics' favorite artists, including **Sara Richard**, **Andy Price**, **Derek Charm**, **Mike Hartigan**, **Christopher Uminga**, **Abigail Larson**, **Morgan Beem**, **Justin Castaneda**, **Tressina Bowling**, **Boatwright Artwork**, **Scoot McMahon**, **Franco**, **Isaac Goodhart**, and **Agnes Garbowska** with **Silvana Brys**.

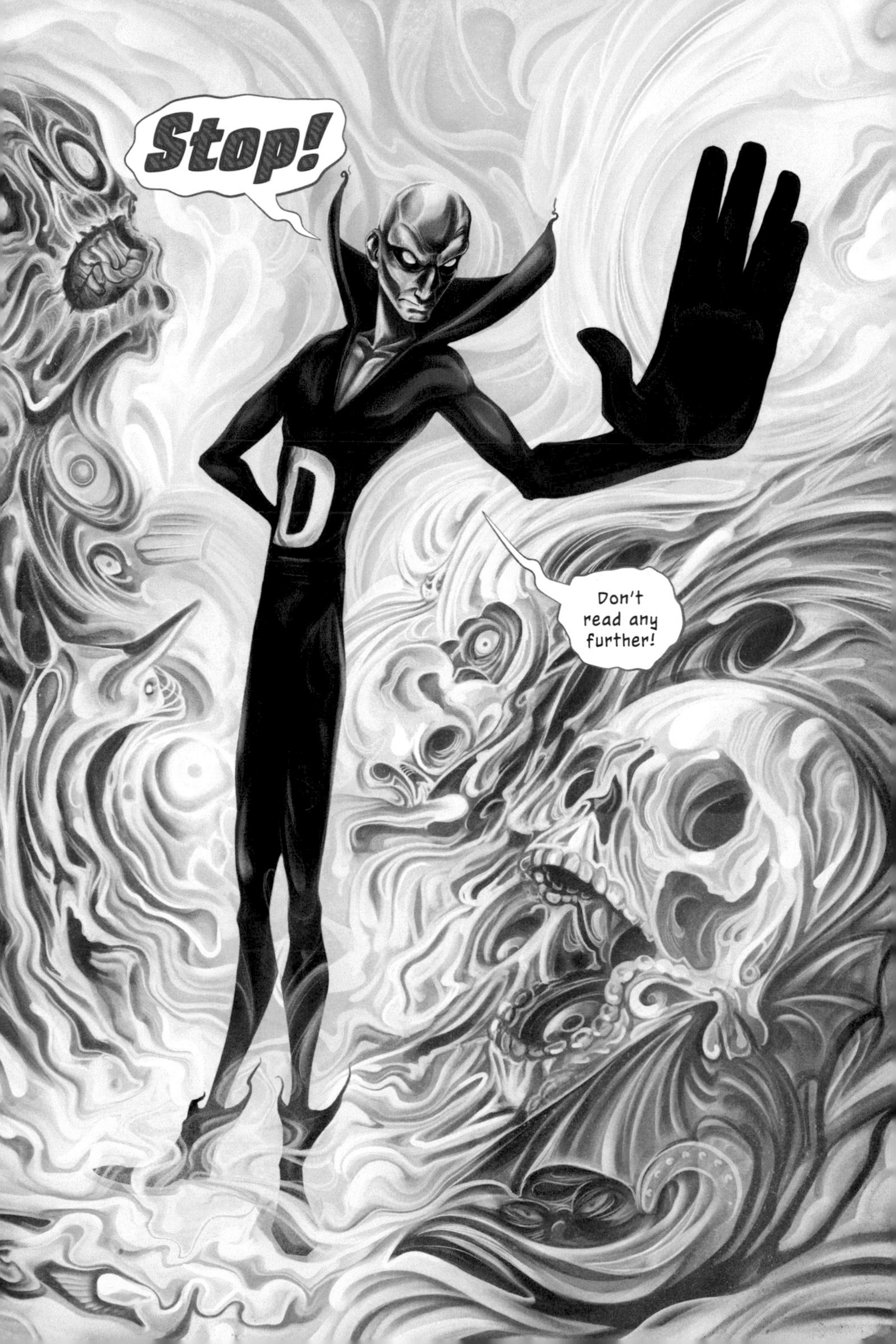
Stop!
Don't read any further!

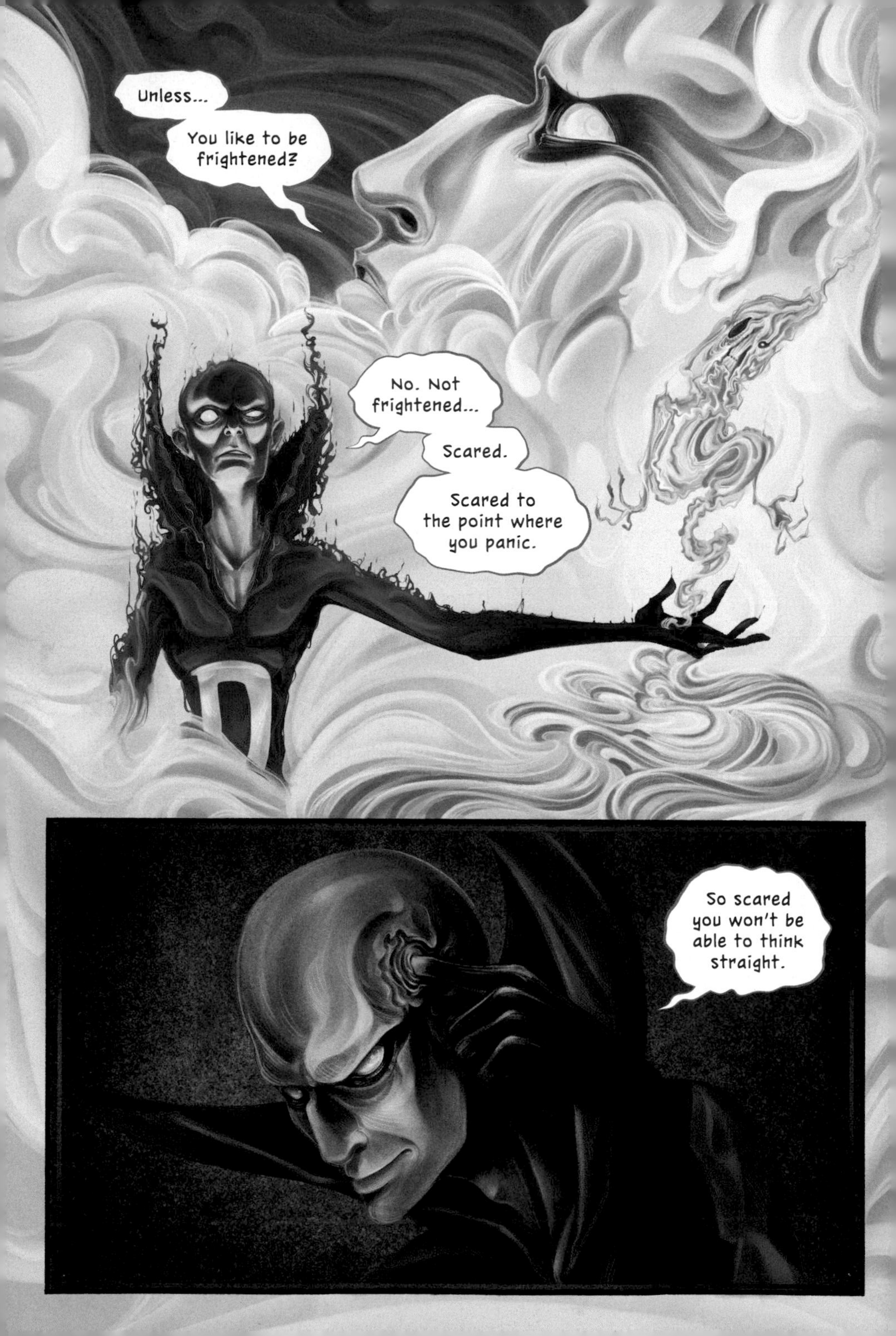
Unless...
You like to be frightened?
No. Not frightened...
Scared.
Scared to the point where you panic.
So scared you won't be able to think straight.

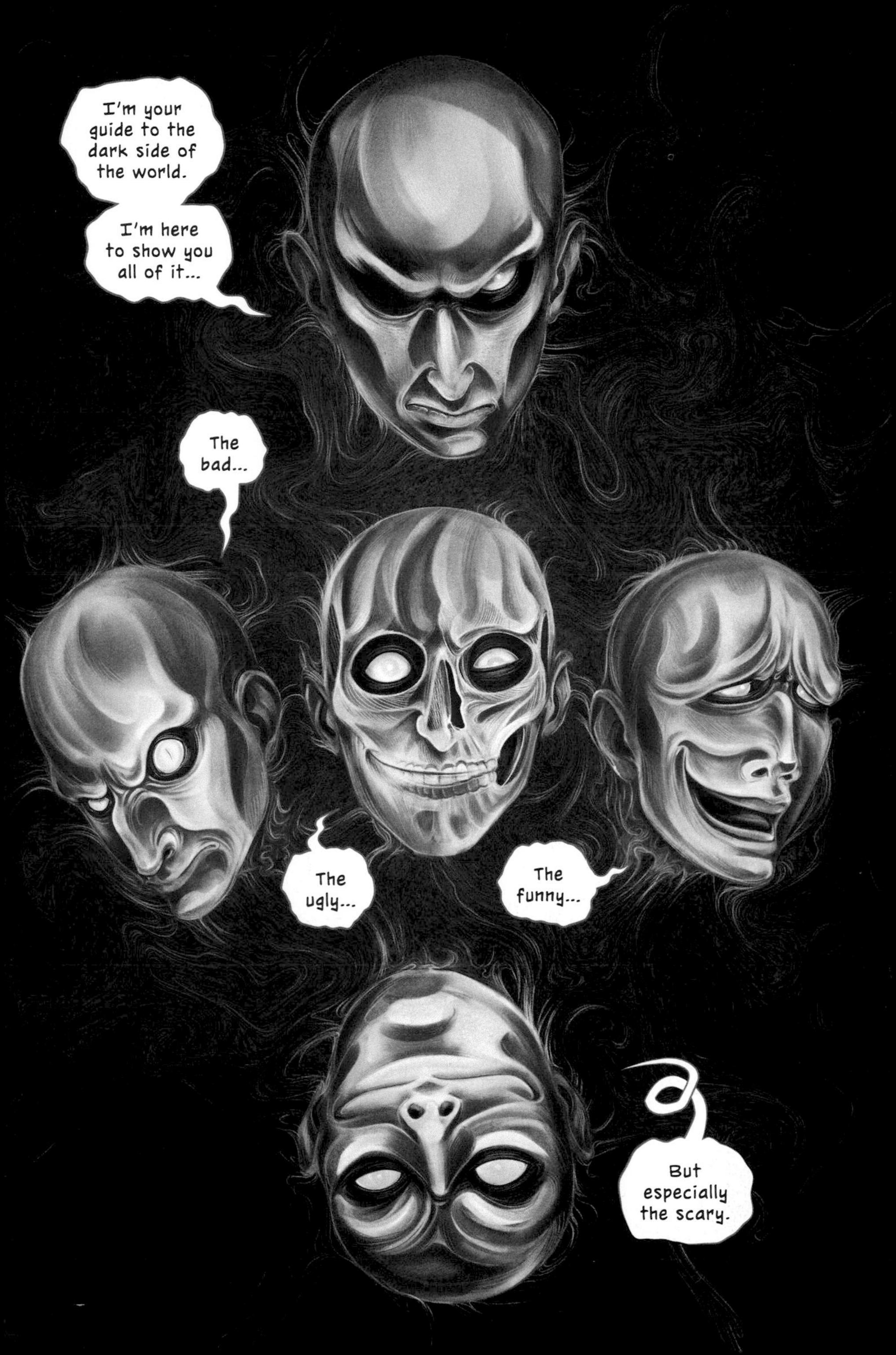
I'm your guide to the dark side of the world.
I'm here to show you all of it...
The bad...
The ugly...
The funny...
But especially the scary.

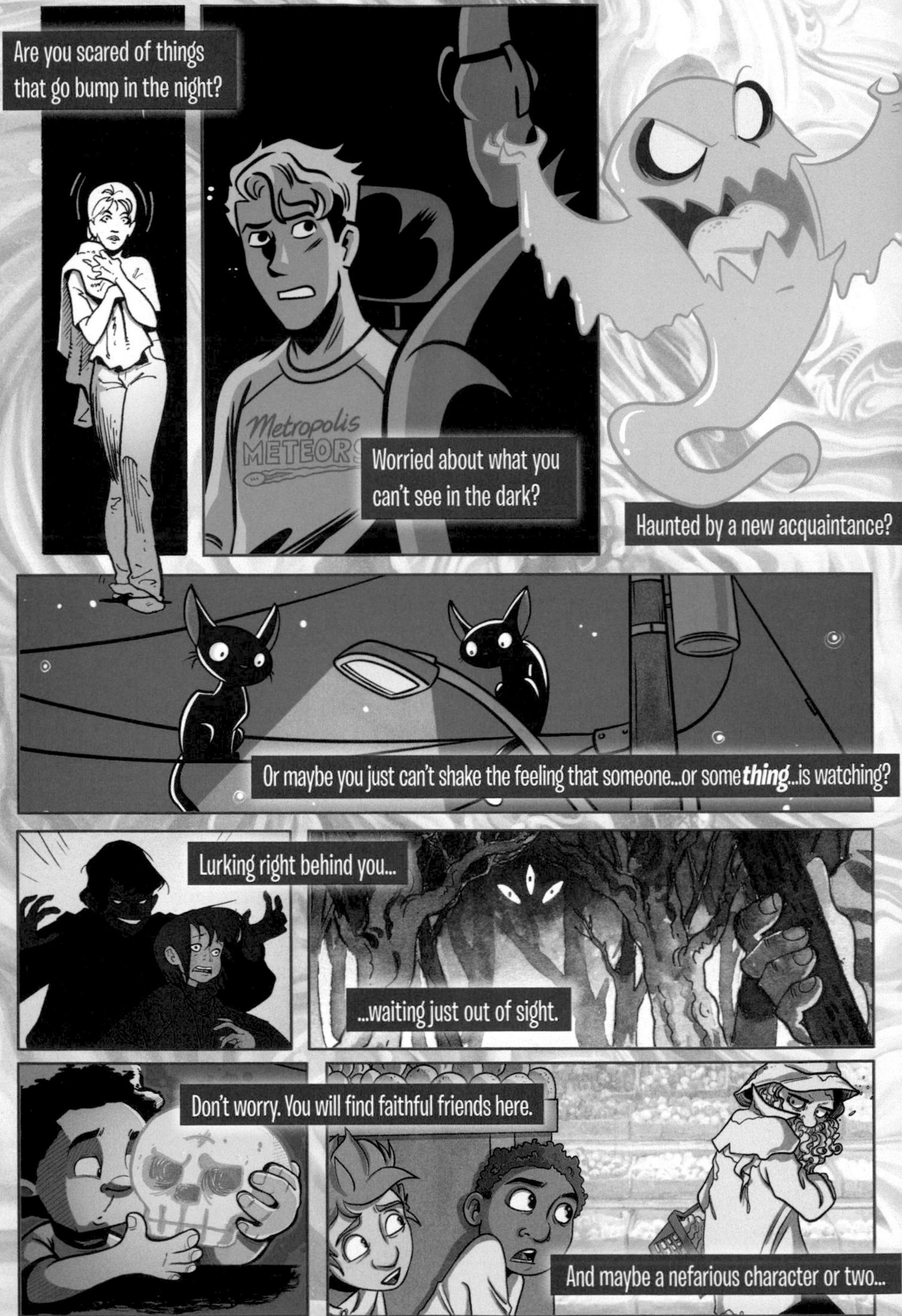
Are you scared of things that go bump in the night?
Metropolis METEORS
Worried about what you can't see in the dark?
Haunted by a new acquaintance?
Or maybe you just can't shake the feeling that someone...or some**thing**...is watching?
Lurking right behind you...
...waiting just out of sight.
Don't worry. You will find faithful friends here.
And maybe a nefarious character or two...

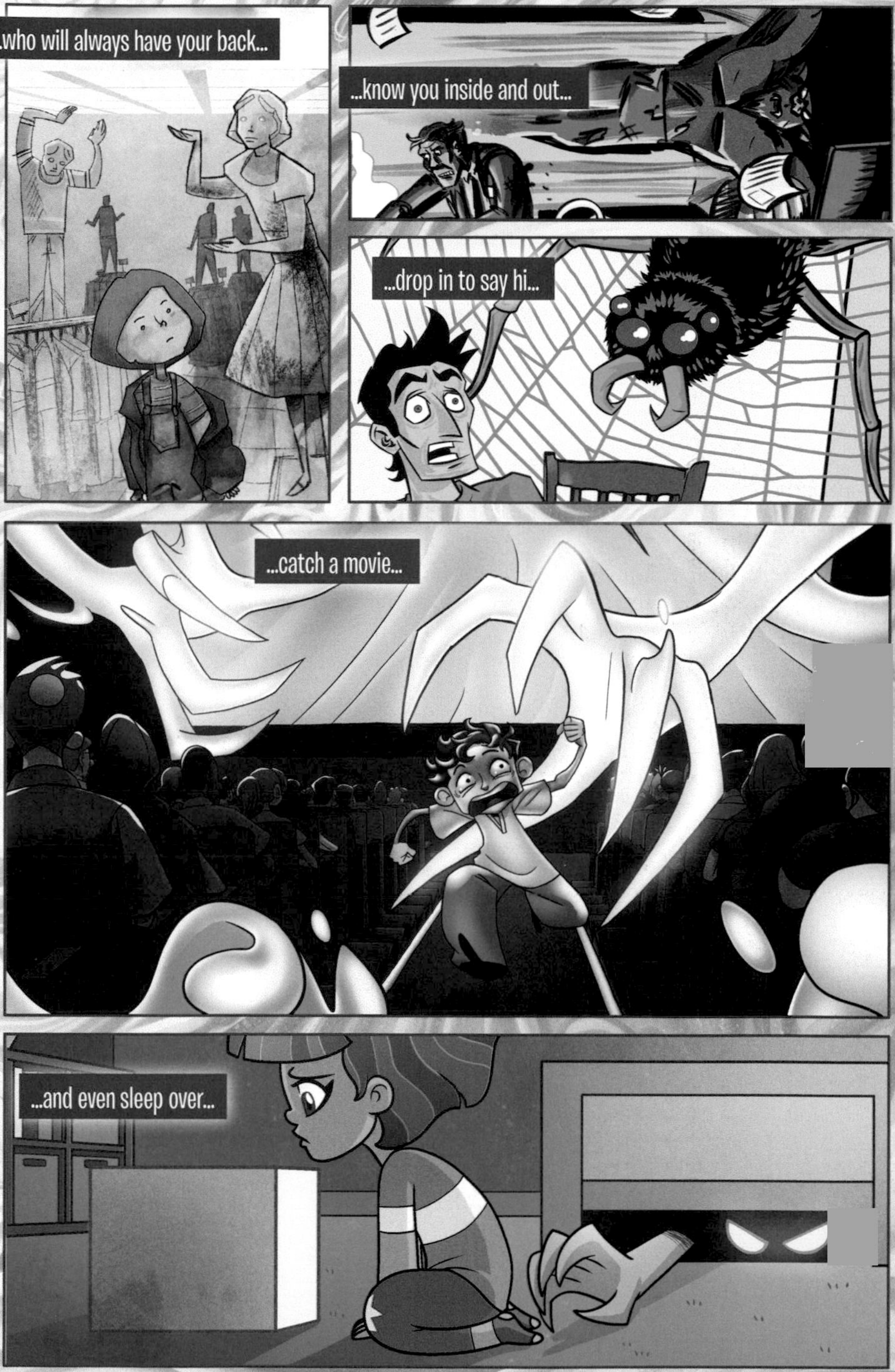
...who will always have your back...
...know you inside and out...
...drop in to say hi...
...catch a movie...
...and even sleep over...

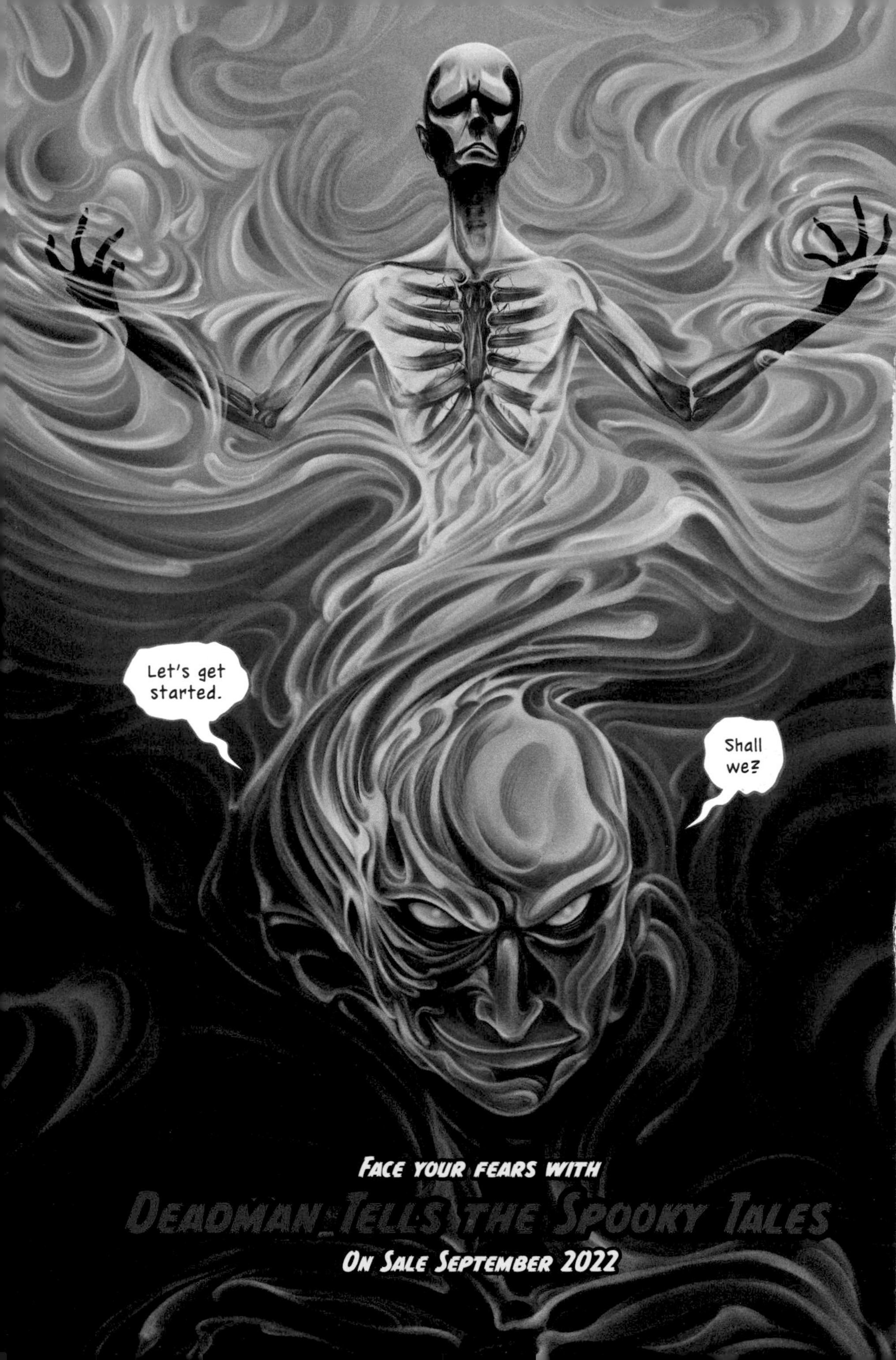
Let's get started.
Shall we?
Face your fears with
Deadman Tells the Spooky Tales
On Sale September 2022